A USEFUL DEATH

Sriram Chellapilla is a writer and screenwriting lecturer. He has a Masters in Communication and lives and works in Hyderabad. His first novel *The Long Reverie of Partha Sarma* (Penguin India) was published in 2006.

A USEFUL DEATH

Sriram Chellapilla

First published by Westland Publications Private Limited in 2019
1st Floor, A Block, East Wing, Plot No. 40, SP Infocity, Dr. MGR Salai, Perungudi, Kandanchavadi, Chennai 600096

Westland and the Westland logo are trademarks of Westland Publications Private Limited, or its affiliates.

This is a work of fiction, Names, characters, organisations, places, events and incidents are either products of the author's imagination or used fictitiously.

ISBN: 9789388689694

10 9 8 7 6 5 4 3 2 1

Typeset by SÜRYA, New Delhi
Printed at Thomson Press (India) Ltd

For my father

1

'They'll find some idiot to blame this on,' the inspector said.

The sub-inspector, who stood a few steps behind him, hesitated before he spoke.

'Hopefully the right idiot,' he offered.

Wrong response.

'A girl's killed herself so somebody has to go to jail?' the inspector said. 'Somebody must have driven her to it?'

'Well no …'

'It's not possible that something was wrong with her head and she messed up her own life?'

'It's definitely possible.'

The inspector gave him a look. 'No, it's not,' he said. 'It's absolutely impossible.'

The sub-inspector didn't seem to be getting anything right that morning.

'It's impossible?' he asked.

'Out of the question. Because such crazy thoughts can only occur to Inspector Pratap. And they only occur to him because he's a lousy bastard.'

Having the wrong response to that last statement was not an option. The sub-inspector stayed absolutely silent and took care to not betray even a facial expression. Pratap glanced back at him.

'Isn't that so, Suraj?' he said. 'I must be a lousy bastard to think it might be her own fault?'

Suraj smiled politely in reply, a well-practiced smirk that could pass for both confusion and embarrassment—a combination of emotions superior officers always found deferential.

Pratap turned away and shuffled restlessly around the room. He walked to the end of the drawing room and came to an uncertain halt. Beyond it was a small dining room, into which a bedroom and kitchen opened out. Through the curtains of the bedroom you could see the forensics team at work.

'Wedding photographers take fewer photographs,' Pratap muttered. 'No hurry—all the time in the world.'

'I told them to be quick,' Suraj said. 'Should I tell them again?'

'So they can tell everyone we rushed them? No need.'

'Yes, sir.'

Pratap's restlessness amused Suraj. He recalled the Deputy Commissioner of Police once calling Pratap 'a bull in a crime scene', stopping just short of saying that he'd damaged evidence. The DCP had to content himself with his little play on words and it rolled right off Pratap's back. The phrase seemed most appropriate that morning, but Suraj also sensed a forced restraint in Pratap, a hesitancy.

'Has the body reached the morgue?' Pratap asked.

'Traffic is slow,' Suraj said. 'Office rush.'

'Ask them to use the bloody siren. If there's a quarter bottle of brandy waiting they use the siren as if someone's dying, but they won't use it when we require it!'

'I'll call the driver.'

Suraj dialled the number and waited. There was no answer.

'The parents are going directly to the hospital, aren't they?' Pratap said.

'Yes, sir.'

Pratap nodded. 'Good,' he said. 'Let the media focus on the family—there's more drama in crying and wailing anyway. Will take the pressure off us.'

The ambulance driver finally answered the call. Suraj simply told him to use the siren and hung up.

'The TV channels won't cover this live, sir,' Suraj said. 'It'll only be in the evening crime-news programme.'

'Wrong,' Pratap said. 'It's being covered live.'

Wrong again, Suraj thought, sighing to himself—this really wasn't his morning.

'It is?' he said. 'But why?'

Pratap didn't answer. He took a few quick steps and entered the dining room; Suraj followed. The ventilation in the dining room was worse than the drawing room. The musty trapped air mingled unpleasantly with kitchen smells.

'Wonder how channels got the news so fast,' Suraj said. 'Our team was here as soon as the landlord called. I reached the place fifteen minutes after you called me—at seven o' clock. The CNEWS crew landed up ten minutes after that.'

Once again, Pratap didn't answer.

'Someone from the station must have tipped them off,' Suraj said. 'Must have heard me talking to you. An actress' suicide is a story.'

'An actress without a single movie,' Pratap said.

'Newcomers are even better for the news—with this industry's reputation for exploitation.'

'Again that victim rubbish!' Pratap turned around to face Suraj. 'Somebody cheated her and so she killed herself and all that other rubbish—what evidence do we have for it?'

'No, sir—that's not what I meant. As of now there isn't any evidence. I'm just saying that that's the sort of thing the media comes up with.'

'That's the bullshit they feed people.'

'Yes, sir—the media's nasty. That CNEWS crew even tried to barge in here. They got on-site first so they think we owe them a scoop. They wanted to get shots of the body here itself, of course. I didn't allow it—you said we shouldn't.'

'The deceased is a young woman—there are sensitivities!'

'The reporters were very upset. But I put constables in the corridor.'

Pratap breathed in deeply and exhaling, let out a short grunt. That usually indicated approval.

'They even tried to talk to the landlord and the girl's friend,' Suraj said. 'I warned them that they couldn't talk to anybody until we had finished taking statements.'

'Where's the friend?' Pratap asked.

'In the landlord's apartment,' Suraj said. 'But I've separated her and the landlord. A woman constable is with her.'

'You've got their statements?'

'Initial information only. The landlord is very upset—half because he thought she was a nice girl and half because this happened in his building.'

Pratap chuckled. 'Rents are bound to fall,' he said.

'Yes. The girl's friend is okay now—she was very upset initially but was able to compose herself. Gave me a clear timeline.'

Pratap wandered in a little further. On a teapoy, next to a red imitation Lay-z-boy recliner, was a stack of head-shots. A photo-frame stood next to it. Pratap leaned over the head-shots resisting the temptation to pick them up. His glance darted between the head-shots and the photo-frame a few times. Suraj walked over and looked at them as well.

The young woman in the headshot had clear, sharp features. Her eyes looked straight ahead and not an eyelash was out of place. Her face was cold and unsmiling but undeniably beautiful. In the photo-frame, the mood was entirely different. Her smile was easy and full. She looked radiant, dressed in a simple salwar-kameez, with a backdrop of hills on a sunny day. A stranger looking at the two photographs would take a moment to make out that it was the same woman in both the pictures. A dupatta was wrapped loosely around her neck and it fluttered in the breeze. She stood poised but relaxed, the look in her eyes genuine and unaffected. She looked happy.

'Poor girl was really beautiful,' Suraj said.

'What is that to us?' Pratap said, grinning slyly. 'It's some industry fellow's loss—not ours.'

Suraj cringed and then twisted his mouth into a polite smile.

'That's the photograph they're going to flash on TV,' Pratap said, pointing to the photo-frame. 'That'll get more sympathy. More than the other photograph anyway.'

Suraj nodded.

'Why is the media treating this as high-priority?' Suraj asked. 'Even if it's a young woman—that too an aspiring actress. You expect the media to get excited, but not this much.'

'There's a panel discussion about this on CNEWS right now—on the day the CM's brother-in-law is holding a press conference about corruption charges!'

'I don't understand why.'

'Because they want to create as much of a stink as possible,' Pratap said.

'But to target whom?'

*

In a palatial house in the most exclusive part of town, men hurried about setting up televisions in a large hall. They placed some of the TVs on tables, the others on the floor. Extension cords were stretched out to plug them all in. DTH receiver sets were brought out from bedrooms and additional cable was grafted on to reach the hall.

Seven screens were set up and turned on. They were set apart far enough to be heard clearly, but the overlapping sounds of all the TVs turned the room noisy. Standing in the centre of the room, a man controlled the rush of activity with quiet authority. His hair and moustache were neatly trimmed and combed; he wore a half-sleeved shirt and trousers over sandals, all three of which were an immaculate white. His gold wristwatch and glasses stood out in strong contrast. There was a robustness about him though he was in his early sixties. He indicated the exact placement of each TV set and assigned a man to it. He was quick to notice the slightest deviation from his instructions and to show his annoyance about it. Once everyone settled down, he had the TVs muted. Notepads and pens were handed out to each of the men sitting in front of the TVs.

'Write the name of the channel you're watching on the cover of the notepad,' he said. 'The moment you hear a mention of a family member, write it down. What was said, at what time, and by whom. Write down the names of all the anchors, panel members, and reporters. In discussions, note down who said what and what their attitude to the whole thing is. Doesn't matter if you don't understand it, but I want it all noted.'

The men gazed at him but did not speak.

'Is that clear?' the man asked.

The men nodded. The man gazed back at them for a few moments.

'Then take the TVs off mute and start watching, idiots!' he said. 'Do I have to tell you everything?'

The men complied. The man in white started to walk away towards the exit. A young man followed after him.

'Stay here,' the man in white instructed him.

'Yes, Ramakrishna garu,' the younger man said.

'Call me the moment the news becomes big.'

'Yes, sir.'

'Keep track of what they're writing. The record needs to be good. The man I'm bringing in will want every piece of information there is.'

'I'll take care of everything. Please don't worry, Ramakrishna garu.'

Mr Ramakrishna shook his head slightly.

'Don't worry, you say,' he muttered. He stopped and turned to look at the men gathered around the TVs. 'And keep these fellows from going into any of the rooms,' he said. 'They are to stay in the hall. Just because they're in his house doesn't mean they have a free run of it.'

*

The constable at the stairway despised the press. Dealing with the CNEWS reporter that morning only strengthened that sentiment. The reporter advanced every time the constable stepped away from the landing entrance. He repeatedly tried to push his cameraman forward, and when that proved futile, he shot video footage with his own cellphone. The constable had to advance on him each time and wave him back, showing his irritation with an odd hissing sound. Earlier that morning, the reporter had backed away more easily, in reluctant deference to police procedure. Like the other reporters he retreated to the stairwell and remained there. As time went by, he began to argue with the constable, demanding that they be allowed to get visuals of the death scene. The constable was sorely tempted to quip that they were not obliged to give them access at all, but he restrained himself. Inadvertently uniting the pressmen was highly avoidable.

'Your forensics team has been inside for over an hour—what's left to find inside?' the CNEWS reporter called out. 'Or is there something to hide?'

The constable simply shook his head and stood his ground.

'Rumour is, an important man drove her to suicide!' another reporter shouted out from the staircase.

The constable did not react. But then there was some disturbance lower down the stairwell. The other constable in the corridor got up from his chair and walked over. A few men were cursing and pushing their way up despite protests from the reporters and cameramen. The sight of one of them made both the constables tense up. He was a thickset man with the brash demeanour peculiar to small-time politicians. Following close behind was a man dressed in jeans and a black t-shirt; he had a shabby, unshaven look about him and his 'fitted clothes' threatened to burst at the seams. A few others—followers, presumably—pushed forward along with them. One of the constables told the other to keep the group away from the apartment; he himself went inside. He found Suraj and Pratap in the dining area.

'The youth wing leader of the National People's Party is here,' he said. 'Seems to have brought some supporters with him.'

'NPP's youth leader?' Pratap asked. 'Wonder what he wants?'

'Don't know, sir. The president of the Junior Artists Association is with him.'

'I don't think the girl was a junior artist,' Suraj said. 'But I'm not surprised he turned up—she was an actress without a released film.'

'Actually, that makes sense—the association is controlled by whichever party is in power,' Pratap said. 'The association must have called the NPP man.' Pratap considered it for a moment. 'Keep them out—doesn't matter if he belongs to the ruling party.'

Suraj shot Pratap a glance.

'Might be better to go out and meet them, sir,' he said. 'They have high nuisance value—they'll say we're covering something up.'

'Why would they say that?' Pratap said, twirling around to face Suraj.

'It's a standard tactic,' Suraj said. 'If they're not given importance, they accuse us of something.'

'Let them say it.'

'It might be better to handle it, sir ...'

'Why?'

Suraj thought it best not to press the matter.

'If you think it's fine …' he said.

But Pratap was in no mood to let it go. He stood aggressively, with his hands on his waist and chest puffed out, and stared hard at Suraj.

'Because they'll say I'm close to Mohan Krishna?' he said.

'Mohan Krishna?' Suraj said, surprised. 'No, sir, that's not what I meant.'

'If you think it, have the courage to say it.'

'Sir, it's just our luck that Mohan Krishna lives within our jurisdiction. People assume that a circle inspector posted here is posted with his consent. He is the Telugu industry's biggest superstar and he's about to enter politics—he's powerful. Do you think some Mohan Krishna loyalist might be named in this?'

'The sons-of-bitches who say I'm close to Mohan Krishna can go to hell!'

'Yes, sir.'

The constable left. Pratap turned and broke away from where he was standing, the nervous energy kicking in again. He went up to the bedroom door.

'Finish quickly!' he said to the forensics team.

'It'll take a little more time, sir,' a voice mumbled from within.

Pratap was about to retort but refrained. He stood where he was, shifting his weight from one leg to the other. Suraj stayed in his place and looked around. From the moment he'd come in, something about the apartment had struck him as being odd. It was as though the objects in the house didn't quite fit together. The furniture was of mediocre quality: gaudy decolam table tops, plastic chairs, and crude shelves. Alongside these were pieces of more contemporary furniture like the recliner, a coffee table, and bean bags. They were imitations of higher-end brands but they were several notches above than the older furniture. Suraj figured the landlord let out the house semi-furnished and the young woman had added her furniture to it. But even her own things didn't follow a set pattern. On the flimsy dining table, porcelain crockery and expensive protein supplements stood alongside old, dented steel plates and glasses, and faded plastic containers. A small, grey fridge hummed in one corner of the room.

Suraj peeped into the kitchen. It was a damp, dark room with smells of copper, steel, and cooking. Utensils were neatly stacked on open racks. But the sink was a mess. Used utensils were piled up to the top; a few tumblers and a plate had been rinsed out and left on the counter. A thin ring of water around the edge of an upturned tumbler suggested it was washed some hours ago. The utensils in the sink were caked, as though unwashed for many days. The dustbin underneath the sink was stuffed with Maggi and biscuit wrappers.

Suraj turned away and wandered into the bedroom. Pratap was already inside. Suraj followed him in. One of the two forensics people left the room; while the other photographed evidence in one corner of the room.

There was an indentation where the body had lain after being brought down. Suraj let his shoulders drop and rotated his neck. He hated being on death scenes so soon after the body had been removed. Things looked eerily normal, just as they must have at any given moment until the person died.

'Straightforward suicide,' Pratap said, looking around. 'The girl hanged herself using a dupatta.'

'There are some questions, sir,' Suraj said.

Pratap didn't react.

The maroon dupatta had to be cut to lower the body but the section of it tied to the ceiling fan was still up there. Books and clothes were strewn about on the bed and stacked on the one chair in the room. A small LCD TV was mounted on the wall facing the bed; its cable TV receiver box was on the floor. Cables ran across the wall and an extra length of wire lay in a loose bundle on the floor by the receiver box. On a dusty dressing table were designer perfumes and other cosmetics. A collection of Bertolt Brecht's plays and a book titled 'Violence and Social Change' lay on the bedside table.

In Suraj's eyes, something was missing. Odd as the mix of objects in the house seemed to him, what was missing from her possessions was far more striking. Their absence was impossible to ignore.

'You've not removed any evidence yet, have you?' Suraj asked the forensics man.

'No, sir.'

'Is the government paying you double overtime?' Pratap said. 'We're practically preparing to lathi-charge the politicians and the press in the corridor and you fellows are working in slow-motion!'

The forensics man didn't say anything.

'I want the place sealed quickly!' Pratap said.

'Sorry, sir,' the forensics man said. 'Just another twenty minutes—maximum.'

Suraj broke in, keeping all traces of impatience out of it.

'You didn't see a cellphone, did you?' he said.

'There's one over there,' the forensics man said, pointing to the windowsill.

An old, black, no-frills Nokia was lodged between the grill and the windowpane.

'I noticed that,' Suraj said. 'It's old and doesn't seem to have any charge. Nobody uses those kinds of phones anymore.'

'I suppose,' the forensics man said.

'Doesn't make sense. Even school children have smartphones these days.'

'There's no laptop either.'

'Yes, I noticed that too. No desktop also.'

'Maybe she didn't have a computer,' Pratap said. 'And maybe she didn't like smartphones and used that old phone.'

Suraj shook his head. 'There's a Wi-Fi router in the house,' he said. 'It was on when we arrived.'

'Hmm …' Pratap said, glancing at Suraj.

'It would be very hard to explain why she had an active internet connection and a router without having a single device to use it with,' Suraj said.

Pratap stroked his chin absentmindedly, his fingers pressing deep into his cheek. The forensics man said he would return in a minute and stepped out.

'No suicide note—is that confirmed?' Suraj asked.

'No suicide note,' the forensics man called from the hall.

Pratap and Suraj were left alone in the room. There was silence for a minute or two. Pratap rocked on his heels and swayed about, his restlessness more conspicuous in the confined space.

'There may be a simple explanation to that,' Pratap said suddenly, looking at Suraj. 'She was depressed and threw the laptop and phone away. Or gave them away.'

'It could be,' Suraj said. 'And there are no signs of a forced entry so we have no reason to believe it was stolen. But until we confirm that, we have to assume someone was here before or after her death and took them. We'll have to treat them as objects missing from the death scene.'

'We will, won't we?' Pratap said slowly.

Suraj stiffened.

'Yes, sir, we will,' he said.

Pratap folded his arms across his chest and was silent. Suddenly, he nodded his head.

'Okay, fine,' he said. 'Let's follow up on this.'

Suraj looked relieved.

'The girl who alerted the landlord should know if her friend had a cellphone and a laptop,' he said.

*

The young woman didn't raise her head. She stared at her hands, wringing them occasionally. She sniffled or let out a muffled sob once or twice. Inspector Pratap watched her for a minute with a deadpan expression.

'She came to the apartment first thing in the morning, sir,' Suraj explained. 'She rang the doorbell but there was no answer. She was worried and informed the landlord something might be wrong. She's a student; her name is Sirisha.'

'What's the dead girl's name?' Pratap asked brusquely. 'Tell me everything you know.'

The dead woman's name was Priya, Sirisha told the policemen, and she knew her from university. Priya was a theatre arts student and had graduated the same year that Sirisha had joined the sociology department as a masters' student. But Priya visited the campus often and they struck up a friendship. The two of them bonded over a common interest in street theatre.

'And you rushed here because?' Pratap said.

The girl seemed almost confused by the question, as though trying to figure out where to begin.

'She's been—I mean, she was—very upset for over a week …'

'About what?'

Pratap watched her very closely. He had interrupted her deliberately; he found taking charge of conversations useful. Uninterrupted, people narrated their own version of things. Sometimes, this version was just their subjective, limited reading of the situation. At other times, their version was a series of lies told deliberately to mislead the police. In either case, it paid to break their pattern.

'Actually …' the woman began.

'Upset about what?'

'She said she'd been used and discarded.'

'How?'

'In the way women are.' There was a note of irritation in Sirisha's tone.

'What way is that?'

'What?'

'In what way?'

'You're asking me in what way are women used?'

'I'm asking you to be clear.'

Suraj broke in at this point. 'Who exploited her?' he asked.

'Because she was repeatedly betrayed—'

'We're not interested in film dialogues,' Pratap said. 'Answer the question directly.'

'I'm trying to!' The irritation had turned to anger now.

'Who betrayed her?' Suraj asked.

'That's what I'm trying to tell you.'

'Don't try,' Pratap said. 'Tell us.'

The girl looked uncertain and angry at once. And then she told them.

*

Pratap and Suraj came out of the apartment and stood in the hallway. The woman constable who had stepped out when they went inside was waiting for them. She told them the ambulance had reached the hospital, as had Priya's parents. They'd driven straight to the hospital from their hometown—which was a few hours drive away—where they'd gone for a brief visit. They had started for Hyderabad the moment they were informed. Policemen at the hospital said that they were distraught and refused to speak to the press.

The noise of the press and people gathering in and around the apartment building had grown louder. From among the disjointed noises, a cohesive sound of voices raised together began to come through.

'Who's shouting slogans?' Suraj asked.

A student group, the woman constable told them. The students had just arrived at the apartment building and were protesting in the parking area. They claimed the police were destroying evidence to protect an important person. The Junior Artists Association and National People's Party activists had joined in. Suraj turned to Pratap who took it all in without a reaction.

'Wait here,' he said to Suraj and walked away. He went to the far corner of the hallway and made a phone call. He could be heard speaking in a low tone and responding in monosyllables. He hung up and returned to where Suraj was standing. He didn't say anything.

'This case is going to be big,' Suraj said impatiently. 'The girl's mentioned some big names. The rumours must be everywhere by now—that's why the media isn't leaving.'

'CNEWS got the news first so they're making a fuss about it,' Pratap said. 'They're the only channel covering every moment live and with a panel discussion in the studio—women's rights activists and all that stuff. Others are covering it as part of their regular bulletins. But they'll increase coverage so they're not left behind.'

'But, sir, if it involves Anil—Mohan Krishna's son!'

Pratap gave him a contemptuous look.

'That girl Sirisha says he's involved,' he said. 'That's all we know right now.'

'You're right, sir. I'm sorry. But if anything that this girl is saying is true—that Priya was supposed to star in Mohan Krishna's home production, his son's debut—then the media will drop everything else and cover only this!'

'It's just her word so far. But look into it. If there are photographs showing her with Anil and others working in the film, collect them formally as evidence.'

'Yes, sir.'

'This girl claims many in the industry knew about the affair, but not one person will talk on the record—take my word for it. But make enquiries.'

'Yes, sir.' Suraj said, a little surprise showing on his face. Pratap was playing all this by the book. There was no open attempt to soft-pedal it, at least yet.

The slogan shouting grew louder.

'Is there any evidence in what we've found so far?' Pratap asked. 'Any mention of anybody?'

'No, sir,' Suraj said. 'Not of Anil, not of anyone else.'

Pratap nodded.

'Then let the media in,' he said. 'Let them get some footage of the apartment. I'm going back to the station. I don't want a word out of any policeman here—no "unnamed sources".'

'Yes, sir.'

'And let's get on the job of retrieving the cellphone and laptop. That's top priority.'

*

At about the same time, in the palatial house, a young man watching a TV screen intently wrote hastily on a sheet of paper. He tore the page from the notepad and handed it over to the man supervising them. The man read it and rushed to the other room.

'In the CNEWS panel discussion, Ramakrishna garu,' he said.

'They mentioned Anil's name?' Mr Ramakrishna asked.

'Yes, sir.'

'Only his name?'

'Yes, sir.'

The man handed over the sheet of paper to Mr Ramakrishna. Mr Ramakrishna picked up his phone and dialled.

'Just when there's a crisis he puts his phone on silent mode!' he said.

There was no answer. Mr Ramakrishna put down his phone with a sigh of exasperation. He raised the sheet of paper and looked at it again. He rubbed his forehead and closed his eyes.

'It's begun,' he said.

2

The 'waiting room' of a film star's house is a place of consequence. Whatever its appearance, it is a place where dreams and fortunes are made or broken. Sometimes it's just a room in the house and at other times an elaborate standalone structure set away from the main home. There, people wait, often for hours on end, for that elusive and consequential audience. The duration of one's wait signals one's importance or the lack of it. Even those offended by the length of their wait never leave before being called in for fear of never being admitted to the room again. To leave before being summoned in is to reject the star's own sense of importance, which is the gravest possible offence in the star system. On a given day one could expect to find anyone from a journalist or a fan-club representative to a director or a film producer waiting with admirable fortitude. Partha hadn't been in one of these waiting rooms in a very long time.

He had the place to himself this morning, which surprised him a little. The film industry was big on shows of support. On a day like this he had expected industry people to queue up in strength and make a display of their concern. But there were no advisors, colleagues, or well-wishers in the room. Perhaps people whose presence wasn't essential had been asked to stay away. If that was the case, Partha approved. The focus had to be on dealing with the problem on hand and not meaningless social gestures. From what little he'd seen so far, it seemed that there was a high level of organisation in the family's response to the crisis.

That morning, the star's personal staff controlled the crowd, manned the gates, and even dealt with the media. It was around 11 a.m. now and the news of the suicide was all over the TV channels. At the gate, fan-club members shouted slogans in support of Mohan Krishna and Anil. There were hundreds of them, which disrupted the traffic severely. The crowd had stopped Partha's car a few hundred metres away from the house. A man stepped forward from the crowd and asked what he wanted. He checked for Partha's name on a list and asked who had called him as a sort of cross-verification. Partha said Mr Ramakrishna Rao and the man crossed his name off the list. Another young man appeared and beckoned Partha to follow him. He ran in front of the car to an empty plot nearby that was being used as makeshift parking that morning. A few fancy cars were parked there—perhaps belonging to close associates and family members now involved in dealing with the situation. When Partha parked his car and returned to the gate he found the man with the list waiting for him. He led Partha into the compound and to the waiting room.

The TV on the wall played HydNews on a low volume. In the studio, anchors interviewed people from political parties, women's groups, and the film industry. At the apartment building and the hospital, NPP activists, students, and the Junior Artists Association members were shown shouting slogans demanding justice. The JAA president and the NPP's women's wing chief gave heated statements to camera crews. The gist of all of it was that Anil was a cheat. He'd toyed with Priya's affections, led her to believe that she'd star in his film, and then abandoned her. He was directly responsible for her death, they said repeatedly. And Mohan Krishna's entire family, which had played along in this deception, were equally culpable. Some commentators went to the extent of saying this was typical of the way the family treated women, and anyone in the industry could attest to this.

The big news that played in a loop was Priya's friend's interview. Sirisha said the normally-cheerful Priya was driven to profound depression in recent weeks. The hurt of being cheated professionally and personally had become too hard to bear. The previous evening, Priya had called her, perhaps in desperation. She spoke briefly and in a diffused manner, and then hung up abruptly. Sirisha called her back several times but Priya did not answer. Though Sirisha could make little sense of Priya's rambling, her defeated tone and talk of death troubled her. Sirisha, being out of town visiting a cousin, tried unsuccessfully to reach some friends to go check on Priya. Unable to disregard Priya's phone call, she took the first bus out and arrived in Hyderabad early that morning. She rushed straight to Priya's apartment. But it was already too late.

The thought that Priya had committed suicide was absolutely devastating, Sirisha said. But it was equally shocking to learn from the police that Priya's laptop and cellphone had gone missing. This was proof enough that somebody had something to hide. It was clear that Priya had been driven to suicide. Only if the devices were traced and their contents revealed could the truth be known. But the police's attitude, Sirisha said, made her wonder if the missing laptop and cellphone would ever be recovered.

Back at Mohan Krishna's house, the HydNews reporter described the situation and the mood. Over visuals of Mohan Krishna's followers gathering outside the house, the reporter confirmed that nobody from the actor's family was willing to give a statement. A few fan-club members, however, lined up and gave soundbites to the reporter. They all spoke in controlled but strong tones. They asked with varying degrees of incredulity if Anil and Mohan Krishna could be held responsible for some random girl's suicide. They also muttered darkly about a political conspiracy hatched by the NPP.

Partha watched this play out for a few minutes before there was a sound at the door. Mr Ramakrishna looked in, squinting to get accustomed to the light. The hassled look on his face eased a little and acquired a hint of geniality. Partha thought he'd gained some weight since they last met but he moved about just as energetically. Partha rose to his feet.

'Thanks for coming!' Mr Ramakrishna said, stepping inside.

'Of course, Mr Ramakrishna,' Partha said. 'Not that you left me a lot of choice in the matter.'

They shook hands.

'You obliged an old friend,' Mr Ramakrishna said. 'Thank you.'

'You're welcome.'

'Follow me. Everything's a rush this morning,' Mr Ramakrishna said. He turned and started to walk away.

Partha followed him out. They walked up an incline towards the main house. With the extensive landscaping the garden resembled a mound on a golf course. At the top was the enormous edifice. It was a mix of styles—minimalist straight lines of glass and steel alongside grand Roman columns. A cobbled path ran alongside the tarred road up the mound. Mr Ramakrishna took the cobbled path at a brisk pace, occasionally turning back to talk.

'Any active work or just consulting?' Mr Ramakrishna said.

'Consulting,' Partha said. 'That's work too, you know.'

'You should roll up your sleeves and get dirt under your fingernails again.'

'No, thanks.'

'Writing protocols and manuals for companies—what kind of life is that?'

'Not much of a life, really.'

'You can be so much more active at your age.'

'I'm ready to retire fully.'

'Rubbish! You're not even forty yet. I'd give anything to have the energy I had in my thirties.'

Partha didn't say anything.

'You'll go crazy without work,' Mr Ramakrishna said. 'Look at me: I'm sixty and still working. And I'll keep working until I die.'

'Good for you.'

They stayed on the cobble-stoned path as it ascended the mound. There it forked, one path leading to the main entrance and another skirting the house. As they took the latter and walked past the house, Partha stared at the marble fountain with a Roman-style sculpture. They'd taken some liberties with the style, painting it gold and a palate of other colours. The effect wasn't subtle.

Mr Ramakrishna glanced back. 'Are you even listening to me?' he said.

'I guess.'

Mr Ramakrishna shook his head and kept walking. Partha thought he'd given offense.

'I got the gist of it—I'm still young and need to work more,' Partha said.

'Semi-retirement hasn't made you less smug.'

'It's even more important for me to be smug now. People mistake it for confidence and hire me.'

They reached a side door to the house. It had its own smaller, columned entrance. They walked through a verandah into a hall where there were about a dozen people. Some watched news channels on several TV sets, took notes, and occasionally whispered amongst themselves. Others stood around or made phone calls. They all glanced up when Partha and Ramakrishna came in, and then they turned their attention back to what they were doing. One man began to walk up to them but Ramakrishna dismissed him with a slight shake of the head. Ramakrishna led Partha through the verandah and into a very small corridor. They went into the first room on the left, a guest room.

Ramakrishna waved Partha in the direction of a chair.

'We have to deal with this before it gets out of hand,' he said. 'I tried to guess what your approach would be—I was only guessing, of course. I'm not an expert like you!'

'Mr Ramakrishna—'

'I've asked those fellows outside to watch who's saying what, to what channel—that sort of thing.'

'I don't want to—'

'I've also asked them to come up with some details about the girl. We can get other information you'll need.'

Ramakrishna looked at Partha expectantly. There was an awkward pause.

'I told you on the phone, Mr Ramakrishna,' Partha said. 'I don't want to get involved.'

Mr Ramakrishna's eyebrows contorted with genuine disbelief.

'These sons-of-whores are trying to destroy the boy's career before it begins!' Mr Ramakrishna said. Under pressure, he tended to slip fluidly from the polite to the abusive.

'Be that as it may be,' Partha said, 'I don't want to get involved.'

'But the real aim is to destroy Mohan Krishna's political career before it starts! And they get to damage the boy's career as a bonus. You do realise that, don't you?'

'Yes, I guessed as much,' Partha said. 'But you have to realise that I couldn't care less.'

*

Mr Ramakrishna stood in front of Partha, throwing his shoulders about in a few half-shrugs before dropping his hands limply to his side.

'But I need your help,' he said.

Partha shifted about in his chair.

'No, you don't, Mr Ramakrishna,' he said. 'Mohan Krishna and his son might, but not you. It's not the same thing.'

'I need to help them, and if you help me do that, you're actually helping me.'

'That's a little too indirect for me,' Partha said with a smile.

'It's not just about my political ambitions!' Ramakrishna's tone had a tinge of indignation.

'I would never suggest that,' Partha said. 'I know you've been close to the family for decades. I know it goes well beyond getting an election ticket.'

'You'll be well-paid.'

'I have enough money.'

This seemed to irritate Ramakrishna further.

'Yes, I hear you got a lot of money and stocks for managing Spectrum Software's problem.'

'I did.'

'That's the kind of situation you like handling, is it? The carelessness of a software giant crashing millions of computers?'

'That's what crisis management is about.'

'Their irresponsibility crashed the computers of millions of people.'

'That's a bit of an exaggeration, isn't it?' Partha said with a laugh. 'It crashed a few hundred computers before they started managing fallout. We got involved because they were being targeted by corporate rivals and politicians. And it was a difficult technical problem to foresee. At least, that's what they explained to me.'

'The huge consultancy fees and stocks made them easier to believe, I'm sure.'

Partha laughed. 'The stocks weren't worth that much when I got them,' he said.

'They are now. Enough to help you go into virtual retirement.'

'That's true.'

'So don't give me some ethical rationale for not getting involved.'

'I didn't give you a rationale.'

'You're being very sanctimonious.'

Partha shook his head. 'Mr Ramakrishna, you did me a favour once,' he said. 'I came here this morning because I'm grateful to you. You used up a lot of political influence for me—you didn't have to do that. And you're right, my work has bailed out a lot of people who did not deserve it. But this just feels wrong, even by my standards.'

Mr Ramakrishna exhaled impatiently and looked away. He suddenly sat down on the edge of the bed.

'What is it about this matter that bothers you so much?' he asked.

'May I speak frankly?' Partha said.

'Of course.'

'We're in Mohan Krishna's house after all?'

'And not in some villain's den! Say what you want to.'

'Your side's defence is that it's Priya's friend's word against Anil's. And that it's being politicised. Fine. Unless a suicide note or some other evidence turns up, we won't know for sure there was an affair. Perhaps the public will give you guys the benefit of doubt. But going by what you, I, or just about anybody in the industry knows about this family—are you seriously telling me the accusation doesn't sound true?'

Mr Ramakrishna looked away from Partha.

'Most actresses who worked with Mohan Krishna despised him,' Partha said. 'He is a sex-addict, he's abusive, and a megalomaniac. He pretty much drove the actress Neela to insanity. He wouldn't let her work except with him, he hit her, and wouldn't let her leave. Then one day he lost interest and left her. Her career was over by then but she was still relieved that he was gone.'

Mr Ramakrishna gave him an annoyed look, an expression he instinctively slipped into when uncomfortable with what was being said. He also kept glancing in the direction of the door.

'My favourite story though,' Partha went on, 'is how he kept a producer and his crew on hold for forty-five days because the lead actress wouldn't sleep with him. They couldn't dismantle the sets or work elsewhere. I hear the producer and director took to standing outside the actress's house begging her to go sleep with him.'

'It's a lie!' Mr Ramakrishna said.

'Maybe. Even if it was, he's done enough things to be despised. The whole family bands together to protect him. That cousin of his, his brother—everyone. And now that he's losing his edge at the box office, he wants a career in politics.'

Mr Ramakrishna didn't say anything for a while. 'What about the poor boy?' he said. 'Even if everything you say about the family is true—which it isn't—I tell you he's innocent.'

'That's why you want me here,' Partha said. 'You're more than capable of managing the political side of things by yourselves. You want me to save the boy's image for the movies.'

Mr Ramakrishna did not reply.

'If the son's anything like the father,' Partha said, 'it probably did play out the way Priya's friend said. She was probably just some girl who fell in love with the movies and dared to believe she could make it. Having that ambition is enough to get the industry folks to say she had it coming. Anil probably did lead her on and ditch her.'

'And what if he didn't?'

'Then he's got his superstar father and all of you standing behind him. He'll be fine. There'll be some bad publicity and a lot of attention, but his film will go ahead. In a couple of years, he'll even be talking about how this suicide forced him to grow as a person.'

Mr Ramakrishna shot Partha a sharp look. 'God, you're cynical!' he said.

'I am,' Partha said. 'I don't want to become any more cynical than I already am by getting involved in this.'

He got up and started to walk towards the door. Mr Ramakrishna got in his way. He held his hands up and chuckled nervously. 'No, no, please stay,' he said.

'Mr Ramakrishna ...'

'You said you respected me and that you owed me,' Mr Ramakrishna said.

'I do,' Partha said. 'But I've already saved one of your companies from a political problem and given plenty of free advice as well. I'm happy to do that sort of thing again but not this.'

'Yes, yes, let's not bring business into it.'

'Unless it suits you, I guess.'

Mr Ramakrishna laughed. He held up one hand.

'Just stay a few minutes longer and meet one person,' he said. 'If you still want to leave after that, I won't stop you.'

'It won't help.'

'It'll only take another fifteen-twenty minutes.'

Partha hesitated. 'Fine,' he said.

Mr Ramakrishna perked up.

'Wonderful! Stay here, don't leave.'

He hurried away, shutting the door behind him.

*

There was no television in the room. A rectangular outline on the wall and a cable with extensions running along the floor and out the door suggested that there used to be one. It was now one of the seven TVs set up in the hall. Partha got onto the internet on his phone. He brushed past his notifications and tried to check a news portal. The signal strength was weak and the page loaded slowly. When it did, he found there was little new information. The portal quoted theatre arts students from Priya's university expressing shock. They described Priya as a talented and dedicated artist; on a personal note, they said she was somewhat reserved but friendly when approached. The comments were largely routine and of no interest, and the internet was a poor substitute for Telugu news television anyway. Partha closed the browser.

He then looked at his notifications. A half-hour-old phone call and a message from his business associate, Seema, were the only things worth noting. Her message simply said: '???' Partha considered calling her but decided against it. 'Meeting,' he texted. 'Be there in an hour.' 'Where are you?' Seema's next text read. Partha didn't reply; he didn't want to get into it all. 'WTF?' Seema's next message said.

He checked Mohan Krishna's Twitter feed. It had been updated in the past half-an-hour. The tweet shared a news clip from HydNews about farmer distress. The accompanying tweet read: 'Those trying to distract public attention with scandal and sleaze should answer the questions raised here.'

Partha cringed. He put his phone away and looked around the room aimlessly. His guess was that Ramakrishna would return with one of the star's family members. Star loyalists believed celebrities could get people to do anything. They couldn't, and Partha wished Ramakrishna would give him more credit than that. In fact, Partha didn't believe celebrities were particularly charismatic. What they were was powerful; that power got them their way, not charm. Charisma, in fact, was just a matter of being polite while exercising that power. As far as Partha was concerned, Ramakrishna had a better chance of convincing him than some celebrity.

Partha wasn't surprised that Ramakrishna was trying as hard as he was to help out the family. His intentions were entirely sincere and they went well beyond staying in the good books of the family. It was true that some of his business interests, and all of his political ambitions, were tied to the family's. But this went beyond community and business ties; proximity to the star's family had become a part of Ramakrishna's identity. To him, an attack on them was an attack on him personally.

Another five minutes passed before the door opened. Ramakrishna walked in first and held the door open. The person who walked in after him was a surprise to Partha. He had expected a brother, cousin, or a brother-in-law—all of whom had some involvement in the film business and were celebrities. But it was a tall, strikingly beautiful woman that walked in.

'You've met Malvika, of course?' Ramakrishna said to Partha. 'Malvika, Partha and I have worked on a lot of problem situations together.'

His casual manner was a bit forced.

'No, I haven't had the occasion,' Partha said.

Malvika extended her hand. Partha rose and shook hands. Malvika was even more beautiful in person than she was onscreen. It had been a few years since she'd retired from the film industry. She quit her career in her mid-thirties when she was one of the top heroines in the Telugu film industry. She just stopped one day, got married to Mohan Krishna's younger brother, and stopped signing any new movies.

'I guess we were waiting for the worst possible occasion to meet,' Malvika said.

'I'm very sorry about the situation your family's facing,' Partha said.

Partha tried to step out of the way so she could take the chair. She waved him back into the chair and sat on the edge of the bed. Ramakrishna sat beside her. She took a few moments to settle down and tucked a lock of hair behind her ear. She was dressed simply in a salwar-kameez, wasn't wearing any makeup, and her perfume was mild. Partha observed that if he had to put her in front of a TV camera right then, he would have no hesitation whatsoever to do so: her appearance was appropriately understated and attractive and she looked totally composed.

'Mr Ramakrishna has told me about your hesitation to get involved,' Malvika said. 'I can understand it, entirely.'

'Thank you,' Partha said.

'I don't expect you to change your mind at my request. Certainly not because I am—or was—a star.'

Ramakrishna nodded.

'I didn't think that was what this was about,' Partha said. 'And you're still a star.'

'I'm a celebrity now.'

Partha didn't say anything to this.

'But do you mind if we speak for a little while?' Malvika said.

'Not at all. But why would you want to do that? Especially on a busy and difficult morning like this.'

'My hope is that you'll change your mind, of course. I know it's highly unlikely, but even if you didn't, I'd benefit from discussing the situation with you.'

Partha didn't answer immediately. 'Alright,' he said.

Malvika smiled.

'"There is great danger in duelling with a person who thirsts for battle more than victory",' she said.

'That's profound,' Partha said, smiling back.

'Just some quotation that came up in a class,' she said laughing dismissively. 'I took a class on Renaissance poetry while getting my MBA.'

Ramakrishna began to look restless. The conversation was a change in pace for the morning and his charged nerves rebelled against it. Malvika glanced at him but his anxiety didn't seem to affect her.

'Your problem with Anil,' she said, 'is that he may be some rich brat who toyed with an innocent girl's feelings?'

'I don't know anything about what happened, of course,' Partha said, 'so it's unfair to jump to any conclusions. It isn't any of my business and I want to keep it that way.'

'But you think that's probably what happened?'

'I know how common it is in the industry.'

'And you buy into the reputation the men of this family have—of being hard-drinking womanisers, that is? People who use women and throw them away?'

'As I said, it isn't my business to judge.'

Malvika broke into a smile once again.

'You are judging, you know,' she said. 'You're even judging the boy. You just won't admit it.'

Partha didn't reply.

'The boy is innocent!' Ramakrishna said.

Malvika touched his hand gently. She turned to Partha.

'It may be hard for you to believe but it's true,' Malvika said. 'The boy didn't toy with Priya's emotions and he didn't drive her to suicide.'

Partha watched her closely for a few moments.

'I'm glad to hear that,' he said. 'Then the boy has nothing to worry about. He has lots of money, political clout, and the top lawyers working for him. He'll be fine.'

'It isn't that simple.'

'That's what bothers me.'

'What do you mean?' Malvika asked.

'I mean, there'll be a lot of stories popping up about the girl now. Things your people will conveniently start feeding the media. Perhaps you have it on good authority that she was using Anil to get a foothold in the industry. Or you know things that make her seem less a victim and more an overambitious or unstable woman. Or that she was having an affair with someone else. I wouldn't want to touch these stories with a bargepole.'

Malvika's look didn't waver a bit.

'Are you ruling out any of those possibilities just because they're politically incorrect?' she said.

'It's the sort of counter-attack used in these situations,' Partha said. 'You can destroy a person—or the memory of a person—with just gossip and hearsay.'

'We don't need you for that kind of advice, Mr Rao. A manager in our studio office could put out such stories. They often do just that—very effectively.'

'That's true. But I think that was a missed opportunity to advance your argument.'

'I'm sorry?'

'Just then, you should have said that the accusations against Anil are also just hearsay.'

Malvika laughed.

'That's true,' she said. 'Now that you've made my argument for me, will you get involved?'

Partha shook his head.

'No,' he said. 'But let's say I was willing to get involved. What is it that you'd want me to do, Mrs Kumar?'

'Malvika, please. If I can call you Partha that is.'

Partha nodded.

'I want you to help save the boy's career,' Malvika said.

'I don't think so.'

'You set the terms of your involvement.'

'I just told you why I won't do it.'

'I don't want you to assassinate the girl's character, for god's sake! In fact, that's one of the things I want to prevent with your involvement.'

This took Partha by surprise. He looked first at Ramakrishna and then back at Malvika.

'That's a good instinct,' he said. 'But why exactly do you want to stop an attack on the girl's character?'

'That lot of cronies out there is itching to do exactly that. They'll attack Priya. Then they'll go raise all kinds of calls to caste and community. They're completely out of touch with how people think these days.'

'It will get a very negative reaction from the demographics where he needs to be a romantic hero,' Partha said. 'I hear that's what he's being pitched as?'

'Yes. And the taint of having driven a girl to suicide will also be tagged to his name.' For the first time, Malvika's look faltered. 'There's very little we can do about that now. But the fallout has to be better managed than what these characters can manage.'

Partha leaned back and considered it. He looked at Malvika for a few moments before he spoke.

'May I speak bluntly?' he said.

'Of course,' Malvika said.

'You're overthinking it and you don't need me for much,' he said. 'I'm sure the kid's already sitting with your lawyers?'

'Yes.'

'Here's some free advice: control the badmouthing of the girl. Stop it. Immediately. Let Anil say he had genuine affection for the girl—but just as a friend—and that he trusts the investigations to bring out the truth. I know you guys will plan to delay the investigation to buy time until public interest dies down. You'll try to get some relief from the courts, get him bail if it ever comes to arrest in the first place. By the time it gets to court and is dismissed, public anger would have diffused or can be managed more easily. It's an abetment of suicide case after all—always hard to prove. And if nothing sensational turns up, he should be okay. There'll be some negative talk but nothing he can't ride out. Put off work on his launch for a year. And if the romantic hero tag doesn't stick, he can take on a slightly tougher image. Either way, if there's no evidence against him, he should be okay in a year or two.'

Malvika looked on straight and didn't say anything.

'I don't mean to be flippant,' Partha said, 'but I told Mr Ramakrishna something similar a while ago. Even if the kid's arrested, his image will survive. Celebrities always do okay. In fact, if he handles it with some grace, he can talk about the trials he went through, how his perspective has changed, how he's grown.'

'That's cynical,' Malvika said, her look hardening.

'That's why I don't do it anymore. That's why I don't want to get involved now. I'm sorry to have wasted your time.'

He began to get up.

'Partha, wait,' Malvika said.

Partha hesitated.

'You don't want to help out with Anil's image, that's fine—we'll handle the media ourselves,' she said. 'But we could use your help behind-the-scenes, finding out what's going on. I know it's that kind of work that's made you successful.'

Partha smiled almost faintly. 'I was a fixer,' he said. 'It's true. But even so—'

'Just help us find out what's going on. Help us find out who's driving all this—who's out to destroy the family.'

Partha hesitated.

'Nothing to do with the media management part?' he said.

'Nothing,' Malvika said. 'Unless you think it's important and want to get involved.'

Partha was not expecting this. He had expected it to be a straight-out crisis management deal, not an offer to poke around behind the scenes. It made him curious. Why would they allow a third party like him, with uncertain loyalties, not even sworn to keeping confidentiality, to dig into the family's affairs?

'How do you know anyone's driving it?' Partha said.

Malvika and Ramakrishna exchanged looks.

'I don't know for sure but I have suspicions with some basis,' she said. 'But if my hunch is correct, there's no telling how far it can go to destroy my family.'

'You'd be right not to rule out anything,' Partha said. 'But you could also be reading too much into it. It may just be that a girl's committed suicide and political parties or other rivals are taking advantage of it.'

Malvika's look was impatient.

'Partha, don't patronise me,' she said. 'You might know about the media and about public relations but I know this family!'

'I'm sorry if that came off as patronising—'

'Doesn't matter. But what I'm asking you to do for me is important. I'm asking you to keep this kid from taking the blame for the sins of another family member!'

Partha leaned forward in his chair. 'Someone else?' he said. 'What're you talking about?'

'Just that. Anil may end up losing his career or going to jail for what an older member of the family has done.'

3

Palace intrigue peaks in times of war. Even as the nobles appear to rally around the king, they size up opportunities to depose him. If the king's position is secure, there are still other battles to be fought and won. A neglected noble may show his worth and rise in the hierarchy. A loyal noble may prove unequal to the demands of war and lose his place. A king under attack may turn suspicious of those he once trusted intimately. With power and money at stake, a crisis for one presents an opportunity for another.

In better times, Mohan Krishna had often compared himself to an emperor. He did it with a certain casualness, as though entirely unaware of the immodesty of the statement. He explained that he ruled the industry and the fans were his people. To the extent that statement was accurate, his empire was now under siege. And the unrest within his palace was heating up.

'Anil's the only son,' Partha said, 'there are no competitors even in the extended family. Who in the family would target him?'

'There are other motives,' Ramakrishna said impatiently. 'See, Priya was in touch with other family members as well. It's convenient for one family member to let Anil take the fall.'

'Why would Mohan Krishna allow that?' Partha said. 'Nobody in the family would dare go against him.'

'Not openly,' Malvika said. 'But all family members are not equal. There are some even Mohan Krishna cannot antagonise.'

'That seems hard to imagine. You'll have to explain it to me in detail.'

Malvika paused to gather her thoughts before she spoke.

'See, Priya was in touch with three or four people in the family,' she said. 'We're certain that someone else led Priya on—had an affair with her—and then cut her off.'

'And this person is powerful enough to get Mohan Krishna to compromise his own son's future?'

Malvika's look hardened.

'Some people in this industry are willing to take chances with a family member's life,' she said. 'Not that Mohan Krishna is doing it …'

'Of course not,' Partha said half-heartedly.

Malvika picked up on the hint of doubt in Partha's tone.

'See, in this industry everything is warped,' she said. 'Some stars believe that a family member has no worth without him, the star.'

'I know,' Partha said. 'They're the sun everything is orbiting around.'

'Exactly. By that token, it becomes easy enough to reason that saving himself is saving the whole family. But saving one family member is saving just that one family member.'

'What does this family member have on Mohan Krishna?'

Malvika didn't reply immediately.

Ramakrishna leaned forward. 'It's not one thing,' he said. 'Mohan Krishna's empire, like any star's empire, is made up of areas of influence. You know how that works.'

'Let me guess,' Partha said. 'The family has stakes in his films, the family runs affiliate businesses with his black money, and some family members set up businesses of their own.'

'That's right.'

'And even in the independent businesses, the family member gives the star a share.'

'Exactly the same here,' Malvika said. 'The family provides a front for the star; the family also allows him to cash in on different aspects of the film business—he's not limited to just his acting fee. Films are produced in family members' names, real-estate projects are run in family members' names, films are distributed and studios run in the same way. Sometimes, the family member runs his or her own business genuinely and invests a part of the star's money. It's a system that benefits both. Within the family, the stardom is milked to the maximum—it increases its control over the film industry. The star gets returns from everywhere and can invest his money in other people's names. What shares the star and the family member get are secret—even other family members don't know.'

Ramakrishna looked uncomfortable with this level of candidness. But he did not interrupt.

'So you're saying,' Partha said, 'that somewhere along the line that star becomes as reliant on the family as it is on him?'

'The star's always more powerful, and everyone defers to him,' Malvika said. 'He perpetuates the family's power. But, yes, at some stage, the star cannot take important family members lightly.'

'I understand.'

'So—'

'So you think Kalla Prakash had a relationship with Priya.'

Malvika and Ramakrishna were thrown by the statement and it showed. It wasn't so much what was said as much as the bluntness with which it was said. Something that had only ever been whispered about had been spoken out loud. Ramakrishna broke into a smile and looked at Malvika. She gave him a quick nod.

'How did you arrive at that?' she asked.

'It's known that he's the most influential man in Mohan Krishna's camp,' Partha said. 'Mr Sivaprasad used to be that but he stopped producing films ten years ago. They also say he's suffering from early-stage dementia now. Anyway, Mohan Krishna no longer needs a mentor. He's still treated with respect, I understand, but is otherwise retired. Your husband, Vishnu, has always been the low-profile one in the camp. He occasionally gets a producing credit but otherwise sticks to managing the administrative side of the studio. Neither of these activities make him powerful enough to blackmail a superstar. He wouldn't, even if he had a chance to. Word is, he's a nice man and very loyal to his brother—unlikely to do anything to hurt him or Anil.'

Ramakrishna nodded. Malvika didn't react.

'Rama Devi, being Mohan Krishna's elder sister and someone he genuinely respects, is powerful but she's not nearly as powerful as Prakash,' he said. 'That makes Prakash the best candidate.'

'Why couldn't it be someone from Rama Devi's family?' Malvika said.

'Prakash recently stole a script Rama Devi was developing and announced the film with Mohan Krishna. Mohan Krishna placated her but did not take the film away from Prakash. Tells you who's more influential.'

Malvika smiled. 'You're well-informed,' she said.

'I read the gossip columns.'

'The news about this film wasn't in the press. Rama Devi is very loyal to Mohan Krishna. She didn't allow even a whisper of this to get to the press.'

'Well, I got it from the grapevine.'

'So that leaves Prakash,' she said.

'It does,' Partha said. 'And it seems in character that he might seduce a young girl like Priya.'

Kalla Prakash was a good ten years younger than Mohan Krishna and good-looking enough to enter the industry himself. But he chose to turn to business instead—his cousin Mohan Krishna's business. He didn't just help out, he virtually ran several of the family companies in addition to those he'd set up on his own. From the very beginning, Mohan Krishna let him have a free run of whatever he was in charge of. And it was the smart thing to do. Prakash's business acumen made the family richer than they could have ever imagined. His negotiation skills and manoeuvering with producers, distributors, and film exhibitors had made huge amounts of money for both Mohan Krishna's family and himself. He quickly became one of the most powerful people in the industry. Along with his success came a reputation for being haughty and extracting every rupee from those he did business with. He set his own terms and wasn't burdened with being scrupulous. If he was disagreeable in his professional conduct, there was little to like in his personal conduct too: he was known to be vain and fond of flaunting his wealth. Over the years, he became something of a hate figure in the entire state and even in the family's community.

'He's involved in every other family business,' Ramakrishna said. 'If he turned against Mohan Krishna ...' Ramakrishna just shook his head to emphasise.

'That's why we need your help—desperately,' Malvika said, looking at Partha keenly. 'There's nothing we can do against him from within the family. Prakash holds all the cards. We can't find out what his role in this whole thing is.'

'You've helped me out in the past, Partha,' Ramakrishna said. 'And while you say I did you a favour once, I don't believe it to be a favour. It was just a friend fulfilling his responsibility. Please oblige me in the same spirit.'

'You don't want to work for Mohan Krishna,' Malvika said, 'and you wouldn't be. In fact, he doesn't know we've approached you—he'd be furious if he found out. He wants to handle it all by himself. But he's in a compromised position—he can't help Anil.'

Partha hesitated. Malvika leaned forward; her look was earnest.

'Please try and find out about Prakash's relationship with Priya,' she said. 'Find out what exactly is happening now and why. We don't want to hide the truth, we want the truth to come out. If it does, Anil will be saved automatically—I don't doubt that for a moment.'

*

There was a knock on the door. A young man stepped in gingerly. He was very conscious of Malvika's presence in the room—he wouldn't even make eye contact with her. He looked only at Ramakrishna and spoke in a deferential tone.

'Sir is about to give a statement,' he said.

'Already?' Malvika asked.

The young man looked at Malvika with an alarmed expression.

'Yes, Madam,' he mumbled.

'Is Anil with him?' she asked.

'No, Madam,' he said, a little more composed now. 'Anil sir is still at home and Mohan Krishna sir went to the studio a little while ago.'

'Is anybody with Mohan Krishna sir?'

'I don't know, Madam. We just saw it on TV—the channels say he's going to give a statement in the studio in a few minutes.'

'We'll come out and watch.'

'Yes, Madam.'

The young man left the room.

'I had no idea he was going to make a statement so soon,' Malvika said.

'It's good to make a statement early on,' Partha said slowly. 'Just that ...'

'Just that what?' Malvika said.

'We don't want him to come off as being either defensive or aggressive,' he said. 'If he sticks to human emotions like concern for his son and sympathy for the girl, he should be fine.'

'Mohan Krishna thinks of everything—don't worry,' Ramakrishna said.

Malvika looked at Partha. She clearly wanted to see what Partha might have to say about that. Partha looked back at her and shrugged.

'I'm sure he's a real genius,' he said. 'Let's see what brilliance he displays now and take it from there.'

Through the frown of stress and concentration on Malvika's face, a smile broke through.

They went out to the hall where the TVs were. A few more men were around by now. The men sitting down vacated their chairs as Malvika approached. Some of them greeted her and stepped back.

The volume on HydNews was turned up and the other channels were muted. The HydNews cameraman had the best angle, and that wasn't a coincidence. The channel was friendly to Mohan Krishna because he owned a significant stake in it through proxies. The background of the studio hall was blank and had no studio symbols or film posters on it. No chair and table had been set up; a low podium with mikes stacked on it was the only visible furniture. This suggested that Mohan Krishna would make his statement standing in front of the mikes and was unlikely to answer questions. Partha thought these were all right choices. It all came down to what he said now.

As they waited for Mohan Krishna to appear, news anchors recapped what was known so far. The latest development was a brief written statement from Priya's parents. They had refused to speak on-camera. They said their daughter was depressed but they didn't know the exact cause. They thought it was because of professional setbacks but they had not seen any signs that she might take such an extreme step. They didn't know any more about the cause of her death and hoped the investigations would reveal it. At this point the statement took on a stronger tone. It said that they wanted no part of any political party or film industry mud-slinging over this. They just asked to be left alone to grieve.

A smaller story also attracting notice was about protesting student groups and National People's Party activists. They were now gathered outside the hospital and growing in numbers. The protests were going to shift to the university the next day. NPP spokespersons made themselves readily available for comment; the occasional student leader also spoke out. The rhetoric was harsher now. They all raised the matter of the missing cellphone and laptop. They now openly accused the circle inspector of misleading the people and destroying evidence.

'These devices are necessities nowadays,' the NPP spokesperson said. 'They're also crucial pieces of evidence that would reveal who Priya was in touch with in her last days and months. And these are the very pieces of evidence missing from the apartment. How convenient for whoever is responsible! And we all know that the local police are under the influence of one family!'

The police, through sources speaking off the record, put word out that they had already approached the phone and internet companies—they were in the process of collecting information about phone calls and Priya's email accounts. They were confident of getting any relevant information even before the devices were found. This response did not placate the protesters. They insisted that these objects would not have disappeared unless they had sensitive information that was not available online.

A casual look at the news coverage was enough to predict that the missing devices would dominate the headlines for days to come. What Partha flagged mentally, however, was the NPP spokesperson's statement. On the surface, the statement sounded harsh but it contained nothing the party couldn't walk back from, even if they could not disown them altogether. Partha could only assume that the NPP's reported negotiations with Mohan Krishna to ally with them in the elections had reached an impasse but were not dead. Mohan Krishna had been disinclined to ally with the NPP from the start. He expected, irrationally, to sweep the elections on his own. That was hardly a possibility but the NPP was electorally the weakest in the very regions of the state that Mohan Krishna was strong in. So it would suit the NPP to use this crisis as leverage in its negotiations with him rather than give the opposition a chance to consolidate in those areas. The NPP wanted to keep open the option of tacit support or secret deal-making—it wasn't ready to burn its boats just yet.

Onscreen, there was a sudden burst of activity as the star emerged from a studio office. Cameramen and reporters jostled amongst themselves. The sounds of scuffling and reporters shouting out questions grew louder. Mohan Krishna walked slowly in their direction. He was dressed in a blue shirt, the top three buttons undone. He wore sunglasses and the usual wig of jet-black hair. He didn't smile, but the look on his face wasn't solemn as much as surly. As he approached the mikes a few jostling cameramen strayed into his path. Mohan Krishna lost his cool—he gestured angrily at the cameraman to step back. He turned to his bodyguards and abused them.

Partha glanced at Malvika. She had tensed up, sat up straighter and gripped the arms of the chair. Her face didn't show any emotion.

The news anchors got worked up by this little performance. They talked in excited tones about how Mohan Krishna had abused the press and his own staff. The scurrying around of people continued as Mohan Krishna made his way to where the mikes were stacked. He had regained some control by the time he got there. He stood at the podium, waiting for the reporters to calm down. He ignored the questions being shouted at him for a few minutes. And then suddenly, his head shot up.

'What atrocity?' he said angrily. 'Are you here to listen to my statement or talk rubbish?'

Once again there was pandemonium. Reporters began to shout back at Mohan Krishna demanding an explanation. A manager stepped in trying to restore order. He pleaded, joked, and requested the reporters to stay calm. Mohan Krishna began to speak animatedly to another one of his managers; he seemed ready to leave. The possibility of his leaving without giving a statement sobered the journalists—a senior reporter began to call out for calm and the others responded.

From Mohan Krishna's body language itself, Partha could tell this wouldn't go well. He seemed irritable and unfocused. It was Partha's guess that Prakash had gotten under his skin already. On occasion, Mohan Krishna was capable of turning on the charm and playing the film industry's elder statesman. Partha had seen him do just that even under extreme provocation or stress. But right then, Mohan Krishna was in no state of mind to make the mature, empathetic statement that was desperately needed of him. If Malvika was right and Prakash was using his influence on the star to shield himself, he may have just won round one.

Mohan Krishna started his statement a few times over until everyone quietened down.

'My son is innocent,' he said. 'It's tragic that a young girl has lost her life. People come to the industry with a lot of dreams—just as I did. I came here with nothing more than a few dreams and my talent. The rest is history, and it is known to you all. Unfortunately, not everyone's dreams come true. What is sadder is that this girl's death is being used to target my son. It is a conspiracy against me and my family.

I've been in the film industry for so many years with no taint on my reputation. Just when my son is about to take his first steps into the industry, to take the burden of his great legacy onto his shoulders, my rivals are targeting him without even stopping to think that he's just a young man. My rivals are people who don't want me in politics because they're afraid of my popularity, because they don't want change in society. They are targeting me using this incident as an excuse. But it will never work. My son is innocent and he'll come through this test by fire even stronger. We will not bow down to blackmail, and we will not shrink from a fight! I urge you all not to pass judgement until the entire truth is known. Don't let this tragic event be misused against my son.'

Partha knew Malvika was watching him for a reaction but he didn't show any. Mohan Krishna had messed up. He'd made the conversation about whether or not Anil was innocent. Instead he could have played for time, generally suggesting that there was no evidence tying his son to the suicide and that they were waiting for the investigation to unfold. He could have taken subtler shots at political parties, saying politicisation was inhumane. Most importantly, he should have used the statement to speak sympathetically about Priya. Instead he'd dismissed her in one clichéd line. Then he'd gone on to expose his own vanity. The greatest damage he'd done however was by centering his counter-offensive in politics. It made it seem as though he was looking at it primarily from a political perspective. There would have been a time for that kind of statement but this just wasn't it. He sounded angry about a conspiracy against him rather than sad about a young woman's death. And he hadn't come off as an upset father at all, he'd just come off as an angry powerful man.

As if the statement wasn't problematic enough, he went on to make more mistakes. Even as his manager tried to wind up the event, reporters began to shout out questions at him. The manager tried to usher him away but Mohan Krishna wouldn't leave. A reporter shouted out something about a cover-up and asked what had happened to the missing cellphone and laptop.

'How would I know?' Mohan Krishna said.

'It is well-known that the circle inspector is close to your family,' the reporter said. 'And the girl's friends are saying that Anil had an affair with her and discarded her.'

'On what basis can you say that?' Mohan Krishna demanded. 'You can say anything you want because you're from the press, is it? And just because I live in the jurisdiction of a certain police station, you can accuse me of influencing the probe? Just because the girl's friends said something irresponsible, am I to give an explanation for it? Is there anything I don't have to give an explanation for?'

'A young innocent girl's life is lost and your family's name has come up—don't you believe you owe an explanation?'

Partha sensed Malvika shift in her chair. This was not going to end well.

'Every year, girls come in the thousands to this industry—am I or my son responsible for all of them?' Mohan Krishna said. 'Some girl commits suicide because she's not able to handle the pressure or is mentally unstable and you people want to drag me and my son into the street like we're criminals?'

Malvika exhaled audibly. She had turned pale. Ramakrishna also looked grim. The men standing behind them didn't make a sound. Ramakrishna turned to Partha.

'It's done now,' Partha said. 'It's just something you have to deal with. An apology to begin with.'

Ramakrishna nodded and looked back towards the screens.

'Wait it out today,' Partha said. 'Shut down all family members' social media accounts—no posts about anything. Let your political party stick to policy issues. When asked about

Priya's death they're to say they'll wait for more information to emerge—at least for the time being.'

Ramakrishna nodded emphatically. He gestured to a young man to take notes. Malvika was composed and alert once again. Partha looked at her.

'And put Malvika in front of the cameras tomorrow,' he said.

Malvika started with surprise. She considered it for a moment and then nodded.

'Is it as bad as I think it is?' she asked.

'It just got harder to keep Anil from being arrested,' Partha said. 'His father has turned every right-thinking person against the family.'

4

Partha called Seema as he drove to the office. He told her he had to meet her and Harish right away.

'Where the hell were you?' she broke in.

'Got a call first thing in the morning—' Partha began.

'And you had to rush?'

'Yeah, there was some urgency.'

'So urgent you couldn't send a text saying you'd be late?'

'I should have—'

'I'm getting very tired of turning up at the office and finding neither Harish nor you here!'

'But I haven't been to the office in a week now,' Partha said.

'That's just it, Partha. I live for Monday morning partners' meetings, you see? That's when I take a moment, shut my eyes, and give in to the fantasy that I don't run the damn business alone!'

'I emailed you all my stuff for this week. I don't think Harish's got an ongoing project either.'

'The Excel Pharmaceuticals meeting is today.'

'That's your meeting.'

'It's a firm meeting.'

'I haven't been in any of the Excel meetings. What're you upset about?'

'I should know where you are or at least be able to reach you.'

'So if you knew I was sitting at home while you were in the Excel meeting, you'd have been fine?'

'Maybe.'

'You do realise we're not married?'

'We're in a workplace marriage! Outside work, I'm out of your league.'

'That's true.'

'I don't like being left out of the loop. You disappear without an explanation. Harish doesn't answer my calls but you always seem to know how to reach him. And I'm taking the boring-as-hell scheduled meetings,' Seema said in one breath.

Partha didn't speak for a few moments as he focused on the road—a motorcycle on the left and a car on the right were overtaking him at once.

'Hello?' Seema said.

'Just a sec,' Partha said.

The motorcyclist overtook him from the left and then wanted to turn right, so Partha had to slow down. Partha settled into a steady pace after that.

'Seema, did you happen to watch any Telugu news channels this morning?' Partha said.

Seema didn't answer right away. 'Yes,' she said.

'And you knew Mr Ramakrishna would reach out to me?'

'Yes.'

'So that's why you texted me.'

There was another pause.

'So we're managing PR for star-kid scandals now?' she said. 'Just this week, I turned away two potential clients saying we don't actively manage crises anymore, that we only do boring manuals and plans. Now we're managing a crisis for Mohan Krishna?'

'Don't get worked up.'

'I'm already worked up! They were both good corporates and very good money. I have a family!'

'We're not managing Anil's PR. Not exactly anyway.'

'What's that supposed to mean?'

'Let me get Harish to meet us at the office. Don't make me narrate it all twice.'

*

A simple grey plaque mounted on the metal gate read 'Enterprise Associates'. It was a sleepy compound in the Banjara Hills area of Hyderabad. There were office and apartment buildings around it, but the lane itself was set off from the frenetic activity of the main road. The mid-sized house with a small garden had now been converted into an office. The structure of the house had been retained as it was, but the insides had been hollowed out and replaced with the glass and steel look of a contemporary office. The front walls were covered with creepers and the garden was tastefully landscaped. A lone, middle-aged guard dozed on a chair in the open garage; an office boy and a driver sat by a car talking.

Inside the building, a small reception area opened out into a well-ventilated hall with a conference room, cubicles, and a lunch area. The room buzzed with quiet efficiency as a few people worked at their stations. A glass door led to a private section. There were three office cabins with blinds, each with a view of the backyard garden.

It was nearly lunchtime by the time Harish got to the office. They met in Seema's cabin.

'So you had the good sense to say no,' Seema said, 'but Malvika batted her eyelashes at you and you said yes.'

Harish nodded. 'I always thought you had a thing for Malvika when she was in the movies,' he said.

'Fine,' Partha said, 'let's say that's what happened.'

'There's no money involved in this?' Seema asked.

'Ramakrishna will pay,' Partha said. 'He'll treat it as work done for his company.'

'Wonderful. He pays peanuts.'

'He's agreed to accept our billing without questions.'

'But we're going to bill him moderately because he's your friend?'

'Because he once used his influence to keep Harish from being arrested.'

Harish stretched his legs out and crossed them at the ankles.

'It's the thing about being a private operative,' Harish said. 'You move about with dubious sorts and sometimes get seen doing it.'

'It doesn't help that "private operative" is a profession you made up, that nobody else recognises,' Partha said.

'People are narrow-minded—doesn't make sense to them if it doesn't show on a drop-down menu.'

'It wasn't expanding people's minds that got your name dropped from that investigation. Thank God, Mr Ramakrishna's contact had faith in his judgement and that did it. '

'His contact had commonsense,' Harish said.

'Well, it would have taken us months to get the police to accept your version of commonsense and clear you, even with all our contacts. With your father's health at the time ...'

Harish nodded loosely. 'So what do you plan to do?' he said.

'I tried to get to a friend in the police department but he didn't pick up,' Partha said. 'I'm just curious to know what they've found out so far. But it's sure to be a dead-end. Nobody's going to talk—the case is too high-profile.'

'I'll find out,' Harish said.

'You believe Malvika about Prakash?' Seema said.

'I'm not sure,' Partha said. 'It explains why Mohan Krishna was disoriented and all over the place in the presser. But other than that, we just have Malvika's word for it.'

'Which is all some people here need.'

'So, I am going to move forward assuming there is a conspiracy.'

'Shocking!'

'How could there not be a conspiracy?' Harish said. 'Malvika said there was one.'

'Sometimes it helps to move forward with a bias,' Partha said. 'We may end up seeing patterns where none exist but there's a lower possibility of missing patterns that are actually out there.'

Harish stretched his hands languidly. 'I can try to get Prakash's cellphone records through contacts in telecoms,' he said. 'But I wouldn't count on it. Network operators have become paranoid about security.'

'I doubt you'd find anything anyway,' Partha said. 'Prakash wouldn't have used a phone that can be traced back to him. He's too careful a man. Find out what you can but don't waste a lot of effort on it.'

Seema looked unconvinced.

'What's the point of doing any of this?' she said. 'If Malvika is right, Mohan Krishna already knows Prakash's secret. But he needs Prakash so badly for business and political interests that he's protecting him. At the cost of his own son, for goodness sake! What good would getting evidence of the affair do?'

'Malvika feels concrete information will strengthen Mohan Krishna's hand. He can get Anil out of trouble then.'

'It's risky,' Harish said. 'If Prakash is desperate, he'll hit Mohan Krishna hard with the dirt he's got on him. We're talking about a major financial and political hit. It may not be worth it.'

'Malvika and Ramakrishna are willing to take the risk,' Partha said. 'If we find something, they're willing to leak it to the press themselves.'

'Two amateurs trying to play the media game,' Seema said, shaking her head.

'They figure they have us,' Partha said.

'We're virtually amateurs ourselves when it comes to the Telugu media. We're in Hyderabad pretending we're in Bombay or Delhi!'

'That's why I kept us out of the PR part of it. They know that part's up to them.'

'Fine. So what's the POA?'

'I wasn't able to meet Anil because he was with his lawyers. I'll go meet him whenever Malvika calls. I've also asked Malvika to be prepared to give interviews. She'll have to check with Mohan Krishna first, of course. I think it's good to give people a glimpse inside the house, show them someone who's composed and sounds reasonable.'

'Oh my!' Seema said.

Harish grinned.

'It'll help show that the family isn't panicking,' Partha said, ignoring Seema. 'That they're not inside their house in a frightened huddle, scheming and plotting.'

'Which they are,' Seema said.

'Yeah, but people don't have to see that,' Partha said.

'And to be fair to them, they've outsourced some of that plotting and scheming to us,' Harish said. 'So it's not all going on inside the house per se.'

'You both make brilliant and useful points as always,' Partha said, 'but if we could get back to what's important.'

'The many virtues of Malvika … ,' Seema said.

'You do realise we're not in high school anymore?' Partha said.

'Oh, a reaction!' Seema said. 'I think we're onto something.'

'Definitely onto something,' Harish said.

'What we want,' Partha said wearily, 'is to show that the family wants justice for Priya. We need that to come out clearly, especially after Mohan Krishna's on-air meltdown.'

'They'll need several good moments to overcome that one,' Seema said.

'We'll have to figure out the best time for Malvika's interviews. In the meantime, Ramakrishna's got a bunch of guys watching the news coverage. I've asked him to see which channel has a head-start—however slight—over the others and let me know. Also asked them to check which channel is the shrillest.'

'Why bother?' Harish said. 'We're not handling their media coverage.'

'This whole situation has arisen because Prakash is under attack and he's trying to make Anil take the fall for it,' Seema said. 'It would help to know who's attacking Prakash. A media outlet is a good place to start and work backwards.'

'Right,' Partha said. 'So I'll wait to hear from him. In the meantime, I'll try to reach out to some journalist friends—see what their sources are telling them.'

Harish got to his feet and stretched a once again.

'Why's Malvika so desperate to save Anil?' he said.

'Ramakrishna says it's genuine affection,' Partha said. 'She's known Anil from the time he was a teenager; he would come to the sets when she was shooting with Mohan Krishna.'

'And she's willing to risk Mohan Krishna's larger interests to save the kid?'

'I got that impression.'

'But why?'

'I don't know. Maybe she hates Mohan Krishna deep down, maybe even his family thinks he deserves to be taken down a few notches.'

'That's nonsense and you know it,' Seema said. 'Malvika and Vishnu want to help get Anil exonerated so they can sideline Prakash and occupy a central place in the family. They'd also have Anil's gratitude, and he's the next star in the family.'

'Makes sense,' Harish said. 'Malvika has been projecting herself as the actress-turned-Ivy League MBA. She may want to play a more prominent role than running a boutique.'

Partha shrugged. 'Anything's possible,' he said. 'Their internal tussles are not our immediate concern. We find out what's happening and pass it along.'

Partha looked at the two of them. Harish nodded. Seema didn't react.

'So, Harish, you'll check about the phone records,' Partha said. 'I'll talk to some journalists; and Seema, please get us something on Prakash's business and political interests.'

As they left the cabin Partha turned around.

'Anything we do has to be done fast,' he said. 'The kid may be questioned and arrested in a day or two.'

*

The bar at the Hyatt Park was virtually empty. In one corner, a man in his fifties sipped scotch and smoked a cigar. Another man, a European, sat at the bar drinking beer. Seema sat by herself at a table to the side. She sipped her glass of Perrier and took in the place. It had the sort of ambience she found alluring back in her twenties. In her late thirties now, with office work to catch up on and a daughter and husband at home, she had no patience for it. She let the restlessness rise within her and run free. It would reach its peak in a few minutes and then subside. She'd learnt to be patient—the entire skill was in waiting out emotions.

She could identify the emotions troubling her: tension, the restraining tug of inertia, and excitement. The three had mixed together to form a single sensation. It was a sensation that rose to the surface every time they got involved in a situation like this. But this time things were messier than usual. She didn't think Anil deserved to be helped out. Perhaps that was unfair to Anil but that was just the way she felt. She didn't like the idea of getting tangled up with megalomaniacal stars and their families. And it did little for their profile; helping out Mohan Krishna wouldn't impress a corporate client in the future. At best, it would enhance their reputation for being unpredictable and edgy, which was a dubious asset to begin with. The whole business made her uncomfortable—it had been a long time since they'd gotten into a difficult, high-profile situation. Her daughter was just five years old and normalcy was pleasant. She didn't want trouble for herself, and certainly not for her family.

This train of thought took Seema a little by surprise. It brought home to her just how much her life had changed over the past ten years. She now had a family of her own, but that was just one part of it. She had also given up a job in business journalism and moved from Mumbai to Hyderabad. She was the managing partner of a consultancy. And an interest in crisis management had turned into a profitable training and consulting business.

Almost all the changes in her life had caught her by surprise, but quitting journalism wasn't one of them. She'd never liked the job to begin with. There was a flurry of frantic activity when a major breaking story came along. She was always up to its demands, but she didn't particularly enjoy the work. She thought of high-pressure situations as things you dealt with without complaint, but not something you glamourised. The culture of valuing adrenaline-rushes and burnouts was lost on her. She much preferred the analytical side of her job, where she could dig into a story and make connections where none were apparent. She had a particular fascination for looking behind the scenes and exploring what happened with companies and business personalities in moments of crisis.

It was while writing on one such crisis that she met Partha. She saw in him someone who could be incredibly effective in a moment of a crisis while remaining strangely detached from it. At the time, he was the founder and head of a small PR agency with a reputation for getting the job done. The agency was pretty much a support mechanism for his work and employed a skeletal staff.

Partha's agency retained Harish's services; this was how Seema came to meet him as well. Harish worked as a freelancer with an unspecified role, an all-round troubleshooter of sorts. Rumour was he had a troubled past—something about activities bordering on the illegal and connections with shadowy characters and organisations.

Very little was also known about the firm's inner workings and about Partha himself. Partha expected companies to repose trust in the firm based on its track record but shared no further information about its everyday functioning. He went to great lengths to keep people from learning anything about himself. It was said he had a dangerous streak about him—that he dabbled in extreme and even violent sports. When asked, Partha always denied the rumours. He'd deny them more vigorously, he said, if they didn't give him an air of mystery. The agency got work steadily, as companies who worked with it tended to stay with it. Even then, Partha worked only on select projects and showed no interest in scaling up the business.

Seema and Partha first collaborated when he approached her with some information about a corporate, a rival to one of his client companies. He offered no inducements but said she should write about it if she thought it relevant. She felt no sense of obligation for the information and used the material sparingly. If it helped Partha's cause, she was unaware of it. From then on, for a few years, they turned to each other for information. With no strings attached.

When the Spectrum Software crisis broke, Seema happened to be in-between jobs, having quit the last one from a sheer lack of motivation. Partha invited her to work with Harish and him on the case. Seema accepted the offer, and she never regretted it. The stakes were high—there was tremendous pressure and it even got dangerous. But they ended up winning, and it paid off big for all of them.

A little later, Partha quit the PR industry and Mumbai to return to Hyderabad. He led a reclusive life anyway; it mattered little to him where he lived. He'd tempted fate often enough, he said, and he wanted to quit while ahead. Seema knew his reasons ran deeper even though Partha refused to discuss them. She felt it was a good decision: going into semi-retirement would be good for him. With the Spectrum Software windfall he didn't need to work that much, so he could freelance when he chose to.

It was Seema's idea to set up a training and consulting firm. All three of them were flush with cash and could afford to try it without a financial downside. She believed in it strongly enough to move to Hyderabad and initiate work on setting up the consultancy. She handled most of the training part herself. The rest of their work was preparing crisis-management manuals and giving some event-specific advice. Occasionally, their consulting went beyond what was on paper. With some clients, they got directly involved, getting their hands dirty. But that was relatively rare and only when unavoidable. The bulk of the work was routine. Seema ran the show as managing partner. Partha and Harish took smaller cuts of the business in return for the freedom to restrict their office and client-service responsibilities. As Partha's record was what brought in clients, he was heavily involved in the designing of crisis plans, protocols, and strategy papers. Harish did some of that too but he remained primarily a troubleshooter. The firm was profitable from the start and they could pick and choose their clients.

Seema had to uproot her young family—her husband and toddler daughter—in moving to Hyderabad. But her husband, Ravi, had found better work with an MNC at Hyderabad. Things had fallen into a steady, relatively predictable routine and though they did get rough a few times in their consulting practice, they were very manageable situations. Her experience of working in consulting was long stretches of routine work punctuated with a few unpredictable times.

With one such uncertain phase looming ahead, Seema couldn't help but be concerned. It seemed to her that even as consulting had clarified her priorities, things had gotten murkier for Partha. She saw crisis situations as necessary evils, something you got through and perhaps benefited from. She attached no additional value to them. She also saw that she didn't like the gritty parts of the business; she preferred the legitimate, corporate, strategic parts. But it was different for Partha. He had to be in the thick of things, he enjoyed taking a hand in difficult situations and in seeing them through to a conclusion. It wasn't that he got a high from it—she knew that for sure. He retained his ability to be be almost coldly detached from a situation. And now, money or a career were no longer primary motivations. Something about a particular crisis lured him in; and then he could not turn away from it. In this particular situation, she couldn't make out what it was that had drawn him in, and that bothered her deeply.

She shook herself out of these thoughts and tried to focus. Her task for now was to gather information and move in the direction they'd decided on. Just then she looked up and smiled. Her contact had just arrived.

*

'Of all the dumbass, despicable people you could be interested in, Kalla Prakash is the lowest!' Prashanth said.

'Come on,' Seema said, 'he's dashing.'

'Allow me to throw up.'

'He still looks like a young guy. Works out like crazy and dresses sharp. There's even a rumour that Mohan Krishna paid him off not to enter the film industry!'

'Even if all that were true—which it isn't—sleaze would ooze from every pore of his body.'

'He's supposed to be a shrewd businessman.'

'Ruthless. That's what he is. Absolutely no hesitation to use dirty tricks. Let me tell you: there isn't a rival producer, distributor, or exhibitor who doesn't hate him.'

'So apart from the film industry he's involved in real estate, power, and TV?'

'Yeah. He's ruthless in all those businesses too.'

'Do you know of any recent spats or long-standing rivalries?'

Prashanth raised his hands in mock helplessness. 'Too many to count!' he said. 'But you probably know about them—there's a lot of gossip out there. Much of it true.'

Prashanth sat back and leaned on the backrest. He reached for his glass and took a big sip of whiskey.

'I'm curious about why you want to know all this,' he said.

'A client wants to know,' Seema said.

'Mohan Krishna's son gets in trouble in the morning and you're asking me this in the evening? Should I read anything into that?'

'My client is curious about the family's business. If the family is in trouble, the fallout on their businesses is relevant to him.'

'Does your client have an interest in the family's businesses doing well or poorly?'

Seema laughed. 'Poorly,' she said.

Prashanth smiled and shook his head.

'I'm invested in Prakash's rivals in the power business,' he said. 'Your answer wouldn't be influenced by that, would it?'

'Of course not,' Seema said, smiling.

Prashanth smiled back but didn't say anything.

'I know it's not personal with you,' Seema said, 'because you represent a giant, impersonal private equity fund. But I knew you'd have a lot of information on him precisely because you're on rival boards. Trust a rival to have all the dirt.'

Prashanth smiled broadly and nodded.

'Still, why should I share it with you?' he said. 'You won't even tell me who your client is.'

'Because we're both professionals without a personal axe to grind. But we both benefit from information. Information like—I don't know—a tipoff about a client preparing to siphon off your fund's investment the moment you made the deal. I remember us talking about some such thing. I'd like us to keep that kind of network alive. Wouldn't you?'

Prashanth nodded again, smiling more easily this time.

'There's nothing much going on in the power sector,' he said. 'The industry is in a damn slump right now. But the word out there is that Prakash is buying stakes in media channels. It's hard to say which channels exactly but everyone just assumes it's for Mohan Krishna's entry into politics.'

'Now, that's interesting. Tell me more.'

*

It was past 9 p.m. when Seema started for home. She called Partha from the car. He was driving at the time.

'Malvika called,' he said the moment he answered. 'Said Anil's going to be left alone for a while now.'

'I suppose you're going to be snuck in,' Seema said.

'Yeah. Perils of working for one faction of the family and keeping it secret from the others.'

'Playing off factions in Mohan Krishna's family. Such a proud moment in all our careers.'

'Tell me about it.'

'I suppose we're hiding not just from Prakash but Mohan Krishna himself?'

'Yeah.'

'That's wonderful. If he finds out we're trying to help his son he'd be furious with us!'

'Well, Malvika says he doesn't want any outsiders involved.'

'Seriously though, Malvika is a taking a big risk,' Seema said.

'I suppose she is. It's admirable in a way.'

'Let's not get carried away.'

Partha laughed. 'So what did you find out?' he asked.

'Nothing earth-shattering. Prashanth says Prakash is buying stakes in some local television news channels. He figures it was part of their strategy for the political push.'

'Not surprising. Mohan Krishna bought a stake in HydNews recently. They'd like more invisible leverage in other channels.'

'Yes.'

'Did he mention CNEWS in some context?' Partha asked.

'CNEWS? No. He said it was hard to know what exact channels they were investing in.'

'Can you try find out who owns CNEWS from other sources?'

'Okay. I was going to check on channel ownership as a whole. But why CNEWS in particular?'

'Remember I asked Mr Ramakrishna to check on who's early on breaking news? Turns out it's CNEWS. Consistently.'

'That's strange. Little-known channel.'

'Unknown channel. Could just be an enterprising reporter, of course. But won't hurt to check if it belongs to a known family rival.'

'Will do. What else is playing out on TV?'

Partha came to a stop at a traffic light. It was past nine but there was still a fair bit of traffic.

'Priya's missing phone and laptop are the biggest story,' Partha said. 'NPP and student groups say the police destroyed them to protect Anil.'

'Okay.'

'Anil drove down to the police station this evening. He was questioned for a while and allowed to go. He's to go back to the police station tomorrow. Another sign of soft treatment, according to political parties and activists.'

'Why are you bothering to go to meet Anil? He's not going to tell you anything he hasn't been coached to say. You can get that version from Malvika or Ramakrishna.'

'I already got that version from them. Now I want to get a sense of what he's like.'

'I suppose he'll claim he barely knew her. That they were just acquaintances.'

Partha didn't respond immediately. The car was moving again now.

'He's already told them they were close friends,' he said.

'Why would he volunteer that?' Seema said.

'His line is that there was nothing between them but she may have gotten the wrong idea about the relationship. He's also going to tell them she hung out with him at their studio and might have met his family members there.'

Seema spoke slowly. 'So her interactions with all other family members become incidental,' she said. 'She was there primarily to meet him and no one else.'

'Yes.'

'God, that's cold! They really are pushing him under the bus.'

'The worst part is, it's unnecessary. He could have said she mingled with all his family members and colleagues freely. But they're making him say it for different reasons. It's to assure someone they're sticking to the narrative agreed upon. To assure them they're not going to try deflect the blame.'

'Prakash?'

'Yes.'

5

Ramakrishna's shoulders were drooped and his eyes weary. It had been a very long day. He'd been at Mohan Krishna's house since early that morning and it was 9.30 p.m. now. He met Partha at the end of the street and led him to the compound adjoining Mohan Krishna's house. The guard let them in without a word and shut the gate behind them. A small board with the names 'Vishnu' and 'Malvika' was fixed to a wall. It was a large, elegantly designed house, with a Zen garden in the front yard. They walked past the house itself to a wicket-gate that led to Mohan Krishna's house. Partha didn't try to engage Ramakrishna in any conversation; he fell in step and remained silent.

The compound, lit up with a few white lights, was quiet now. It was empty except for a few guards and drivers at the gate. Even the crowd of fans had gone. Ramakrishna insisted they walk close to the compound wall. They walked in the shadows for a distance, then Ramakrishna suddenly picked up the pace, striding quickly towards the house. They came to a small door that looked like a service entrance. Looking at it, Partha wondered how they ever kept track of all the doors in the house and how long it took to lock up every night. Ramakrishna opened the door and ushered Partha in. There was a small verandah, with two doors leading from it. Ramakrishna opened one of them and led Partha into a small room, this one more cramped than the one Partha had been in that morning. It had a two-seater sofa in one corner and few chairs around a small, circular table at the centre. It seemed to be a card room.

Malvika was seated on the two-seater sofa, Anil next to her. Anil looked up when Partha came in but no reaction registered on his face. He had on a plain t-shirt and jeans. Anil was tall and fit, as young movie stars tend to be, and even though he sat limply in his chair, in a dazed state, there was an air of physical power about him. What was immediately evident was that he didn't have the raised-hackles arrogance of a star-kid. In fact, he seemed quiet and reserved, with even a hint of hesitancy. Partha's sense was that Anil's insufficiency ran deep and wasn't merely the result of the current circumstances. Sitting on a chair at the table was a man in his forties. He was dressed somewhat formally, wearing a half-sleeve shirt tucked in, formal trousers, and black loafers. One could immediately make out the family resemblance with Mohan Krishna, only this man was not as handsome. The exuberance and charisma one associated with Mohan Krishna were missing in this man—in fact, there was a distinct air of the understated about him. He rose when he saw Partha but didn't make eye contact or speak. He seemed uncomfortable even being there. Malvika nodded at Partha in greeting and then looked at the man. The man extended his hand.

'Vishnu,' he said simply.

'Partha.'

Vishnu nodded and sat down. Malvika gestured Partha to a chair near the sofa. Ramakrishna slumped into a chair at the table, next to Vishnu.

'I've told Anil you're helping us out,' Malvika said. 'But he says he doesn't want to narrate the whole thing again. He's totally exhausted.'

Anil's eyes stayed down on the ground. Malvika said something in his ear. Anil didn't react.

'I won't keep him long,' Partha said. He leaned towards Anil. 'Anil, I'm really sorry about Priya's death,' he said. 'And I'm sorry about the situation that's developing with you. But we can help out and hopefully end this thing quickly.'

Anil nodded but his eyes remained downward cast.

'Here's what we'll be able to do for you,' Partha said. 'One, look high and low for any information that will take the heat off you—any scrap of evidence that helps. Two, we'll find out who's attacking the family. If there is a conspiracy, we'll get to it. And then we'll hit back. Either way, anything we find will take the heat off you. That's what we're here to do. Okay?'

Partha felt a bit like a salesman—this was the kind of pitch he'd given too many times to remember. But he needed Anil to open up to him; he needed him to share whatever he knew. Anil looked up for a fraction of a second and nodded slightly.

'I need you to be forthright with me,' Partha said. 'I need you to tell me what your relationship with Priya was. Don't be afraid, don't worry about an official version—just tell me the truth. That'll help us anticipate and prepare for any revelations that may turn up.'

Anil made as if to speak and then stopped. He was nervous.

'You can trust him,' Malvika said. 'Tell him.'

Anil quickly glanced in Vishnu's direction. Vishnu nodded.

'We were good friends,' Anil began. 'I first met her through our director, Keshav. He introduced her to me as a possible actress in our film. He didn't say she'd star in the film, but he said it was possible.'

'Do you know how she got the part?' Partha said. 'At least, how she got into contention?'

Anil didn't seem to understand the question.

'I mean, you don't just walk up to a director and ask for a role,' Partha said. 'How did she even get access?'

'A guest lecturer at her university knew Keshav. He asked her to send in a portfolio and put in a word.'

'Oh yes, I forgot she was a theatre arts student.'

'She is—I mean, she was.' Anil's eyes darted about for a moment and then he went on. 'Keshav auditioned her and he was very impressed.'

'Okay. Sounds like she had more luck than most.'

'It was a dream start,' Malvika said.

Partha glanced at her.

'Terrible how it finally turned out for her, of course,' Malvika said.

'Yes ...' Partha said. Malvika looked a little embarrassed.

'Priya had a way with people,' Anil said, speaking a little more easily now. 'She had tremendous energy and spirit. It was hard to ignore her.'

'She was really ambitious,' Malvika said. 'She just wouldn't give up. She would call people a hundred times if it meant getting what she wanted. Even if they treated her like dirt she would call back. She seemed to hate every moment of it but she'd do it anyway. It was as though she'd decided this was what she'd signed up for and so she'd go through with it.'

'Did you interact much with her?' Partha asked Malvika.

'A little bit,' Malvika said. 'She made a point of getting to know as many of us family members as she could. She took the initiative, made the effort. She could turn on the charm when she wanted. Whether you liked her or not, she was determined—you had to give her that.'

Partha absorbed that for a moment.

'Doesn't sound like a girl who'd commit suicide,' Partha said.

'No,' Malvika said.

'But...' Anil said. 'She was like that only some of the time.'

'What do you mean?' Partha said.

'Sometimes she would disappear for weeks. She could also be a total—'

Anil broke off and looked at Malvika.

'A bitch?' Partha said.

'Moody,' said Anil.

It was Partha's turn to be embarrassed. 'Okay,' he said. 'Was she depressed?'

'I suppose she was. I didn't think it was depression though.'

'Not until this morning, at least,' Malvika said.

Anil continued, 'Yes, not until this morning. I just thought she was too ambitious. She wanted to succeed so bad she was holding on too tight. She would get stressed out. I'd tell her to chill but she couldn't be detached and just enjoy the process.'

'I see,' Partha said, trying not to cringe at all the clichés. Sweeping generalisations about 'the process', 'living-in-the-moment', and 'not worrying about success' were lines young stars were coached to mouth during promotional interviews. They were expected to have Zen-like detachment while managing to be 'passionate' and 'ambitious' as well.

'I tried to be there for her—as a friend, that is,' Anil said, 'but she would never say what was bothering her.'

'Were you guys close enough to share a lot of personal information?' Partha asked.

'No,' Anil said quickly. 'I would meet her at the studio and if she seemed down, I'd ask if something was wrong. That's about it. She would never answer though.'

'So you never found out if she was suffering from some psychological condition?'

'No. But she would always bounce back. I just thought it was an ego problem.'

Partha nodded. Anil's response was appropriate for his age. At twenty, everybody else's troubles were the results of ego problems entirely absent in oneself. It was also easy enough for Anil to talk about detachment when opportunities were being gift-wrapped and delivered to him. For an outsider like Priya, the stakes would have been incredibly high. Losing this opportunity would have probably relegated her to being an industry outsider. There was nothing to guarantee she'd get another chance.

'Let me run what I know by you,' Partha said. 'I gather from your aunt and Mr Ramakrishna that you guys were tentatively cast together in a film. It wasn't formally announced, but you started rehearsing for it. But you say she was not guaranteed the female lead role?'

'It wasn't guaranteed,' Anil said, hesitantly. 'Keshav told her very clearly that it may not happen—that casting was not entirely in his hands. But he assured her she'd act in the film. A supporting role if not the lead.'

'And she was okay with that?'

'She was a newcomer,' Vishnu said. Everyone turned to look at him. 'She had no reason to believe she was owed anything more than that.'

'I guess, but it's a big step down from being the star,' Partha said. 'Question is, had she reconciled to it mentally?'

'She didn't like it,' Anil said. 'But she seemed to accept it. Actually, she seemed very confident of getting the lead role.'

'You said the casting wasn't up to Keshav,' Partha said. 'Who was it up to then?'

Anil tensed a little. Partha fixed an unwavering look on him.

'Your father and Prakash?' Partha said.

Anil again looked at Vishnu and then at Partha. Vishnu nodded.

'Yes,' Anil said.

'Okay,' Partha said. 'So you guys rehearse for this film for several months. In this time, Priya is closely in touch with you and gets to know some of your family members?'

Vishnu uncrossed and crossed his legs again. He didn't speak. Anil looked Partha squarely in the eye.

'She interacted mainly with me,' Anil said, no hesitation in his voice this time. Malvika leaned in and whispered into Anil's ear. Anil was silent for a moment before he faced Partha again, scowling a little, like a stubborn child. 'Yeah, she came into contact with some family members,' he said.

'And around this time, it starts appearing on gossip websites and blogs that the two of you are in a relationship?' Partha asked.

Anil nodded.

'It's a standard publicity ploy,' Malvika said. 'Especially for debutant pairs. Doesn't mean it was true.'

'So there was absolutely no truth to it?'

Anil shook his head.

'So we're not going to have photographs or emails of you guys turning up somewhere?'

Anil shrugged, 'There are some photographs taken in the studio. But nothing ...'

'Controversial?'

'Nothing controversial. Most of them are group photographs.'

'Good,' Partha said. He thought for a few moments and said, 'So let me understand this: you guys were spreading false rumours about an affair between you two on the assumption that she would be cast—'

Anil realised where Partha was going with this.

'There was no assurance—' Anil said.

'But there was an assumption,' Partha said.

'She was right for that particular role, in that particular story.'

'What changed then?'

'What changed,' Vishnu interjected, 'was that they scrapped this script altogether and picked up another. Keshav was upset and broke off with our studio. But he couldn't get anyone else to produce the film either. This kind of thing happens all the time in the industry. And this new film just didn't suit Priya. So the decision wasn't about keeping her out, but just that this was a very glamorous role and she was wrong for it. She was more of a homely type.'

Partha had to restrain himself from smirking at the mention of 'homely type'. It had been a while since he'd heard mention of the homely-glamourous binary.

'She was a trained actor,' Anil said. 'Very intellectual. The earlier script would have been okay but the mainstream role wouldn't have worked for her.'

'Did she think she could pull it off?'

'Yeah.'

'Was there a supporting role she could have hoped to get if not the lead?'

'No, not in this movie. She could have had a minor role as a sister character. But she wouldn't have dreamed of doing it.'

'Makes sense. But for the next several months she continued to hope she'd get the part.'

Malvika narrowed her eyes.

'Yes,' Anil said.

'Why?' Partha said.

'What?' Anil said, tensing up once again.

'You've explained to me that it was Keshav who brought her in. It was Keshav who gave her an assurance of some prominent role. But his project was scrapped and he left. But Priya continued to pin her hopes on your studio, confident for several months that she'd star in a movie. Why would she assume she was in the running at all?'

Anil looked lost for a moment.

'I don't know—she just assumed!' Anil said.

Partha noticed Anil was trying to refocus and steady himself.

'What makes you say Priya thought we owed her a chance?' Anil asked.

Partha watched Anil keenly.

'You just told me,' Partha said.

'It's because Prakash led her on!' Malvika said. She looked angry; perhaps she was upset with the tone Partha had taken with Anil.

'I'm not trying to interrogate you, Anil,' Partha said.

'Sounded like interrogation,' Vishnu said.

'I'm sorry if it did,' Partha said, looking at him. 'This is exactly the kind of thing that will come up in the investigation and even in a press conference. And their tone will be a lot harsher. Why did the girl still think she was owed a starring role in the film?'

'People get their hopes up,' Vishnu said. 'It isn't reasonable, but they do.'

'That's true. But from an outsider's perspective, it would look as though she drew her confidence from a source other than Keshav.'

Malvika looked upset.

'Who was in a position to give her such an assurance?' Partha said. 'They'll say it was Anil. The man she was rumoured to be in a relationship with. I believe Malvika when she says Prakash led Priya on, but Anil gave the police a different version. He told them he was the only one in the family Priya knew well.'

Anil didn't speak for several moments. 'She just wanted to believe that it was going to happen,' he then said. 'She had some attitude issues—I mean, mental issues. I can't explain it beyond that.'

Partha sat back. Anil had been thoroughly coached not to mention Prakash. He was dodging even with Malvika and Vishnu assuring him that Partha could be trusted. He'd been tutored to say that Priya had deluded herself into thinking she deserved a part in a film, that she had some attitudinal problems. Both dangerous statements to make as far as the perception game went. Partha decided against saying so in Anil's presence. Even if he was a star-kid trying to play tough, he was a young man under tremendous strain. Mohan Krishna had set his son up to take the fall, and Anil's role now was to be tough, toe the family line, and take the hit.

*

Anil stepped out for a few minutes. Partha waited for him to return. He didn't know when he'd have access to him again and wanted a few questions answered.

'It's really messed up,' Malvika said, almost to herself.

'Looks like they're insulating all other family members,' Partha said. 'So he's the face of it.'

'What can we do?' asked Malvika.

'I don't think he should say Priya was mentally disturbed. And definitely not that she had a bad attitude—nobody wants to hear about the right attitude for success in the film industry from a star-kid. Let him say she was disappointed but he didn't realise how badly.'

'And about her expectation that she'd be cast?' Vishnu asked.

'He can only say she kept her hopes up,' Partha said.

Vishnu was impassive. Anil returned to the room, looking a little more collected.

'What else do you want to ask him?' Malvika said. 'He's had a terrible day. I'd like him to get some rest. My sister-in-law will also come looking for him if he's not seen for long.'

'I'll keep it brief,' Partha said. 'Anil, when did you last hear from Priya?'

'Last month,' Anil said. 'She called twice. First time, she said she'd finally accepted that she would not get the film. She said I was a nice guy and that I should not turn cynical like other film people, especially my family.'

Vishnu frowned at this.

'I told her it was one film and there would be others,' Anil said. 'She said it wasn't just the film, that everything was going badly—she broke down and hung up. I tried to call her back but she wouldn't answer.'

'Did you call from your cellphone?' Vishnu asked.

'It was from the prepaid phone I use to talk with outsiders,' Anil said.

Vishnu looked relieved.

'So that number's not going to be traced back to you?' Partha asked.

'No,' Vishnu said. 'We have these prepaid numbers that don't have clear owners. We don't like our regular numbers known.'

'Why all the cloak and dagger?' Partha asked. 'The police are going to ask which number she would contact you on. That you were calling from a mystery number only makes it seem sinister.'

Vishnu met Partha's gaze but didn't say anything.

'Don't you know paranoia is part of a star's vanity, Partha?' Malvika said. 'This family is soaked in it.'

She looked at Vishnu. Vishnu appeared surprised at the harshness of her tone and her look. After a moment of uncertainty he smiled at her in a conciliatory manner.

'It's done now, Malvika,' he said. 'I know it sounds bad now but what can we do?'

The pressure was beginning to tell on Malvika now. Partha hoped that she would be her poised self by the next day. Word had been put out to journalists that she might be willing to give interviews. She would be required to be calm and clear-headed through them.

'What about the second time Priya called?' Partha asked.

'She sounded better,' Anil said. 'But it still wasn't normal.'

'In what way?'

'She kept saying that she had to figure out the purpose of her life. She said that I kept talking about the small picture—like a career or one particular film. She said she was thinking of bigger things now. Something to live for and to die for.'

Partha frowned at this.

'Did she ever talk about such things before?' he asked.

'No,' Anil said. 'I was a little freaked out. I said stay positive and things like that. She just laughed at me. Like I was some shallow kid. She said I knew nothing about the world. I got pissed off and hung up on her.'

'You don't have to volunteer that information,' Vishnu said.

Anil's shoulders gently slumped, and he stayed that way for several moments. Nobody spoke. It seemed as though the entire stress and tiredness of the day was hitting him at once. When he looked up his eyes were filled with tears.

'I didn't know she was going to kill herself!' he said. 'She was my friend!'

His face twisted as he tried to control himself.

'I didn't know what kind of pain she was in! Imagine what she must have been going through. I just didn't know. And I hung up on her. If only I'd known, I would have talked to her. I'd have reached out to her somehow!'

He tried to control himself. He kept his eyes down and nervously wrung his hands and feet, but he didn't allow himself to break down fully. Malvika put an arm around him and whispered to him gently. Partha looked at Vishnu to see how he'd react to this display of affection. He expected him to look away. But Vishnu's eyes remained on Anil. He got up slowly, walked over to the side of the sofa, and stood by Anil for a moment; he then extended his hand and stroked Anil's hair.

'It'll be alright, Anil,' he said. 'There was nothing you could have done. You're a good boy. You couldn't have known any of this would happen.'

Anil fought to recover his composure.

'That's all I know,' he said hoarsely.

'I need to ask just one last thing,' Partha said gently.

Anil gave a slight nod of the head in response.

'Her cellphone and laptop are missing,' Partha said. 'Do you have any clue who might have taken them or what might be on them?'

Anil shook his head.

'So even if those are found,' Partha said, 'we're not going to find any embarrassing photographs, conversations—nothing of that sort?'

Anil shook his head again. He then put his face in his hands. His exhaustion was now complete.

'I'm really sorry about all this,' Partha said. 'But believe me, we'll do everything in our power to get ahead of this.'

Anil's eyes stayed on the floor. 'I have to be strong for tomorrow,' he said. 'Especially at the police station.'

'You'll do fine,' Partha said.

Anil looked at Partha.

'This is now attached to my name forever,' he said. 'Even if I have a career after this ...' his voice trailed off. 'Sounds selfish to think about it now. But they'll always say I drove her to suicide. Even if the truth comes out and I am let off, they'll say I got away with it because I'm rich. People will always look at me and wonder if I drove Priya to suicide. That's what I'll have to live with now. That's what I'll have to go through. I have to be strong.'

*

The young man looked unwashed, unshaven. The two-day stubble was shabby and his eyes were bloodshot. He stared out of the bus as the outskirts of a city rolled by in the early morning light. The khadi kurta he was wearing was badly crumpled and his jeans were streaked with grime. He'd spent the previous day waiting in the bus stop of a mofussil town; the night before that he'd travelled in a truck. He was worn out with stress and travel but he could not sleep. Every time his eyes closed for a few moments, he awoke with a start.

He reached into his kurta pocket. From it, he pulled out a cellphone and looked at it. He delicately touched the power button. The touch was gentle, taking care to depress it only lightly: the purpose was to ensure that it was turned off, not to turn it on. Reassured that it was powered off, he returned it carefully to his pocket.

Outside, a sign appeared in Kannada. A little further down, a board said: 'Bengaluru welcomes you.' The young man stared at the board vacantly until it passed.

He reached to his left and put his hand on the backpack lodged between him and the side of the bus. He ran his hand over the surface of the backpack and dug into the backpack with his fingers. He felt the contours of a laptop computer. It was still there. He pressed his fingers deeper into the backpack. He felt the shape of another, smaller laptop. And then he felt the contours of a smartphone. He began to open up the bag to peek in. Then he hesitated. He closed the backpack up again and rested his elbow against it. He leaned to the side tiredly, his head against the window bar.

6

Around the time the bus was rolling into Bangalore, the news story in Hyderabad seemed to be heating up. Studio discussions got shriller and more combative, anchors and panelists made serious allegations, and they insinuated much more—no conspiracy theory was off-limits. Panelists faced-off with marked aggression; they refused to let each other complete sentences and wagged fingers in each other's faces.

In one studio, a Mohan Krishna supporter jumped up and grabbed another panelist by the collar. He slapped the man twice before studio hands were able to separate them. The clip ran all day and was analysed threadbare.

Through the morning, the news channels were building up stories in anticipation of a demonstration the National People's Party (NPP) was planning to hold outside Mohan Krishna's house. They were to be joined by women's and students' groups. A line of OB vans took position outside the house early in the morning and stayed through the day. To counter the protestors, Mohan Krishna's fans also gathered in large numbers. Regional heads of Mohan Krishna's fan club told news channels that Mohan Krishna had warned them against getting into scuffles or slanging matches with student groups, as Mohan Krishna fully understood the students' sentiments. He only sought an opportunity to speak with them and explain the political game being played out behind the scenes. On the other hand, the fan club heads warned NPP activists that they would be countered move for move—whatever that entailed.

The police were on high alert to keep NPP workers and Mohan Krishna fans apart. A few skirmishes did break out but they were quickly contained. The drama and tension on the streets made for exciting news. The story came alive: there was a sense of urgency about it.

But anyone watching the studio debates with a keener eye could sense that Mohan Krishna's opponents were growing nervous. While the fire and venom around the story served as kindling, the real victims, the young woman's parents, had shut themselves off entirely. No information or support for the story was to be had from that source. More crucially, absolutely no information connecting Anil and Priya romantically had come to light even twenty-four hours after her death. All that the news channels had to go on were two photographs. Both of them showed Anil and Priya with Keshav, the director, and other cast members. The photographs were taken at the family-owned Swayamabhu Studios. Anil and Priya weren't even standing together in those photographs. The family wasn't defensive about the photographs in the least. In fact, they had been handed over to the police by Anil himself. The family's managers went around offering copies of the photographs to journalists and pointed out to them how flimsy the so-called evidence against Anil was. The worst news by far for the family's opponents came from police sources who told journalists that they had absolutely no grounds to arrest Anil. Even public belief in Anil's guilt was wavering.

The family's opponents countered with allegations of a cover-up. They claimed the missing laptop and cellphone contained romantic messages between Anil and Priya. They insisted that the police was either concealing them or going slow on efforts to recover them. Mohan Krishna supporters hit back, simply pointing out that the NPP was in power in the state and was responsible for the police investigation. This effectively blunted the NPP's attack and it was left to the women and student groups to raise the pitch. They targeted the circle inspector, stopping just short of saying he was on Mohan Krishna's payroll.

Partha called Malvika and asked her to postpone any press interviews. Even as the noise around the story grew shriller, the story was stalling by itself. Malvika would be of greater use at a later time, when there was some adverse publicity to counter. Instead of interviews, a press note on behalf of the entire family was released. In it, family members reiterated their sorrow at Priya's death and offered condolences to her parents. It briefly mentioned the highly-politicised but futile efforts by some political players to implicate Anil in the case. The statement called on all parties to be sensitive and lower tempers, so a fair investigation could take place. In conclusion, the family offered its complete cooperation with the investigation.

Early that morning Partha came into the office and stayed there, watching the story play out on the news channels. He left the TV in his office cabin on in the background as he worked on a crisis plan for an oil company. He stuck to watching CNEWS even as the same panelists droned on and the same news stories played out hour after hour.

A little before noon, Pratap, the circle inspector, stepped out of his police station with a statement. The inspector waited for the press to calm down before he began his statement. Partha turned towards the television and raised the volume. It was significant that the inspector was addressing the press. Higher officials were usually deputed to do it, especially in high-profile cases like this one. It was most likely a political decision to let him do the briefing. The NPP, for the time being, was sticking with its strategy of keeping the pressure on Mohan Krishna but also restraining itself from alienating him altogether. So for the present, the case was being handled at the operational level and that too by someone seen to be close to Mohan Krishna.

If the circle inspector felt the pressure of scrutiny and the suspicion of bias, he didn't show it in the least. He had a grasp of the facts and narrated them fluidly. He confirmed that the police were treating it as a suicide. However, there was an obvious attempt to obscure evidence as objects were missing from the death scene. Adapters for the devices were also missing from the apartment. The service provider had confirmed internet usage even after the time of death, so the objects were, most likely, removed from the apartment only after Priya's death. The police had ascertained the brand and other details of the devices and had gotten serial numbers from the dealers. The death scene was examined once again to check for signs of tampering or erasing of marks. There were clear signs that someone had tried to erase prints from the doorknob and some other places inside the house, especially the Wi-Fi router. The suspect might have had a key to enter the apartment as there was no sign of a forced entry. Also, the door was locked by the time the landlord came up to check on the girl. The inspector assured everyone that the missing laptop and cellphone would be traced.

'Do you have CCTV camera footage?' a reporter asked.

'Could Anil or Mohan Krishna's people have removed the devices?' another reporter asked.

'There's no CCTV footage,' Pratap said. 'There was no camera in the building. We're trying to check CCTV cameras in the area to see if anyone connected to the case was there.'

'But could Mohan Krishna's people have taken the laptop and cellphone?'

'We believe we know who may have taken the devices,' Pratap said.

The noise from the crowd dropped off for a moment. Pratap didn't wait for it to pick up again.

'We spoke to a lot of current and former university students,' he said. 'Many of these people knew Priya directly. We've learnt that a current university student by name P. Varaprasad used to help Priya with her laptop computer. He would visit the house sometimes and may have had a key. We've found only one key to the main door in the house, no duplicate. The landlord confirms two keys were given to Priya. We've been trying to find the student. He's missing from his hostel and his mobile phone is switched off. His parents have also not heard from him. We're getting ready with a press release—his photograph and other details will be in it. We'll release it this afternoon. We request the public or fellow students to come forward with information if they have any.'

There was chaos as reporters shouted out incoherent, unfinished questions even as they tried to absorb this new information. Pratap ignored the questions and continued to speak.

'Many students were understandably reluctant to speak to us,' he said. 'They don't want their friends to get into trouble. We request them to cooperate with us. Even if your friends have done something wrong, hiding it from the police will only make it worse. Let them come forward and we'll do our best to help them.'

'What kind of help did Priya need with her computer?' a reporter said.

'We don't know,' Pratap said. 'We're going to try analyse her online activity and carry out other investigations to find out. We're told Varaprasad is a Masters of Computer Applications student. He may just have helped her if she had a problem with her computer. That's all we know.'

'Why would he steal the laptop and phone?' another reporter demanded.

'We're not necessarily saying he took them,' Pratap said. 'He may have had access to the apartment. He's probably had access to the devices we're looking for. And he's currently missing. So we're looking for this student to find out what he knows.'

Pratap turned to go even as reporters shouted out more questions at him.

'Inspector sir, is Varaprasad being named to divert attention away from Anil?' a reporter shouted.

Pratap turned for half a second and shot the reporter a look. He didn't say anything though and walked away.

Partha leaned back in his chair. This new information was good for Anil. So far, it had been easy to insinuate that the devices had been removed by Mohan Krishna's people. The fact that Varaprasad was a university student helped weaken that impression. Pratap had come off looking professional and in control; that helped lower suspicions of police inaction or bias. Things had gone well for the Mohan Krishna camp this morning.

But Partha's hunch was that there would be a counterattack. And very soon.

*

A little past one-thirty in the afternoon two university students appeared on CNEWS. One of them was Sirisha, the young woman who was at Priya's house the morning of the suicide. With her was a young man, another student, Biren, from the English department. They claimed to have been close friends of Priya's, even though they had joined the university after she graduated. Priya had mentored them both in street-theatre workshops for some time. She was always eager to encourage students with an interest in theatre arts, they said, and so the three of them had grown very close.

The lies Anil and Mohan Krishna were spreading had become unbearable, Sirisha and Biren said, so they felt compelled to come forward. Anil had told the police that he and Priya almost always met at the studio and that too along with other cast members. It was a lie, and they had proof.

The anchor cued a visual. The photograph that appeared onscreen was a selfie taken by Anil. He and Priya were sitting close on a couch, laughing into the camera. The background was a plush hotel room.

'Anil has a copy of this picture,' Sirisha said. 'He would—it's a selfie he's taken. Then why didn't he hand it over to the police along with the other two? Because it didn't fit into his story that they'd met only at the studio and in company of other people.'

The room visible in the background, Sirisha went on to say, was the hotel suite Mohan Krishna's family kept permanently. This could be easily verified. It was ostensibly used for story settings and business meetings. Here, Sirisha paused.

'Are you saying Mohan Krishna's family uses it for illicit purposes as well?' the anchor asked.

'Yes,' Sirisha said after a pause. Biren nodded emphatically.

'The casting couch?' the anchor asked.

'Yes,' Sirisha said.

Sirisha went on, with Biren occasionally chipping in with a detail. Priya had told them what happened on the day that photograph was taken. It was supposed to be a rehearsal of sorts. She was nervous from the start because it was to be just her, Keshav, and Anil. When she got to the hotel, Keshav wasn't there. Anil said Keshav had to cancel but insisted that they run through their lines. He had been flirting with her openly for weeks before that. And in an alien and high-pressure environment like the film industry, Priya reacted in a manner she had not anticipated—she allowed herself to be flattered by his advances. It was just the relief of feeling finally accepted into that hostile world. Anil had her convinced that he was falling in love with her, and that evening they slept together for the first time. They met in that hotel room a few times after that.

'Do you have any further proof?' the anchor asked.

'Priya said there were other photographs,' Sirisha said. 'She said Anil had secretly filmed her in the room.'

'He was blackmailing her with them,' Biren broke in. 'Threatened to leak them if she told anybody about their affair. The anxiety drove her to—'

'She was heartbroken,' Sirisha said.

The anchor nodded. 'Please be specific,' he said to Sirisha. 'Tell us exactly what Priya told you.'

This made Partha smile. This was an anchor with a story to tell. His questions sounded interrogative but that was merely for appearances' sake. The guests were there to say certain things and the anchor's role was to facilitate it.

Sirisha said Priya had told her of the affair a few months back. She had fallen in love with Anil and believed that he was in love with her. Then, about a month before she died, a distraught Priya called Sirisha.

Anil had begun to distance himself from her. Not long after that, she was dropped from the film. When she tried to call Anil, she found that his number had been disconnected. She was later told the SIM card wasn't even Anil's. None of the family members—those she thought she knew well until then—would take her calls. Other actors and technicians working in the film also avoided her. When she grew upset and began to show it, a man who worked for the family approached her. He showed her intimate photographs that Anil had taken of her. If she didn't quietly fade away, she was warned, the photographs would be all over the internet. She was helpless to do anything about it.

Initially, Priya would call Sirisha and Biren on and off. But then she began to cut herself off. They could see she was sinking into depression. Every attempt they made to approach her was rebuffed. She withdrew further into a shell and rarely left her apartment. For several weeks, she was unreachable.

Sirisha next heard from Priya only on the night she committed suicide. She said the apartment walls were closing in on her, and she spoke of death and dying. When Sirisha grew concerned and expressed it, Priya hung up. She did not take her calls afterwards. That's when Sirisha rushed to Hyderabad.

The interview concluded shortly after that. The two students left the studio and held a press conference nearby. They were ringed by students' groups who kept others at a distance. They stuck to repeating what they had said in the studio and refused to say much else. They were then escorted away by other students. Student representatives gave a quick statement that they would accompany them to the police station, where they would give statements to the police.

In the studios, the news story exploded once again. Spokespersons and representatives trooped back in. The term used most often now was 'casting couch'. This was a blatant, shameless example of it, they said. A star brat toying with a girl's affections and discarding her like an object. The treatment meted out to Priya was common practice in this film industry, they said. This was how the industry punished women for trying to assert themselves—they blackmailed them and even former colleagues cut them off as though they were the perpetrators and not victims. This was exactly how the industry elite drove people out of the industry. Mohan Krishna's family was particularly good at these tricks—they'd ruined several actors' lives. Most panel members demanded that the police arrest Anil on the basis of these statements.

The story was alive once again.

*

A little after 2 p.m. that afternoon, just before he left the office for his appointment, Partha walked into Seema's room. Telugu news channels were running on a low volume in her office as well.

'Could you try and find out CNEWS's ownership on priority?' he said. 'I did a preliminary check and it's a sham. Not a single eminent journalist onboard. The editor is networked but no serious journalism credentials. Reporters look like a bunch of untrained, inexperienced kids. A few experienced anchors—again, second-rungers, not serious journalists.'

'A talented reporter on the story, maybe?' Seema said.

Partha shook his head. 'Going by the notes Mr Ramakrishna's people made, the guy who initially covered the suicide scene isn't the one covering the story now,' he said. 'And several reporters seem to be on the story—the story's being passed around. It's not the reporting that's driving the story. Most likely, the editors and owners are driving it.'

'So you find the owners, you find who's directing the attack at Mohan Krishna's family?' Seema said.

'It's a good place to start. Of course, someone with a stake in the channel could have just asked the management to be sympathetic to this story. That may be why people with something to say are taking their stories to CNEWS. Certainly possible, but in a charged environment like this—unlikely. Especially when the stakes are so high.'

'I agree with that. But you're assuming this is a conspiracy? That someone with influence in CNEWS is either seeking out information and broadcasting it, or even masterminding this attack?'

'Yeah. It's a bias I'm consciously working with.'

'And the fact that these two students went to the CNEWS studio first to break the news and only then held a press conference confirms it?'

'It fits. CNEWS is a controlled environment for them. They get the story out in the form they want; say very little else at the press conference. It was exactly the kind of thing I was looking out for.'

Seema smiled.

'So you've been watching this crap journalism all morning?' she said.

'Wasn't easy,' Partha said, shaking his head, 'but it had to be done.'

'You've inflicted worse content on people.'

'That's true. Sad, but definitely true.'

Seema then tapped on a stack of printouts on her table.

'I've started looking into CNEWS's ownership,' she said. 'Lots of smokescreens. It's all very unclear.'

'Probably means we're onto something. Keep on the trail.'

'Will do. What're you up to?'

'I'm going to meet Vishwanath at the Telugu News Network.'

'You mean TNN?' Seema said with a smile.

'Yeah.'

'You think a rival editor will know who owns CNEWS?' she asked. 'I doubt Vishwanath even looks at CNEWS as a competitor. It's too tiny.'

'I know,' Partha said. 'But TNN is behind on all the major revelations so far. So they must have analysed it, tried to figure out who's driving the story and why CNEWS is getting the breaks.'

'That's true.'

Partha checked a message on his phone. It was the confirmation of his appointment.

'So you thought the kid was genuine?' Seema said. 'You think he's telling the truth?'

Partha looked up.

'He had the family line pretty well-internalised,' he said. 'But yeah, I believe him. He even broke down at one point—talking about Priya. I don't think it was just the stress.'

'He broke down?'

'Yeah.'

'And you believe it was genuine sorrow about Priya?'

'Yeah. I know he's supposed to be an actor, but still.'

'Yeah, well. It can't be easy being Mohan Krishna's son. Having to cover up for Prakash because his father says so. And this scandal won't go away anytime soon. The suicide will come up every time his name is mentioned.'

'He knows that.'

Seema steepled her fingers and gazed at them for a few moments.

'The kid's sadness about Priya must be genuine,' she said.

'You think so too?' Partha asked.

'Yeah.'

'I felt bad for him.'

Seema shrugged awkwardly.

'Yeah, whatever …' she said. 'He couldn't have pulled off that convincing a performance. That family has stars but not actors.'

Partha laughed.

'We'll have to put Malvika on today, after all,' he said. 'I've shared a document with you about it. I'll speak to her as well.'

'I'll look at the document.'

'After the CNEWS story, we need to get back in the game.'

'We'd better,' Seema said.

7

The afternoon traffic moved sluggishly, picking up pace for small stretches in between bottlenecks. Partha was running a bit late for his appointment, but not enough to have to dash. He had spoken to Malvika at some length before leaving and that had delayed him. The traffic remained slow-moving until Partha crossed a major junction and then the traffic moved more steadily. He was able to maintain that pace until he came within a few kilometres of his destination. The approach to the TNN office was through congested lanes with several twists and turns.

As Partha was turning off a lane, he caught sight of a motorcycle turning into it. It wasn't the first time he'd seen the rider that day. He'd seen him on his drive to work that morning, and it was the second time he'd spotted him since he set out from his office. Partha took care not to look in the rearview mirror for long; he glanced at it and then refrained from looking. The rider was careful to maintain a safe distance, as he was earlier that morning.

Partha reached the TNN office a few minutes later. He waited at the reception for about ten minutes before Vishwanath came down to meet him and Vishwanath was about a decade older than Partha but looked much older. His indifferently brushed hair and his overgrown moustache had both turned grey for the most part. He would have been described as lanky at one time but with middle-age, the thin frame had filled out generously.

An attendant brought in two cups of machine coffee.

'What's so important you just had to meet me urgently?' Vishwanath said. 'It's a busy day.'

'What're you busy with?' Partha said. 'It's not like this Priya–Anil story's that hard to manage. Put a bunch of reporters around the police station, Mohan Krishna's house, and Priya's parents' place. The rest of the action is in the studio.'

The casualness with which Partha said it irritated Vishwanath.

'Trying to get to the parents,' Vishwanath said shortly. 'They're locked up in their house—won't speak to anyone. Usually victims' families themselves seek us out!'

Partha knew this was important to Vishwanath. He needed an exclusive on this story desperately.

'Why aren't the parents talking?' Partha asked.

'They're in shock, of course. They don't want to be part of the drama. That's understandable. They also think media coverage of deaths is insensitive and does nothing to increase the chances of justice being done.'

'Fair enough.'

Vishwanath gave him a sharp look. 'I also hear they had some concerns about the girl's mental health,' he said.

Partha didn't react. He didn't want to increase Vishwanath's suspicions by asking questions about it. Partha noted that it was good for Anil if her parents themselves had doubts about her mental state.

'How do you know all this?' Partha asked.

'Their family friends,' Vishwanath said. 'These friends are preparing another statement. I'm pushing them to get the parents to speak in front of the camera.'

'Dignified silence is not a bad option. You and I both know they're not wrong about the media coverage.'

'They'll talk eventually. Did you hear what that friend of hers said today? All that masala about hotel suites and seductions? How long are a dead girl's parents going to keep quiet with this kind of speculation going around? '

'You have a point,' Partha said.

'I've got a good reporter and cameraman parked outside

the house,' Vishwanath said. 'When they do speak, I want us to be first.'

'I thought you would. You guys have been behind on the story so far.'

Vishwanath ran a hand across his forehead roughly.

'We're late on every bloody thing with this story,' he said.

'Any idea what that statement might say?' Partha asked.

Vishwanath eyed Partha for a moment. He then rolled his eyes exaggeratedly.

'Come on, Partha,' he said, 'I'm not telling the Mohan Krishna family PR guy.'

Partha shrugged. He had anticipated such a response. At his core, Vishwanath was an honest and sharp journalist. But he was also a realist and there usually was some scope to make a deal. Vishwanath understood the realities of the media business and knew how to operate within its constraints. He was what Partha liked to call a 'transactional journalist'. He did his job honestly and did not tolerate much interference or influence. But in a given situation, he was open to playing the game, taking an opportunity if it promised to put him or his organisation ahead. This was why he had agreed to meet Partha in the first place and why he was drawing the line right now. Vishwanath knew only too well that a journalist's main influence came from information and he would not part with any of it without reason to do so.

'So your guy saw me go into Mohan Krishna's house?' Partha asked.

'Not one of my guys. It was Afroze from CityNews.'

'Okay. I should call Afroze sometime. How's he doing?'

'So you're handling Anil's PR?'

'Would I have had the time to drop in like this if I was? I'd have been making phone calls to you and a hundred other journalists.'

'You're not helping them with the story?'

'I've retired from the PR business. Didn't want to get involved in this kind of story anyway. Told them I have no reach amongst local journalists, especially since my retirement.'

Vishwanath gave Partha a sardonic smile. 'So what's your interest in all this?' he said.

'Mr Ramakrishna—you know him—he wants me to write media strategy papers and a whole bunch of stuff for Mohan Krishna's entry into politics. Could be big money for my firm.'

'So to make sure you get that consultancy you want to feed them some information?'

'I just said no to working full-time to help save the man's son. I can't just wash my hands off and do nothing.'

'Okay.' Vishwanath's face was impassive.

'I need to give them something,' Partha said. 'It's going to be a big media push for them when Mohan Krishna formally gets into politics. The works: TV channels owned by them and proxies, huge ad buys—everything. They'll be the most glamorous family on the campaign trail. Interviews with them, heads up on stories—every detail will have to be figured out. Guys like you and me can't afford to miss out on that kind of action.'

Vishwanath's expression didn't alter a bit.

'You're going to have a say in all that?' he said.

'They're pushing Mr Ramakrishna to head the media cell.'

'Disaster.'

'I know that. More importantly, he knows that. That's why he wants me involved.'

Vishwanath's expression stayed frozen as it was.

'So I thought I'd reconnect with old friends like you,' Partha said. 'And also make a show of loyalty to the family.'

'Two birds with one stone,' Vishwanath said. 'Efficient.'

'Very.'

Vishwanath gazed at the space above Partha's shoulder for a moment.

'What do you want to know?' he asked.

'Just want to tap into the journalistic grapevine,' Partha said. 'Obviously, there is some coordination in the story against Anil—the NPP guys, the junior artists' union, the way stories find their way to CNEWS first. Who do you think is organising it?'

Vishwanath shook his head. 'Don't know,' he said.

'Do you know who owns CNEWS?'

'They say some Singapore-based NRI called Chari. Wants to change his home state for the better apparently. Don't they all?'

'Know anything about him?'

'I know he hasn't been to India in two years. From Singapore, for god's sake!'

'Maybe that's his way of changing India for the better.'

Vishwanath let out a gruff laugh.

'Yeah,' he said. 'He claims to be a finance guy but has no real track record to show for it. He's made a lot of money somehow though.'

'Must be a money-laundering front. Any links to the NPP?'

'Not that I am aware of. His operation is all legitimate on paper, I'm told.'

Partha nodded. He leaned forward slightly.

'I'm just asking you now,' he said. 'A hunch is good if you don't know exactly. Who do you think is coordinating this attack?'

'Don't know,' Vishwanath said, shrugging expressively. 'Mohan Krishna's got a lot of enemies.' He gave Partha a keen look. 'In fact, I'd like to know who you think it is,' he said.

'I'm still trying to figure it out,' Partha said. 'His bitterest rival in the film industry is Vikram Kumar—the hatred runs deep there. Vikram has media interests as well, but I'm not able to find any link. And then there is the NPP, which faces a tough election. They want to pressure Mohan Krishna into an electoral adjustment. I can't think of any others.'

'I'd suspect those two myself. The people who're doing it, they're hiding their hand pretty well.'

Vishwanath's phone rang. He picked it up and listened for a few seconds.

'Hold on,' he said.

He stepped out of the conference room. Partha tried to listen through the slightly open door. Vishwanath was speaking in a moderate tone, loud enough for Partha to hear if he strained.

'You tell them they can't stop journalists,' he said. 'We'll run stories and discussions about it for a week. Maybe even do an investigative report on their functioning—something like proper process not being followed in appointing the registrar. Mention that exact example. Tell them they won't enjoy us poking around the university administration for stories.'

Vishwanath came back inside the conference room. He looked a bit charged up. He didn't sit in his chair.

'Look, I have to get back to work,' he said.

'Sure, I understand,' Partha said, getting up. 'Just one more thing though. Apart from trying to get the girl's parents to talk, what else are you following?'

'Come on, Partha, I'm not telling you our strategy.'

'Fair enough. No harm in asking.'

Partha shook Vishwanath's extended hand.

'Strange, don't you think,' Partha said as he left, 'that Priya left university two years ago but was so attached to it still?'

Vishwanath pulled a deadpan face. 'She was?' he said.

Partha gave him a puzzled look.

'Of course,' he said. 'These two students on CNEWS earlier today didn't go to university at the same time as her but she was close to them. Didn't you notice that?'

'Oh yes, that's right! You're right. Absolutely. It's very strange.'

*

He went to the lodge because the owner only ever watched Kannada movies. A year earlier, he'd accompanied his father from their village to Bengaluru when his father needed to see a heart specialist. They chose the lodge because it was cheap and close to the bus station. But through the fog that had surrounded him since that terrible moment in Priya's apartment, the image of the lodge's lobby came to him. The image grew stronger as the bus entered the city.

He recalled clearly that the owner sat behind a small counter near the entrance. Day or night, the TV played, even when the owner had dozed off. In the three days and nights that they'd stayed there, never once had he seen anything play on the TV but Kannada movies. The man did not speak Telugu either. That meant he did not watch Telugu news.

Nothing had changed in the past year. The manager asked for an ID, but it was perfunctory. He merely glanced at the driving license that Varaprasad held out and nodded. The sixteen-year old Varaprasad in the photograph—the license being for a gear-less vehicle—held no more than a family resemblance to the twenty-three year old man he was now. The owner didn't object, and he didn't ask to make a copy of it.

'I'll pay cash by the day,' Varaprasad said.

The owner nodded once again. When Varaprasad made to enter his name in the register, the owner placed a hand on it to stop him. He pulled out a thinner register from the other end of the table and pushed it forward. Varaprasad had counted on an off-the-books arrangement like this. In places like these, despite regulations, people liked to show no identification, pay cash, and have no formal record of it. Owners valued this kind of business—they too liked to have some business with no formal records. Varaprasad scribbled his name with a deliberate spelling mistake. The owner collected the cash for the first day and handed him a key. He then turned away to face the TV.

Varaprasad watched wistfully as the owner put the cash away. He had withdrawn most of the money in his bank account; and there wasn't much in it to begin with. Since then, he had had to spend more money than he would have liked. He had to pay the truck driver who gave him a lift; and then he'd taken a bus to Chennai from the town he'd gotten off at. He'd gone to Chennai just to throw anyone looking for him off the trail. He got there in the evening. He ate at a roadside restaurant and walked around to blend into the crowd as much as he could. Then he took a bus to Bengaluru. These were the right choices, he knew. The diversion bought him a precious few days. But it had depleted his meagre cash reserves severely.

The room, though bare and dismal, still sent a wave of relief through him. It was the first place he'd felt secure in since he'd set foot in Priya's apartment that night. He knew that the sense of security was illusory and the clock was ticking, but he allowed himself to enjoy it for the moment. He looked forward to having a wash and sleeping for a few hours—the exhaustion was overpowering him now. He could also feel the first rumblings of hunger. The previous day and that morning, it had seemed entirely out of the question. He'd forced himself to eat only from the fear of passing out. He quickly washed up and collapsed on the bed.

He awoke a little past two in the afternoon. He forced himself to get up. He had to go eat lunch nearby and return to his room quickly. Then, he'd get to work. He had very little time to get it all done, very little time before they came for him.

8

The motorcyclist stayed with him as Partha drove back to the office. He was a man in his thirties with an unshaven look; he wore slippers and a black t-shirt with a garish *Avengers* picture on it. He could have been mistaken for any average idler. He was disciplined about maintaining a safe distance from Partha's car but he kept up. He didn't panic, hurry, or do anything to attract attention to himself—he had clearly done this before. An unsuspecting mark wouldn't notice him, but to the watchful eye, he was obvious.

Partha knew better than to underestimate low-end methods like this. Whoever was having him followed now knew that he'd gone to TNN. They would also try to find out whom he met there. That was as easy as asking around in the office or finding a source they could pay off. Their having that information didn't concern Partha too much: they would assume Partha was trying to manage media coverage for the Mohan Krishna family.

Who was having him followed was difficult to guess. Partha had nothing to go on so far other than the motorcyclist's appearance and methods. The man following him looked like any unemployed or underemployed young man who joined fan club associations. At best, he was a notch above that—a man with skills the fan club found useful from time to time. Partha didn't waste time trying to guess beyond that. He could be working for Prakash or the NPP or whoever was out to attack the family. He could just as easily be working for Ramakrishna or Malvika. It was common enough for business families to hire someone for a task and then have them spied upon.

Partha drove into the office garage and saw Harish's black Audi A4 parked in its place. He parked in the space next to it and walked towards the office. Partha himself drove a Volkswagen Jetta, which he thought was a great car at all times that it wasn't parked next to an Audi. He had considered buying a higher-end car himself, but decided against it ultimately. Envy wasn't the best reason to buy an expensive car he had little use for. There were times he didn't set foot out of his apartment for days or even weeks. An Audi was definitely wasted on someone like that.

Partha walked in with a sense of anticipation. Harish turning up at the office was significant as he only came in when had something important to convey. Perhaps he'd learnt something. It was common enough for Harish to disappear for long stretches of time without explanation and then to reappear with a valuable piece of information.

Partha found him sitting in Seema's cabin as she moved about hurriedly, sorting some papers into folders.

'I'm about to leave for Mohan Krishna's,' Seema said, as she collected a sheaf of printouts from the tray.

'You remember there are sensitivities about our presence there?' Partha said.

'I've already worked that out with Ramakrishna.'

'I discussed the general message and logistics with Malvika a little while ago. Especially about countering what Priya's friends said but you'll have to go over it with her. Can't be too careful with the press.'

'Really? Wow!'

Partha smiled. 'Sorry,' he said.

Harish grinned.

'Why're we helping out with PR stuff anyway?' he asked. 'I thought we were staying out of it.'

'They're screwing it up,' Partha said, 'and we need a little more time to figure out what's going on.'

Seema had gathered her papers and her things.

'Seema, I had a quick question,' Partha said. 'I assume all you could dig up about CNEWS is that it's invested in by some NRI called Chari?'

'Yeah, classic laundered-money operation,' she said. 'Dummy companies with vague addresses here. Mauritius or Cayman Island routes for the money. A skeleton board of directors with Chari and two others. The other two may as well be invisible. Hardly any information about them.'

'Any idea what Chari's political affiliations are?'

'He's close to everyone. He has contacts in the NPP but he's also got strong connections to the opposition.'

'Well, Vishwanath doesn't know why CNEWS is getting the breaking news,' he said. 'Aren't you hearing any buzz? Nothing about a professional rival like Vikram Kumar or the NPP—nothing about moves being made in the industry?'

'There's absolutely no buzz out there. News is being fed to news channels but nobody knows by whom.'

Seema picked up her phone and began to leave.

'I had one more favour to ask,' Partha said hesitantly.

'Something to keep me occupied?' Seema said sarcastically. 'To ensure that I'm not bored with all the time on my hands?'

'It's just that I'm going to use India Post for my journalistic credentials,' Partha said a little sheepishly.

'And you'd like me to ask them to spruce it up a little?'

'That'd be a huge help! I can't talk to that woman, Neha.'

'I should find out what she's doing and replicate it,' Seema said. 'I'll talk to her on the way. I better get going now.' She gave Harish a quick, harried look. 'Was there anything you wanted to talk to me about, Harish?'

Harish shook his head.

'What I already told you,' Harish said. 'That Partha's being followed.'

'How'd you know?' Partha asked.

'So it's true?' Seema said. She was still in a hurry but curious as well. 'How did you find out, Harish?' she asked.

Harish waved the question away. Partha pulled a chair and sat down.

'Oh, it's supposed to be some dangerous, secret thing you boys can't trust little me with?' Seema said.

'I didn't say that,' Partha said defensively.

'Even he doesn't know how I know,' Harish said, waving dismissively in Partha's direction.

'I want to know how you found out,' Seema said. 'I don't have time for this, so tell me now!'

Seema looked at Harish impatiently. When he didn't answer, she raised an eyebrow. Harish shifted about in his chair.

'When we're in the middle of something like this,' Harish said, 'I keep an eye on you guys.'

Seema stared at him.

'You mean to tell me that if some outsider isn't having us followed, then you are?' she said.

Harish shrugged awkwardly.

'What the hell's wrong with you, Harish?' Seema said.

'It's for your own safety,' Harish said.

'It's an invasion of my privacy!'

'It's not a big deal. A few trusted, well-vetted guys follow you around and keep track of your movements. That's all ...'

'Just when I think I'm getting used to you, you creep me out, Harish. You know that?'

'A good kind of creepy?'

'There's no good creepy! I don't want strangers keeping tabs on me and reporting to you.'

'Why not?'

'What do you mean "why not"? Isn't it obvious? I come and go as I please!'

'I suppose. But why the secrecy?'

'They're not secrets; it's just none of your business. Maybe I want to start another firm—with partners who have boundaries. Maybe I'm having an affair. Either way, I don't owe you an explanation!'

'You're not the cheating kind.'

'Thank you, Harish. But that's not what I meant.'

'Not once in all these years have my guys seen you doing anything of that sort.'

'Years!'

'He's kidding, Seema,' Partha said, pushing his chair back. 'Why don't you go on ahead to Mohan Krishna's house now? I'll call you later in the evening.'

Seema lingered at the door.

'Trust me, Seema, Harish is not having you watched,' Partha said.

'Okay,' Seema said. 'So there's no one trailing me or my family?'

'Of course not,' Harish said. 'But I can turn it on as easy as flipping on a light-switch. Just let me know if you want your husband followed or something.'

'She has your phone number, Harish—she'll call if she wants her husband followed,' Partha said. 'And, Seema, if he ever needs to have you watched for safety reasons, I promise he'll check with you first. Okay?'

Seema shook her head and walked away.

'I was already running late,' she said, 'and with all this nonsense!'

Harish smiled as he watched her leave.

'Wonder how she manages to keep it all together,' he said.

'God knows we do our bit to help,' Partha said.

They got some coffee from the common area and went into Partha's cabin.

'I need to head out soon as well,' Partha told Harish. 'How did you find out about the guy tailing me? I just noticed the guy myself.'

'My guys on this street,' Harish said. 'I told them to be on the lookout for someone hanging around too long at the tea shop, watching offices, asking questions—that sort of stuff. They noticed this guy watching our office all morning. He took off after your car, so they informed me.'

'No idea who's set him after me?'

'Working on it.'

'Was that what you came in for—to inform us about the guy trailing me?' Partha asked, a little disappointed.

'That's all I have right now,' Harish said. 'Just wanted to drop in so I did.'

'Okay,' Partha said. He sensed there was something on Harish's mind but, as was characteristic of him, he wouldn't bring it up. And Partha preferred to leave things undiscussed as well. Proponents of good communication might disapprove but it was his experience that people could constitute extremely effective teams without having to agree on everything.

'No progress on the mobile phone side either,' Harish said. 'I'm working on it but my source is extremely cagey. He's agreed to confirm leads but no more. I'm wearing him down.'

'That's fine. I didn't expect much from it anyway.'

'Most of our contacts have been off-retainer for over a year now and we don't have the resources of a big client behind us. Everything's harder to find out this way.'

'We can't retain that kind of reach and infrastructure if we're not doing corporate wars,' Partha said.

'That's why we should have never left.'

'We all agreed to leave.'

'I went along with the majority decision.'

Partha hesitated before he spoke.

'We had to quit while ahead,' Partha said.

'Now we're behind,' Harish said. 'I'm just pointing it out.'

Partha nodded.

'I wasn't able to hack it anymore,' he said, a little awkwardly.

'I wasn't talking about that,' Harish said.

'I was getting worse—I wasn't getting any help for it.'

'You could have gotten help and we could have kept going.'

'I don't think so.' There was a long pause and then Partha said, 'I know it's been harder on you than—'

'That's my issue to deal with. Has Rachna been talking to you and Seema about it again?'

'A while ago. Just something about benders in Macau.'

'I should break up with her.'

'You're not crazy.'

'Too bad.'

'Give the slower pace a chance, Harish.'

'I liked what I was doing.'

'You got into fixing by chance. You wanted to be a police officer!'

Harish didn't reply. Partha could see the jaw tightening. After all these years, it was still a sore point with him.

'Look,' Harish said, leaning forward. 'You guys have been good about it. You've got no problem with me working with others—you let me use our contacts, our office even. It's not your fault that stuff hasn't worked out. Now let it go. It's my problem to deal with.'

'Fine.'

There was another pause. Partha got up.

'I've to go to the university,' he said.

'To try to get access to those students on the news?' Harish said.

'I doubt I'll get access to those two. That story was a classic media counterattack. But there'll be other students there. If I can find out who approached the students, who led them to CNEWS, or anything along those lines it'll be a step forward.'

'Won't be easy. The press will be all over.'

'I have a ticket in.'

Partha picked up his car keys. Harish didn't move.

'Go to the university tomorrow,' Harish said. 'Let me get a better sense of what's going on there.'

'I'll get a sense of what's going on when I get there.'

'Fine.'

'What're you going to do?'

'Going to Chennai.' Harish stretched and made to get up.

'What for?' Partha asked.

'That boy, Varaprasad,' Harish said. 'They think he made for Chennai. At least that's what a guy from the police department says. I'm trying to crosscheck. He went by road, so I'm driving down myself.'

'Okay. Keep me posted.'

9

Earlier that day, Vishnu and Malvika had gone to see Mohan Krishna. Vishnu initiated the topic of Malvika doing press interviews, made a case for it and ran through the list of reasons. But Mohan Krishna's response was an absolute, ominous silence. Vishnu said they needed to put a family member's voice out there, that Malvika was popular with women and young urban people (both important demographics for Anil's career), and her speaking out would help douse some of the anger. He assured Mohan Krishna repeatedly that Malvika would play safe and keep out of controversy—no matter what the provocation.

Mohan Krishna watched Malvika as Vishnu spoke. After a while, he cut Vishnu off with a slight wave of the hand. He looked at Malvika with a hint of mockery in his eyes.

'In your eagerness to prove yourself,' he said, 'don't bite off more than you can chew.'

Malvika stared blankly for a moment. She then nodded quickly.

'As if this whole problem wasn't enough, I have to deal with family members who think they can play in the big league now.'

'No, no, she wants to help Anil—' Vishnu began.

Mohan Krishna glanced in Vishnu's direction and Vishnu fell silent mid-sentence. Mohan Krishna turned to Malvika again.

'You can give the interviews,' he said. 'But keep two things in mind all through. First, don't mess things up—not even in the slightest. Second, in your eagerness to play a part in this, don't interfere with what I'm doing. Anything you learn, any bright ideas you get—you bring to me. Understood? Only I can get Anil out of this mess—no one else can. Don't entertain any delusions about what your role could be. Is that clear?'

Malvika's face had turned crimson. She nodded very slightly. Mohan Krishna turned to Vishnu again.

'Anything else?' he said.

'About your statement yesterday ...' Vishnu said.

'What about it?' Mohan Krishna's eyes were cold and still.

'The media distorts what you say and then makes a fuss about it,' Vishnu mumbled. 'We could try to give a clarification ...'

'She'll go out there and say I'm sorry for what I said?' Mohan Krishna asked, his tone calm.

Vishnu nodded his head slightly.

'Or something else,' he then mumbled.

'That I was a bloody idiot who didn't know how to react to the situation?' Mohan Krishna said.

'No, no,' Vishnu said in a low tone.

Mohan Krishna gazed out the window as Malvika and Vishnu waited in complete silence. For over a minute, Mohan Krishna stared out into emptiness.

'There'll be no apology,' Mohan Krishna finally said, not looking back in their direction. 'Say I was misinterpreted.'

Vishnu nodded, as did Malvika. They left the room without another word.

*

That morning, Partha had called Malvika, asking her to keep journalists dangling with the prospect of an interview, but effectively putting them off for the time being. Later in the day, after CNEWS's breaking news with the two students, Partha called again. He said they should do the interviews immediately so they could catch the evening news. He had a few specific points about countering what the students had said. A little after 3 p.m. Malvika began a series of interviews. It was a deliberately chosen time. It served well to retake the news cycle as it built up to evening primetime. Left undisputed, the students' interviews would have dominated the news all day. Immediately, intimations were sent out to journalists, especially the news crews waiting outside.

The interviews were set up in an austere hall in Mohan Krishna's house. Some household activity, like staff and family members moving about could be seen in the background. They hurried across the frame when they strayed in, but in the process they helped establish a semblance of normalcy—the image of a functioning household. Every hint of opulence was taken out of the camera's gaze. The sofa that Malvika sat on and other furniture in the room was elegant but simple. They took care to set up the interviews in a hall without expensive chandeliers, artworks or carpets. Malvika was dressed in a simple cotton sari—a white sari with black embroidery. She spoke to one TV crew at a time while the next crew waited in a room nearby. When she was done with the TV interviews she met with a few print journalists. It was a well-coordinated operation; no one had to wait for long.

The previous evening, Partha and Malvika had discussed the details of handling the media. But Seema got into the specifics with Malvika. They first got into the strategy to counter CNEWS. Then she picked out the exact location, decor, and clothing. She even identified a restricted path through which the media were allowed into the house. What they saw had to be carefully controlled.

They were to only see the workings of a regular household, things that would make audiences look past star power and wealth to see just another family. A family with a child in crisis. The natural grace and attractiveness of Malvika was to help win over the audience, make them fall a little bit in love with her, just like in the movies. As Malvika spoke earnestly about what her family was going through, at least some in the audience would see another dimension to the story, something beyond the predictable narratives being spun inside TV studios. It had the potential to shift public opinion in a moderate but critical way. To pull this off, Malvika would need to be credible. If she got carried away or came off as making an argument, the effect would be lost. It was this perceptional sweet spot she would have to find.

Over the afternoon, in interview after interview, she was asked about Priya and the circumstances of her suicide. The tones of the interviewers varied but the questions fell into a pattern. Malvika replied in flawless Telugu; a listener could not tell that it was not her mother tongue.

'Did Mohan Krishna's family know Priya?'

'Of course, many of us met her. Unfortunately, we didn't know her very well. I met her at our studio two or three times. She seemed like a wonderful girl and a talented actress.'

'They say she was depressed. Did you get the sense that something was wrong?'

'I didn't interact with her enough to sense something like that. Yes, I've heard these reports about her being depressed. But I have to say that whenever I met her she was cheerful. You could never imagine something like this happening. She was excited to join the industry and very curious to know how things worked. She seemed very intelligent.'

'Do you think it was untreated depression that drove her to kill herself?'

'A terrible, tragic thing has occurred. Priya is not with us anymore. I think we should wait for the police to investigate and for all the facts to come out. Any speculation would be wrong. We don't know whether she suffered from depression or not. Even if she did, we don't know if that's what caused her death. In life, these are very personal things. I don't think we should we violate that privacy because Priya is no more. If anything, we should be even more careful about what is said.'

'The alternative version of the story is that she killed herself because she lost the part in Anil's movie?'

'The movie idea itself was dropped and another was picked up. It's not that she lost the part in the movie.'

'But the effect is the same—she no longer had a starring role.'

'The whole film idea was changed and Keshav—the director of the first film—himself left the project. He took his script with him. He is working on a different film now. So the whole team had changed. As it happened, Priya would not have been suitable for the role in the new film. Everyone involved with the rehearsals of the earlier film swears by her talent and beauty. We would have liked to cast her in a future project.'

'Was she given such an assurance?'

'No. No other film project was under development at the time.'

'Keshav is only a first-time director. Don't you think Priya would be more disappointed about losing a prestigious film with Anil, a superstar's son?'

'As you would know, projects often get shelved in the industry. Casting also changes. An intelligent and talented girl like Priya would know about these things. She struck me as a positive, determined young woman. One disappointment would not have driven her to such an extreme step. That's my real concern about all this speculation about the cause of her death—so much of it is unfair to her. We don't know what she was going through. Hopefully we'll find out through the investigations.'

'That just leads to the question: was there more to it than just a film part? Was there an affair?'

'I can tell you with absolute confidence that Anil and Priya were not in a romantic relationship. Priya seemed a very positive, extroverted girl. Anil is also very cheerful boy—he has no ego hassles, and makes friends easily. They worked together for some months and obviously got along well. But they were not in a relationship.'

'So are the two university students lying?'

'That's a very strong word. We don't know what transpired between Priya and them. I can tell you what we as Anil's family members know. I can tell you what Anil's friends know and tell us. Or I can tell you what their colleagues at the film rehearsals tell us. They all confirm that Anil and Priya got along well but they were not romantically involved.'

'So you're contradicting their statement?'

'See, Priya was focused on building a successful career. Anil is focused on his career, and proving himself a capable successor to his father. They were both so focused on their careers, they didn't allow themselves any distractions.'

'But are you saying the students' statements are false?'

'There is certainly a contradiction between the two statements. But as I said, the inquiry is on and it'll give us a clearer picture.'

'Why is Anil hiding? Why hasn't he come out into the public and addressed the press?'

'It's not correct to say he's hiding. But let's keep in mind that a friend of his has just committed suicide. He's in shock. He's a young man having to go through a lot—including allegations and insinuations. His priority was to give all the relevant information to the police. He met with the police yesterday and did that. He's with the police again today, available to provide any information they need. I'm sure he will speak to the press when the time is right.'

'If he's being so cooperative, why didn't he share the picture the students revealed today? Didn't he try to conceal it because it shows him with Priya in a hotel room?'

'I'm glad you brought this up. The photograph was a selfie taken by Anil but not from his phone. He doesn't remember having taken it in the first place and he didn't have it with him anyway.'

'Whose phone was it taken from then?'

'He doesn't remember. He feels it might have been a crew member's or Priya's. The police can verify it. Or the crew member on whose phone it was taken can come forward.'

'Would any crew member dare come forward? They're all afraid of Mohan Krishna's family!'

'Why would we be upset at a crew member coming forward? It would only confirm that Anil and Priya weren't alone there, wouldn't it? Personally, I think this kind of speculation about a woman just because she's in a room with a man is most unfortunate.'

'They say the picture is backed up to an account connected to an email account. This was accessed from another SIM card that Anil used to use but has since destroyed. That's why it's not available on his current phone or email accounts.'

'I don't understand how all that "backing-up" works. I don't know about any fake SIM cards. But if Anil was so paranoid, he wouldn't have allowed himself to be in the photograph at all. As for the rest of it, I can only say that I don't really understand technology that well.'

'How do you think this will affect Anil's film career?'

'I don't think this is the time to think of such things. A young, promising life has been cut short. All other things are not of significance just now. My heart goes out to the girl's parents. As a family, our thoughts and prayers are with them.'

'If the family is really so concerned about Priya and her parents, why was Mohan Krishna's statement yesterday so disrespectful? He hasn't even apologised so far.'

'It was not at all intended in that way. He was also dealing with the sudden news so it may not have been framed as he intended it. He was referring to the fact that actors work alongside a large number of people and so come into contact with a lot of people. It may have gotten phrased incorrectly in the moment.'

'Does he apologise?'

'He didn't say what is being suggested in the media.'

'Mohan Krishna and his entire family have a bad reputation when it comes to how they treat women. His statement reflects this attitude.'

'I don't agree. That image is a media perception. As a woman who belongs to the family, I can tell you that is not at all their attitude towards women.'

'Isn't it true they wouldn't allow you to marry Vishnu for a long time?'

'That's off-topic but I'll answer it. No, not at all. I was winding up films on hand at the time so I could take time off for the wedding. The family has accepted me entirely. I've been happily married for over five years now. And what greater evidence can there be of the respect the family accords to women than that I have been designated to speak on behalf of the entire family? That too at a difficult time like this.'

'You weren't allowed to act in films though.'

'Producers stopped approaching me for major roles after I got married. I would have worked if I'd gotten offered the kinds of roles I was getting offered earlier.'

'There are rumours that Mohan Krishna is trying to sabotage the inquiry.'

'Everything is under the gaze of the public. We're people who live in total public view and we need their goodwill to survive in the industry. How can we do anything to lose that trust? And how can anybody influence the police? We just want a quick and transparent inquiry so that Anil's name is cleared.'

'Rumours are that the family is keeping Priya's cellphone and laptop from surfacing?'

'I think all parties should be responsible while questioning a police investigation. There are procedures about handling evidence and keeping records. Things can't disappear just like that. I myself don't know much about these procedures but an investigation being conducted under such intense public gaze cannot be manipulated just like that.'

'What do you make of NPP's statements?"

'The NPP is the party in power in this state. The investigation is in their government's hands. I would request them to hasten the investigation rather than taking to the streets like an opposition party. But what really saddens me is that at the heart of this whole matter are two very young people. They're just in their early twenties. There's a young woman who's not here to speak for herself, but all kinds of speculations are on about her personal life. And there is a young man yet to set out on the journey of his life who is being accused of terrible things. Surely, all parties have to be careful and responsible.'

'How is the rest of the family taking it?'

'When the child of the family faces a problem like this, the rest of the family is shattered. I feel particularly bad for my sister-in-law, Anil's mother. She's a wonderful, cheerful, and strong lady. She is very spiritual and her faith is keeping her strong at a moment like this. But a mother's suffering is of a different level of intensity. All of us in the family are going through our routines but feel distracted and saddened. But we know the truth will come out, and the truth is Anil is not responsible for this tragic turn of events. Until then, we're determined to support Anil emotionally and we're not going to leave any stone unturned in bringing the truth to light.'

By the time the interviews were done it was late evening. As the journalists left, Seema prepared to leave too. Malvika came up to her and gave her a hug. Seema smiled awkwardly.

'Thanks for everything, Seema,' Malvika said.

'You're welcome,' Seema said. 'You did good.'

She started to leave. She hesitated and turned back to Malvika.

'You were fantastic,' she said.

10

The drive to Hyderabad City University went through the city's congested roads. The route wasn't particularly scenic. Like in many other parts of the city, the streets were narrow, shops and houses were all squeezed together, and road maintenance was poor. The city wasn't always that way. A few decades earlier, the roads appeared wide, sprawling bungalows stood on sleepy streets, and office buildings stood comfortably apart. But that was before the city became another boomtown on the information technology highway. Space that was once ample became scarce overnight. The roads were marginally widened over the years, but they were never designed to accommodate the numbers of cars and motorcycles that now plied on them. Very quickly, every bit of residential and commercial space was built up, producing a rather claustrophobic effect. It was as though a newer, more commercial city had been forcefully superimposed upon the frame of the old one. To add to the city's troubles, the ongoing construction work for the metro project worsened the traffic flow. There was some irony in the slowing down of traffic for several years in order to speed it up later on, but it was lost on the city's residents.

Around the time Malvika sat down for the first of her interviews, Partha set off from the office. In the slow traffic, Partha easily spotted the motorcyclist tailing him. Once again, Partha took care not to glance into the rearview mirror too frequently. Pearl Jam and Radiohead songs played on the car stereo; Partha tapped out rhythms on the steering wheel and hummed along. When he stopped at traffic lights, he checked his emails and messages on his cellphone.

Fifteen minutes later, he reached a stretch of road with several traffic bottlenecks. The metro construction had affected this area particularly badly. Partha worked his way to the right lane and picked up speed, overtaking several cars as he did so. These were not broad, straight roads: they were uneven and ran for short stretches before turning in other directions. To keep Partha in line of sight, the tail would have to speed up. When Partha stopped at the next traffic light, he was right in front and the motorcyclist was out of sight, somewhere behind a turn in the road.

The moment the light turned green, Partha took off. He built up his lead steadily, taking care not to appear to be rushing. He slid into gaps in the traffic and pushed ahead, extending his lead. In a little while he had extended his lead enough to lose the tail entirely. At the next traffic light, he was lucky to catch the green and he kept going. At the distance of a few hundred metres, he saw the turn he was looking for. He slowed down dramatically.

*

The 'tail' tried to speed up. Initially, he was calm and picked up pace skillfully. But when he couldn't spot Partha's car for a few minutes, he began to grow nervous. He blared the horn at people in front of him and darted about the road trying to get ahead. And then he came up against a red light at the next traffic signal. He followed several other riders as they powered their bikes onto the pavement and tried to cut ahead, but too many other riders had the same idea and soon, the pavement was jammed. Motorcyclists inched forward, propelling their vehicles with their legs. The tail beeped his horn and yelled at those in front of him, almost getting into a fight with one of them. The tail backed down, displaying remarkable and uncharacteristic restraint and good sense. Instead, he settled for eyeballing the man in front for a few moments. It was more inconvenient for the man in front to do and he turned away in a little bit.

The tail then made a phone call.

'I'm stuck at a traffic light,' he said into the phone. 'He's gotten ahead.'

'Motherfucker, I didn't send you out there to follow traffic rules!' the voice at the other end said. 'Catch him!'

'I would have gone through the red light,' the tail said defensively, 'but I'm caught in a traffic jam!'

'Stupid bastard! I should never have sent you! Do you know how important this is?'

'I'll catch up—he's going to the university. It's a straight road from here.'

'The university?'

'The light's turning green! I'll call you later!'

The tail shoved the phone into his shirt pocket. As soon as the traffic began to move, he manoeuvred forward, almost wriggling through the traffic in his way and then picking up speed.

Up ahead, right beyond a small incline was a clear stretch of road. The tail raced towards it, knowing that he would have a clear view of a straight stretch of road from there. If he could catch even a glimpse of Partha's Jetta, he could relax. He could then slow down his pace and gain on him steadily.

He rose to the top of the incline and immediately applied the brakes. His high-speed dash forward had pitched him too close to Partha. A few hundred metres away, a metallic-grey Volkswagen Jetta was turning off the road, into a residential lane. He was certain it was the car he was following.

Relief showed on the man's face. He eased the bike into a lower gear and rode towards the lane. Off the main road, he found a sleepy residential colony, a few rows of squat apartment blocks stretching out from the main road inward. The buildings were several decades old. Constructed by the government, they were allotted to retired teachers and non-teaching staff in government institutions. Each two-storeyed block contained four apartments and was separated from the next by a two-car garage. Ground-floor apartments had small gardens that once had hedges or bamboo meshes for borders, but now whitewashed brick walls had taken their place.

At this time of the afternoon, the place was deserted. The tail rode through the colony, looking out for the car in the lanes. In the second lane, he caught sight of it. He rode right past the lane and looked for a place to park. The next lane was the last in the colony; a chest-high wall marked its boundary. He turned into the lane, riding at a very slow pace and looking around. Suddenly, he braked hard.

Partha appeared from behind a compound wall and stood not two feet from the bike. Before the man could react, Partha moved forward and reached out with his left hand. The tail felt his right wrist wrenched off the accelerator grip. Then he felt the pain. Partha had the arm in a crushing grip and he simultaneously twisted the arm upward. Partha then took a few short steps forward. Now he had the man's hand pinned behind his back. With his right hand, Partha took a hold of the tail's collar from behind. The man let out an angry shout but could do little else. The move was too sudden and extreme for him to react.

'Who the fuck are you?' the man managed to say. 'Let go, bastard!'

Partha did not answer. He tightened his grip on the man's arm and twisted it to maximise the pain. The move was precise and targeted. It was no longer severe pressure on the arm, it was a crushing force. The man flailed his other arm and stood up. He stood unsteadily, his feet not evenly planted on the ground. He felt the weight of the tilting motorcycle on his lower thigh. The bike began to slip down towards the knee. The man struggled to find his footing.

Partha could sense the man's experience in physical combat beginning to kick in. From the crude but strong conditioning of the arms and the torso, he knew that the man could fight. But from the way he moved, it didn't look like he had much agility. He knew the man would now wring the torso and kick around wildly to break free. He had to be tackled before he could move. Partha kept his grip on the left arm tight and shook free his right arm. He hit the man with a quick jab to the back. The wind went out of the man's lungs. Partha hit him again—same force, no more, this time closer to the centre of the spine. The man's legs buckled—the motorcycle's weight fell on the knee and then the calf. The bike crashed to the ground, hitting the man's ankle on its way down. Partha kept his grip on the man's arm and dragged sideways, making him crash to the ground. The man was totally winded. His arm was twisted and his ankle was hurt.

Partha took a quick look around. Nobody was around and he couldn't make out anyone looking out of the windows. Still, he knew he didn't have much time. The man turned over, still trying to regain control. Partha knelt over him.

'Who sent you?' Partha said.

The man grunted but didn't speak. Partha held down the man's right hand with his knee and grabbed his collar. He slapped him across the face. He hit him again before he could recover. The move was quick and brutal. He then grabbed the man's ear in a fist and pulled upward.

'It's going to start getting painful now,' Partha said. 'Who sent you?'

Partha raised his hand again.

'Satya *anna*!' the tail said.

'Who's that—your pimp? Who the fuck is Satya?'

'He's my friend!'

'What the fuck is that to me? Who the hell is he?'

'He's big in the Khairatabad area! Everyone is afraid of him there.'

A local tough. That made sense: it was how these things were done. The job would come down from a client to a local area goon who would put his people to work. It provided an effective buffer between a client and the guy on the street. Partha's eyes stayed cool and on the squirming man in front of him.

'Who told Satya to follow me?' Partha said.

'I don't know!' the man said.

Partha slapped him again.

'I swear I don't know!' the man said, gasping. 'Promise!'

Partha believed him. He was just a small-time street thug. He wouldn't have anticipated any more danger than a few thrown punches. Now he'd been attacked—ruthlessly and efficiently—and he lay injured and in pain.

'You tell Satya,' Partha said, his tone low, 'that if I catch you or anybody else following us, I won't be this gentle. You understand?'

The man nodded vigorously.

'Give me your phone,' Partha said.

The man reached into his pocket tentatively with his left hand and handed it over to Partha. Partha let go of him and stood up.

'Go pick your bike off the road,' Partha said.

The tail looked at him for a moment.

'I said pick your bike off the road,' Partha said, his voice a tone lower now.

The man struggled to his feet and took a few steps gingerly. He then grappled with the bike. Partha looked at the recently dialled numbers. There were several calls to a 'Satya Anna'. Partha punched the number into his cellphone and saved it. He scrolled down randomly through a few more names but found nothing familiar. Partha looked around the contacts and amongst the messages but found little that seemed at all pertinent. From the corner of his eye, he saw the man finally get a grip, haul up the bike and put it on the stand. The man cringed from the pain. Partha pried open the back cover of the phone and extracted the battery. He threw it over the boundary wall.

The man picked up his bike and looked in Partha's direction, uncertain of what to do next.

'Next time I see you, I'll rip your arm out—you understand?' Partha said. 'That goes for anyone else Satya sends. You tell him that.'

The man stared at him. There was fear in his eyes. Partha dropped the phone on the ground in front of him. The man took a few tentative steps forward and picked it up. Partha jerked his head for him to leave. The man went back to the bike. He winced as he took the accelerator grip with his right hand. He began to push the bike away.

When the man had turned the corner, Partha began to walk as well, through a small gap between buildings, to the next lane, where his car was parked. He looked up and noticed a teenager watching from an apartment window. He grinned at Partha as he passed.

*

Partha walked back to his car in the adjoining lane. He pulled down the sun visor so that the 'Press' sign he'd taped to it could be seen through the windscreen. From the glovebox, he pulled out an ID tag and visiting cards of the web portal 'India Post'. These documents conferred upon him the designation—'editor-at-large'. He then started the car and drove out of the lane. He arrived at the university ten minutes later. He stopped at the check-post, gave the guard details of where he was going, and then drove in. He went past the roadside canteen towards the humanities building.

Students milled about the canteen. One of them watched as Partha's car drove by. He pulled out a cellphone from a pocket and dialled.

'He's entered the campus,' he said.

11

The humanities building in the University was one of the newer constructions on campus. Its designers, who were tasked with blending the modern and the traditional, decided to build a large, rectangular edifice with arched windows and turrets. Inside, its corridors were wide, and apart from a few smudges and hand-marks, the recently-painted walls were well-maintained. They looked nothing like the graffiti-and-spittle-marked walls of Partha's university days. It took him a little while to find out where Prof. Hussain's office was. It turned out to be on the first floor, at the far end of a corridor. A simple plaque read 'Prof. Hussain, PhD'.

Partha knocked. Almost immediately a muffled voice asked him to come in. At his desk, Prof. Hussain was winding up his lunch.

'Partha, come in,' Prof. Hussain said.

'I can come back in a couple of minutes,' Partha said.

'No, no—not at all. Class ran late today, so lunch did as well. Please come in.'

Partha took a seat across the desk. Prof. Hussain wound up his lunch box and put it away in a cloth bag. He then got a drink of water and settled back in his chair.

'I must say, Partha,' Prof. Hussain said slowly, 'your return to journalism came as a bit of a surprise to me.'

'I wouldn't call it a return,' Partha said.

'True. You weren't in journalism long enough for your departure to count. Yours was more of flirtation with journalism, wasn't it?'

Partha smiled. 'You could call it that,' he said. 'This assignment—it's just a service I'm providing.'

'What kind of service?'

'I have contacts who want to write longer pieces on Priya's suicide. Some of them are picking up feeds about this story sitting in Mumbai and Delhi and even abroad. They want me to supplement their information.'

'So you just snoop about for information. Like an investigator digging things up?'

'Something like that.'

'You conduct interviews with sources for your journalist clients?'

'Yes.'

'But you identify yourself as a journalist as well?'

'It's a difficult role to explain. Easier to just go in as a journalist.'

'It opens doors?'

'It does.'

Prof. Hussain rested his chin on his palm.

'You're a PR man, Partha,' he said. 'Who's hired you?'

'Not getting involved in this story on the PR front, Prof. Hussain.'

'Please don't insult my intelligence.'

'I'm not. I've retired from that business. I write crisis-management manuals and stuff like that now. I take on work like this to stay in circulation. I have to stay useful and stay in touch to keep my contacts alive.'

Prof. Hussain's expression did not change.

'Let's say I take your word for it,' he said. 'What is it that you want me to do for you?'

'Put me in touch with any students who can get me background information on Priya. Present students or alumni.'

'Anyone in particular?'

'No. I know access to the two students who just spoke on TV is very difficult. I understand they returned to the campus after the press conference but are not talking to anyone.'

'I don't want to get involved in any of this.'

'I just need a few introductions. I wouldn't ask you to even put in a word for me. If I'm not able to convince them to talk to me, that's the end of it.'

'That girl, Priya, was not even from my department.'

'Sir, almost all theatre department students are in touch with you. There's no one more knowledgeable about English and vernacular theatre. Some of these students must have known Priya.'

Prof. Hussain raised his head awkwardly and angled away from Partha.

'I learnt a long time ago not to get involved in murky things like these,' he said.

'Not even involved enough to put me in touch with a student?' Partha said. 'An introduction to another faculty member is good too. I can seek out further introductions from him or her.'

'No.'

'Is this story really that toxic? Usually, you have a hundred people willing to tell you what they know or think. You just have to promise to keep it anonymous.'

'I don't want any part of it.'

Partha could tell that it was pointless arguing. He nodded.

'I understand, Professor,' he said. 'I'm sorry. I shouldn't have bothered you.'

Prof. Hussain nodded stiffly.

'Please say hello to Ayesha for me,' Partha said. 'She spoke to me a few weeks ago.'

'I will …' Prof. Hussain said.

'She'd called for some inputs on her South strategy,' Partha said.

'Did she?'

'She wanted to know how companies are held out here. I was able to give her a little information. More importantly, I put her onto a partner at our firm who's more knowledgeable about such things.'

'I see.'

'We're not the best act when it comes to local media. But we have some ideas on strategy and we have some useful local information. Information we don't have, we usually manage to get.'

Prof. Hussain ran a hand through his hair.

'Well, thank you for your time, sir …' Partha said, getting up.

'Would you mind waiting outside for a moment while I call Ayesha?' Prof. Hussain said.

'I'd be very grateful if you did,' Partha said.

Partha went out, closing the door behind him. He leaned against the parapet wall and waited. He hadn't anticipated this much resistance from Prof. Hussain. Putting him onto some student and letting him take it from there shouldn't have been this big a deal. But, Prof. Hussain seemed on edge. Partha had brought up Ayesha, Prof. Hussain's daughter, and a friend of his from his university years, as a desperate measure. That was just a shot in the dark, a ploy. The truth was, Ayesha hadn't called him in a very long time.

Ayesha was a journalist initially, but she'd changed tracks, gotten a prestigious MBA, and was now a powerful executive in a media company. She was on the verge of establishing herself as a major player at the national level. Her project at present—one that she was being tested on—was supervising the expansion of her company's reach in southern India.

Partha waited, wondering if Ayesha would be able to take her father's call in the middle of the afternoon. If not, Partha would luck out. If she did take his call, she would tell him not to entertain Partha for a second.

*

Prof. Hussain came to the door just a few minutes later. He beckoned Partha back inside.

'I forgot that Ayesha's travelling today,' Prof. Hussain said. 'She's on a flight to Amsterdam.'

'I need to move on the story today, Prof. Hussain,' Partha said. 'You know time is of the essence.'

'Sit down, please,' Prof. Hussain said, waving Partha to a chair and returning to his own.

Partha saw an opening here, but he would have to be careful not to trigger Prof. Hussain's suspicion again.

'I do understand how you and Ayesha might be helpful to each other,' Prof. Hussain said. 'She has mentioned it on occasion. But you do understand my sense of caution?'

'Of course, sir.'

'Things are charged over here right now.'

'Are they? I'm a little surprised. This doesn't involve any intra-university dynamics. I mean, Priya had already left university. Anil is an outsider with no connection to the university. Why are things tense here?'

Prof. Hussain threw up his hands loosely.

'Things are always tense here,' he said. 'You know that.'

'I knew that different university factions would react differently,' Partha said. 'But they usually do call a temporary truce—university insiders versus outsiders sort of thing—at least put on a pretence of pulling together.'

'The pretence is there. But the radical Left unions wanted more agitations. They wanted intense pressure on Mohan Krishna's family. But the other unions said it wasn't a student issue and stayed away. There were even some scuffles over this.'

'I've got no political interest in it. I'll write up whatever they say and pass it along.'

Prof. Hussain took a while to respond.

'It's political to them,' he said. 'Sirisha, the girl who discovered Priya's body, has a lot of friends who're from the

Left Students' Union. I suppose she's a member herself. She was understandably traumatised about the death and is worried about the fallout. The Left Students' Union has taken it upon itself to insulate her. It's a good gesture of student solidarity.'

'Nothing I'm going to ask students has any political overtones,' Partha said. 'I want to find out if other students knew about Priya and Anil. If they have some idea—or theories—about what is on the missing devices. They can speculate wildly if they want and I'll pass it along to my contacts. I also want to know a little bit about Varaprasad. That's it.'

Prof. Hussain nodded.

'The students are suspicious,' he said. 'A former student is dead, another is on the run. If I put you onto somebody and anything goes wrong ...'

'It won't go wrong.'

'The union is screening whom Sirisha and Biren will speak to or not. In fact, they approach news channels and journalists—not the other way around.'

'Let me talk to the union people.'

'You'll win them over with your journalistic credentials, I suppose. Or the fact that you run a PR consultancy will win their trust?'

Partha laughed. 'Leave it to me to convince them, sir,' he said.

'I suppose I could trust you to win over some students,' Prof. Hussain said. 'But my concerns are different. May I be frank with you, Partha?'

'Please do, sir.'

'I don't really trust your motives, Partha. It seems very plausible to me that Mohan Krishna would approach you to get his son out of trouble. You'd be just the sort of man who can get it done.'

Partha leaned back.

'They did,' he said.

Prof. Hussain's mouth tightened.

'I turned them down,' Partha said.

'Yet here you are.'

'Yes.'

'Why?'

'To get to the truth. Find out what really happened with that young woman.'

Prof. Hussain raised his eyebrows animatedly, his expression stopping just short of outright incredulity.

'Let's say you do find out,' he said. 'What do you intend to do about it?'

'What I can.'

Prof. Hussain drummed silently on the desk.

'You say you turned Mohan Krishna down?' Prof. Hussain asked. 'Why did you do that?'

'I'm retired.'

'That's not an answer.'

'Prof. Hussain, I'm retired from a business I could be making a lot of money in. I quit when I was at the top. I have enough money to get by without a lot of work—without any work, in fact. I'm also partner in a firm that makes a lot of money. So Mohan Krishna's offer in a sleazy case like this doesn't tempt me. I've turned down ten times that amount from big corporates and political parties.'

'That's very impressive. But it still doesn't tell me why you want to find out the truth about Priya.'

Partha gazed at Prof. Hussain and then looked away. His shoulders dropped just a bit.

'A young woman is dead,' he said. 'There are rumours and innuendos about her affair with Anil. There are rumours floating about now that she was having an affair with someone else. There are rumours being planted as we speak that she was mentally unsound and killed herself. Different camps are planting versions that suit them. If any of these versions is true—fine, it's just another tawdry news story. But if they're untrue—look at what they're doing to her memory. It isn't right to let people do that and just walk away. It is not right that they get to benefit from her death.'

*

Prof. Hussain had tea brought in as they waited. It was the typically thick, cloying university tea available in campuses everywhere. As Prof. Hussain looked through some papers desultorily, Partha tested his Dictaphone and looked over some notes on a legal pad. He'd scribbled out a list of questions just before he left the office.

As he went through the motions, like an actor getting into character, Partha had the distinct sense of being at a disadvantage. The university was likely to play a big part in this story, but the dynamics of this university were difficult to make out. There were several unions, different ideological strands, and everything was potentially controversial. Prof. Hussain's hesitation in getting him a contact suggested that the roots of this trouble ran deep in the university community. It was tricky terrain and what Partha was trying to do came with significant risks. If things went wrong here, it could be a major PR disaster.

Partha had limited interest in interviewing students. He did want to know a little about Varaprasad and if he'd shared information about Priya with anyone. But gathering tidbits of information was a small part of Partha's purpose.

His real aim was to inject himself into the environment. Partha knew his so-called cover story wasn't hard to see through, but that was just as well. He looked like an investigative reporter at best, and at worst, someone snooping around for information. Either impression was fine with him. The real objective was to successfully enter the students' world and elicit a reaction from it. That reaction would give him a glimpse of the power structures operating on the campus. Studying that structure would hold clues about who controlled it. Partha was willing to be patient, to go where the student contact led him, and to deal with whatever reaction awaited him. It was a calculated risk: one that he would take and then try to manage the fallout if there was any.

A few minutes later, a student came into Prof. Hussain's office. There was no knock on the door, no greeting.

'Yes, sir?' he said.

The scrawny young man was dressed unlike most other students. He wore a formal striped shirt, which was tucked into his trousers, and rubber slippers. His face was gaunt and he wore glasses; the eyes were alert and darted about constantly. He held a smartphone nervously in his hand and shifted from foot to foot.

'Raghav, Mr Partha Rao here is a journalist,' Prof. Hussain said. 'He wants to meet some students—especially union members. He also wants to interview Sirisha and Biren if possible. I told him they were being taken care of by the union.'

Raghav looked at Partha and then back at Prof. Hussain.

'Can you put him in touch with the union leaders?' Prof. Hussain said.

'They don't want any interviews right now,' Raghav said.

'You don't have to introduce him to the Sirisha or Biren; introduce him to the leaders. Let them talk to Mr Rao directly. I don't want him roaming around campus randomly. If the union wants to talk to him, they can. If they have some problem talking to him, let them convey it to Mr Rao.'

'I should tell them you sent him?'

'Tell them Mr Rao came to see me and I've sent him to the union.'

Raghav absorbed that for a moment and then nodded.

'Yes, sir.' He looked at Partha. 'Come with me.'

*

Raghav walked a few steps ahead of Partha. He didn't look back or make any conversation.

'Must be tense times at the campus,' Partha said after a while.

Raghav shot him a glance but did not reply.

'It's great to see students taking responsibility for other students.'

'This way,' Raghav said.

He turned left past a building. They walked away from the main university streets into a by-lane. Here, the structures were smaller, often flat and single-storeyed. It was an area thick with brush and trees and large spaces separating buildings. Beyond it, in the distance, was the campus's afforested area, the Green Belt, spread over several acres. It was in that direction that Raghav led Partha. A few students, moving about in ones and twos, could be seen in places but the area was otherwise deserted. As they drew closer to the tree line there was no one around.

Raghav looked back at Partha more frequently now. If he was looking for any signs of nervousness he didn't find them. Partha walked at that same steady pace, tinkering with the elaborate camera he was lugging around but could barely operate. He also pulled out his cellphone and sent Seema a message saying he was at the university and she shouldn't wait for him. Raghav stopped.

'Please put the phone away,' he said.

'Why?' Partha said.

'You cannot use your phone or your camera without permission.'

'I won't take pictures of any students without their permission.'

'No, you can't use it from now itself.'

'I need some pictures to accompany my story. I'd like to ask the union leaders if they're okay with it.'

Raghav was clearly inclined to say no, but he just looked away with irritation.

'If they agree,' he said brusquely.

Partha nodded, smothering a smile. Deciding whether Partha could use his phone was above Raghav's pay grade. Raghav began to walk again and Partha followed.

At a little distance, at the edge of the Green Belt, two young men could be seen. One of them was sitting on a parked motorcycle and the other on a low wall. They both wore kurtas and jeans. When they saw Raghav and Partha approach, the conversation amongst them ceased. Raghav picked up his pace.

'Wait here,' he said to Partha without turning back.

He went over to the bike and spoke to his comrades in a lowered tone. Partha caught bits of the exchange. 'Journalist, he says,' Partha heard him say. 'Prof. Hussain has sent him.' The man straddling the motorcycle cut Raghav short, silencing him—there was something imperious in the manner he did it. He looked past Raghav at Partha—there was just a trace of contempt in the look. He got off the bike in an unhurried, deliberate manner and walked in Partha's direction. Raghav and the other man followed.

'Journalist?' the man said to Partha.

'This is Vikranth,' Raghav said, pointing to the man who'd addressed Partha.

Raghav seemed to believe that to be an adequate introduction.

'Yes, I'm a journalist,' Partha said.

'Don't look like one,' Vikranth said.

'Don't I?'

'No. You say you work for a web portal?'

'Yes.'

'That makes you a journalist?'

'You want to see the website?'

This threw Vikranth off-rhythm. He'd set himself up for a confrontation and he wasn't expecting a non-defensive response. He didn't reply; he stood where he was, a sullen look on his face. Partha had the 'India Post' website already pulled up on his cellphone. He clicked the browser icon and it came up on the screen.

The website had an unremarkable stream of features on current events, most of them economy or business-related stories. Partha scrolled down to two articles—one an inside story of fraud in a major Hyderabad-based pharmaceutical company and the other describing political wrangling over land allotment in a Special Economic Zone. In both, Partha was credited as a contributor. He clicked around a little more and showed Vikranth his profile on the website. It claimed he was a 'contributor and editor-at-large'. The profile also listed his background in advertising and PR but did not elaborate on it.

'Looks like a fly-by-night operation,' Vikranth said.

'A lot of portals are,' Partha said with a laugh. 'These guys pay up on time. That's how I tell the difference between the real ones and the fly-by-night operators.'

Vikranth had regained his poise by then. He eyed Partha languidly, smiling and cocking his head to indicate disdain. He had the air of a young man convinced of his being worldly-wise, the sort who could see through the cons of the world. Armed with a sarcastic grin and a general sense of suspicion he felt ready to call the world out.

Partha tapped on the phone screen again and pulled up another page. He scrolled down the entire list of journalists and contributors. There were some known names: TV journalists and prominent business reporters and commentators.

'These are big names,' Partha said. 'They wouldn't associate with a fly-by-night operator. So are you guys going to talk to me or not? Any chance I can get an interview with Sirisha?'

He wanted to force Vikranth into a decision but Vikranth wasn't willing to be hurried.

'If I clear you,' he said. 'you'll meet with the Union General Secretary—he'll decide.'

Partha nodded impatiently.

'I take it you're the General Secretary,' he said.

Vikranth's sneer didn't alter but his mouth tightened a fraction.

'Don't play games with me,' he said.

Partha shrugged dismissively.

'I'm a journalist,' he said. 'You think I'd turn up at the university without checking out who was who? The students on TV this morning are being protected by the Left Students' Union. You think I'd turn up for a story with them without knowing who the General Secretary was?'

Vikranth was less cocky now; he directed a hard stare at Partha.

'Spare me the cloak and dagger,' Partha said. 'I'm not a rookie reporter breaking his first story. You let me in, talk to me, and I'll tell you why it's good for your cause. Or you tell me to get lost and I'll find some other way to write about this story. You're not the only source here.'

As he spoke, Partha subtly adopted a more confrontational physical posture. He was taller than the other men by a good half-a-foot and he projected a certain physical strength. Vikranth's stare grew more hostile, but the change in Partha's demeanour was not lost on him. Vikranth's cockiness was fed by indulgent faculty members and fellow students and he was unused to being confronted or talked down to.

'It's bullshit,' Vikranth said. 'There's nothing you can do for us.'

'How much national-level attention have you gotten so far?' Partha said. 'None. A mention in the second-rung headlines was as high as you got. And now that's dropped to the lower-end of the channel webpage. Don't fool yourself: local reporters of national news channels can't get you any more play by themselves. I've shown you who our contributors are. I've shown you who I've worked with. I can pick up the phone and give any one of them a call and get them interested. My people can get you the national spotlight.'

Vikranth looked at Raghav and the other man who was sitting with him. The man looked like a student but was heavily-built—without a doubt, the product of a small-time boxing gym. Vikranth turned back to face Partha and stayed locked in his confrontational pose for an uncomfortably long time. The other two students shifted about in their places.

'What's your interest in taking this story national?' Vikranth said.

'What's that to you?' Partha said. 'I know you students believe Mohan Krishna's family is getting away with murder. It suits other people to bring out the truth. As long as your interests are aligned, what do you care?'

'We know how to take this story national,' Vikranth said.

'You do?' Partha said. 'There's no evidence of it so far. Do you understand that from Delhi this story looks insignificant? Some right-minded editor will run it for a day considering it's a woman's issue. But other than that, what is it but some controversy surrounding a regional star's family? And nothing sensational is coming out—the national media has already half-lost interest. Local reporters must be pushing the story hard but nobody's bothered in Delhi. You think there isn't a geographical disadvantage? If this were happening in Delhi, you think it wouldn't be the lead story?'

Vikranth wiped his upper lip with the back of his hand.

'What do you propose to do about it?' he said.

'Get a respected journalist to champion the story. That'll make it hard for everyone else to ignore it.'

Vikranth considered this for a moment. He looked at the other two. Vikranth swallowed and looked at Partha again. Just as he was about to speak, a strange, loud tune blared out from nowhere. The hyperactive tune only grew shriller. It took Partha a moment to realise it was Vikranth's phone.

'Nice ringtone,' Partha said drily.

Vikranth glared at him and picked up the phone.

'Yes, anna,' he said, his tone deferential. 'Yes,' he said again.

He gave Partha a look and then walked away. He tried to do it casually, but it was obviously intended to get out of earshot of Partha. He stopped a distance away and spoke for a few moments. When he hung up, he didn't turn to look at Partha or the other two waiting with him. He stood staring away for over a minute. He then walked slowly back to the others.

'You'll leave your camera and phone here,' he said to Partha brusquely. 'With Raghav.'

'Fine,' Partha said.

Raghav came up and collected them from Partha.

'We'll need you to turn out your pockets,' Vikranth said.

'You've got to be joking,' Partha said. 'Nobody—especially students—is in any danger.'

'We set the terms.'

Partha took the contents of his pockets out with a shake of his head. Partha held up a handkerchief.

'I'd leave this with you if I hadn't blown my nose into it,' Partha said.

Raghav shrunk away from it. Partha grinned and put it back in his pocket. Without a word, Raghav began to walk away with Partha's things.

'Hey!' Partha called after him. 'How do I get my things back?'

Partha looked questioningly at Vikranth and the other man. Neither bothered to assure him they would be returned to him. Vikranth just gestured in the direction of the Green Belt and started walking.

'We're going into the Green Belt?' Partha asked.

'It's a shortcut,' Vikranth said.

Partha seemed to ponder over it for a moment and then he followed Vikranth. The other man walked behind them. As they entered the wooded area, Partha was unsure what Vikranth was up to. The possibility of national attention had tempted him but he was still undecided about what to do next. It was the phone call that had clinched it for him. There was no way of guessing what had transpired in that phone call.

12

He knew Priya was dead even before he opened the door. A dim light was on in the hall, and he could see a light in the bedroom. The rest of the apartment was dark. Fear coursed through him—a paralysis set in and every move became a struggle. His mouth was dry, his stomach was knotted up and he thought his knees would give way. The dark spaces in the apartment terrified him—though he'd never known fear of the dark even as a child. He shut the door behind him even as his instincts resisted violently.

He moved towards the bedroom slowly. He knew she was there. Another step and she would be in view. Then he saw her. Her feet were suspended inches above the bed. He recoiled from the sight. He felt himself gagging even as another part of him fought to regain control. For several minutes he could do nothing but sob. But through the fear a single thought broke through to him: he didn't have much time. They would be coming soon.

Again, Varaprasad forced himself to move. He looked around the room, willing himself to think again. The cellphone and the computer. He knew none of the photographs were printed out, there were no pen-drives in the house, no printouts of emails—but there were things on the devices. Some of their contents were already backed up, but the most important, most recent communications were not. If they weren't secured now, they would be lost forever.

There was a sound at the door. Varaprasad didn't even dare breathe. Suddenly, he felt very cold. There was a noise once again. Had the man come to the apartment? He was supposed to wait at the meeting point—that too an hour later! That meant they suspected his loyalty! They knew he was going to run. Or was it someone sent by her lover? Did they know she was dead too?

The impulse was to break down in terror. To give up entirely. He had never known fear like this. But deep within himself he knew he couldn't allow weakness to overcome him now. If he did, he would be dead soon. And the truth about what had happened to her would never come to light.

He forced himself to move. With great difficulty, he moved towards the main door. He was careful to stay close to the wall and in the shadows. He inched closer, struggling to control his breathing, afraid to make the smallest sound. He could hear muffled talking and movement outside. Very carefully, he raised himself to the peephole. His heart almost stopped—there were men outside.

He pulled away. There was no reaction from the other side. They had not seen him. He stayed there, barely breathing—he remained that way for a couple of minutes that seemed to drag on forever. Nothing happened. It was then that it registered in Varaprasad's mind that the men were half-turned away from the door. They were standing in the middle of the hall but it was possible they were looking in the other direction. Very slowly, he leaned forward to look out of the peephole again. He saw them more clearly now. The two men swayed a little and moved about uncoordinatedly, like they were drunk. Now they were at the entrance of the apartment across the hall. They managed to open the door; went inside, and shut the door behind them.

Relief surged through him like a wave. It eased the terror a little bit and helped him focus. He turned around; he had to work fast. He went back to the bedroom door. He fought through the resistance and nausea and entered the room. The laptop and the smartphone were both on the bed. The laptop was still on.

Once again, he stopped cold. Was it still running? Would he be seen if he faced its camera? How did the man know Priya was dead for sure? When he'd received the phone call a few minutes earlier, the man was sure she was dead but had warned him to wait for a while by way of precaution. Was he still online watching?

He moved forward gingerly and peered over the top of the screen. There was no glow. He leaned a little further forward. The screen was dark; the laptop had gone into power-saver mode. He allowed himself to breathe—there was no Skype call on. He gently shut the laptop, sending it into hibernate mode.

He did not dare look up at the body. He could not bear to see the face. Through the haze of fear that had engulfed him, he reached for the cellphone and the laptop and stumbled out of the room. He was being inefficient and clumsy—he told himself to get his act together and focus. He needed the connecting cables and adapters. He went back into the room and looked around; he found them on the bedside table. He picked them up, careful not to touch anything else and retreated into the hall.

He had to work fast. His hands were unsteady and his nerves were frayed, but he was clear about what to do now—handling computers and technology was second nature to him. Even in his current state of mind he knew what had to be done. He could get to the bulk of the contents of the laptop later but the cellphone could never be switched on again. Its contents would have to be transferred now. But even more important was a file on the laptop in a concealed folder deep within the system. He had to check that it opened and that it was backed up—it was simply too important to lose. At another time he would have found it in a matter of seconds, but in these circumstances, it felt like a superhuman task. He had to marshal all his attention and navigate the screens.

When he found the file, he clicked on it. It played, the audio was clear. The voice on it made Varaprasad shudder. He shut down the media player and reached into a pocket of his backpack to extract a pen-drive. He plugged it in and saw that it had reached almost full capacity. But he didn't need a lot of space—he needed just that one file. He copied it onto the pen-drive. He ejected the pen-drive and then connected the cellphone.

He knew this would not take long: he knew his way around the phone well. He knew Priya had very little stored in the phone's memory. But he had to back it up fully right now. He connected it to the laptop and navigated through the folders and transferred the contents in bulk. In particular, he made sure he had the WhatsApp and SMS folders copied. When that was done, he opened up WhatsApp. The video that Priya was to send out was there. That message could be important too.

From time to time he glanced in the direction of the bedroom. And then it began to sink in. She was really dead; she was really gone. He looked away, determined not to lose control.

As the contents were transferred, he checked Priya's email account. She was already logged in. He changed the password, made a note of the new password on a piece of paper and logged out. He then changed the password of the Skype account and logged out.

He then logged into another email account. With this one, he hesitated. Changing the password for this account could trigger a response immediately if its owner received an alert. It was unlikely he would though because Varaprasad was the one who handled the settings. But just then, at this moment, he could not be a hundred per cent certain. And if the owner got the alert, Varaprasad realised his escape itself would be jeopardised. He refrained from changing the password and signed out.

When the transfer was done, he unhooked the connections and wound them up. He then looked through her phone quickly, assured himself he'd copied everything, powered it off and put it in the backpack.

He went back to the sign-in page of the email account. He noticed the anxiety well up within him. He could delay no longer; he entered the user ID and the password. He quickly checked the inbox, sent, and draft folders—there was nothing of interest to him. He then clicked on the Google Drive icon. He quickly scanned it to see if any new documents or videos had been uploaded. He couldn't see anything he wanted to download. He closed the Drive page. Back on the email page, he went into settings. He went into the reset password section. He took a deep breath; he had to secure this email account as well. He changed the password. That was his own declaration of war.

Now he had no time to lose whatsoever. He quickly put the laptop into an inner pouch in his backpack, next to his own laptop. He hoisted the backpack onto his shoulders.

Then, without any real cause, he wondered if he had touched the router on his last visit to the apartment. He took out his handkerchief and brushed the router thoroughly. He couldn't stop at that. He looked around and brushed down some other places he thought he might have touched. Even as he did, he knew his mind was playing tricks on him. But he couldn't stop himself.

At the main door, he brushed the doorknob to get rid of any prints. He turned around and looked in the direction of the bedroom one last time. He turned away and cautiously opened the main door. He locked the door behind him, using the handkerchief all along. He then put the key in his pocket and hurried away.

Thinking back to that night, now secure in his lodge room in Bengaluru, Varaprasad could still feel the nauseating sensation of despair he had felt that night—of knowing that Priya was dead in the next room. But he tried to shake it off. He knew he had little time to act. All his efforts would come to nothing if he allowed those memories to paralyse him now. He got off the bed, put on his shirt, and then picked up the backpack. He needed to move fast. Every time he stepped out, he increased the danger that somebody would recognise him. But he had a very important task to do.

*

An area with rows of eucalyptus trees formed a buffer to the Green Belt. It stretched out for a few hundred metres and then there was the natural forest. The vegetation in this region was scrub and the trees tended to be short, but it was lush and dense. A small path ran through it.

They fell into a steady rhythm. Vikranth in the lead, Partha a few steps behind, and the third man bringing up the rear. The vegetation grew thicker as they walked on and then they changed direction. Partha made a mental note of it, visualising what to look for if he had to return by himself.

He knew this was no shortcut, of course, and that didn't surprise Partha. What surprised him was that the boys weren't more suspicious of his willingness to go along. Partha felt at once alert and curious but not particularly threatened by the students. Their aggressive posturing was half-amusing. It definitely came with the risk that they might spring an attack or a trick on him. But it would be a risk worth taking if it revealed the opponent's hierarchy at least to the next level. It could be a step forward in figuring out who was calling the shots at the university.

A little farther into the forest Vikranth came to a sudden stop. The area was more spacious here—though still under the trees—the foliage creating a dome high above. Vikranth stood around uncertainly. Partha felt the adrenaline stirring within. He controlled it; staying focused. He became highly aware of what was happening around him. The man behind him hadn't moved much so far. Partha waited, resisting any urge to take evasive action. In these situations, he knew it paid to hold back while retaining the intensity of the sensation. It was before an attack that even the opponent was tense, it was the time the opponent made mistakes. It was the time when a hidden opponent grew restless and showed his hand.

Then he heard movement in the thickets. It came from different directions. A man emerged in front of him. There was a scar on the man's eyebrow, running up across the forehead. Partha felt movement behind him. Before he could turn around, a powerful hand went over his shoulder and around the neck. The hand pulled back forcefully.

*

Seema disliked Partha's university plan from the start. So after the last of Malvika's interviews, she returned to the office just to check on things. It was about five in the evening. Initially, she'd planned to go home from Mohan Krishna's house, but when she saw his text message she thought it better to return to the office.

She now understood why Partha wanted his India Post profile updated. She'd gotten that done on the way to Mohan Krishna's. The online 'editor', Neha, enjoyed playing the part though she was more website admin than journalist. She responded with characteristic resentment and said she wouldn't be ordered around by contributors. But having interacted with her for over a year by then, Seema had her figured out. She listened politely and sympathetically but stayed firm that this had to be done and done immediately. Neha got to work reluctantly. Seema thought the updated profile was a little cut-and-paste but adequate to impress laypeople.

Seema had forgotten all about the university as she and Malvika got caught up in the interviews. Once done with them, her unease returned. Her main problem with Partha's plan was that he was a bad choice to go to the university. She should have gone instead. She had the journalistic experience—Partha's was short-lived and he was an indifferent journalist to begin with—and she had the ability to extract information without ruffling feathers. Both skills would be crucial in a university with excitable students and tempers boiling over—skills Partha wasn't very adept with.

She tried calling Partha. There was no answer. She then called Harish. He didn't answer either. When she received Partha's message telling her not to wait for him, she forwarded it to Harish immediately. His reply was characteristically staccato: 'I know. Advised putting-off until I'd checked out Univ. Said he'd handle it.'

This didn't make her feel any easier. It was not like Harish to suggest caution unless he had a reason for it. And it was a risky move to begin with: if Partha was discovered to be in touch with Mohan Krishna's family, his snooping around campus would be the big story going forward. It was unlike Partha to disregard Harish's warnings or to be careless about perception. It didn't add up.

She sent Harish the emergency text message they'd agreed upon. She sent it both as a regular text and as a WhatsApp message. She then sent him another text saying Partha had gone off the grid. While she waited to hear back, she got online and checked the tracker installed in their cars. The tracker showed that Partha's car was parked in the Hyderabad City University and that it was parked a while ago. She searched for the tracker on their phones—the tracker that could be traced even when the phone was switched off. She found that this was also static but in a different location, somewhere in the middle of campus.

She decided to wait for a while, see if she heard back from either Partha or Harish. She called Ravi and asked him to pick up their daughter from a friend's house. She then informed her driver that it was likely to be a long evening. He was used to changes in plan at short notice; he got himself a tea and snack in the office canteen and waited.

After a little while Seema tried Harish's phone once again. He didn't pick up, and Seema began to get irritated. It seemed to her that Harish's taciturn, distant nature was hard to take in a fully-grown man. In one's twenties it had a certain intensity and charm about it but in anyone older than that it was just tiresome. Even as she let that thought build up, she knew she was being unfair. While Harish had that non-communicative quality about him, in situations that mattered he had always been reliable. At this moment however, she wasn't very charitably disposed towards him.

Her irritation then turned on Partha. Seema guessed he'd gone to the university in a rushed, unprepared way, in part, to make the point that he didn't need a bodyguard. The dynamic between Partha and Harish included these infuriating displays of bravado. They played out elaborate self-reliant tough-guy routines even if there were safer ways of doing things. If Harish had accompanied Partha to the university, both of them would have been fine. But alone, Partha may well have walked into something bigger than he anticipated. Seema trusted her instincts and they told her that both Partha and Harish were underestimating the seriousness of what was going on. They seemed to be treating it as a relatively simple conspiracy to target a star family. Seema was certain it was so much more than that. This thing was dangerous.

Her phone vibrated and lit up. Seema picked it up—a text message from Harish.

'Will find out,' it said simply.

She picked up the phone immediately and typed a message.

'Any alarming trends at university?' she wrote.

Harish, with his network of contacts, usually managed tip-offs and even tidbits from intelligence reports. The university being so much in the news, he was bound to have checked.

The phone vibrated again. Harish again.

'Don't worry about Partha. He'll be fine.'

Seema exhaled loudly. It was intended to be a long, calming breath but it had come out quick and short, like a whistle. It didn't have the effect of calming her at all—that taciturn, tough-guy rubbish again!

*

Even as the hand firmed its grip around Partha's neck, he felt his knees buckle. They were trying to kick the legs out from under him. But Partha found his feet and dug in. He struggled and dragged forward in order to remain standing. Another man took his right arm, twisting and trying to pin it; he felt a punch or two fall on the side of the torso, but they were weak and undirected. Partha kept his footing and rooted himself. He reached for the hand around his neck with his left hand but it was taken hold of and pinned down by the man holding him. The right arm was twisted more forcefully.

Vikranth stood where he'd been. The man with the scar ran up to Partha. Partha barely saw the fist; and then he felt its impact on the solar plexus. He'd barely had time to tighten his muscles or brace for the blow. A flash shot through his eyes and the breath went out of him. As he tried to catch his breath, he saw the man cock his arm to hit him again. Partha twisted away as much as he could. This one caught him on the chest. Partha wobbled and struggled to stay on his feet. The man cocked back his arm again. It came at his face.

Partha restrained himself for a fraction of a second and turned his head as much as he could to the left. The blow caught him on the left side of his face but not with the entire intended force. The man came closer and raised his fist again.

'Enough!' Vikranth said.

The man with the scar didn't stop. The grip tightened on Partha from behind. This time the man hit him straight up on the mouth. The lip burst and felt warm, the taste of blood was in his mouth. His head dropped.

'I said enough!' Vikranth said.

Vikranth ran up to the man and pushed him aside. The man with the scar and Vikranth faced off, the scarred man's stare was livid. Vikranth glared back. Suddenly, the man with the scar grinned; he patted Vikranth's chin mockingly and saluted. He gestured 'all yours' to Vikranth and stood aside. Vikranth flashed angrily at him. It took a few moments for him to collect himself. He then turned and stepped closer to Partha.

'Do you think we don't know who you are?' Vikranth said.

Partha didn't reply.

'You thought we'd believe you were a journalist? You think we're fools?'

Partha stayed silent.

'We knew who you were the moment you entered campus,' Vikranth said.

The pressure on Partha's shoulder was growing painful. Partha straightened a fraction, trying to ease it. The men tightened their grip, the pressure increased. Vikranth drew closer.

'You think we don't know you are working for Mohan Krishna, Mr Partha Rao?' he said. 'You think we don't know you sneaked into Mohan Krishna's house twice yesterday?'

Partha held Vikranth's gaze but did not respond.

'You're the one who's going to save—what are they calling him—"the Next Generation Sensation"?'

'You think the name's a bit much?' Partha suddenly said.

'What?' Vikranth said.

'I thought I'd ask, as I have a captive audience of young men.'

'You're the captive.'

'It would appear that way,' Partha said, nodding.

The man with the scar stepped in line again. He slapped Partha across the face.

'Think that's funny, bastard?' he said.

'Being cheerful never hurt anyone,' Partha said.

The man moved towards Partha again.

'I said that's enough!' Vikranth said.

Again, the scarred man and Vikranth exchanged angry looks. Vikranth turned to Partha.

'Where are the cellphone and the laptop?' he said.

'What?' Partha said.

'I said, where are Priya's cellphone and the laptop?'

'How the hell should I know? They're wherever that missing student is.'

'Tell me the truth or we'll hurt you.'

'That is the truth.'

The man who held Partha's right arm tried to manoeuvre it into a twist. Partha pushed backwards and strained hard against it and kept it in place.

'You scum think you can manipulate anything with money, don't you?' Vikranth said. 'Your dog, that circle inspector, he has them?'

'I don't know anything about it,' Partha said.

The man who held Partha's neck jerked his arm backwards. Partha struggled to stay on his feet.

'You read the papers?' a deep voice said from behind.

'Yes,' Partha said hoarsely.

'You ever read about bodies being discovered here in this forest?'

'Yeah. A student leader not too long ago.'

'Talk. Or they'll find yours.'

The grip eased on Partha's neck. Partha nodded slightly.

'Talk,' the voice from behind said again.

'I think there was no harm done,' Partha said.

'What?'

'I think that dead kid would have made a lousy union president.'

The arm closed around the neck and this time it was hard. He felt a slap or two land on his face. Partha held on. The man with the scar waved and the pressure came off. The scarred man paced about excitedly.

'What bullshit are you people wasting time with?' he said. He grabbed Partha's face roughly, his nails digging into the skin.

'Give me a list of journalists who're with Mohan Krishna,' he said. 'Which channels does he control and which does Prakash control?'

Partha didn't speak. The fingers dug deeper.

'What does the family know about Priya's last days?' the man said.

Partha looked at him without expression. The scarred man's face flushed with rage. And then, just as suddenly, his face broke into a smile.

'We're doing this the wrong way,' the scarred man said. 'Threats won't work on him. We need to do some permanent damage.'

He walked over to one side of the clearing and bent down. He struggled to get a grip a rock with both hands and then straightened up.

'Hold out his right leg,' he said, breathing heavily.

Partha stiffened. Vikranth hurriedly stepped in the way.

'What's in the devices?' Vikranth said. 'What do you know about Varaprasad's whereabouts?'

'Get out of the way!' the man with the scar said, his voice strained.

'Are your people chasing Varaprasad?' Vikranth demanded. 'Do you people know where he is? What're you going to do with him?'

'I don't know where Priya's devices are or what's on them,' Partha said. 'I don't know where Varaprasad is and I don't know what Mohan Krishna's family knows.'

Vikranth grabbed a clump of Partha's hair.

'Tell me the truth!' he said. 'I know you know—the police is helping you! Tell me where Varaprasad is!'

There was a thud on the ground. The scarred man had dropped the rock on the ground. He ran over to Vikranth and grabbed his collar and pulled him away.

'I told you to get out of the way!' he said.

Vikranth grappled with him. The scarred man slapped Vikranth twice.

'Bastard, you do as I tell you!' the scarred man shouted.

The student who had accompanied Vikranth and Partha tried to separate the two. The two men holding Partha also began to shout at them.

Partha let his head drop limply. A fraction of a second later, his head snapped back up. This time with electric force. His captor had made the mistake of easing his hold on the neck and leaning forward. That was enough for Partha to strike with serious power. The man's nose was broken. Blood gushed out.

Partha now used the power of the stance and the momentum created by the blow he'd just landed to launch himself backwards. The mass of three men—himself, the man holding him from behind, and the man holding his right arm—fell backward. The suddenness and power of Partha's move caught them entirely unawares. The heap of men crashed onto the ground hard. Partha's weight landed entirely on the man who held him from behind. The man was strong and of large build, but his nose was broken and he was entirely winded with the fall. The man holding Partha's right arm had also let go as he stumbled and fell to the ground. Partha raised his elbows and thrust downwards. He heard the scream and then the gasping of the large man. He would not pose any threat immediately.

These men weren't professional fighters. They were at best street scrappers—even the scarred man's punches had lacked serious power or direction. Even then, Partha had to move fast to keep the advantage. Partha turned and got on his knees just as the man who had grabbed his right hand tried to get up. Partha knew he would get only one shot at this. He hit him with a short, powerful strike. The man jerked back and then he fell forward.

Partha swung around and got to his feet. He faced the other three men. Vikranth and the other student held back a little as the scarred man approached Partha. The man threw a punch. It missed Partha entirely. Partha hit him with a full-fisted hit to the skull. It wasn't a dangerous blow but it was powerful and painful. The man yelped, held his head, and fell forward.

Vikranth rushed forward. Partha threw a hard, poorly-directed kick. It caught Vikranth on the knee. He fell and grabbed his knee. Vikranth was just not used to being in fights. The last man, the heavily-built student with Vikranth, came towards Partha. Partha could see the hesitation—the student looked intimidating and may have been a boxing gym hanger-on but he didn't like fighting. The student lunged forward. Partha swung sideways, raised his hands slightly in front of him to grab the oncoming man's collar, and he used the man's momentum to deflect him. Partha's feet were in position now, he swivelled just slightly. The man went flying. He landed several feet away, hitting the ground hard. He didn't move. He wasn't badly hurt; he was just scared and hoping Partha would leave him alone if he stayed still.

Partha looked around to take stock. The guy who'd taken hold of him from behind was in no position whatsoever to move. He was still gasping for breath, his nose was bleeding profusely and he probably had a broken rib. He stayed down. Vikranth lay on the floor, more from fear than pain or injury. The man who had held Partha's right arm was also bleeding and stirring about on the ground. The fight had gone out of him too. The scarred man was the only one who showed the initiative to get up. The blow to the skull had disoriented him but things were beginning to clear up for him just then.

Partha looked at Vikranth. Partha shook his head slightly: another hotheaded student leader caught up in things he had no control upon. Partha had no desire to hurt him but he was going to make him answer some questions if he could. While he didn't particularly want to hit Vikranth, the desire to hit the scarred man came easier. Partha walked over and took a hold of him by the scruff on the neck and held him up.

'Who told you I was on the way to campus?' Partha said.

'Fuck off,' the scarred man said.

Partha hit him square on the mouth. The lips split and blood shot out. The man let out a shout.

'Not fun, is it?' Partha said.

'Fuck yourself!'

Partha hit him again. This time it was lighter but a glancing blow across the right eye.

'I'm enjoying this,' Partha said. 'Or I'd have hit you with a full-shot and knocked you out. Now, I'm going to break your nose.'

Partha looked at Vikranth.

'Who tipped you off about me?' he said.

Vikranth was up on his feet. He had a scared look on his face.

'No?' Partha said.

Partha hit the scarred man on the bridge of the nose. It was a clean break.

'You know, you don't look like a student to me,' Partha said. 'I'm being too gentle with you.'

Partha hit him again. The man fell. Partha let him slump to the ground. When he looked up, Vikranth stared at him with naked fear.

Partha took a few steps towards him. Vikranth backed away, still holding his knee. He straightened up and put weight on his knee. It was fine. Partha took a step forward, Vikranth's eyes widened. He turned and ran into the forest.

*

Seema locked her office cabin and asked the guard to lock the main door. Her driver was waiting by the car.

'Let's go to the university,' she said.

All Seema knew was that Partha had gone to meet Prof. Hussain. So, she called him. They were acquaintances so she expected him to respond. She had to call several times before Prof. Hussain picked up the phone. His tone was standoffish.

'I've come to learn that Partha is working for Mohan Krishna,' Prof. Hussain said. 'That means he got a student's contact from me on false pretexts.'

'We're not working for Mohan Krishna, Professor,' Seema said, 'we're making our own enquiries.'

'Yes, he told me the same thing. Unfortunately, I allowed myself to be misled. Do you know what kind of position it puts me in with students?'

'I can understand, Prof. Hussain, but even we're not pushing Mohan Krishna's agenda.'

'Whose agenda are you pushing then?'

'We just want to find out what happened.'

'You people have worked out an entire routine! You people have deceived me and put me in an awkward position once already. I'm not going to allow you to do it again.'

'Fine, Professor,' Seema said, picking her words carefully. 'I can't make you speak to me. But, like you, there might be others who believe Partha's working for Mohan Krishna. He's going around asking questions in an already tense university. If students take matters into their hands, we won't hesitate to prosecute.'

Prof. Hussain did not reply. Seema thought it promising that he didn't hang up either.

'He's carrying a valid journalist's ID—he has a right to be there,' Seema said. 'We won't let the thought of bad publicity hold us back; we'll go after any student that's involved.'

Prof. Hussain cleared his throat.

'I won't tell you whom I put him onto,' he said. 'But I will make some enquiries.'

'I would prefer you give me a contact who can help me trace him.'

'Ms Kapoor, we're dealing with young people's futures here. I can't just give you names and let you go around campus looking for them.'

'Professor, Partha may have voluntarily switched off his phone, he may well be fine. I'm just making sure. Nobody's necessarily in any trouble.'

'Even if it's as minor as a scuffle, I would rather the student got the benefit of the doubt. I had warned Partha that the atmosphere here was charged and that it wasn't good to stir things up. He wouldn't listen and now I'm being hassled as a result of it.'

'Will you contact somebody? And will you get in touch with me and let me know what's going on?'

Prof. Hussain was silent for a few moments.

'I'll get in touch with you if needed,' he said.

He hung up before Seema could say anything. Seema stared at the phone for a moment and then put it in her purse and stared out of the window. The sun had almost set.

*

It was almost twilight but, under the trees, it was as though nightfall had set in. Partha ran full tilt. He could vaguely make out Vikranth running ahead of him. From time to time, in clearings where light streaked in, he caught sight of him. Vikranth was running fast and without any hesitation, like he knew his way around these paths. With the adrenaline, the bruised knee didn't slow him down. Partha knew he couldn't catch up with Vikranth if he didn't trust his instincts outright. He'd learnt that in situations like this it was a mistake to think you could figure your way about. The senses were better guides.

Partha felt his arms hitting thorns and branches, bushes and rocks struck his shins and he almost tripped a few times. But he didn't the let pace flag. When one slowed down, the reliance on instinct dropped, and with it the edge. He knew he would have to keep up the pace for only a little while longer. Vikranth didn't have a lot of stamina. He was already tiring and he had a hurt knee. If Partha stayed close to him, not allowing him a chance to hide, he could not get away.

They were running up an incline now. Partha tried to pick up speed—with Vikranth already running out of steam, this would be the best time to close the gap. It wasn't easy. Partha had taken a few body blows and then there was the skirmish with the men; to keep fatigue from setting in was near impossible. They were running almost entirely in the dark now. Partha was closing in on Vikranth. And then, the vague apparition-like figure of Vikranth just went out of sight.

Partha's instinct told him to slow down. Even though he knew better than to second-guess his instincts he hesitated for just a moment or two. He felt an uneasy sensation as he slowed down. The sensation came to him just one step too late.

He extended his right foot and came down. In thin air. He started to fall down a slope. He tried to fall as loosely as he could, minimising the damage from impact. He felt the undergrowth cut at him and then the impact on his right leg.

He slid several feet down the slope and came to a stop. He just lay there for a few moments. He caught his breath and raised himself to his feet uncertainly. The leg was hurt but he was lucky not to have twisted it. His vision was better now, his eyes well-adjusted to the darkness. There was a narrow pathway that started in the clearing and went all the way to the top of the hillock. Partha shook his head slightly, trying to marshal his attention. He listened closely for a sound from Vikranth. There was nothing. There was the sound of crickets and an occasional breeze rustled the leaves and obscured all other sounds. He looked up and down the path to see if there was any sign Vikranth had fallen down along it as well. There was none. Partha guessed that Vikranth, knowing the hillock well, had ducked out of sight and was hiding somewhere near the ridge. Partha began to walk up.

He walked slowly, securing his footing the best he could. He listened intently for a crack of a twig or a branch, sounds of movement, animals—anything. The breeze that was occasional till then, had grown steadier now.

Partha drew closer to the ridge. He moved even more slowly. The breeze eased up; it seemed like it would start raining any minute now. And then he heard something that made him slow his pace. He didn't know what the sound was but it was close. He prepared to take another step. He heard the scattered sounds of raindrops falling. They slapped against the leaves on the trees and the dead leaves on the ground. The wind picked up again. The rustling of leaves drowned out everything else. Then he heard it again.

Beneath all the sounds the wind had stirred up he heard the sounds of twigs breaking and then of hurried breath. It was coming directly at him. By the time he could pick out its source in the darkness, it was upon him. There was a muffled cry and he could make out a man rushing right at him. There was no time to get out of the way.

Partha didn't try. He swerved to weaken the impact and tried to guide the man away using his own momentum. The move worked. The man didn't have enough force to push Partha off the ridge, and Partha's evasive move propelled the man to lurch forward. Partha let go—the man took off and fell several feet away, on the slope. Partha rushed down after him. At the bottom was Vikranth.

He was in no shape to put up a fight; he just lay on the floor. He was exhausted and in pain. Partha took an arm firmly.

'Get up,' he said.

Vikranth didn't move but Partha could feel him stirring. He pressed down on the arm. There was a sharp cry.

'I said get up,' Partha said.

Vikranth pulled himself up to his knees.

'Not such a tough guy on your own, are you?' Partha said. 'Even with darkness and the advantage of surprise, you don't count for much. Perhaps you'd like to take another slide down the hillside?'

'Please!' Vikranth said.

His voice was just a gasp.

13

Partha dragged Vikranth to the edge of the clearing and propped him up on a small mound. There was still light enough to see in the open. From the look of it, Vikranth was shaken up, scratched, and bruised, but otherwise alright. Partha stood over him.

'My turn to ask the questions,' Partha said.

Vikranth looked up weakly. Partha could tell he was struggling with himself, at once scared and upset with himself for being scared.

'No,' he said.

He cowered in anticipation of a blow.

'I'm not going to hit you,' Partha said. 'And you'd have been hurt a lot less if you hadn't run.'

Vikranth didn't say anything. He looked up once and then dropped his head.

'How many of those guys back there were even students?' Partha said gesturing loosely in the direction of the forested area.

'Two.'

'Let me guess: you and the guy who was with you at the bike. And the rest?'

'Activists.'

'They're goondas. Just criminals—political thugs.'

'You people brand political opponents goondas.'

'And what do you call them—soldiers? I've seen too many like these. The only thing they've got to sell is brawn and that's what they bring—to political parties and street-side gangs. They've got no ideology. Did you really think you controlled them?'

Vikranth's gaze was confrontational.

'I am the general secretary of the union!' he said.

'Tell that to the guy who was slapping you around.'

Vikranth glared but did not retort.

'That's what makes it pathetic,' Partha said. 'Winning the election means something. Being led along by these thugs doesn't.'

Vikranth remained silent. He avoided eye contact, pulling up a torn sleeve and examining the scratches.

'I'm guessing they told you you'd be in charge. That fell through pretty quickly, didn't it? I enjoyed watching you try to give orders.'

Still no reaction from Vikranth.

'Think about this though,' Partha said. 'You were the one who lead me into the Green Belt. You and other students are the face of this little operation. These other guys, they only appeared in the forest.'

Vikranth stopped examining his wounds. He looked down and didn't speak.

'And the questions they wanted to ask me were very different from yours,' Partha said. 'They had their own agenda. But who was it that asked you to confront me? What did they want you to do—make a news story out of me? To say that I was spying or trying to influence students for Mohan Krishna?'

Vikranth finally looked up. He sneered with deliberate effort. His self-confidence was returning rapidly.

'You seem to have a lot of questions,' he said. 'You can go to hell.'

Partha smiled back at him, shaking his head.

'I've already learnt a lot from you,' Partha said. 'That someone with campus connections is tracking my movements, that you don't know what's on the devices, that you're clueless about Mohan Krishna's counter-strategy, and that despite your man-in-command delusions, you're just a flunky being used by a higher-up.'

Vikranth's sneer disappeared.

'Fuck off,' he said.

'Why wasn't your boss here doing his dirty work himself?' Partha said.

'I don't have a boss.'

'You think you don't. What do you think you serve—an ideology?'

'Something you know nothing about!'

'This ideology of yours involves using goondas and acting like one yourself. I'm okay without it.'

'Those others were not party members. And it's justified for dealing with people like you.'

'You can tell yourself that. Your ideology lets you pick a side and tells you who your enemies are. After that, anything you do to win is alright.'

'And you're some moral beacon?'

Partha didn't respond immediately.

'You're right about that,' he said. 'I have helped some despicable people. I helped them put a good face on very cynical things at times.'

'Is this honesty supposed to disarm me?' Vikranth said.

'No. But think about this: in the world that I work in, it's understood that there is deception. It's understood we're manipulating opinion, that we're chasing selfish interests. And I should have been prepared for what it does to you as a person—my guard should have been up. But it wasn't. It wasn't easy to handle when it finally hit me. And I thought I was a smart guy. Just like you do. But here in the university, they don't even expect your guard to be up.'

'What's your story got to do with me?' There was just a hint of uncertainty in Vikranth's tone.

'If you treat something like a war, you better be prepared to do things that you can't justify to yourself. Things that you wouldn't do as a normal, moral human being. That's the situation you found yourself in today. If you think these compromises are not changing you as a person, you're wrong. Calling it an ideology doesn't excuse you from making choices on the path. You either make your own choices or get manipulated by someone else.'

Vikranth didn't retort; he just looked away once again.

'I believe Anil didn't drive Priya to suicide,' Partha said. 'So I'm trying to find out who did. Ask yourself if these people who're supposedly fighting for her genuinely want justice. If you believe that—fine. If not, you're being used to target political rivals. Then you have to drop these illusions about a moral cause. Then your objective is not to get justice. It's to use this girl's name—and use her death—as weapons in a political war.'

'It may still get her justice,' Vikranth said, after a few seconds.

'If Anil is responsible, yes,' Partha said. 'If not, the one who drove her to suicide, drove her to such extreme despair, will go free. He'll probably even benefit as a result of this. And an innocent man will go to jail, lose his career and name. The only bright side for you then will be that your side won the political game.'

Vikranth slowly got to his feet. But he didn't make any move.

'I find the idea of helping your side more distasteful than your opponents being untruthful,' he said.

Partha nodded.

'That's a choice for you to make,' he said. 'I'll get to the truth with or without your help.'

'It'll have to be without me then.'

'Fine.' Partha indicated the road. 'You're free to go.'

Vikranth hesitated for a moment and then started to walk. He had a limp and he cringed in pain. Partha began to feel the pain of his own wounds and a wave of tiredness. So far, he'd been alert just in case any of the men from the clearing caught up with them. The beatings they'd taken were severe but he was cautious just in case. Now he felt very tired. He walked slowly towards the road himself.

Vikranth stopped and turned.

'We're worried Varaprasad won't be found alive,' he said. 'Do you know if he's alive now?'

'I don't have any information about him,' Partha said. 'But I've not heard anything to suggest he wasn't alive.'

'Does he really have Priya's devices?'

'Yes. The police certainly don't have them. Our sources say he's got them.'

'Can you give us an assurance that Varaprasad won't be harmed by Mohan Krishna and Prakash's goons?'

'I can assure you as far as my associates and myself go. We'll protect him if we find him. I have nothing to do with Mohan Krishna or Prakash's private armies.'

'You'll excuse me if I'm not convinced.'

'That's really your concern.'

The streetlights came on in the distance. A faint light reached where they were.

'What made you so sure I was taking instructions from someone?' Vikranth suddenly said.

Partha sensed insecurity in his tone again. The cynical exterior was extremely fragile and beneath it lay a lot of doubt. The situation he'd gotten caught up in was volatile and had raised his insecurities to their peak. It also indicated to Partha that he'd touched a nerve, given voice to a thought that had already occurred to him.

'You got a phone call just before we headed into the Green Belt,' Partha said. 'There was a change in your attitude from then on. And it's also obvious two different agendas are playing out here. From the start the questions you were asking were about Varaprasad's safety and getting justice for Priya. You weren't interested in questions of strategic advantage like that other man was. Somebody must have teamed you up with those men; somebody must have called and told you who I was and what to do.'

'I can't tell you who that was,' Vikranth said.

'I'd guess it was someone respected on campus. Maybe a more politically connected student or even a faculty member like Prof. Hussain.'

Vikranth laughed.

'Why would he send you to meet us in the first place?' he said.

'Is there a better alibi?'

'Your conspiracy theories are amusing.'

'I know. They're also very addictive.'

Vikranth was silent. He spoke after a little while.

'Varaprasad used to help out Priya sometimes,' he said. 'I don't know with what exactly. He was very disturbed about her a few weeks earlier. He was always secretive about it and wouldn't say about what. If what the police say is true then he must have run with the devices to keep them from being destroyed. Or he may be afraid that they'll frame him.'

'He hasn't been in touch with any of you?' Partha asked.

Vikranth shook his head. Vikranth started to say something but he stopped himself and stared at Partha in confusion. He turned abruptly and started to walk away.

Partha knew he wouldn't get any more out of Vikranth now. He began to walk towards the street himself. He'd taken only a few steps when he sensed something. He knew he was too late to react to it. He'd lost clear awareness of his surroundings and hadn't kept track. Even as he made to turn, he felt the strike to the side of his head. Partha felt himself falling.

*

The university had a forlorn air about it in the evenings. Cheerless buildings, poorly lit by dull, white tube lights—the sight had always depressed Seema. In her student days, she'd longed to be free of the university system. And having graduated, she never looked back at those days with nostalgia. Entering the humanities building that evening, preoccupied as she was, she felt that sense of gloom descend upon her.

She went up the stairs and looked around for Prof. Hussain's office. There were no sign boards and so she went down the wrong side of the corridor and had to walk all the way back. Walking back, she almost walked past the innocuous title board without noticing it. She found the office door shut and padlocked.

It was over half-an-hour earlier since she'd spoken to Prof. Hussain. With moderate traffic, they had reached the university in reasonable time. Prof. Hussain hadn't called her back and she hadn't heard from Partha or Harish either. She knew for sure now that something was wrong. When out making enquiries like these, they had a system of updating their status every few hours. Partha hadn't done that.

Seema hoped that her presence on campus would pressurise Prof. Hussain to act. If he gave her any information, she would seek help from the police. She had contacts who would put in a word for her. Her Plan B was to show the police the location of Partha's phone. But she wanted to avoid sharing that information if she could. The option open to her now was seeking Prof. Hussain out at the faculty quarters, and if she couldn't locate him, going to the police.

She started down the dimly lit stairs. As she walked down the second flight of stairs, she saw a man walking up. He was in his late fifties and had the bearing of a senior faculty member. He had a somewhat thickset frame, though he was not fat; he panted a little with the effort of climbing the stairs. With thick, old-fashioned spectacles and a trimmed, thin mustache, he fit the image of a university professor. When Seema passed him on the stairs, he stopped and stared at her.

'Excuse me,' he called, when Seema had reached a landing.

'Yes?' Seema said.

'Are you here for Prof. Hussain?'

'I am.'

'If you don't mind, may I ask who you are please?' He spoke in a measured tone. The rhythm and pace of his sentences was steady but never self-consciously slow.

'Seema Kapoor.'

'Oh,' he said simply.

Saying no more, he walked down the stairs to where she was standing.

'I am Prof. Ramdas,' he said. 'Are you looking for a Partha Rao, by any chance?'

'Yes!' Seema said, almost allowing herself to be relieved. 'Do you know where he is?'

'Unfortunately, I don't,' Prof. Ramdas said. 'But students tell me Prof. Hussain had put Mr Rao in touch with a few students. I've heard rumours about some of those students turning up with injuries. Other students are still missing.'

'Injured?'

'Yes, we're trying to find out more.'

'Do you know where Prof. Hussain is?'

'Prof. Hussain left for Delhi unexpectedly.'

'Delhi! I spoke to him less than an hour ago!'

'He must have been on the way to the airport when you spoke.'

'That's ridiculous,' Seema said. 'I'm going to call him now.' She took out her phone.

'You could do that,' Prof. Ramdas said. 'But my priority is to find the missing students, so please excuse me.'

He started to walk away. Seema considered it for a moment and hurried after him.

'Prof. Ramdas, finding them is my priority as well,' she said.

Prof. Ramdas stopped.

'You do understand that if your friend has harmed the students, we will lodge a police case?' Prof. Ramdas said.

Seema nodded.

'And we'll lodge a case if Partha's been harmed in any way,' Seema said.

'Your friend came here by himself,' Prof. Ramdas said, folding his arms across his chest, 'and was unnecessarily interfering in student matters. Now you're threatening students with legal action?'

'If he's been attacked—yes.'

'Rumour is that your friend—and perhaps you yourself—have been contracted by Mohan Krishna. If this is true, his presence on campus is suspicious. If he's been in a fight with students, we will ensure charges are filed and that the story reaches the press.'

'The rumours are wrong. We're not on Mohan Krishna's payroll. Partha has valid journalistic credentials and he was working on a story. So if the press has been attacked, we'll go to the media before you do. And we'll prosecute any student involved in it.'

Prof. Ramdas's stare was cold.

'The publicity is not a bad thing for the students' cause,' he said, his tone low. 'We as faculty will support them in this.'

'They're welcome to the publicity,' Seema said. 'Then we'll cooperate with Mohan Krishna's people and counter-spin it as the presence of antisocial elements on campus and as an attack on the press. They'll be very happy to get a breather with this sideshow.'

Prof. Ramdas didn't respond.

'And we'll dedicate the next few years,' Seema said, 'and all the resources at our disposal, to getting convictions for assault.'

'That you could be so callous about students' futures is shocking,' Prof. Ramdas said, his tone dropping even lower.

'Not as shocking as faculty members who don't know the difference between activism and goondaism. Not as shocking as faculty members who think it's their job to help students get away with violence.'

Prof. Ramdas's face darkened.

'Your friend may have been the one who turned violent,' he said.

'We don't know that it wasn't your students,' Seema said.

They were at an impasse.

'Since Prof. Hussain's run off and you're not willing to help find Partha,' Seema said, 'I'll get help from the police.'

She started to walk away. Prof. Ramdas called after her.

'If I am to assist in finding your friend,' he said, 'I would want assurances that the students do not suffer. That any skirmish or altercation that took place is forgotten. We can come to some arrangement here itself. But the police and the media are not to be involved.'

Seema nodded.

'If nothing very serious has happened, I assure you we won't make an issue of it,' she said. 'But if we need to get police help in finding them, I insist we do.'

'Of course.'

Prof. Ramdas gestured for them to move out into the university building portico. They walked on through the path as thousands of night-insects danced frantically around the lights.

'How did you find out about this situation?' Seema asked.

'Some students approached me,' Prof. Ramdas said. 'I then tried to reach Prof. Hussain. He spoke very briefly, said he was on his way to Delhi and that he would speak upon his return.

The students told me that Prof. Hussain had contacted a student called Raghav. Raghav was seen walking in the university by-lanes along with this gentleman, Partha.'

'Any idea who they were going to meet?' Seema said.

'Student union leaders,' Prof. Ramdas said. 'In connection with getting an interview with other students, perhaps even the students who were on TV today. The union has taken their protection upon itself—both from media harassment and threats from Mohan Krishna's people. They screen anyone seeking an interview.'

'Any sign of Raghav?'

'Raghav was seen sitting in a canteen and he later went in the direction of the hostel. He's not in his room and he's not answering his phone calls. It's a large hostel and we can't go door to door, so we're at a loss about what to do.'

Seema immediately thought of the tracker showing Partha's cellphone at the centre of campus. But she didn't want to mention that immediately, just when Prof. Ramdas was opening up.

'What about the union leaders?' she asked.

'They're not to be seen,' Prof. Ramdas said, his expression grave. 'As I said earlier, I hear some students were injured but nobody has details.'

'If it's just students, I wouldn't be very worried, Professor,' Seema said. 'Even if they got into a fight, Partha wouldn't hurt them badly. So that's the best-case scenario. But if he's not to be heard from, then it's worrying—both for him and the students. I suggest, we try to reach at least one of the students in the group that met Partha.'

Prof. Ramdas raised his hands and let them drop to his side. 'How do you suggest we do that?' he said.

'Let's find Raghav,' Seema said.

'I already explained to you—'

'I might have a way of finding him.'

'How would you—?' He stopped. Then he nodded. 'Some kind of gadget,' he said.

'Yes.'

Prof. Ramdas's face hardened.

'I don't approve of these tricks and invasions into students' privacy,' he said. 'That's why I don't like outsiders entering the campus.'

'It is a safety measure,' Seema said. 'What we do gets dangerous sometimes. Can we please find this Raghav now?'

14

There was something steel-like about the man, a sense of coiled power. He was lean and over six feet tall, his face sharp-edged, almost gaunt. His strength was not the sort built up in a gym or a martial arts studio. There was a functionality about it, as though it was developed through sheer physical endurance. He wore a green shirt with a black undershirt, cargo pants, and simple sports shoes.

He dragged Partha by the hands, away from the open area and into the Green Belt. He showed no signs of exertion. Vikranth stood transfixed for a few moments and then ran after him.

'What're you doing?' Vikranth said. 'Why did you knock him out?'

The man didn't stop or answer. When they got past the front line of the trees, he let go of Partha. Partha was knocked out cold for a few seconds but he came to soon afterwards; he lay in a groggy, semi-conscious state, hardly able to move. A scattered drizzle fell on the foliage and was now dying out. After all the wind and lightning, heavy rain had not materialised. The man turned on a small torchlight and held it in his mouth.

'Take his feet,' the man told Vikranth.

Vikranth squinted in the dark and hesitated.

'I said, take his feet.'

Vikranth, wincing with the pain of his own injuries, bent down and took hold of Partha's legs. In the limited glow of the torchlight, they carried Partha a short distance, over a small incline and down the other side. There they set him down. The man began to check Partha's pockets.

'What're you going to do with him?' Vikranth said.

'Make him disappear,' the man said.

'What does that mean?'

'What you think it means.'

Vikranth gave the man a frightened look. Partha by now began to regain some control of his limbs but his movements were weak and poorly coordinated. His head pounded with pain and it was dark all around, but he was vaguely aware of what was happening. He tried to get up. The man just brushed Partha's hands away and pushed him back down. The man undid Partha's shoelaces and began to tie his legs up. His task, tying knots in the darkness, demanded all his concentration.

'But why did you have to hit him at all?' Vikranth said. 'He let me go; he was about to leave!'

There was silence. Vikranth felt hollow in the pit of his stomach.

'You gave away too much with your stupid talk,' the man said. 'You were leading him to us. I'm managing the damage.'

'You told me to lead him into the Green Belt!'

'I told you to get a student into a fight with him and get it on camera.'

'He walked right into our trap. I thought we'd get some information before we did.'

'He walked into your trap? He went into the forest so he could learn what was happening. He wanted you to do something so he could see why you were involved and what the organisation was. All of which you conveniently showed him.'

Vikranth's discomfort grew.

'Your man, Chandu, also wanted to question him,' Vikranth said. 'He didn't stick to the plan either. He was also becoming very violent.'

'He at least knew what was important,' the man said. 'He was focused on the missing devices.'

'How do you know all this?' Vikranth asked, frowning.

'My people got out of the forest and reported.'

'What about my friend?'

'Don't know. Chandu says he went the other way. Must have gotten out.'

'Chandu hit me.'

'You had to be kept in line. If you had even a bit of sense you'd have arranged a small fight, got it on camera, and run away. We'd have had a news-story and stopped this man. But you think you're a star—you wanted to get information for yourself.'

Vikranth started to say something but stopped himself.

'I'm sorry,' he said sullenly.

The man did not respond. He was looking through Partha's wallet and ID card in the torch's light. He chuckled.

'He's very careful,' the man said. 'His driver's license is a laminated copy of the original. One credit card, some money, and this press card—that's it. Not a lot of details about him.'

'We have his cellphone and camera.'

'They'll be hard to break and they'll have hardly any data on them. And they will be tracked.'

'They're switched off.'

'Doesn't matter.'

'They're with Raghav.'

The man untied a large towel from around his neck and wrapped it carefully around his head and over his mouth. He sat Partha's head up on a tree root and began to slap his face lightly.

'What're you doing?' Vikranth said.

'Now that you've allowed trackers onto the campus, we don't have much time. I'm going to show you how to extract information from a man. And then we're going to make him disappear.'

'Disappear?' Vikranth's voice had a slight tremor. 'You're going to kill him?'

'We, not me. But don't worry—not immediately. My people will hold him—just in case we need information or a bargaining chip. But we'll get some information out of him first. We can dispose him off when we've achieved the goal.'

'I don't want anything to do with this! I said I didn't want any violence!'

'Really? And why would people believe you don't? You led him into the Green Belt and had him attacked? Three witnesses will say what I tell them to say.'

Vikranth was stunned.

'But, it wasn't my—'

'Shut up.'

'But he doesn't know anything! We don't have to harm him. We can leave him right now and not escalate it!'

The man ignored him.

'Please!' Vikranth said.

The man spoke without turning towards him.

'Control yourself. If you didn't have the stomach for the big fight, you should have kept out of it. This man knows about the union now. You know who he is—we have to deal with him.'

The man slapped Partha's face several times. Partha opened his eyes and shut them again.

'I know you're awake,' the man said, 'sit up now.'

Partha was entirely conscious by now. Vikranth stood completely paralysed. In the dim light, he watched as the man extracted a long-bladed knife from his back pocket. The man placed the torch on the floor so that the light fell on Partha's torso and face. He pulled out the long blade and held it against Partha's ear.

'You better show signs you can hear me or you'll lose an ear,' he said.

He thrust the knife up slightly, up against the earlobe. A streak of blood ran down Partha's chin. Vikranth watched in horror. It was all too much for him to take, physically or mentally—too much had happened over one evening. He stood undecided for a moment. He just had to get away from there. He turned and ran as fast as he could.

The man turned around and cursed under his breath. He stared after Vikranth into the darkness but didn't try to follow him. He turned to face Partha again. He pushed him higher on the tree root and slapped him harder this time. Partha's eyes shot wide open.

'You're stronger than that,' the man said. 'I heard you almost snapped a man's wrist on your way to the university.'

He picked up the torchlight and flashed it in Partha's eyes. Partha's eyes clamped shut.

'And then you beat up a good number of people right here,' the man said. 'So I won't believe a little hit to the back of the head knocked you out too badly. I didn't hit you that hard.'

The man put the flashlight back down.

'You'll now answer my questions,' the man said.

He picked up Partha's left palm and held the index finger. He held the fingernail between his forefinger and thumb. He then squeezed down. Partha gasped in pain. It was like thousands of volts coursing through him.

'You're awake,' the man said. 'That always works.'

He placed the blade of the knife at the base of the finger and folded the finger down over it.

'You'll lose the finger if you don't answer,' he said. 'Where's Varaprasad?'

Partha didn't reply. The man cupped the finger and knife with his hand. He began to squeeze down. Partha felt the knife begin to cut into his finger.

'I don't know,' he said.

'I don't believe you.'

The hand kept squeezing.

'I don't know,' Partha said again.

'Okay, lie,' the man said. 'It's your finger.'

Partha tried to raise the other hand but the man saw it and swatted it aside. He tried to move but the man pushed him back into place. Partha tried to kick and trash but his legs wouldn't move. He couldn't see his legs but he realised they'd been tied to something. He tried to speak. The voice barely came through.

'I'll tell you!' Partha said trying to raise his voice.

The man eased the pressure but not fully.

'We know he went by road somewhere,' Partha said. 'That's all we know.'

'I think you don't value this finger very much,' the man said, raising the knife back to the ear. 'Perhaps you value your ear more.'

'We don't know anything yet.'

The knife began to dig deeper into the earlobe. Partha squirmed. He felt the warmth of blood roll down his cheek.

'Your colleague, Harish, is the one searching for him?' the man said.

They had done their homework about the firm. Partha did not to show any reaction.

'Where is he now?' the man said. 'What has he found out?'

Partha didn't speak.

'I'm patient,' the man said. 'And you're going to be with my men for several days now—you'll suffer less if you speak early on.'

Partha didn't reply. He held on. He knew the plan couldn't be to extract some information and let him go. If there was any fight left in him, this was the time to use it—this was about survival. There weren't a lot of things he could do. His hands were free, perhaps simply because the man had nothing to secure them with, but they were always in view. His only real chance would be to summon every bit of strength he had and grab the knife. And then he couldn't let go. The state he was in, Partha didn't fancy his chances. But he knew it was better to act than to be passive.

The knife dug deeper into Partha's ear.

'What's on the laptop?' the man asked. 'What are your police sources telling you?'

'I'll tell you.' Partha's voice was weak and defeated.

The knife eased but stayed wedged in his skin. Partha first shut and then opened his eyes. He tried to catch his breath.

'The laptop would have information about her relationship,' Partha said.

The man didn't react for a moment.

'What else?' he said.

'That's all we know about it,' Partha said.

'I don't believe you. What else is on the computer?'

'Nothing else.'

'Wrong,' the man said, leaning in.

Partha made his move then. He lunged forward. His left hand went for the hand holding the knife. The other hand went for the man's throat. Partha grabbed the hand with the knife perfectly, but the right hand missed the throat. He threw it again, taking hold of the man's collar. He pulled at the collar but his hand slipped and fell. The man pulled his arm back to aim a punch. Even the hand holding the knife began to twist away from Partha's grip. Partha slumped just a little and the man's punch ricocheted off his shoulder. The shoulder exploded in pain. Partha knew he didn't have another chance. He threw all his energy into the right hand. It was a short, powerful jab in the direction of the voice. This found its mark. It was weaker than it could have been but it landed perfectly, right on the throat. The man's head dropped down sharply.

It was Partha's hope that the man would be disoriented at least for a few seconds, giving him the chance to regroup and attack. But the man was still. He had recovered immediately. He wrenched his hand with the knife free; he was in a position to slash or stab. Partha, who had thrown his all into that one manoeuvre, was entirely exhausted and out of options.

*

A little earlier that evening, Seema and Prof. Ramdas entered the men's hostel building. They were headed to the location indicated on the tracker. Identifying the exact floor was difficult—they would have to climb up level by level and walk around a few steps, gauging from the relative angle of the target if they were on the right floor or not . Locating the room would be an easier matter. Prof. Ramdas climbed the stairs at a steady but slow pace. At his age he had to be cautious, he explained. Along the way, Prof. Ramdas made his displeasure with Seema's methods apparent.

'Your friend, Ms Kapoor,' he said, 'came to the campus trying to deceive or intimidate students for information. Now we're invading their privacy.'

'Almost every phone these days has a tracking feature, Prof. Ramdas,' Seema said, 'this software is just a bit more sophisticated.'

Prof. Ramdas grunted dismissively.

'And Partha wasn't trying to intimidate them,' Seema said. 'Yes, he wanted to get some information from them. But if you want students protected from such external influences—'

'I know what you're going to say. That we should encourage them not to get involved in situations like this. That we should smother the idealism out of them. Students have always played a role in bringing about change, Ms Kapoor.'

Seema started to say something but didn't. As they walked up, some students looked at the two of them curiously. Seema became particularly aware of the attention she was attracting. The attention was unpleasant.

'You have something to say to that, Ms Kapoor?' Prof. Ramdas said.

'Please, Seema is fine.'

'Well, Seema, I see you are not happy with what I said.'

'It isn't that, Professor. And I appreciate your help—I know you disapprove of our methods, but you're helping us out in spite of it.'

'But go ahead and say what you wanted to say. I encourage even my students to speak freely.'

They stopped on a landing.

'Well, I see that it's not you or Prof. Hussain out there protecting the students on TV today or dealing with external pressures. You could insulate the students and take up the cause through lawyers or public movements. This could be a teachers' movement or a civil society movement. But all of you like student movements. You give them support and try to score ideological points through them. You're in the background, like generals, leaving it to the students to face the consequences.'

'And your point is?'

'My point is that when the stakes are high—as they are in this case—these external pressures will come. They will not back off because it happens to be at the university. Why don't you deal with it and protect the students? Is it because you don't think you could mobilise anybody? So you latch onto a students' movement and try to shape it?'

Seema walked up a few steps up. She noticed Prof. Ramdas wasn't following; she stopped and looked back down.

'I'm just catching my breath, that's all,' Prof. Ramdas said. 'It's not that I am outraged by what you said.' He laughed. 'Though I must confess, that asking students—or anybody for that matter—to stand up to me doesn't make it easier to palate what they say!'

'I hope I haven't offended you,' Seema said a little sheepishly.

'No, no. I disagree with you entirely, but I am not offended. We all have our roles to play, and I like to think a teacher's is to inspire.'

He started to climb the stairs again. After one more flight of stairs, they reached the third floor. The arrow on the tracker looked closer here. They walked down the corridor to the room in one corner. There was no answer to their knock on the door. They waited for a few minutes. Two students emerged from a room nearby. They greeted Prof. Ramdas.

'Prasad!' Prof. Ramdas said. 'Is this Raghav's room?

'No, sir. It's Vikranth's room.'

'Have you seen Raghav this evening?'

'Yes, sir,' Prasad said. He looked at Seema uncertainly for a moment. 'I saw him go in there, in fact—into Vikranth's room.'

'How long ago was this?'

'About an hour ago.'

They heard a minor movement inside. Prof. Ramdas knocked on the door firmly.

'Raghav, this is Prof. Ramdas,' he said. 'Open the door immediately!'

Again, there was silence for a moment. Then came the sound of deadbolts being drawn slowly. The door opened.

'Why didn't you open the door?' Prof. Ramdas said.

Raghav looked at Seema suspiciously and then at Prof. Ramdas.

'Answer me!' Prof. Ramdas said. 'And honestly. We don't have time for any nonsense right now!'

'Yes, sir. Sir, Vikranth told me to go to his room and stay out of sight until they got back.'

'Do you have Partha Rao's cellphone and camera?'

Raghav looked extremely nervous.

'Bring them,' Prof. Ramdas said.

Raghav went inside and brought them back with him. Seema grabbed them from his hand. She turned on the phone to check if there were any new phone calls or messages made after his leaving the office. There were none.

'Now, Raghav, there is no time to lose, so tell me immediately,' Prof. Ramdas said. 'Where did Vikranth and Partha go?'

Raghav's eyes darted about and he swallowed hard.

'Tell me immediately, Raghav!' Prof. Ramdas said.

'Sir, to the Green Belt,' Raghav said.

Prof. Ramdas closed his eyes.

'When will you all learn not to behave like street-side hoodlums!' he said.

'We just thought we'd get some information.'

'And you put yourselves in danger! Yourselves physically and your careers!'

Prof. Ramdas turned to Seema.

'Once again, I can only hope your friend hasn't harmed Vikranth and any other students,' he said.

'I'm sure he hasn't. Even though it seems he had enough provocation for it.'

'But they're young and impulsive!'

Prof. Ramdas shook his head and looked deeply upset.

'We have to go to the Green Belt immediately,' Seema said.

'What good would that do?' Prof. Ramdas said.

'We'll have to get the police involved.'

'No. Let's go there as you say and get a sense of what's going on first.'

*

It was the darkness that gave him that slightest of chances. The small torch lying on the mound of sand cast a weak light on Partha and left the surrounding area dark. The man, holding the knife in his right hand, took a loose stab at Partha. Barely able to see it, Partha raised his hand instinctively. Entirely by accident, his hand hit the other man's. Not expecting the block, the man dropped the knife. In the darkness, it took him several seconds to find it.With the other hand the man grabbed Partha's neck, holding him down.

The man clutched the knife firmly. This time, he wasn't taking any chances. He pulled his arm back. The knife was raised, ready to strike. There was a rustle in the undergrowth. Partha braced himself.

From the darkness something rushed out and slammed into the man with great force. The man fell sidewards, away from sight and into the darkness. As Partha strained to hear, the sounds of a struggle became clearer. The man with the knife cursed and his breathing grew laboured.

Partha knew there was no time to lose. He crawled sideways and reached for the torch. He had to get his legs free first. He had to retain focus, sticking to the task rather than let the sounds of the battle or its outcome trouble him.

Partha stretched out and grasped the torch. He then pulled himself forward towards his toes, like in a crunch. The pain was severe and he began to sweat profusely. He shone the torch in front. He saw his feet disappear into the undergrowth; he had to part the branches to see better. His laces had been tied together and then secured to the branch of a slender, sturdy shrub. The branch was almost parallel to the ground.

Partha didn't have the focus or the reach to undo the laces. And he didn't have the time to try. He pulled himself forward, closer to the tree branch, and lined up his feet squarely against it. He pulled his legs back as far as the laces would allow and kicked at the branch. It moved but there wasn't much of an impact. He aimed the torch more carefully. He pulled his feet back again and kicked, this time closer to the base of the branch. It shot back more sharply now. He kicked three or four times with equal force. The branch began to crack. But it didn't snap. Rather it had broken and twisted, the branch's fibres holding on. Partha was exhausted. He waited to catch his breath.

Partha moved forward again, kicking at the branch repeatedly. When the branch finally gave way, he let his feet drop to the ground. He didn't bother trying to unlace his shoes. He loosened them just as much as was needed and pulled his feet out. He was free. He picked up the torch and tried to get up. He struggled to walk in the direction of the fighting.

He held the torch up. The weak light fell on the man's face. The towel he'd covered his face with had come loose during the fighting; it hung around his neck. The face was thin and bearded, the eyes hollow and still. Partha kept the torch focused on the man's face. The man suddenly threw a punch and broke free. He ran deeper into the forest. The other man followed him into the distance. And then he stopped. Partha could hear his deep, painful gasps of breath.

Partha moved forward and pointed the torch in his direction. Harish doubled over, kneeling on the floor, still trying to catch his breath.

'Lower the light; you're marking me out for a target,' he said.

Partha kept the torch switched on but trained it on the ground.

'Was just getting the upper hand,' Harish said, through laboured breaths, 'and he broke loose. Just landed a serious punch to his head.'

'You get a good look at his face?'

'Little bit—it's dark. You?'

'Yeah. Got a decent look.'

Harish walked in the direction of the light. He took the torch from Partha and turned it on him.

'Oh fuck!' he said.

'That bad?' Partha said.

'Worse.'

'Long day.'

'Any serious damage?'

'No.'

'Hope it was worth it.'

'It was.'

'Can you walk?'

'Of course I can walk.'

'We better get the hell out of here. The guy probably won't take both of us on by himself but seemed crazy enough to do it.'

*

The sight of the Green Belt dispirited Seema. It loomed dark and ominous and was stretched out over a huge area. The handful of students who'd accompanied them didn't want to go in, which was understandable. Campus security could only spare two people to go with them as the rest of their personnel were deployed on specific duties. Seema managed to flag down two constables on patrol through the campus. They weren't perturbed about entering the Green Belt, but they wanted to be sure Partha was in there first.

Seema argued with them for a few minutes. She explained that nobody really knew where Partha was, but as he was last seen entering the Green Belt, it was logical to look there. The constables accepted that. They told the campus security personnel to go with them and asked the rest to remain outside. As they started for the Green Belt, Prof. Ramdas called after them.

'You won't find any students there,' he said, 'but if you do nothing must happen to them.'

The policemen ignored him.

'The university authorities must be allowed to deal with them!' Prof. Ramdas said.

A few steps down, they stopped and appeared to be trying to train their torchlights on something.

'Somebody's there,' Raghav said.

The light from the torches fell on dry grass and bushes, but just beyond it they could make out some movement. The constables quickened their pace. Light beams fell on a man limping, being helped along by another.

'Harish!' Seema said.

She quickened her pace and went up to him.

'What're you doing here?' she demanded. 'I thought you were halfway to Chennai!'

'I was waiting—'

She turned on her cellphone's flashlight. She looked at Partha for a few seconds.

'You look terrible,' she said.

'That's what I said,' Harish said. 'I said it better though.'

'Why the hell didn't you call me back if you were coming here?' Seema asked Harish. 'And I called you so many times!'

'I told you not to worry,' Harish said. 'I thought you'd assume I would do something about the situation.'

'Why would I assume that?' Seema demanded.

Harish looked surprised by the question.

'Because I always do,' he said.

15

They sat in a room on the ground floor of the humanities building. An inspector joined them. Most of the students who had tagged along were told to wait outside, only Raghav was allowed inside. Two students were sent out to look for Vikranth. A few minutes later, news came back that he was at an uncle's house in the city. He was asked to give Prof. Ramdas a call to confirm he was well. The call materialised in a few minutes.

'There were some others in the Green Belt,' Partha said to Prof. Ramdas. 'Some of them were injured.'

Prof. Ramdas asked Vikranth about it. He listened for few seconds.

'He says there was one other student there,' he said, 'and he seems to have gotten out safely.'

'We'll need to speak to this boy, Vikranth,' the inspector said. 'And the other student with him as well.'

Prof. Ramdas looked concerned. He covered the cellphone with his hand.

'Is that necessary?' he said.

'Of course, it's necessary,' the inspector said. 'We need to find out who attacked this man in the forest.'

Prof. Ramdas spoke into the phone in a muffled voice and hung up. He then turned to watch Partha intently.

'Did this boy Vikranth lead you into forest?' the inspector asked Partha.

'Yes.'

'And then he and his friends attacked you?'

'How can you come to that conclusion?' Prof. Ramdas said.

The inspector gave him a stare. Prof. Ramdas stared back at him.

'We were attacked by outsiders,' Partha said.

'Outsiders?' the inspector said. 'How do you know they were outsiders?'

'Vikranth didn't know them. They attacked us—me and the two students who were with me.'

The inspector shook his head.

'Half the fights and attacks on this campus happen in that Green Belt,' he said. 'Most of these incidents involve students. But you're telling me the attackers were outsiders?'

'As I said, Vikranth didn't know them.'

'Why did you go into the forest in the first place?'

'I was told we were taking a shortcut.'

'And you believed them?'

'I did.'

'There are no shortcuts through the Green Belt.'

'That's not true,' Prof. Ramdas said. 'You could enter through where they did and approach the back of the science building. It is much shorter than going along the road.'

The inspector gave Prof. Ramdas a tired look.

'Okay,' he said. 'Let's accept you were taking a shortcut. Why were they leading you anywhere? What did you want?'

'I wanted to interview some students—perhaps even the two students who were on TV today.'

'Did you get any interviews before the attack?'

'No. We were attacked pretty soon after we started off.'

The inspector smiled sardonically at Partha.

'What did these "outsiders" hope to gain by attacking you?' he asked.

'I don't know. They went after Vikranth first but when I started to fight back, they turned on me.'

'You don't know why they attacked?'

'I have no idea. I also don't know whether the man who knocked me out was with them or not. I suppose he was.'

'There was another man?'

'Yes. After we fought the attackers off, we were walking out when I was hit on the head from behind. Vikranth ran.'

The head constable let out a small laugh and shook his head.

'You were knocked on the head from behind,' he said slowly, 'but you were able to see that Vikranth ran?'

'I wasn't totally knocked out.'

'Why're you making all this up? Why're you trying to keep that boy out of trouble?'

Partha shrugged and shook his head.

'He didn't know what was going on,' he said. 'I would have told you if I thought he did.'

'We will speak to him tomorrow morning.'

The inspector looked at Prof. Ramdas expectantly. Prof. Ramdas looked reluctant but nodded. He dialled Vikranth's number again. He told him he would have to report at the police station the next day and hung up. The inspector turned to Partha.

'This man who hit you on the head—he was not with the other attackers when they first attacked you?' he said.

'No,' Partha said. 'He seemed to be operating by himself.'

'How is it you were able to find your friend?' the inspector said turning to Harish.

'I got a text from Seema saying Partha had gone off the grid,' Harish said. 'So I parked outside and entered the campus. I knew the union had formed a ring around the two students. So I took a chance and enquired if anyone had seen the union leaders around. With so many journalists on the campus, most students didn't cooperate. Then I just got lucky. One student told me he'd seen them go towards the Green Belt. When I described Partha, he confirmed a man of that description was with them. It was almost dark by then, so it took me a long time to track Partha down.'

'And this man was torturing your friend?' the inspector said, pointing loosely in the direction of Partha's face.

Harish shook his head.

'It didn't look like that to me,' he said. 'He was just pounding Partha's face pretty badly.'

This made Partha cringe. Seema could barely suppress a smile.

'Luckily for Partha, I got there in time to save him.'

'He seems to have cut your ear a little,' the inspector said to Partha.

'Revenge for thrashing his people,' Partha said.

'And he got his revenge,' Harish said. 'He was beating the crap out of Partha.'

Partha stared at Harish coldly. Seema covered her mouth to conceal her smile and looked away.

'Anyway, we better get Partha checked up,' Harish said.

'This second attack is very surprising,' the inspector said. 'Two separate, random attacks on the same set of people, in the same location.'

'As Mr Rao has explained,' Prof. Ramdas said. 'The man saw that his friends were beaten and so he attacked Mr Rao. Also explains why he hit him from behind.'

The inspector looked unconvinced.

'This other man sounds like the sort of vagabonds who hang around in the Green Belt,' Prof. Ramdas said. 'We've been complaining to you people about them hanging around in the forest. They take drugs, form gangs and carry out crimes on campus. We've asked for more patrols, but you don't seem to take it seriously.'

'If it's so dangerous, why did your students go there?' the inspector said.

'So students deserve to be attacked if they go there?'

The inspector grimaced irritatedly. He looked at Partha and raised his hands in disgust.

'All of you can go,' he said. 'But your students have to be at the police station first thing in the morning. We'll find out if this man's story matches up.'

*

As they left the humanities building, Partha, Harish, and the policemen were the last to step out. They stayed back so that the police could take a detailed description of the man in the Green Belt. In the portico, they found Prof. Ramdas waiting with Seema.

'I appreciate your protecting Vikranth,' Prof. Ramdas said when the policemen had left. 'Students may be impulsive but they don't deserve to be treated like criminals.'

Partha gave a slight nod.

'He'll have to come up with some explanation tomorrow morning,' he said.

'Yes, he has to get himself out of that one. But it is a relief to know you're not complaining against him. It would have had severe consequences for him.'

'I've no interest in getting students into trouble, Professor.'

'So it's understood that neither side will take this to the media either?'

'It's understood. It suits both of us and keeps the police out of it. I have no issue with the students. What I'm really interested in is who's coordinating this news story from behind the scenes. This kind of access to a TV channel and airtime doesn't just happen.'

Prof. Ramdas didn't say anything.

'There are all kinds of political and corporate forces at play in this game,' Partha said. 'These students are bound to get used.'

'Don't forget social forces, Mr Rao,' Prof. Ramdas said.

'Those too, I'm sure. The students will get dragged into whatever it is.'

'All these matters are happening off campus,' Prof. Ramdas said. 'Let's keep them there.'

'Now it involves students and unions. The story is on campus now.'

'That's true, unfortunately. It has reached campus.'

'It's interesting Prof. Hussain hasn't gotten in touch,' Seema said. 'Not even a casual enquiry about how things turned out.'

'I'm sure he's waiting for me or someone else on campus to update him,' Prof. Ramdas said.

They reached Seema's car. Partha would ride with her while her driver drove Partha's car back to his apartment.

'Thanks so much for your help, Professor,' Seema said.

'Of course,' Prof. Ramdas said. 'Though I must confess that my real motive was to keep my kids from getting into trouble.'

'Even so, we appreciate your help,' Partha said.

'You're welcome.'

Prof. Ramdas began to walk away.

'Professor,' Partha called after him.

Prof. Ramdas turned.

'I think Vikranth will be able to concoct some story for the police tomorrow,' Partha said. 'I'm sure he'll have your help to come up with one.'

'I'll do my best,' Prof. Ramdas said, with a smile.

'Good. The thing is, I heard Vikranth speak to the man who was torturing me. They definitely knew each other.'

Prof. Ramdas folded his arms across his chest.

'What do you mean to suggest?' he said.

'Vikranth ran. He didn't cooperate with the man. In that sense, he may well have done me a favour. Now I've returned it.'

'That's good to know.'

'But if the man who attacked me doesn't forgive Vikranth, he may be in serious danger.'

'Vikranth must learn to be more careful,' Prof. Ramdas said. 'All these students must.'

'I know you don't believe in police protection for ideological reasons,' Partha said. 'I just hope the union and the faculty will be able to protect Vikranth.'

Prof. Ramdas nodded.

'I hope so as well,' he said.

16

The next morning, the rumour was that Anil would be arrested. News channels rushed reporters to Mohan Krishna's house and the police station. Pressure was mounting on the police to act on the televised statement of the students. The police refused to comment on it on record. Off the record they said they hadn't come across any real material tying Anil to the suicide. They felt trapped between growing public resentment and a politically influential family. On balance, they said they couldn't act without some kind of evidence. What gave credence to the rumours of arrest, however, was a political leak from the State Secretariat.

The leak said the state's chief minister had discussed the case with the home minister. This was seen to be a significant development. The NPP was in a complicated situation as far as this case was concerned. The party was in power in the state of Telangana and hoped to make significant gains in the neighbouring state of Andhra Pradesh in the upcoming elections. The two states, until a few years ago, had been a combined state; upon bifurcation, the NPP had come to power in Telangana and was the main opposition party in Andhra Pradesh. Hyderabad was the common capital for ten years; and as yet, media houses, the film industry, the business community and even political parties hadn't fully become region-specific. Movie stars and businessmen were still popular and influential across state boundaries.

In Andhra Pradesh, Mohan Krishna was a serious political rival, or at least a political disruptor. The Andhra Pradesh NPP saw an opportunity in this crisis. On the face of it, they demanded strong action against Anil, but behind the scenes they were using it as leverage in their negotiations with

Mohan Krishna. To the Telangana NPP it was not a matter of great importance, so they obliged the Andhra Pradesh NPP's requests. Now, however, the perception of passivity in this case was beginning to hurt the government.

As this speculation played out in the morning hours, Partha stayed at home. The effects of the previous day's exertions and attacks were telling on him. He was on painkillers and had slept in late. When he finally got out of bed, he turned on the television and watched the news for a few minutes. He then checked his phone and saw that he had a few missed calls from Malvika.

He washed up and drank a couple of cups of coffee. He then got himself a slice of toast and another painkiller. When he thought he'd found his bearings to a degree, he called Malvika. She picked up on the second ring.

'I hesitated to call,' she said. 'Seema messaged this morning—said there was an incident at the university. But all these rumours going around have got me all nervous. Did anything come up at the university?'

'I think we're onto something,' Partha said, 'but nothing that will help stop the arrest. If it's going to happen, that is.'

'Nothing?'

'I'm afraid not. It's a political thing. You must be trying to handle it?'

'We are. And legally. We're trying to get anticipatory bail.'

'Good.'

There was silence for a long moment.

'Seema said you were injured,' Malvika said. 'Are you alright?'

'I'm okay.'

'Is there nothing more we can do at the media level?' Malvika's voice betrayed a touch of desperation. 'Our party people are spinning this around community pride and stuff like that. I don't think that's good for Anil's career.'

'Tactically, what your party's doing is not bad,' Partha said. 'It'll keep the political constituency together. Not a bad move when your back's to the wall. The political base will buy into conspiracy theories and twist facts to suit their version of the story. If it gets enough of a response, the NPP will risk alienating that section of society. That'll give you guys some bargaining power.'

'It's not good for his career to be identified with a single community like this.'

'It isn't. Especially in an angry, aggressive context. It'll alienate a lot of people—especially the urban middle-class.'

'But we just live with it?'

'You don't have a lot of good options right now.'

'But there are options? Give me one—any option, even if it's a bad one.'

'I've got one. But you're not going to like it.'

'Tell me anyway.'

*

Partha felt better in a little while. The right arm was a little sore and he'd taken a few punches to the face and the body. But when the painkiller started to take effect he felt alright. He did a stretching routine, taking care not to strain any injuries. Through the years, he'd learnt the counterintuitive fact that it helped to actively retake control of the body rather than wait. He ate again—leftover rotis and vegetables from the previous day and a breakfast bar—and drank more coffee. Half-an-hour later, he felt revived. He showered and put on a fresh pair of pajamas. He wandered about the house aimlessly, which was what he did when he wanted to think things through.

The house was bare, showing few signs of being consistently inhabited. This was odd because Partha travelled infrequently and, when in town, spent much of his time at home. The furniture, fittings and the interior design were tasteful but, on the whole, the apartment looked more like a hotel room with a few personal items strewn about. The second bedroom, which also served as the study, had a few book shelves. But even here, most of the reading was done on tablets and the two laptop computers that were on the desk. In the main bedroom, clothes were neatly arranged in the closet and the bed was always well-made. There was no TV in the bedroom but there was an expensive iPod dock. What made the apartment pleasant was that it was high up, on the thirtieth floor, and had a view of the city unimpeded by buildings.

Partha shuffled about from room to room, occasionally sitting down. He found a message from Seema on his phone. It said she and Harish would follow up on things and he could stay home and that they should have a conference call when he felt up to it. Partha replied to it saying he would probably come into the office that afternoon. This morning, however, he just wanted to try to figure out some of what happened the previous evening. In the car ride back, Seema had told him how she'd traced him to the Green Belt. Now he had to put his experience together with hers and try to make some sense of it.

The first task Partha set himself to was looking back at his interaction with Prof. Hussain objectively. This was not easy. Ayesha was a friend from their days as students at the university. As professionals their paths had diverged and sometimes been at odds, but at the personal level they had remained cordial. For a while, during their college years, Prof. Hussain was even concerned that Partha and Ayesha were romantically involved. He had expressed this concern to Ayesha in a roundabout way. Partha had a pessimistic worldview, he'd told her, and expressed the hope that she would retain some idealism about her chosen field, journalism. The two of them were never romantically involved. The truth was that, back then, Partha was a bit in love with her, but that never led to anything because she was involved with someone else. Ayesha dismissed her father's concerns as hilarious and he took her word for it. Reassured that they were not involved, Prof. Hussain had warmed up to Partha. But when Prof. Hussain saw him as just another student, their rapport improved dramatically. Prof. Hussain began to discuss issues with Partha patiently even though they had very different worldviews.

After he left university, Partha's interactions with Prof. Hussain became infrequent. When they met, they spoke cordially. But as Partha's career in the corporate world took off, Prof. Hussain's disapproval of his work became more pronounced. He found Partha's work cynical and manipulative. This didn't particularly bother Partha: most people thought of his work in that way. However, it did irritate him to think that Ayesha often did identical things in the course of her work, something Prof. Hussain remained in denial of. Partha took care not to say as much to Prof. Hussain. A father, he figured, was entitled to some illusions about his daughter's ethics. But once the undertone of discomfort became pronounced, Partha distanced himself from Prof. Hussain. Over the years, they became mere acquaintances. It was something Partha looked back on with some regret. It would be overstating it to say that Prof. Hussain was ever a mentor to Partha. But Partha did see him as an important influence during his university years.

That morning, it troubled Partha to think that his personal regard for Prof. Hussain had blinded him to his true motives. He had disregarded the fact that Prof. Hussain had a stated dislike for Mohan Krishna and his family. He had gone so far as to have written a series of op-eds against Mohan Krishna's entry into politics. Partha had discounted its importance, chalking it down to ideological antagonism and not something that would affect Prof. Hussain's actions.

Partha had also underestimated Ayesha's professional interests in the Mohan Krishna story. She was known to be close to the National People's Party and so her interests were arrayed against Mohan Krishna's. Partha had considered some of these aspects when invoking Ayesha's name to convince Prof. Hussain to give him a contact. If Prof. Hussain had succeeded in reaching her, Partha's gamble would have failed and Ayesha would have asked her father not to help him. But even here, Partha had factored it in loosely—that Ayesha would merely be upset at her father being dragged into this. He hadn't considered the possibility that Ayesha had a direct stake in how the story played out. He had never considered the possibility that Ayesha could be the bridge between the students and CNEWS, facilitated by her father.

Putting in perspective what he'd heard transpire between Vikranth and the man who'd attacked him, Partha figured Prof. Hussain sent him to Vikranth—after feigning reluctance—with the purpose of creating an incident. With that one action, they would have a news story against Mohan Krishna's camp and knock Partha out of the game. It could well have been Prof. Hussain who had instructions issued to Vikranth just before they entered the Green Belt. Partha could not be sure of this, because Prof. Hussain could just as easily have made a phone call the moment he and Raghav left his office. But the delay could be explained. Prof. Hussain had exercised caution—he had made the man in the forest call Vikranth rather than call him directly.

Once in the forest, Vikranth had overplayed his hand and upset the plan. He hadn't focused on getting into a fight and getting it on camera. Partha's fighting back and easily overpowering Vikranth's men disrupted it further.

When things didn't go according to plan, Prof. Hussain probably panicked and left the campus. It could have occurred to Prof. Hussain that Partha had anticipated the possibility of an incident being orchestrated and was confident of dealing with it. Also, his cover story of being a reporter was enough to drum up outrage about a journalist being assaulted and that had made him feel even more secure. Then Prof. Hussain had possibly asked Prof. Ramdas to go looking for Seema—to contain the fallout, to see that a negative story didn't get into the media. Going by the regard Prof. Ramdas seemed to command amongst the students, it was reasonable to assume he was close to the union as well. Prof. Ramdas however seemed to be motivated more by the interests of the students than ideology per se. He was the sort of faculty member university administrators hated—the one constantly arguing on behalf of the students.

The fact that the man who'd attacked him later that evening knew about his confronting the man tailing him also tied into it all. The man in the forest had mentioned Partha almost snapping a man's wrist on his way to the university. So they knew he was headed for the university and had lain in wait to manufacture a media incident. When things went bad, the muscle of the operation tried to take Partha hostage.

Partha didn't see two aging university professors sending people out to tail and attack people, let alone torturing or taking them hostage. But university professors loved nothing more than a chance to meddle in the real world. Trapped as they were in a world of ideas, they loved imagining their knowledge was actually power. But people in the world of politics, films, and even the media, on the other hand, could easily have such criminal elements on payroll. This was probably an instance where these two worlds intersected.

So it appeared now that the university was a big part of the story they were caught up in. In figuring out the connection between the university and the outside world would lie important keys to unravelling it. Seema and Harish were actively pursuing the media and corporate connections. Any loose ends they could tie up could give them a breakthrough. Partha got dressed and headed out.

*

Partha took an Uber to the office. The driver reacted to his beaten-up face with a quizzical look. Partha grinned at him, making the sight even more grotesque. The driver didn't ask what had happened. At the office, Seema considered his bruised face for a moment.

'You look hot,' she said dryly.

'I know,' Partha said.

'I'll try keep my hands off you.'

'You must—for the good of the firm.'

'The sacrifices we make for the common good.'

'Heartbreaking.'

Partha filled Seema in about the suggestion he'd given to Malvika that morning. She thought about it for a few moments.

'It's a risky move,' Seema said. 'And there will be blowback as well. But it could just help his image.'

'It will tie his image up with Priya's suicide indefinitely,' Partha admitted, 'but that's already the case. He can try getting out of it when things have cooled down a little. Right now, his biggest problem is that he's passive and seems like a brat with a feudal community base. This move makes him more active and human. At least some people would give him the benefit of doubt.'

They discussed it a little while longer and then retired to their cabins. They decided to meet once Harish got in. Partha worked on a detailed memo for Malvika. All through, he left CNEWS playing in the background.

There was no mention of the incidents on campus in the news. The main thrust of the coverage that day was the likelihood of Anil's arrest that day. Panelists spoke about how the arrest was already overdue. A major criticism was that Anil was virtually in hiding from the time the story broke. He had not faced the press. To not face the press, they argued, is to not face the people. The family had put forward Malvika but were unwilling to expose Anil to the spotlight because they were afraid. It showed just how the son of a powerful father could abuse the law. The other story in the news was of Mohan Krishna's lawyers seeking anticipatory bail in the High Court. On the whole, nothing new had come up—the story was in passive mode.

Harish came in about an hour later. He said he'd spent the morning on a relatively sedate task—accompanying his girlfriend on a routine doctor's appointment. Even though Partha and Seema had known Harish for years, the contrast between his mundane domestic existence and the rest of his life always took them by surprise.

'All good?' Partha asked. 'The doctor's appointment, I mean.'

'Yeah, all good,' Harish said. 'Physiotherapy though.'

'Okay.'

'The doctor was more alarmed with my bruised face and stuff. Wanted me to get an X-ray.'

'Did you?'

'No. I feel fine.'

'You know best.'

'Yeah,' Harish said. 'You still look like crap though. You could have stayed home.'

'I'm fine,' Partha said.

The three of them went into the conference room. Harish asked Partha for a quick rundown of all that had happened the previous evening. So much of what they'd heard had come in bits and pieces, he wanted a clear picture of events. Partha started with how he'd confronted the man tailing him and ended with the attacker in the Green Belt.

Harish then narrated how he'd found Partha. What he'd told the police the previous evening was largely accurate. What he hadn't mentioned was that he had a few sources in the university. The moment the two students had given interviews on TV, he'd reached out to his contacts. He learnt that the union was controlling access to the students and he knew the atmosphere was tense. His sources had also mentioned that suspicious outsiders—trouble-makers with connections to political parties—had been spotted around campus over the past few days. That's why he was keen to get a little more information before Partha went in there. When Partha insisted on going, he told his sources to be on the lookout for him. He was wary of sending any outsiders onto campus so he made do with university employees—clerical and other category staff. They could be his eyes and ears but not the muscle.

Harish himself had put off starting for Chennai until he'd received some confirmation that Varaprasad had actually gone there. When he got the text message from Seema, he decided to go to the university campus instead. His contacts had seen Partha walking through campus with Raghav but they hadn't seen him enter the Green Belt. One employee saw Vikranth's bike go in the direction of the Green Belt and ventured a guess that they'd gone in. Harish checked the tracker and asked the contact if the location was anywhere near the Green Belt, which was where Partha was last seen going. He'd then traced the tracker's history to check the path the device had travelled to be at its current location. He saw it had skirted the Green Belt. He figured Partha's phone could have been extracted from him there. It was most likely that Partha had gone into the Green Belt.

He instructed a contact to be on lookout near the Green Belt access. He himself entered the Green Belt from a different direction and moved in the direction of the access point. He'd been at it for a while when his contact called saying Partha and a union leader had emerged. They were a distance away from the access point, but within view. And then something seemed to happen—he didn't get a clear view—and they disappeared into the forest again. This narrowed down the location. Harish got to the area and began to scour around. It was lucky he'd reached Partha when he did.

'Anything we can do about finding the guy in the forest?' Partha asked.

Harish wasn't optimistic.

'Wish I'd been able to keep a grip on him,' he said. 'Once he's out there, we can't get to him without the reach of the police. I'll try find out from my contacts in the department but it's a long shot.'

'Maybe it's because I took some punishment from him,' Partha said, 'but it seemed to me he was a trained fighter. Ex-defence services or something.'

'Not defence,' Harish said. 'He had some training though. I wouldn't go so far as to say terrorist camps, but he'd been in something similar.'

'So we forget about him for now?'

'I'll get his face sketched and put it out there. It's all we can do right now.'

'You think we'll get a lead on Varaprasad?' Seema asked.

'That won't be easy either,' Harish said. 'But we have one advantage in this case: the kid's face is on TV and he's got a bunch of people after him. If he doesn't have some easy place to disappear to, some lodge owner or landlord will call in. A detective agency I'm in touch with is confident that Varaprasad travelled to Bengaluru from Chennai. They're trying to confirm it. If he's there we should at least get a whiff of it.'

'Stay on top of that,' Seema said. 'Finding him is the key to everything.'

'The agency's top notch. They're our best shot. They're expensive as hell though. Rules say I get charged even though I own a stake—one of the foundational rules of the agency. Only privilege I get is priority.'

'We'll bill it to Mr Ramakrishna,' Seema said.

Partha was silent. Harish looked at him.

'Pay them,' Partha said. 'We'll figure out the money later.'

Seema frowned. 'Ramakrishna will pay, right?' she said.

Partha rubbed his hands together and shrugged indifferently.

'He'll pay if we resolve the matter to his satisfaction,' he said.

'What if we don't? We're professionals—we expect to get paid.'

'It's a film industry practice,' he said. 'They don't pay up in full if the film doesn't succeed.'

'So not only are we involved in this sleazy affair, we might be paying out of our pockets?' Seema said.

'For some of it. It's a risk we run.'

Seema gave him an incredulous look. Partha pretended not to notice. He gave Harish the phone numbers of the man who was tailing him and his boss, Satya. Harish would try track him down. This too was an important lead, it had the potential to reveal who was having Partha followed and who connected the university to the outside.

Harish took the responsibility for getting a sketch drawn of the attacker in the Green Belt. The sketch artist would be at their office any minute now. Harish caught a partial glimpse of the man's face, so he could augment Partha's description. He also volunteered to give instructions to the Bengaluru detective agency; and then he'd get on the trail of Satya through his network in the city.

'And what the hell are you guys going to do?' he asked.

'I guess we'll follow up on the university thing,' Partha said. 'Perhaps go to the university and talk to Prof. Ramdas.'

'Both of you?' Harish said.

'Seema made an impression on him,' Partha said.

'You didn't do too badly either,' Seema said. 'Refusing to blame Vikranth for the attack would have won him over.'

'Don't do all the heavy lifting all by yourselves,' Harish said sarcastically, folding his arms across his chest.

'I have to do the heavy-lifting with the sketch artist,' Partha said defensively.

'It'll be a miracle if Partha has the energy to make it to the university after that,' Seema said.

'Thank you, Seema,' Partha said sarcastically. 'I could talk to the detective agency guys if you like,' he offered to Harish.

Harish didn't look too keen. He liked to be in direct contact with his sources. He didn't trust others to be as thorough as he himself was. Though he thought highly of Partha's skills, he preferred not to leave such tasks to him.

'Never mind,' he said. 'You two go tag-team your elderly university professor.'

Harish left right after they were done with the sketch artist. Both Partha and Seema got immersed in things they needed to get done before setting out. Every moment she could spare, Seema was focused on trying to establish the ownership pattern of CNEWS. Partha had to get detailed guidelines to Malvika as soon as possible so she could go ahead with the plan he'd suggested. This time, he didn't believe it was a good idea to have Seema at the location—it was becoming important not to be seen to be directly involved with the Mohan Krishna camp. But the memo he was writing was urgent. The event Partha had in mind was contingent upon receiving Mohan Krishna's consent; if it did, they would have to roll it out immediately.

*

The man raised his right hand and gently touched the area around his lower ribs. A rib was definitely broken. On his cheek was a deep gash from when he'd fallen against a stone. His arm was still sore and it hurt when he lifted it. The scuffle the previous evening had been harder on him than any fight he'd been in, in recent years.

The man observed the injuries as though from a distance. He knew how to divert his mind from the pain. It helped to think of injuries objectively, as though they had happened to someone else. If you did that and moved about without impediment, as though you weren't injured at all, you would be able to get most things done as though you weren't injured. Within reason.

He brought his arm down. He considered the incidents of the previous day with that same sense of objectivity. The two men knew how to fight. His men had told him about how Partha had fought back. Two of them were students but the others were hired men. They were riff-raff but they knew enough fighting to be able to restrain a layperson, even someone with some training in the martial arts. A white-collared man, a media person of sorts, should have been easy to handle. But his men had proved to be no match for him. Even on his way to the university, Partha had dealt ruthlessly with the man following him.

The second man—whom the man assumed was Harish—was lethal as a fighter. He was definitely trained. It wasn't just about formal training in martial arts but he'd used them in serious confrontations—one could just sense that quality in people. He had come across such men in the past. They wouldn't give up even in the face of a firefight. They would keep going until the objective was achieved.

He would have to deal with both of them quickly and decisively. The strikes would need the element of total surprise. There was no scope for error. He would have to lead the attack himself. He could not afford to make the mistake of delegating it to others.

He had already planned it all out. His leader had initially been reluctant to even talk about it. But he had approved a tentative plan, which could be put into action whenever his leader thought it appropriate. The two men would disappear and their bodies would never be found. The blame would carefully be shifted—through insinuation more than anything else—onto a criminal group. But the leader thought it was too dangerous to try right now.

He also had to deal with Vikranth; the idiot they'd given so much importance to. He had been given control of a few men to help him restrict access to Sirisha and Biren. He took this to mean absolute control. It was loathsome dealing with amateurs like this. But he had no option in this matter either. Once again, his leader had urged restraint. They'd deal with Vikranth in time, he assured him. But right now, anything happening to a student leader would raise hell. But when the chance arose, either Vikranth or someone close to him would have a very unpleasant experience, something that left no ambiguity about who was in charge.

But first, in order to see the current business through to the end, the retrieval of the laptop and cellphone was essential. All his people were on the job of tracking down the student on the run. There had been some promising whispers, but nothing concrete. He had to warn his people to deliver results quickly. The news story was dangerously close to flagging. Without the material on the devices, they were losing most of their bargaining power.

New information suggested the boy had gone to Bengaluru from Chennai. He had asked for a confirmation within the day. The moment he heard back, he would act. In the meantime, he had another task to deal with. He had to deal with the fallout of incompetence. The task that filled him with some pleasant anticipation.

17

The morning after the incident in the university Green Belt, Prof. Ramdas was by Vikranth's side as he spoke to the police. Vikranth stuck to Partha's version and told the policemen that the men who'd attacked them in the Green Belt were outsiders. The police didn't believe him, but in the absence of a complaint from Partha, there was little they could do.

The police were more insistent when it came to the second attack on Partha. Vikranth played safe answering this: he narrated the entire story again. He said they were taking a shortcut through the Green Belt when they were attacked by some unknown men. They managed to get free of them and were finding their way back. Just as they reached the edge of the forest, Partha was hit from behind. This was exactly what Partha had said so that should have been the end of it. But the campus police wouldn't let it drop so easily.

'So you ran?' the inspector said.

The question irritated Vikranth.

'Partha Rao was out and I couldn't fight the other man off,' he said.

'So you ran and didn't even go get help?'

'I wasn't sure what to do.'

'This is a man you led into the Green Belt. The two of you are attacked. He fights them off—I doubt you had that much to do with it—and you are safe. Then he's hit on the head and dragged away by some unknown man. But you don't even call for help? You should have done it out of gratitude at least!'

'Now that's unfair,' Prof. Ramdas said. He was sitting next to Vikranth at the inspector's desk. 'The boy was shaken and ran. I'm sure he would have called for help once he regained his composure.'

The inspector didn't react to Prof. Ramdas.

'This man who attacked Partha was strong?' he said to Vikranth.

'I thought so,' Vikranth said.

'What did he look like?'

'I don't remember.'

The inspector reached into his desk drawer. He took out a photograph and placed it on the table. It was a photograph of the man who had attacked Partha.

'Was this him?' he said.

Vikranth's eyes flickered. 'I didn't get a proper look,' he said.

'Partha said you were almost out of the forest and there was still some light outside,' the inspector said. 'How is it you didn't see him?'

'I was taken by surprise and didn't observe.'

'You just ran.'

'What do you expect him to do?' Prof. Ramdas said. 'Fight this thug off with his bare hands? He's only a student, for God's sake!'

The inspector smiled at Prof. Ramdas. 'I didn't say he should have fought him,' he said. 'I said it was surprising that he didn't even catch a glimpse of him.'

'This kind of speculation is endless!' Prof. Ramdas said. 'And who is this man?'

The inspector's smile stayed as it was.

'One of the criminal sorts you at the university periodically make complaints about,' he said. 'You think we don't act on them but we're very sensitive about such things. We take photographs or get pictures from CCTV camera footage. This man was recently spotted on campus and the descriptions given by Partha Rao and his friend last night matched this photograph.'

'And who might he be?' Prof. Ramdas said.

'Why should I go into all that?' the inspector said. 'Especially when Vikranth is here to answer my questions and not the other way around?' The inspector looked at Vikranth. 'Any idea why you were attacked twice—or more specifically why Partha was attacked—on the same day, and almost at the same time?'

Vikranth shook his head. 'I don't know who attacked us and why,' he said. 'In both instances.'

'A few men had X-rays and even a scan done last night at a small private hospital about five kilometres away,' the inspector said. 'The timing matches up—we think they might be the men who attacked you. We're going through that CCTV footage. When we do find them, I hope we don't find glaring differences between their story and yours.'

Vikranth's head shot up but he didn't say anything.

'They'll have the same story, I'm sure,' Prof. Ramdas said. 'Inspector, if you don't have any other questions, I would like to take Vikranth back to the hostel now.'

'I have no questions for him now,' the inspector said. 'But I have questions.'

'What do you mean?'

'This young man seems to remember nothing about what happened last evening. He's either the most unobservant young man I've seen or he's lying.'

Vikranth fidgeted with his hands. Prof. Ramdas smiled coldly.

'You're describing any student suffering from the shock of an unexpected attack,' he said. 'It's your prerogative to read more into it, but I find that unfortunate.'

The inspector's smile was replaced with a humourless stare.

'We're going to talk to the other students,' he said, 'especially the boy who accompanied Vikranth and Partha into the Green Belt. We're going to be talking to a lot of people on campus, and we're going to be looking out very closely for this man on the run. If any discrepancy comes up, we'll be talking to Vikranth again. And this time, I won't allow him the moral support of having his professor with him.'

'Maybe a lawyer can be with him.' Prof. Ramdas's smile was undisturbed. 'And I fully intend to accompany the other student when he reports to you later today.'

'I don't mind. And Vikranth is welcome to bring along his lawyer.'

'The university community will be watching you very closely, inspector. We won't have our students harassed.'

'I have some bad news for you, Professor, I play entirely by the rule book. That might sound like a disadvantage but it actually gives me great strength. I don't break the rules, I don't take shortcuts—I just investigate the case. If I talk to Vikranth again, it'll be because I have something on him.'

Vikranth's fidgeting got worse. He looked sideways, at Prof. Ramdas, and then down at his hands. Prof. Ramdas's smile tightened.

'You'll find nothing inspector, because the boy is innocent,' he said. 'Now can we go?'

The inspector shook his head firmly. 'Vikranth will write out his version of the story in its entirety before leaving,' he said.

'But you've just heard him tell his whole side of it!'

'Now he'll write it.' The inspector looked at Vikranth. 'You saw me taking notes while you spoke, Vikranth. Don't let me find any discrepancies between what you told me and what you're going to write.'

Vikranth's mouth trembled a little.

'You're pressurising the boy!' Prof. Ramdas said.

'I've been extremely understanding in letting you be here, Prof. Ramdas,' the inspector said. 'Please don't take that to be a weakness. Don't interfere with my inquiry.'

Prof. Ramdas's eyes hardened.

'Fine, inspector,' he said. 'Go through your process.' To Vikranth, he said: 'Write it as you remember it, Vikranth, don't worry about anything.'

Vikranth stared at Prof. Ramdas blankly.

It was an hour later that they left the police station. Prof. Ramdas and Vikranth walked in silence up to the road. As Prof. Ramdas's car pulled up, he placed his hand on Vikranth's shoulder.

'Partha Rao is keen to drop the whole thing,' he told Vikranth. 'He also understands that outside people were involved and he doesn't want to equate students with them. It is in his self-interest, of course. He knows their side will lose sympathy if students are targeted. This issue will die out quietly. Don't worry about anything.'

'The police are going to compare versions of different people,' Vikranth said, agitation telling in his breath. 'They know the story I told them was made up. They're going to have something or the other to harass me with. And that's only the police—'

'Don't worry about all that. Without Partha's complaint, they have nothing to go on. And this has always been a liberal campus; we won't let the police harass you.'

'And what about people outside the campus?'

'You're unnecessarily panicking, Vikranth. Go to the hostel and stay there. Stay on campus until things cool down. Here, you're amongst people who care about you, people you can trust.'

Vikranth shook his head; he looked very disturbed. He pulled away and Prof. Ramdas let his arm drop. Prof. Ramdas watched him as Vikranth walked away. He thought it better to let him be for the time being. He then got into his car and told the driver to take him to the humanities building.

He looked out of the window as they drove along. This was not a bad outcome. He doubted the police would make trouble for Vikranth. The only troubling thing this morning was Vikranth's state of mind—he appeared frazzled and vulnerable. He seemed full of self-doubt and disillusionment—two qualities that put people at risk. Prof. Ramdas just hoped Vikranth wouldn't do anything rash. He would have to ask other students to keep a close eye on him.

*

The easy part was buying the pen-drives. He'd gone to a small stationery shop and asked for three 4GB drives and two envelopes with cloth lining. He picked the cheapest pen-drives, but even then, he paid the shopkeeper with a twinge of regret. Varaprasad was acutely aware that in addition to what he'd have to pay for the room and meals, he had some significant expenses coming up. On impulse—actually as a precaution—he also bought a small stack of paper, another expensive buy. On his way back to the lodge, he bought a packet of food from a street-side vendor and took it back to the room. It suited him: he didn't want to be outside any more than he needed to be, and he didn't have the money to buy anything fancier. He got back to his room and bolted the door.

He felt the sweat on his brow and his heart beating fast. Every moment he was outside the room, he felt there were eyes on him. He constantly imagined a hand landing on his shoulder and a hostile voice calling out his name. He was troubled by images of someone pursuing him through the streets. At night, he woke up in a panic imagining there were people outside his door. During the day, he listened fearfully for sounds in the corridor. His senses were heightened all the time now; he heard the slightest of sounds, sometimes even the inflection of a voice down the corridor. There were times he felt completely overwhelmed and he thought he would collapse. Sometimes it was too much to bear: he sat by the bedside and allowed himself to break down.

Only the task he had to get done kept him going. He couldn't weaken now. He had to make copies of the material on the laptop. And then there was the challenge of sending it out. After that, he didn't care if he was caught. He didn't care what happened. Anything was better than the terror he lived in now.

*

Early in his teens, Satya was accorded the honorific 'anna'—elder brother—even by people older than him. Whether or not it was a sign of respect was debatable, but it was definitely a sign of fear. By his early twenties, he was the most prominent goonda in his area. About a decade later, he had graduated to a more entrepreneurial role. A bunch of boys worked for him now and did the muscle work while he himself became a contractor of sorts. His role was getting clients, supervising his men, and reporting back to the client. He'd been doing this for over a decade now. Things ran smoothly enough most of the time. This morning though he had an issue to deal with.

The task he'd assigned his man, Yaddiah, had been simple enough. Yaddiah was to follow a man and track his movements. But he'd made a mess of it. Satya had instructed him to take precautions, to swap the task around with some of the other boys so he wouldn't easily be spotted. He'd also told him to be extra cautious on the job. He had done none of that. Looking back, Satya regretted not shuffling the shifts around himself. Once boys got comfortable with a task, they stuck to it, not wanting to switch to more strenuous work. Yaddiah said the mark had observed and confronted him; in fact, he said he'd beaten him. Yaddiah claimed that the man had crushed his arm, knocked over his bike, wrenched away his phone, and threatened him. Satya discounted this account heavily. It was more likely that the man rushed Yaddiah and he fell, his bike landing on him.

But it was a major goof-up. The moment he heard about it, Satya had behaved professionally. He called the client and narrated Yaddiah's version of events to them. He also told them that Yaddiah had given up the information that he was his man. Satya felt it was the professional thing to do: give the client full information to make their next move. Tough as it would be to lose an important client like this, Satya believed that being honest made things easier. It was better for the client and for his own reputation in the long run.

Yaddiah was told to come meet Satya at his house that morning. He was to give a more detailed narration and also tell him how he'd undo the damage he'd caused. Then, if Satya deemed it necessary, he would face any punishment meted out to him. But about an hour earlier Yaddiah had called. He was unwell and in pain, he said. He had important information to give him but could not come see him. Satya told him to stay put and that he would come over instead. He wanted details about the incident immediately. Any information that might help him win back his client was welcome.

Yaddiah lived in a slum close to where Satya lived. A part of the slum had developed quite well, with rows of two or three-storied houses springing up. Yaddiah stayed in a room on a building's top floor—a single room in a corner of the terrace. Yaddiah liked to complain that this room was the only place he could afford but Satya knew he wouldn't move even if he could afford better. The place suited him. He could come and go as he pleased; the apartment had its own access to the terrace through an external staircase. The other perk—one he valued even more—was that the landlord's daughter came upstairs to hang out the clothes to dry. Yaddiah hung around on the terrace for that if he could and only afterwards, around lunchtime, would he turn up at the marketplace tea stall that was the gang's hangout. He would dreamily describe the way she looked that day and how gracefully she went about her work. The other boys would make lewd jokes, which sometimes upset him and led to altercations. But on most days, they were received in good humour and everyone had a good time.

By the time Satya reached the top of the stairs he was winded. He knew he was getting out of shape, but he thought of it with no serious regret or intent to change. He had tried calling Yaddiah a few times but got no response. As he passed the bathroom door on the way to Yaddiah's room door, Satya banged on it. No answer. Satya paused outside the bedroom door. It was slightly ajar and the room was dark inside.

'Motherfucker, come out,' Satya said tiredly.

There was no answer. But Satya thought he heard some sounds of movement within.

'Bastard, if I come in and find you doped—' Satya said.

No answer. But again some movement. Satya was angry now. Satya had rules for his boys: drinking was fine but no drugs. And not even drinking in the day time, except on festival days and special occasions. He knew many of them did drugs and drank behind his back, but to do it when Satya was expected was going too far.

Satya tried to open the door but it wouldn't budge. It seemed something was wedged in between. Satya turned sideways and positioned his shoulder carefully, aiming for the edge of the door. He leaned back and lunged forward. The door didn't budge. It hit something soft but heavy. The door stayed where it was—unopened. Something was blocking it from inside. Satya tried to peer in but it was very dark. But he heard something. A choking sound it seemed. Satya instinctively recoiled. After a moment of thought he leaned back and crashed his shoulder into the door again. The result was much the same. The door opened marginally more than it had the last time. Satya braced for another blow to the door. Before he could plunge forward, the door opened a little more by itself. Satya stopped himself.

He leaned forward towards the door and tried to push it open a little more. He then stopped and pulled a knife from his back pocket. He tried again to peek inside to get a better look. A rough curtain had been drawn across the small window in the room—it was too dark to see clearly. Satya felt the pleasant rush of adrenaline. Whether it was Yaddiah or someone else inside, whoever was playing these games would pay. He leaned back and lunged forward again, leading with his shoulder.

Suddenly, Satya had the sense of losing balance, pitching forward. The door had been pulled back open a little wider and he had lost his footing. He fell to the ground hard. A kick hit him squarely in the ribs. Before he could react, a powerful kick hit him in the stomach. Satya struggled for breath; he was in serious pain. He felt himself dragged in and the door shut behind him.

Satya blinked, trying to get accustomed to the darkened room. He saw a figure loom over him. The figure reached down. Satya struggled but his strength hadn't returned yet. He felt the man grip his throat and pull upwards. He got to his knees. Then Satya felt a hit to the body; he fell forward. Satya's hands were free, so he reached for where he'd been hit. His palms wrapped around a man's hand. The man's hand was firm and warm with blood. The man's other hand was on Satya's shoulder. Satya felt the knife drawn out of him and then it struck again, this time deeper and pushing upwards. Satya's eyes opened wide. The little struggle he'd put up came to a stop. It was over.

The man pulled out the knife and let Satya slump to the floor. He walked over to the end of the room and pulled the curtain. Not five feet away was the wall of the adjoining building. The little sunlight that shone through into the room was just about enough to see. The man turned around and sized things up. His gaunt face looked grotesque in the dim light. A gash showed on a side of his face.

His eyes turned in the direction of the door. Standing gagged and tied, his legs barely holding him up, blood flowing down his shirt side, was Yaddiah. A rope was tied noose-like around his neck. He was tied right behind the door, just about half-a-foot away from the hinges to allow for movement. He was put right in position to block the full impact of Satya's thrusts against the door. Even his face was battered.

The man walked up to Yaddiah. He looked at him for a moment and then stabbed him. The first, he held for a while. He then stabbed him twice with quick, efficient strikes. The body shuddered and fell forward, the rope tightening around the neck.

18

Partha and Seema set out for the university once again. Prof. Ramdas had agreed to see them that afternoon. They also tried to reach Prof. Hussain, knowing fully well that there'd be no response on his phone. A call to the office landline was answered by an office attendant who said Prof. Hussain was out of town.

With the driver taking them, Seema tried to catch up with some phone calls. Partha looked out of the window and seemed preoccupied. Seema turned to him when they were about halfway. Seema cleared her throat. Partha didn't notice or turn to look at her.

'Not going over to the dark side, are you?' Seema said.

'What?' Partha said, looking at her.

'Are you? Is something getting to you?'

'No, no. I'm fine. In fact, I feel okay when this stuff's going on.'

'Can you tell what brings it on? What triggers it?'

Partha shrugged awkwardly.

'It's not a fixed pattern,' he said.

'Should I not have brought it up? Is it insensitive? '

'Not at all. Don't worry about it please. Perfectly fine to ask about it or joke about it.'

'I don't want to joke about it. I'm just trying to understand it.'

Partha shrugged again and hesitated as though he was fighting a deep resistance to talking about this subject.

'I'm sorry to have brought it up,' Seema said. 'You don't have to talk about it.'

Partha waved her apology away.

'Thing is,' he said, 'it's always been there, underlying everything I did—what you call the dark side. I thought work helped ease it. Then I realised it just buries it. And actually makes it worse.'

'Nobody you deal with can tell there's something going on.'

'I myself couldn't tell for a long time.'

'True.'

There was an uneasy silence.

'Aren't you worried about bringing me along?' Seema said with laboured levity. 'You got battered yesterday, they'll think you brought me along for protection.'

'That is why I'm bringing you along,' Partha said.

'Harish told me not to let you out of my sight. Said he wasn't around to protect you today.'

'I would've handled it.'

'Were you waiting for a special incentive before you "handled it"? Just look at your face!'

'Don't you have more phone calls to make?'

'I'm done.'

'For some reason, I do feel the dark side coming on now.'

'So you need Harish to keep you out of trouble, you need me to get Prof. Ramdas to talk—what exactly can you do by yourself?'

'I did manage to make breakfast this morning. Toast.'

'Looks like you have an alternate career lined up.'

Partha smiled.

'So what were you thinking about?' Seema asked.

'Just wondering what Prakash's next move would be,' Partha said.

'Why should he do anything right now?' Seema said. 'He's got Mohan Krishna where he wants him and doing his bidding.'

'Indefinitely?'

'You mean he'd prepare for a time when he doesn't have an upper hand over Mohan Krishna?'

'He has to. See, our assumption throughout has been that Prakash has solid leverage on Mohan Krishna—as far as we know, it's business interests that are very closely intertwined. But what happens when this matter is over? When his position is strengthened, Mohan Krishna will want revenge. Prakash has to prepare for that eventuality.'

'So he's got to keep the leverage on Mohan Krishna.'

'Exactly. So suppose we get the devices and hand them over to Mohan Krishna. He could use them to exonerate Anil or force Prakash out in the open. Do business interests sound like reason enough not to?'

'You know, from the very beginning business interests didn't seem like reason enough to sacrifice Anil.'

'Right. And if Anil is exonerated, Mohan Krishna's political clout could actually soar. Then he could make up for any financial losses that Prakash inflicts upon him.'

'That's true.'

'Prakash would have anticipated all this. So he must have an insurance policy.'

Seema nodded. 'Something Mohan Krishna desperately wants to hide,' she said.

'Just consider this: maybe Mohan Krishna's camp needs us to get hold of the devices so that the material on them and what Prakash has on Mohan Krishna cancel each other out.'

'Interesting.'

'It is,' Partha said. 'But it leaves another question wide open: what if we don't get to the devices first? Someone else—like that guy in the Green Belt yesterday—gets them. What would Prakash do then?'

'He'd have to cut a deal with whoever has them,' Seema said. 'Even if it means burying the family.'

*

They found Prof. Ramdas waiting for them in his office. His office was larger than Prof. Hussain's. It had the additional luxury of a small sofa set and a coffee table.

'We hosted an international sociology seminar here once,' he explained, almost apologetically. 'I couldn't very well meet delegates in a tiny office. So they thrust this burden upon me. The furniture came as part of that funding. It's too grand for an academic.'

They sat on the sofa and Prof. Ramdas sent out for some tea. Prof. Ramdas asked Partha how he and Harish were feeling after the previous evening's incident. Partha said they were both fine and asked how the visit to the police station had gone.

'There are holes in Vikranth's story,' Prof. Ramdas said with a laugh, 'but with you refusing to lodge a complaint, they're not in a position to do anything about it. They're trying their intimidation tactics, of course, but we'll not let them act on them.'

'I won't change my statement,' Partha said. 'So Vikranth can relax.'

'I genuinely appreciate that,' Prof. Ramdas said.

'It's not a problem.'

'Good.'

Prof. Ramdas looked at Partha expectantly and Partha returned the look. After a few seconds, Prof. Ramdas laughed.

'So what is it you expect in return?' he said.

Seema smiled. Partha didn't.

'Call it quid-pro-quo if you will,' Partha said, 'but we need to know what's going on here.'

Prof. Ramdas leaned back in his chair and interlaced his fingers and wriggled them around. He frowned and then nodded, almost to himself.

'It's not so simple, Partha,' he said. 'The university is a self-contained ecosystem. We may disagree fiercely amongst ourselves, but ultimately we have to live together. Our loyalty must be to each other.'

He looked in the direction of Seema.

'We can appreciate that, Professor,' Seema said. 'But as you saw yesterday, your students are getting drawn into things way too dangerous for them to handle. They're definitely being used by some vested interests. You may not believe that we want to help but if you at least believe we're not trying to harm them, then you should give us a chance.'

'You think I should cooperate with you?' he said.

'If you believe that we don't mean the students harm,' Seema said.

Prof. Ramdas placed his elbows on the armrests and twiddled his thumbs for a little while. A canteen assistant brought in cups of tea; he placed them on the coffee table and left.

'I won't volunteer anything by myself but I'm willing to answer questions you may have,' he said. 'But I'll consider each question on its merits.'

'That's fine with us.'

Prof. Ramdas nodded his head slightly. Partha leaned forward.

'Is Prof. Hussain mentoring these students?' Partha asked.

'We all mentor them,' Prof. Ramdas said.

'Yes, but is he their ideological mentor?'

Prof. Ramdas looked at him and shrugged.

'Some faculty members are very passionate about their subjects,' he said. 'About their beliefs as well. They express themselves forcefully, emotionally. Others are less animated. Students react to such vocal teachers better—it's youthful idealism.'

'And Prof. Hussain is such a teacher.'

'He is very committed to his beliefs.'

'And his extreme ideology appeals to a lot of students?'

'I said he was passionate, not that he was extreme.'

Partha smiled.

'Come on, Professor,' he said. 'It's passion when you agree with those beliefs and it's chauvinism, extremism, and unreason when you don't.'

Prof. Ramdas smiled back at Partha. 'You're a cynical man,' he said.

'No, I passionately believe this to be the case.'

Prof. Ramdas laughed. He picked up a cup of tea from the coffee table and took a sip.

'His ideology is certainly not mainstream to everyone—as in what's circumscribed entirely by the Indian Constitution,' he said. 'And yes, a lot of students do take him to be a mentor.'

'Especially the union?' Seema said.

Prof. Ramdas nodded.

'Is he their main connection to the outside world?' Partha said.

'How do you mean?' Prof. Ramdas said.

'Is he the one who connects them to media sources, to political parties—that sort of thing?'

Prof. Ramdas replaced the tea cup on the table. He let his hands drop into his lap and straightened his back against the rest.

'I'm not comfortable with this question,' he said. 'But to be honest, he has no such connections.'

'But his daughter does.'

'He never interferes with her work, and he doesn't need connections. And I'm going to ask you to stop this now. I agreed to answer a few general questions, not to indulge in kite-flying about a colleague!'

'That's not what we're trying to do, Professor,' Seema said. 'Even Prof. Hussain may be getting dragged into things he doesn't understand. Professors tend to be idealistic and they're used by politicians and other interests—we see that all the time in our line of work.'

'Even so.'

'What you say isn't likely to incriminate him in anything, Professor,' Partha said. 'But his behaviour is suspicious. He puts me in touch with students who already know who I am and have a view on why I might be on campus. The students lead me into a trap of sorts—'

'Which you deliberately entered!'

'Fair enough. But are you saying Prof. Hussain's intention was that I be led into a fight and be made a news story of?'

Prof. Ramdas didn't answer.

'In any event, that's how it played out,' Partha said. 'I'm attacked. At the same time, Seema gets in touch with him asking for help. He responds by leaving the campus and stops answering his phone. And then he leaves town.'

Prof. Ramdas spoke carefully.

'When I called him about rumours about injured students,' he said, 'he did ask me to be available in his stead.'

'You helped us out yesterday evening,' Partha said. 'Prof. Hussain, whom I've known for years, whose daughter I've known for years, hasn't even sent me a text message. Doesn't all this strike you as being odd?'

'I don't want to talk about this anymore.'

'Sir,' Seema interjected. 'Partha told you yesterday that Vikranth knew the man who attacked him in the forest. If the students are being dragged into a dangerous situation like this, I would have thought you'd want to stop students being used like this.'

'And we already know how strongly Prof. Hussain feels about the Mohan Krishna family,' Partha said. 'He writes about it. He rails against Mohan Krishna for being the corruptor of an entire generation. He attacks him for his collaboration with the National People's Party in the 1980s.'

Prof. Ramdas didn't meet Partha's eye. He stared at his palms nervously.

'So you think,' he finally said, 'that when the students got involved in the aftermath of Priya's suicide Prof. Hussain sensed an opportunity? That he's using the students to fix the Mohan Krishna family?'

Partha didn't reply.

'I will have you know,' Prof. Ramdas said. 'That Prof. Hussain is a man of the highest integrity. He would never be party to conspiracies! I think any attempt to suggest otherwise is despicable!'

Partha waited before speaking.

'Maybe Prof. Hussain believes he's got a chance to make something right in the real world,' he said. 'I think he's mistaken though.'

Prof. Ramdas smiled coldly at Partha and then at Seema.

'That is your belief, isn't it?' he said. 'That we don't make any difference in the real world and can't pass over a chance to meddle with its workings?'

'That's not what I meant,' Partha said.

'That's not the case, Professor,' Seema said.

'Teachers are happy doing their work,' Prof. Ramdas said. 'They teach, and write, and research—they live in a world of ideas. And if they change someone's mindset, they're achieving their lives' purpose. They don't need to make an impact on the so-called "real world".'

'But you're talking about the good ones, sir,' Partha said. 'I'm talking about someone who's lost perspective.'

'Perspective? That's very glib,' Prof. Ramdas said. 'You'd be less glib if you knew what Prof. Hussain lived through in the 1980s.'

*

It was almost an hour later that Partha and Seema left the humanities building. They walked silently to the car. What they'd heard was troubling and it had forced them to think of things beyond the narrow rush of events they were caught up in. It reminded them that what was playing out was far more complex than they'd ever imagined, and that it had its roots far in the past. It reminded them that things tended to build up, they bubble beneath the surface for years, decades even, and then burst onto the surface. There were larger things at play here. Not just politics and media, but the past itself. In that past were people's lives, lives too little to be noticed in history's relentless march forward. But each life, significant in itself, and for itself, remembered the wounds inflicted upon it. And at a time long forgotten by the perpetrator, a victim had found the opportunity to strike back. Prof. Hussain had not forgotten. And if their assumptions were correct, Prof. Hussain's rage, seeded all those years ago, had now become a weapon capable of striking directly at Mohan Krishna and his son.

Seema had her hand on the car door handle. She stopped, stayed where she was. Partha looked at her.

'There's really no way of justifying it to ourselves,' she said. 'We're on the wrong side of this one.'

'We're on Anil's side,' Partha said.

Seema's stare was incredulous; a hint of frustration and even anguish flashed across her face.

'He isn't directly responsible, Seema,' Partha said. 'It's right that Mohan Krishna pays—and for all his power he's unable to protect his son and he's being blackmailed by a former hanger-on. But even then, if Anil is innocent, he shouldn't have to pay for it.'

'But it's not that simple, Partha,' Seema said. 'Let's just suppose we are the first to get hold of the cellphone and laptop. Suppose it has incriminating evidence against Prakash. You think it's ever going to come out? Mohan Krishna and Prakash will call a truce because they'll have leverage on each other. And then what? The reason Priya died will never come out. Once again, that family will get away with it just like they did all those years ago. And we'd have helped them do it!'

Partha didn't reply. He leaned against the car and looked away.

'So what do you want us to do?' he said. 'Get out?'

'I don't know,' Seema said.

Seema took a long, slow breath.

'That girl is dead and we're going to become a part of the cover-up,' she said.

'No, we aren't,' Partha said.

'How can we not become party to it if we stay involved?'

'We won't. Trust me.'

Seema nodded and got into the car. They rode for several minutes without speaking a word. The silence was finally broken by the sound of Partha's phone ringing. It was Harish.

'Higher stakes now,' Harish said.

'Did you manage to track Satya and the other guy down?' Partha said.

'Yeah. But they're both dead.'

19

For the first time after the news of Priya's suicide broke, Anil faced the cameras. As hundreds of flashbulbs went off, Anil sat behind a table looking down occasionally but otherwise gazing steadily into the middle distance. He'd been instructed not to wear sunglasses, so he struggled to look up for long. He wore a plain polo shirt and chinos and sat silently as the frenzy built up around him. Once again, the venue was the family-owned Swayambhu Studios.

Vishnu sat next to Anil. Initially, he looked more uncomfortable than Anil himself but he settled down after a few minutes. He continued to look stiff but no longer fidgeted about as much. As he and Anil sat and waited, the managers tried to calm things down. They struggled to soothe fraying tempers as cameramen and reporters elbowed each other out of the way. Reporters began to shout out questions to Anil even though they'd been informed that a statement would be read out first.

The questions were along expected lines: 'Did you have an affair with Priya?' 'Are you responsible for her death?' 'Will you be arrested today?'

Anil didn't respond. His face was set but not entirely impassive. He didn't smile, but his expression had a soft quality about it. Even as reporters tried to force a response with provocative questions or direct taunts, Anil's expression did not alter.

After a few minutes, Vishnu leaned into the camera and spoke from a written text:

'We thank friends from the media for attending this press conference. As you know, it's been a very difficult time for our family, so we appreciate your understanding and cooperation.

Anil has come to an important decision today and wants to make an announcement to all of you. When Anil first told us family members of this decision, many of us were upset and opposed to it. But when we considered Anil's sentiments we realised it was the right decision—a decision he was able to arrive at before we did. It is a major step for a young actor to take, and it is not a choice he has made easily. We are all proud of him and support his decision.

'You will all appreciate that he's a young man who has experienced loss and great strain over the past few days. You are also aware that there is a police investigation in progress. Anil has consistently tried to help the police get to the truth. But he does not want to say or do anything that could distract from that investigation. So we request that you accept the format of this press conference. Anil will make a statement but he will not be answering any questions.'

'Why are you wasting our time then?' a voice called out. 'Why can't he answer questions?'

'What's he hiding?' another reporter shouted out.

Vishnu raised his hands defensively and made an apologetic face. He spoke into the mike again.

'I request you to please allow Anil to make his statement now,' he said. 'Copies of the statement will also be handed out to all reporters.'

With that, Vishnu gestured to Anil and slid a sheet of paper across to him. Reporters continued to shout out angrily. Anil didn't react for a few seconds. He then leaned forward towards the mike; he looked at his uncle and gently pushed the sheet of paper back towards him.

'Please,' Anil said, as the noise continued, 'I know it's unfair to set these conditions in a press conference. But please bear with me because these are extraordinary circumstances.'

His tone was steady and while he wasn't assertive, there was no nervousness either.

'I wouldn't wish the past few days on an enemy,' Anil continued, going on without waiting for the noise to die out fully. 'I've lost a dear friend. I'm in shock personally. But I'm also saddened that we've lost a wonderfully-talented actress in Priya. I am also heartbroken to hear rumours suggesting we were in a relationship. We were friends and to have speculation about our relationship after her passing has been deeply upsetting. My family has already denied these rumours and I don't have anything to add to that. The matter is under police investigation and I don't want to do anything that creates more rumours and speculation. The one thing I will say is that I have been cooperating with the police every step of the way. I was at the police station this morning as well. They informed me that they were making progress on recovering Priya's computer and cellphone. Nobody would be happier than me if they are found. There have been rumours that I'm to be arrested today; I was not informed of any such thing when I went to the police station. I have great respect for the police and will go along with whatever course they see fit. I've even asked my family to drop legal proceedings to obtain anticipatory bail.' He broke off at this juncture. 'I never imagined I would be addressing a press conference to talk about Priya's death,' he went on, 'but to imagine I'd be talking about my possible arrest in this context is just a nightmare.'

'People have even speculated upon why I didn't hand over one particular photograph to the police,' Anil said. 'I would have if I had it with me or recalled its existence. But I didn't have it, and I don't recall taking it. I sincerely request whoever might have it on his or her phone—any cast or crew member—to come forward. On the other hand, it if it was taken with Priya's phone, then we'll have to wait for the police to complete their investigation.'

He paused to take a breath.

'But this is not what I wanted to talk to you about,' he continued, 'I am here today as an actor. As my uncle said, I have made a decision. It was not an easy decision to make, but I think it's the right one. In these circumstances, I find it particularly painful that there is so much speculation about my career and the prospects for my debut film. I understand that such speculation is logical but it all seems wrong to me. At a time when a friend's life has been lost, I find the prospect of discussing careers and films just distasteful. What's happened here is too big, too tragic. I don't want to contribute to the trivialisation of it.'

He paused and took a breath.

'So I would like to announce,' he said, 'that I have suspended my launch in the film industry until the investigation of Priya's suicide is completed. However long that takes, however many years it takes. There are things that are more important than careers. Certainly a lot more important than my career.'

There was a semblance of silence. The reporters too seemed uncertain how to respond.

'I know this is open-ended,' Anil went on. 'I know I'm putting my life in others' hands. I know this may drag on for years and it may even end my career before it starts. But I owe my friend this much. I can't treat her death as some obstacle I have to surpass to have a career. I want justice for Priya. Until the truth about her death comes out, I will not sign a film. I apologise to all the producers who've approached me, I apologise to my father's fans, and I apologise to my family. But I must tell them, with all humility, that my decision is final. If it helps get justice for Priya in any way, that's all I want. Thank you.'

With that, Anil leaned back from the mike. Vishnu put his arm around him. The reporters began to shout out questions once again. Anil rose and stood there for a few moments and then he walked away, steadily and without hesitation.

*

The Speed Post centre was his best bet: they almost never asked for an ID. Varaprasad had taken all the precautions he could think of. He'd written his correct name, using initials instead of spelling out the surname just in case they asked for ID. Then he put down a fake return address. He had also taken care to use much larger envelopes than he needed to, wrapping the pen-drives heavily in paper so they were undetectable to the touch. He'd seen booking clerks depress or even bend envelopes to ensure that there were just documents inside.

The thought of the booking clerk discovering the pen-drives troubled Varaprasad. He wondered just what he would do if that happened. It seemed to him the best way to handle it would be to quietly pick up the envelopes and walk out. But then he wondered what he would do if the clerk asked more questions and didn't return them quite so easily.

The sight of the booking counter triggered a flutter of anxiety within him. This one had a glass partition through which you had to slip the envelope through to the clerk. You couldn't just retrieve it and walk away. It made him deeply uneasy but he had to give it a try anyway. A private courier service seemed like more trouble and less dependable.

He moved forward in the queue. Then another fear began to trouble him. He had the uneasy sense that a man in the queue was glancing in his direction occasionally. The man was holding an envelope addressed in Telugu. Varaprasad knew that all the Telugu channels aired in Bangalore. And Telugus tended to watch them regularly, including the news channels, even though they lived in a different state. If this was a man who had watched Telugu news recently, in all probability, he would know his face. Varaprasad had discreetly bought a Telugu newspaper the previous day. This particular paper did not have his picture but it did mention the missing devices and that he was thought to have taken them. The man in the queue glanced in his direction once again. It was with difficulty that Varaprasad kept his nerve about him and remained in the line.

When he got to the counter, he slipped only one of the two envelopes through the slot. The clerk barely looked up. He asked if the telephone number mentioned on it was correct, to which Varaprasad said yes. The clerk typed out the address details on the computer, printed out a label, and told Varaprasad what it cost.

'I have another,' Varaprasad said.

'Why didn't you give them both at the same time?' the clerk said irritably.

'I thought you'd do one at a time,' Varaprasad said.

The clerk nodded and extended his hand. Varaprasad slipped the second envelope through. The clerk went through the motions again and told him the total charge. Varaprasad pushed the money through the counter slot.

'What's in them?' the agent asked.

'Documents. I mean, papers.'

The agent ran his fingers over the envelope, applying pressure. Varaprasad felt his throat constricting. The agent ran his fingers across the length of the envelope. He then flipped the envelope over, picked up the other envelope as well, and tossed them into the heap of outgoing packages.

Varaprasad left the counter as soon as he was done, glancing once more at the outgoing pile. He felt a sensation he could only describe as elation. He then looked back to see where the Telugu man was. He was still in line and didn't turn to look at Varaprasad.

With the two envelopes on the way and with no formal record of his having sent them, his work was done. It was perhaps the most important and difficult thing he had ever done. But even through the sense of peril he felt, Varaprasad knew it had been worth it. The video of the recorded Skype conversation was the most important thing on the pen-drives. But the phone had another important message too. A little before she'd killed herself, Priya had recorded a video message for Prakash—accusing him of shutting her out after their brief affair, and then she'd sent it out to him. Varaprasad had not known of its existence until the night of her death. These two pieces of information were not backed up on the cloud. They were now on their way to safer places on these two pen-drives; and there were copies of the files on his laptop and in the third pen-drive he'd bought. When the time was right he'd make his own attempts to get online and post the files he had with him. But for now, he had done as much as he could have.

He ripped up the Speed Post receipts and threw them into a dustbin and walked out of the office. The two people he'd sent the envelopes to, were to follow the instructions he'd written out. He couldn't be entirely sure they'd take the risk he was asking them to, but he was convinced they'd do their best. Even as he thought this, he knew the data wasn't entirely safe yet. If he was caught and tortured, he knew he would end up revealing the names of the people to whom he'd sent the pen-drives. In any event, he'd done his best and it was a moment of dizzying relief for him.

At the same time, he knew he was still in danger. His task now was to get out of Bengaluru. He was lucky to have gone undiscovered in a lodge for this long. He couldn't afford to push his luck. Also, he was fast running out of money and had no choice but to undertake a risky journey. If he made it, he could possibly find a place from which he could plot his next move.

*

As soon as the three of them came into their financial windfall from Spectrum Software, Harish had made a significant investment. He bought a twenty-five percent stake in an investigating agency with branches in all the major states in southern India. He got a fair return on it, but more importantly it gave him considerable control over it and expanded his reach. A rule strictly enforced in the agency was that all work was billed, even if it was for a part-owner. But he could expect the agency to deliver what he asked for, especially when it was urgent. It was with that expectation that he turned over the task of finding Satya to the agency. Even after he had, he could not rest easy: he needed to get as many hands on the job as possible. So he put his own sources on the job as well. Whether they were the agency's people or Harish's own informants, the method employed would be the same. They'd approach young men in the gang's usual hangouts, preferably acquaintances of the targets, on the pretext of having a task for Satya. It was a highly effective method, one that almost always led back to the target.

The story they reached out with was that a young son of a rich Marwari family was at odds with the rest of the family over business and property matters. He needed people to keep tabs on his parents and brothers, and for protection. The men might even be called upon to aggressively secure properties. No other details would be given until he met face-to-face with Satya. This was promising enough to get Satya to evince interest and not demand a lot of details. If he revealed his location or committed to an appointment, Harish would be able to get to him. He had come up with this story about a Marwari family because he knew such men were wary about the people they met. But a business family at war was too good a prospect for a contractor of muscle power to resist. It lent believability as well: with an ongoing family feud, someone in the family would be forced to reach out to a new contractor.

The entire morning, there was no news to be had. As Harish began to check in around afternoon, word was that Satya had had a matter to deal with—a problem with one of his people. One of his men had been attacked the previous day and he had gone to find out what exactly had happened. Guessing that Satya had gone to deal with the fallout of Partha's handiwork, Harish doubled down on that source to get information about Satya's recent movements. He asked to be updated every half-an-hour.

Around mid-afternoon, there was a disruption. People Harish called didn't pick up his calls or said they'd call him back. This went on for the better part of an hour. Harish waited patiently. Then the news began to come in. One of Harish's most trusted sources was the first to call in. He told him with absolute certainty that Satya and one of his men had been found dead.

When both Satya and Yaddiah failed to answer their phones, one of the boys had gone over to Yaddiah's room and there they were, both dead of stab wounds. Yaddiah had suffered the worst of it, with signs of torture on him. There were hardly any other signs to suggest who might be responsible. When aggressively questioned by Satya's group, the landlord's daughter said she saw a tall, strongly built man, with short hair and a beard climb up the stairs. How long he stayed and when he left, she did not know.

Harish immediately knew it was the man they had confronted in the Green Belt the previous day. His first thought was of the safety of Varaprasad. From the time he'd faced off with the man, Harish knew they were dealing with a professional. After that confrontation, Harish was in no doubt about just how lethal things could turn. If this man or his people were on the student's trail, he would not be able to survive for long.

Harish made a call to Mr Kumar, who headed the private investigative agency. He was a retired director general of police and was based out of Bengaluru. Mr Kumar had built the agency by drawing together the best forensic scientists and officers as they retired or quit the police department. Harish had already sent them a sketch of the attacker in the forest. He was also in touch with them about locating Varaprasad.

Harish's true hopes rested on this outfit more than any other. Their contacts ran deep in police departments across the country, from the highest level to the smallest police station. This gave them an edge other agencies just couldn't match. They had access to information at the operational level that no other agency could hope to have.

When Mr Kumar answered his phone, Harish quickly told him about the murders in Hyderabad. He requested them to speed up the identification of the man whose sketch he'd sent out but he had a second more important request. He asked the agency to put all its resources to work to locate Varaprasad.

'I told you we're no good for a manhunt, Harish,' Mr Kumar said after hearing him out patiently. 'Only the police department has the scale for that. Even with our contacts, we wouldn't come up with much.'

'I understand, sir,' Harish said, 'but this man is bound to be on the lookout for that student. We need to find him now. He's still here in Hyderabad for now—the murders were committed just early this afternoon. That gives us a window of opportunity to find the student. It might be the only chance we have to reach the student alive.'

'If this criminal gets scent of the boy, he'll be here in a matter of hours. A little longer by road.'

'Yes, sir.'

'It's very little time for us to work with. I have my people checking in on lodges and things. But it's hard to find a lone man in a city this big, with such a large floating population.'

'I understand, sir.'

'But we'll intensify our search.'

'Sir, I'd request you to piggyback on the police department if you can—any whiff they get, please give me a heads up. Even if you can induce the police to find him on a priority basis, that's good for us. At least he'll be safe.'

After the call, Harish spoke to his informants and had copies of the man's sketch sent out to his entire network. He sent people out to the Hyderabad and Bengaluru airports to be on the lookout. He didn't bother with the bus and train stations—he just didn't have the resources to put people on the lookout there.

He then reached out to his sources in the Hyderabad police department. He had sent them scanned copies of the sketch as well. His sources simply said they'd check and get back to him. The source he got on the phone was particularly circumspect given the high-profile nature of the case.

'No real leads,' the source said. 'We're going through all of the girl's things and we might ask Anil for a DNA sample—that sort of thing.'

'You've found nothing yet?' Harish asked.

'Not really. But the moment we find the slightest thing, we arrest him.'

'What about the student? Any idea where he is?'

'Nothing yet.'

'Is it true he's in Bengaluru and not Chennai?'

'Lots of rumours—it's not very clear yet.'

Harish knew the police were under some pressure to get to Varaprasad first, or they wouldn't be this unwilling to speak.

'What about the sketch I sent you?' Harish asked.

'We are trying to get his record,' the source said. 'Our Hyderabad City University campus police seem to have some photographs of him.'

'That's where I ran into him.'

'We're trying to confirm his identity. Should not take too long—tomorrow sometime.'

'You need to get that on priority.'

'Hmm ...'

'Listen to me—this guy is probably going to go after that student, Varaprasad, who's on the run.'

'How can you be so sure?'

'I just am.'

'You're too sure of things.'

Harish knew he wasn't going to convince him this way.

'Well, I'm sure about another thing too,' he said. 'You find this guy and you'll have a breakthrough on the double-murder in the Banjara Hills slum.'

The policeman was silent.

'How do you reach that conclusion?' he asked.

'I tend to be too sure of things,' Harish said. 'You know that about me. But trust me on this.'

He hung up. He knew he had the man's attention. He knew how policemen thought. They were trained to cut through the chaff and focus on promising outcomes.

Harish then headed back to the office to wait to hear from any of the sources. He hated this part of the job. The part where you just waited around while things outside move along rapidly.

*

By the time Harish got to the office, Partha and Seema had returned from the university.

'Looks like we were headed in the right direction,' Partha said. 'Just the two guys we wanted to talk to turn up dead.'

'Yeah, they could have led us back to the media or political interest in the story,' Harish said. 'They were willing to kill to keep us from it.'

'Their approach to tracking Partha was so slack, so amateurish,' Seema said, 'I didn't think it was very serious.'

'It's safer than putting their own people on the job,' Harish said. 'If Partha had cornered one of their own guys like he did Yaddiah, we'd directly know who the involved party was. Here, they have a buffer.'

'A buffer?' Seema mumbled.

'I know, doesn't sound so benign when it's the murder of two people,' Harish said.

'How do we pick up where this trail got cut off?' Partha said. 'Can we get to someone valuable in Satya's network? He must have confided in some subordinate about who the client was.'

'I'm already on it,' Harish said. 'The entire gang will try to disappear now. But we're on the job.'

'I think we should also locate Prof. Hussain,' Partha said. 'Find out where he is and whom he's talking to. If we find someone remotely connected to the media or film industry talking to Prof. Hussain, we have a lead.'

Harish nodded but looked sceptical.

'I'll put the agency guys on it,' he said. 'but I wouldn't get my hopes up. We're not going to get access to phone records so easily, and he can always deal with the media through his daughter. I don't want to devote too many resources to a dead end.'

Partha nodded but he wasn't happy. Prof. Hussain's moves would be important and not having eyes on him was a serious constraint.

'I can check on the corporate moves Ayesha's making these days,' Seema offered. 'Anything interesting could be a tip off.'

Partha nodded. Harish got up to go into his cabin.

'I've got phone calls to make,' he said. He turned to Seema. 'I've put a watch on your house and on you individually. On Partha's apartment as well.'

Seema didn't respond.

'These guys are serious,' Harish said. 'We should be too.'

Seema nodded.

'Should we be worried about Vikranth's safety?' Harish asked.

'Prof. Ramdas says he's holed up in the hostel with friends around him,' Partha said. 'And he won't talk to anybody, certainly not us. We'll have to assume he's safe in that company.'

'That kid Varaprasad is the key in a lot of ways,' Seema said. 'He's in real danger.'

'Nothing we can do about that until we get a lead,' Harish said, 'and then hope to reach him first.'

*

Anil had followed the given suggestions to the letter. Both Partha and Seema were impressed with how he'd handled the press conference. Watching a recording of the press conference, they observed right away that the organisation of the press conference was extremely professional. But the real revelation was Anil himself. He came across as sincere, genuinely emotional at times, and grounded all through and his statement looked spontaneous and heartfelt.

'He did very well,' Partha said.

'He did,' Seema said. 'Either he's really genuine or we should be prepared to find incriminating material about him on the laptop.'

Partha laughed.

'Let's hope it doesn't come to that,' he said. 'I hate it when a hunch is proven wrong.'

Partha got on the phone to check with the two research agencies he'd commissioned for quick, discreet polls about how Anil's statement had been received. He was told they'd hear back in a couple of hours. He then called Malvika. He could sense the jubilant mood she was in. She was trying hard to keep it out of her voice, but not quite succeeding. The press conference was her event: she'd handled everything from behind the scenes. She had prepared the statement for Anil, coached him on what to do. She had even instructed Vishnu on how to conduct himself. The coverage was largely positive except for news channels clearly against the family.

'You think you can control the messaging from Mohan Krishna's camp?' Partha asked. 'We don't want anything to queer the pitch now.'

'No problem,' Malvika said. 'Leave it to me.'

'No triumphalism or hero-worshipping Anil. No statements of anger against rivals for Anil's career being put on hold.'

'Leave it to me.'

Partha could hear the confidence in her tone. She had just won a significant victory. Mohan Krishna had entrusted her with a big task, he'd taken a risk on her suggestion, and it had paid off.

'The next day or two are crucial,' Partha said. 'Things just turned very serious. Two men were murdered today.'

'In connection with this?' Malvika asked, a hint of strain entering her voice.

'Yes. Two men we were looking for because they could lead us to who's behind all this. They were found dead.'

'Oh my God, it's turning brutal,' Malvika said.

'This whole thing will be over in a day or two,' Partha said. 'We can't afford not to be alert. And it's time Mohan Krishna shared some information with us.'

Malvika didn't reply.

'Mohan Krishna and his people must have their own sources,' Partha said. 'If they know who was having me followed, this is the time to share that information.'

'He doesn't want any interference. He'd be upset to know you're working on it actively.'

'He's taken my advice on media tactics twice this week.'

'Yes.' Malvika's tone had turned stiff.

'I'm pretty certain we're ahead of his people in terms of information,' Partha said. 'But if he wants his son helped out, he's got to trust us more. He's not doing us any favours, but we're doing him some.'

Once again Malvika was silent.

'I might need to meet him soon,' Partha said.

'Give me a little time—'

'I need to know soon.'

'Fine,' Malvika said. 'I'll call you back and tell you when might work.'

Partha hung up. Seema looked at him with a raised eyebrow.

'Playing hardball, is she?' she said.

'Usual film star nonsense,' Partha said. 'The fearsome brother-in-law finds use for our services but won't give us an audience or share information or even acknowledge that we're helping him.'

'It's providing him our services that bothers me right now.'

'Not still hung up on what Prof. Ramdas told us, are you?' Partha said. 'We have a situation on hand.'

'I know, I know. I wasn't thinking about what Prof. Ramdas said just now. There are other things about being in his service.'

'Like what?'

'Like the price we might end up paying for being involved. I was thinking about this murderer on the loose.'

'What about him?'

'He killed two people today.'

'Yeah. We can't think about all that right now.'

Seema got up and walked towards the door.

'Harish's got you protected, Seema,' Partha said.

'I know,' Seema said. 'I was just thinking he meant to kill you yesterday.'

'Yeah. But it all worked out alright.'

Seema didn't say anything. She nodded and went back to her office.

20

Amongst the crowd at the bus-stop, Varaprasad felt particularly vulnerable. He just knew there were people out there looking for him. How would it play out if they spotted him? Would they grab him right then and there? Would they wait until the bus reached a deserted spot outside the city before they made their move?

He made his way towards the ticket counter. There was a short queue and he joined it. It moved along quite quickly but to Varaprasad it seemed excruciatingly slow. He felt out in the open, exposed. He had no option but to stand where he was and move along the line, even though panic was rising within. By the time he got to the ticket counter, his palms were clammy.

'Kadapa,' Varaprasad said hoarsely.*

'What?' the man behind the counter said.

'Kadapa,' Varaprasad said, more clearly now.

The man at the counter took the money and printed out a ticket to Kadapa. Varaprasad took it and moved away. It would be a while before his bus arrived; in his anxiety not to miss it, he'd arrived too early. He knew this bus well, he'd taken it before. It reached his hometown late at night, at a most inconvenient time. In the current circumstances it was an advantage.

As he waited, he tried to convince himself that the crowd made him secure rather than expose him to danger, but a voice inside him told him that it was false comfort. Being in a crowd made him physically secure for the time being but it also dramatically increased the chance of his being discovered. He then told himself to focus on staying safe moment to moment. He would avoid secluded spots—he would stay where other people were—and try to be inconspicuous.

---

*Kadapa is a town in Andhra Pradesh.

It was half-an-hour before the bus arrived. There were very few passengers onboard; Varaprasad went right to the last row. From there he watched other passengers board with a mixture of suspicion and fear. A few minutes later, the bus was ready to leave.

As the bus began to pull out of the stop, a young man who'd been waiting near the ticket counter ran up and jumped in. He looked around quickly and took a seat.

*

Partha found it useful at times to remind himself that things beyond his control were happening all around and all the time. It was a fact easily forgotten in the rush of events, but one that was useful to remind oneself of, because it helped to consciously disengage oneself and gain perspective.

It was Partha's experience that in the midst of a crisis there were a few slack periods, times where one could do little more than wait. It was very important, he felt, to do nothing at such times. To create activity for the sake of activity was not only wasteful but frustrating. This evening was one such gap in time before this crisis took its next turn. It was important not to waste it.

Partha lay on the sofa in his office with his eyes shut. He tried to ease the whole problem out of his mind. After a few minutes of this relaxation, the thoughts would lose some of their charge. They would return eventually, but by then they could be looked at with greater objectivity. After a few minutes of relaxation Partha allowed his thoughts to run free.

It seemed to Partha that in this particular instance they were working under constraints they were quite unused to. They didn't have a giant corporation's resources and contacts. They had worked with comparable constraints in the past, in situations where people within the organisation could not be trusted, or where the organisation was too small to be of significant help, but they had never faced such severe limitations in access to information. It had always been possible to get cellphone records or have computers hacked. Harish managed to get a great deal of it done still, but telephone and internet companies were harder to deal with now. And then, an additional constraint in this instance was Mohan Krishna wanting the pretence of an arm's length distance between him and them. This was ostensibly on account of fear of Prakash finding out about their activities, but it was also a way of shielding Mohan Krishna from Partha, of not allowing him anywhere near his secrets. Partha expected this pretence to continue for the time being.

These constraints not only slowed them down but limited their options. The latter part was not necessarily a bad thing. Another lesson that years of managing crises had taught Partha was the danger of being paralysed by a multiplicity of options. It was critical to define a line of action and pursue it to the end, even at the risk of that choice turning out to be incorrect. The obvious pursuit for them in this case was the retrieval of the devices from Varaprasad. They were trying to do that but too much was out of their control on that front. Until they had something to act upon, they would have to work on the next level of priority. That was finding a connecting link between the university and the outside world. This lead had the potential to reveal much, just like following a cable right to the detonator.

This was a good option to explore for several reasons. One, it could lead them to the source of the attack on the Mohan Krishna family, which would allow them to form a counter strategy. Even exposing the conspiracy could help exonerate Anil. Two, the search for Varaprasad and the happenings at the university were not unrelated. The man who had attacked Partha in the Green Belt knew Vikranth and had a connection to the university and the union. He had even tried to extract information about Varaprasad. Third, the news story could still be manipulated through the interviews of Priya's supposed friends. If they hoped to counter that at all, they needed access to the campus.

Their connections so far were tenuous. They had gotten leads but no serious access. Vikranth was opposed to them, though Partha now hoped for some goodwill there for keeping his name out of the police records. Prof. Ramdas too could prove valuable if he thought it was in the interest of the students, but he would be cautious and guarded.

So, until they heard back about Varaprasad, the university was the angle they would have to work on. Partha's guess was that Varaprasad would be found very soon. He had too much going against him to continue to be on the run for long. It appeared that he was entirely on his own, even the union and his friends didn't know where he was. That meant that he probably didn't have easy access to money, phones and internet, or places to stay. It was also likely that he would run out of money soon. He was a student on scholarship and the media said his parents had a very meagre income. So even with access to an ATM—which would disclose his location—he was unlikely to have a lot of money to go on. Then there was the pressure of being on the run, in danger, and alone. These pressures would add up and get to him. In all likelihood, he would try go to his hometown or contact someone from the campus. Partha just hoped that when he finally did, Harish's contacts would be the first to learn of it. If not them, at least the police. If it was anyone else, he would be in serious danger.

With the whole game set up to be won or lost with the discovery of Varaprasad, it was difficult to focus on things like the university or media ownership. But Partha was aware that patience under pressure was a virtue. It was a difficult discipline to adopt but one that often paid big rewards. Their job now required them to stay focused even as events moved rapidly outside the sphere of their control.

*

The rhythm of the bus travelling on the highway lulled Varaprasad to sleep. He had resisted it as long as he could but sheer fatigue pulled him into deep slumber. Around him others dozed or tinkered with their cellphones. The odd man in the crowd read a newspaper.

Several rows ahead of him, a young man typed rapidly on his cellphone screen. He read through the text he'd written out and hit send.

'Bengaluru-Kadapa road. Bus registration number no. KA 11 T 2243. Starting time: 8 p.m. Confirmed.'

A minute later he sent another text.

'Confirmed. Confirmed. Confirmed.'

The second message drew a response.

'In Kadapa.'

*

By eight-thirty that night, they hadn't heard back from anyone. They'd stayed at the office late, hoping something would turn up. They even ordered dinner. They then sat in their cabins, winding up small tasks, preparing to leave. As Harish turned off his laptop and packed things into a backpack, his phone rang. It was Mr Kumar from Bengaluru.

'I have two bits of information for you,' Mr Kumar said, direct to the point as was his wont. 'The first is about the student. It's urgent. You'll have to make note of a number.'

'Yes, sir,' Harish said, going to his desk and pulling up a stack of Post-Its.

'One of our regular informers sits at the ticket counter at a bus station in Bengaluru. It's a hub for intercity buses but not the main bus-stand. This man is on our payroll, and we sent out Varaprasad's photograph to everyone who works with us. He thinks he saw the boy about an hour ago.'

'Yes, sir,' Harish said.

Harish's impulse was to enquire how certain the source was but desisted from asking. Mr Kumar was thorough. He would not be passing this information along if he weren't satisfied with its quality.

'He says his stubble was overgrown and his kurta was crumpled and dirty,' Mr Kumar continued. 'But definitely him he says. The boy's showing good sense. He didn't go to the main bus stop and he apparently stood in a corner without drawing any attention to himself.'

'Sir.'

'That's why we keep people at the smaller bus points. The people we're looking for are more likely to go there.'

'Yes, sir, I agree.'

'Our man says he bought a ticket for Kadapa.'

'Sir.'

'The bus number is KA 11 T 2243. Time of departure is eight.'

'Sir!'

'Did you get that?'

'Yes, sir.'

'I take it Kadapa is his hometown. He's probably run out of money and is exhausted, so he's going home?'

'His hometown is actually near Anantapur, sir. But Kadapa is nearby. He's trying to be cautious again. He'll get down there and either stay with someone he knows or work his way back home.'

'Nothing wrong with that logic. But he's made a mistake. This is the bus stop most buses starting for the Kadapa-Anantapur side take. So it's likely it was being watched. If they saw him get on the bus, the journey will be a dangerous one for him.'

'I'll be at Kadapa by then hopefully.'

'Because you plan to beat the laws of physics?'

'If it isn't a Volvo, we have a shot at getting there soon after he does.'

'He has a shorter distance to cover and a head-start. Anyway, you'll have to take your chances. Take some people with you.'

'Sir?'

'That relates to the second bit of information I had for you. That sketch that you sent me—I have a name. Shiva. The police records about him are a trunk-load.'

'I thought he might be a known hand.'

'It's not just that he's a criminal. He's associated with radical groups.'

Harish absorbed this for a moment.

'Leftists, sir?' he asked.

'Yes. But not the regular ones. Not even the known extremist groups. I'm talking about ultra-Leftists, if there is such a thing.'

'I'm a little surprised, sir. We think these people are tying up with local players to have an impact at the political level. This kind of deal making is not the sort of thing you expect with radical groups.'

'I agree. But his affiliation is not generally Left, as in one side of an argument or fight. It's a fanatical splinter group that broke away from the Naxals in the area.'

'Not radical enough for them?' Harish said.

'In a sense. This group has a single-point agenda: the overthrow of the State. That is their fundamental and only goal. They are not interested in, say, peasant and workers issues specifically. They are interested in a violent upheaval.'

'Revolution?'

'Not exactly. Revolution thinks forward enough to ask who's going to take control when the battle is won. This group has some mumbo-jumbo in that regard but nothing serious. Their only reason for organisation and existence is to strike at the State, to contribute to all attrition against it.'

'I see.'

'Killing, collaborating with drug dealers, criminals, terrorists—all fair game.'

'Sir.'

'They've also killed off other Left factions that went against them. They've been involved in killings of activists of every other Leftist group. Their strategy seems to be to kill off competitors and take over all violent Left movements.'

'I'm sorry, sir, but how's that possible? They can destroy the other groups, not take them over.'

'That's the brilliance of it. There is a substantial Left block out there—everything from political parties to activists to terror groups. These are organised groups. Many of them in trouble with the law. You muscle your way right to the top in this world, eliminating people who're against you, then you become the group to fear. You cannot leave that world: you're either killed or you surrender to the police. So you are left with one choice—join the group that's killed off your leadership.'

'What's the success they've had so far?'

'They've definitely made a dent. But they seem to be in rush now.'

'How do you mean, sir?'

'They've stepped up killings in the past year or so. Not uncommon when elections are coming up—these groups sense opportunity at such times. It seems that this group is just one major victory away from becoming a dominant force.'

'So they'll go all out to win this?'

'Yes. And remember, Harish, that these people have very elaborate networks—these are organisations with cadres and hierarchies. So, if they're looking out for this boy they will likely have sources, just like we do.'

'Is this Shiva a commanding figure in the hierarchy?' Harish said. 'If they found Varaprasad, you think he'd know immediately?'

'I can't be sure, of course. But the fact is that he's a war-hardened veteran. He's senior in the organisation but he's also active in the field. Often works by himself. If this target is as important as you believe he is, he'll definitely be in the know. And he will move on it.'

'Yes, sir. Would you happen to know if he's had any serious combat training?'

'Rumour is that he crossed into Nepali territory and from there to China many years ago. I personally doubt it. He's more locally taught and hardened in the field. That makes him particularly dangerous.'

'I've had a run-in with him. He's not elegant, but he's very dangerous.'

'He's thought to be personally responsible for eighteen murders. Prefers knives. Known to be sadistic.'

'I'd notch it up to twenty today. And he also tortured a victim today.'

'As I said, take someone good along.'

'I will.'

'That's all I have for you.'

'Sir, that's a lot! It's a huge lead. Thank you.'

'Remember what I said, Harish, be careful on this thing.'

'I will, sir. Can I request just one more thing?'

'No, you may not.'

Harish didn't say anything.

'Harish, you know as well as I do that if I call people on the ground and try to have the boy protected, I could inadvertently be doing him harm. I don't know the people at that level. With political stakes this high, I wouldn't risk it.'

'Yes, sir. Sorry, I mentioned it. I understand your position entirely.'

'But you just had to take a shot.'

'Yes, sir.'

'Good try though.'

'Thank you, sir. I really have to get moving now.'

*

Harish made a few calls from his office and then rushed into Partha's office. Seema was already in his office. She'd just walked in with a bunch of printouts and her notebook. Seema opened up a notebook for every project they worked on. It contained the minutiae they dealt with as they worked through it. It would be filed away in her cabinet when the situation was resolved. She sometimes liked to retrieve these old notebooks and leaf through them. She said she enjoyed seeing that something that was once current and even life-and-death could be completely innocuous at another.

As Harish rushed in, he wasn't particularly delicate about the possibility that he was interrupting.

'This is big,' he simply said.

The other two looked at him, Seema with irritation.

'We have the best possible lead on Varaprasad,' he said. 'He's on a bus right now, and if he gets to the destination in one piece, we can keep him from harm.'

The others stared at him.

'Are you serious?' Seema said.

'Just got off the phone with Mr Kumar,' Harish said.

'That's fantastic!' Seema said.

'Partha, I know you're still beat up but I'll need you to go with me,' Harish said.

'Of course, I'll go,' Partha said getting to his feet.

'Remember how I told you we should start keeping guns around?' Harish said.

'You want to start now? Why?' Partha said.

'Because the guy from the forest--his name is Shiva—is more insane than we already know him to be,' Harish said. 'And he might be bringing some friends along.'

Partha raised an eyebrow.

'Okay ...' he said. 'You can carry guns if you like.'

'Fine,' Harish said, shaking his head slightly.

'You found something?' Partha asked Seema.

'It'll keep,' Seema said. 'You boys go play good guys–bad guys games. I have serious money laundering to figure out.'

21

They stopped at the mouth of the Outer Ring Road to pick up Singh Saheb. Harish quickly told him what they were trying to do and pulled out a picture of Varaprasad they'd gotten from an internet news website and showed it to him.

'This is whom we're looking out for,' Harish said.

Saheb looked at it and nodded. Harish then showed him a picture of Shiva that Mr Kumar had sent him on WhatsApp.

'He's trying to get to the boy before we do—if he does, the boy won't make it,' he said. 'We're going to try and catch the boy in Kadapa before this man does.'

'We have to drive really fast,' Singh Saheb said simply.

Looking over in Partha's direction, something caught Saheb's eye. He leaned forward to get a better look.

'What happened to your face, Partha sir?' he asked.

'This guy did it to him,' Harish said, holding up Shiva's picture. 'Hopefully we don't run into him.'

'Good chance to return the favour if we do,' Partha said.

Singh Saheb sat back.

'If it doesn't interfere with our overall purpose,' he said, 'then why not?'

Partha was at the wheel. He pushed the car well above the speed limit, and without much concern. Keeping up the pace on the highway would be difficult. The highway wasn't always well set off from habitation and often went right through villages. People and vehicles strayed onto it all the time, sometimes in the wrong direction. But Partha was good with this sort of driving. Still, Harish looked at him with concern once or twice.

'What?' Partha said.

'You okay to drive?' Harish said. 'You've popped a few painkillers, and your face is making me nervous.'

'I'm fine.'

There was a pause.

'It's not fine though,' Harish said.

'What?' Partha said.

'The state of your face.'

'Seema said I looked hot.'

'I worry about her.'

When they got off the Ring Road and onto the highway, their progress slowed down. Partha kept the pace as steady as he could. Saheb strapped on his seat belt and went to sleep. He had the ability to switch off and get rest whenever he could. A habit he had learnt in the Army.

'It was a guy at the bus station who spotted Varaprasad for us,' Harish said, after a while. 'I'm hoping this Shiva character has not found out about it as well.'

'Varaprasad's made a mistake,' Partha said. 'They'll definitely be watching his hometown.'

'I just hope they don't stop the bus on the way and try to get him.'

'Let's just hope the presence of other passengers deters them.'

Partha kept the speed high. He had to strain to see on the sometimes poorly-lit roads. He was also watchful when trucks came barreling down the opposite side, often overtaking one another. After a little while, they hit a straight patch of the highway that was also relatively empty.

'Why is this radical group interested in bringing down Mohan Krishna?' Harish said. 'It makes sense that they're interested in the university for political reasons but why're they after Mohan Krishna's blood?'

'Fits right in with what Prof. Ramdas told us,' Partha said.

'Are you serious?' Harish said.

'Yeah. Some stuff Prof. Ramdas told us. We filled out the rest of the picture by looking things up,' Partha said. 'This whole thing goes back to radical Left politics in the 1970s and early 1980s.'

'1970s and 80s? What the hell are you talking about?'

'It goes that far back. The 1970s were a total mess—'

'Like the 2010s aren't a mess.'

'Yeah, but think about it. It was the peak of the Cold War. Huge unemployment and disillusionment with post-Independence India, poor economic growth, rural unrest, Naxalism…'

'Yeah.'

'In rural areas, most political seats were controlled by local feudal chiefs.'

'Still the case in many places.'

'Yeah, some difference in degree.'

'I guess.'

'So, there were rural uprisings, usually Leftist. There were several strands of these groups. Naxalism was one of the strongest, but there were other factions as well. This group that we now know Shiva belongs to was one such. It was particularly powerful in the Andhra and Telangana regions.

'This group killed police officers and district officials and also bombed major state events. Even back then, they were considered a particularly murderous group. While other factions tried to justify their killing on ideological lines, this group targeted just anyone.'

'Sounds exactly like Mr Kumar described it,' Harish said.

'Yes,' Partha said. 'In many places, local district administration and forest officials abandoned their posts. They were just too afraid to serve in the interior regions. The State was under serious threat.'

'I've read a bit about it too,' Harish said. 'Some historians think it was a precarious time for India.'

'It was. But around the late 1970s that tide began to turn. The State began to hit back hard.'

'Not always scrupulously. Free hand to police and security forces, encounter killings—I know all about that.'

'Yeah. But that's where general knowledge stops,' Partha said. 'It's one of those little pockets of time that get glazed over. If you were reading about it in any account of that period, it would simply read that the security forces were given a free hand and the tide began to turn. A lot of specifics get missed out.'

'I suppose.'

'So the time Prof. Ramdas told us about, several violent incidents occurred, the movement gathered steam, but the revolution never panned out. The reason such movements fail is usually complex—it's never just one factor. You can argue about the importance of each factor but you'd never get a clear answer.'

'True.'

'The area near Srikakulam became particularly important at the time. As you know, it is a transit point out of AP state, to Orissa.'

'Yeah.'

'So all Leftist factions were active in Srikakulam,' Partha said. 'They ran a parallel administration. But as the security forces began to strike back, a few other things went in favour of the forces. The government had put a lot of development schemes in place and many—mostly tribal people—started participating in them. Prof. Ramdas didn't mention all this but it's a fact. Word had also begun to spread of the Leftists' excesses. But the revolutionaries had one huge advantage. Many of them were student leaders and were seen to be honest. They lived with the people and they took risks for the cause. That kept them popular. They had, in a way, caught the imagination of the people, especially the youth.'

'Yeah, I've read about it. There were even fears that a whole generation had gone over to radical ideology.'

'Correct. This area, Srikakulam, became something of a centre for radical students and activists to gravitate to. One activist leader who arrived in Srikakulam to lead the movement was Ahmad Hussain.'

Harish whistled almost involuntarily. 'So it falls into place,' he said.

Partha slowed the car down. A truck overtaking another in the opposite direction had dipped its lights, requiring Partha to move to the side. Even after he had, the space on the road was inadequate and the left wheels of the car went onto the gravel on the side of the road. The moment the truck passed, Partha got back on the road and accelerated.

'It does fall into place,' Partha said, 'but it's not all of it.'

'The Mohan Krishna connection,' Harish said.

'Exactly. You must have made the obvious connection already?'

'He's from the Srikakulam region.'

'Right. Do you also recall when he rose to fame?'

'Established himself in the late 1970s and became a huge star in the early 1980s. So this was the time his popularity was on the rise.'

'His rise in the industry was entirely unexpected,' Partha said 'Nobody gave him a chance at success—he was a total outsider—but within two years, he was one of the most promising stars out there. He had three hits in a year at the time.'

'Must have been huge for young people,' Harish said 'An alternate narrative.'

'Its effect was supposed to have been electric,' Partha said. 'Suddenly a young man from this obscure part of the country becomes one of the biggest stars in one of the largest states in the country. There was even talk of his working in Hindi cinema—becoming a national star.'

'I can imagine the scale of it.'

'It was huge for the regional identity in the Srikakulam area. It also had an huge effect on people from his own community. The government latched onto this.'

'Used him to wean young people away from the movement?' Harish asked.

'Yeah. They launched a bunch of schemes for young people and had Mohan Krishna push them. It was incredibly powerful apparently. How much of it was the effect of his stardom, how much of it was frustration with the Leftists, and how much of it was about the government's initiatives—there's no way of telling. People have different interpretations.'

'But it worked?'

'Dramatically. Once people turn against a movement, the fallout is quick and harsh. The same people you control and are your foot soldiers start turning informers. Your ranks deplete and run out. You no longer have shelters, safe-houses, information—nothing.'

'Right.'

'Mohan Krishna became incredibly powerful at the time. He even got married to the local MLA's daughter and became a prominent member of his community. He could pick up the phone and call anyone in the state government and expect a response. State chief ministers and central ministers would visit him.'

'Thank goodness he is a humble guy by nature!'

Partha laughed. 'He used his power ruthlessly, of course,' he said. 'Put his family members and cronies in positions of power all over the region. And he enforced their power with the help of political parties, particularly the National People's Party, and the police.'

'And that's where Hussain comes in?'

'Yeah. Hussain held on determinedly. He was active in the region around Mohan Krishna's village. He was trying to dislodge Mohan Krishna's family from the control of some agricultural land. Hussain held on even as his comrades were killed and he was betrayed repeatedly. He's said to have suffered a great deal, living in the jungles primarily.'

'Sounds heroic. Wouldn't be able to tell just looking at him.'

'No. Here's where it becomes even more personal. He was betrayed and fell into the hands of Mohan Krishna's family.'

'Wouldn't want to know what that entailed,' Harish said.

'Everything you'd expect. Brutal torture for two days. They planned to kill him of course, but wanted to make an example of him first. But here they blundered. It gave his supporters enough time to rally around and stage a rescue.'

'Lucky for him. But how did a guy with this kind of record of radical activity end up with a university job?'

'I guess his luck changed. There was a new superintendent of police in the region who didn't like the police being used as Mohan Krishna's private army. He refused to hunt down Hussain and even tried to move against Mohan Krishna's family. My understanding is that there was some amount of local rancour against Mohan Krishna's highhandedness building up by then. Even politically, Mohan Krishna had already served his purpose. The tide had turned and he was no longer needed in the same way. Local political leaders of the NPP also had also had enough of Mohan Krishna. So Hussain was able to get away.'

Partha continued, 'Hussain escaped from the region and resurfaced in Hyderabad. The SP refused to have any false cases foisted upon him. A few years later, to encourage more students to rejoin the mainstream, cases were closed against them.'

'That allowed him to apply to the university?'

'Yeah, so many of the applicants had similar backgrounds it wouldn't have mattered by then.'

'Mohan Krishna didn't try to get at him?'

'He didn't have that much clout in Hyderabad. It was only in the 1980s that the film industry started moving here from Chennai. And his clout also waned with his relationship with the NPP souring. He would have seen the sense in letting things go. Anyway, Hussain was in no position to touch him back then—he was just a young university employee. Hussain got emboldened to speak out against Mohan Krishna only in the 1990s. He kept a low profile for several years.'

'Why did he join the mainstream at all?' Harish said. 'Someone so committed to the cause that is?'

'Prof. Ramdas says it was a mix of practicality and disillusionment. On the one hand, he saw the revolution had fizzled out. He had parents and siblings to take care of, who had suffered at the hands of the authorities when he was on the run. He needed to work and live a normal life. On the other hand, he saw betrayals all around him. Friends turning on friends. Plans leaking to the police, people testifying against their comrades, and high-profile surrenders in large numbers.'

'So all this is about karma catching up with Mohan Krishna,' Harish said.

'There's another kicker,' Partha said.

'More?' Harish said.

'The most brutal of Prof. Hussain's torturers…'

'Prakash?'

'Prakash! According to Prof. Ramdas he was just working his way into Mohan Krishna's good books. He'd do anything for him. His enthusiasm, let us say, was not easy to endure.'

'Sounds psychotic.'

'So this is how I figure it. News of Priya's suicide breaks; Mohan Krishna's family is on a very weak wicket; Priya is a university alumnus with strong ties to the campus; Prof. Hussain has media connections through his daughter—he makes his move. And he uses his clout with students to push things through.'

'Gives Mohan Krishna a hell of a choice: give up Prakash and risk losing the bulk of his empire, or watch as his son's career, freedom, and reputation are taken away. And Mohan Krishna is all heart, so he's yet to make a choice!'

'If this kid, Varaprasad, hadn't gone on the run, they'd have had enough to destroy the family by now. They could've straightaway taken out Prakash or got Prakash to turn on Mohan Krishna.'

'So right now they're keeping the story alive until they find the material?'

'Yeah. There's lot riding on this missing cellphone and laptop.'

'We better count on finding a reception committee for Varaprasad then.'

*

It was past 2 a.m. when they reached Kadapa. They'd made excellent time, having started out from Hyderabad a little past 9 p.m. that night. They had a good chance of meeting the bus Varaprasad had boarded. It was a relatively slow bus, taking about seven hours in all to get to Kadapa including a stop along the way. Partha drove through the town to the other side, which would be the approach for a bus coming in from Bengaluru. He parked away from the road, taking care to stay in the shadows and out of line of sight. The hinterland provided good cover, even though it was a clear, full-moon night.

Harish woke up Singh Saheb. He was instantly alert; there was no sign of drowsiness or lethargy from the moment he woke up. He took another look at Varaprasad and Shiva's photographs and then the bus's registration number. He then gazed out of the window.

'If Varaprasad requests a stop on the way, we're screwed,' Partha said.

'I'm guessing long-distance bus drivers don't entertain a lot of request stops,' Harish said. 'They may just make a stop on the outskirts to let out people who don't want to go into the city. Not a lot of people will ask to get off in virtual wilderness this late in the night. Anyway, we'll follow the bus here on into town.'

'We'll have to maintain a safe distance. He'll be on the lookout.'

'Either way, he'll have the fright of a lifetime when we catch up with him.'

They turned the engine off and sat with windows lowered. Occasionally, they stepped out and peered onto the road, taking care to stay in the shadows. They were watchful, always looking and listening hard for any hint of others hiding by the roadside.

Twenty minutes later they saw headlights in the distance. It was definitely a bus. Partha got behind the wheel, ready to start off at a moment's notice. Harish and Singh Saheb went forward at a crouch, standing close to the road, but staying behind the undergrowth so they wouldn't be seen in the headlights. Singh Saheb quietly slid to a side, at an angle to the road, and looked through a pair of binoculars, trying to get a glimpse of the bus's license plates. Harish followed him there. Singh Saheb lowered the binoculars and shook his head. Not the bus.

The bus went by. Harish watched the background for any movement—any sign that anyone else was waiting by the roadside. There was nothing. From his position in the car, Partha too watched the road intently. He too strained to look at the background to discern any sign of movement. He couldn't make out any. A few trucks passed by and things were quiet again. A single car drove by, and passed their location at a high speed. Someone likely pushing on to Hyderabad.

The three of them stayed in their positions. About ten minutes later, another set of headlights appeared. Another bus.

As it drew closer, its shape and form became more visible—it seemed old and ill-maintained. Singh Saheb peered through the binoculars again. He looked up and signalled to Harish. It was their bus. Harish nodded and stayed still until the bus went past them. They stayed in their place for a minute and then slipped back, careful still, and returned to the car. Partha had started the engine but kept the headlights off.

'Careful as we turn onto the road,' Harish said. 'Hang back for a little bit.'

They waited a minute on the roadside and then turned onto the road.

'Careful, Partha boy,' Harish said, 'you'll be driving blind initially.'

The road was poorly lit here; much of it wasn't lit at all. They couldn't see too far in front of them. Partha had only the moonlight to steer by. He would have to trust his eyesight growing accustomed to the dark. Oncoming traffic was as much a danger now—they were driving in a black car with the lights turned off. At one point, a truck came hurtling down the middle of the road from the opposite side. Partha pulled over to the side until it had passed.

Partha was now confident enough to turn on the headlights in low beam—they had given the bus enough of a lead. Even if someone in the bus was keeping watch it would seem unlikely that they were following it. And even if a car following the bus came up from behind, they would look like any other car driving on the highway.

They drew close enough to see the bus at a fair distance down the road and Partha maintained that distance. The tail-lights disappeared from time to time but Partha would take care to hold his pace steady and not hurry. In a little while, the lights would reappear.

The streets of the town were deserted in the middle of the night. The bus kept up a moderate speed, carrying on in the direction of the bus stop. With the twisting and winding of the city roads, Partha was forced to draw closer to keep the bus in sight. They were all the more alert now.

'Surprising they didn't keep anybody on the city outskirts,' Harish said.

Partha nodded. Singh Saheb leaned forward.

'If it were me,' he said, 'I'd have watched his native village and Kadapa bus stop—not the approach road. Then I wouldn't have to watch the streets or roam around at night and won't be taxing my people too much. And I would also be fairly certain I'd catch him before he reached home. If I kept a few people in and around the bus stand, I could just get lucky and catch him when he got down unsuspectingly.'

'That makes sense,' Partha said. 'Let's assume they have people waiting at the bus stop and approach quickly after the bus stops there.'

'Let me off near the entrance,' Harish said. 'I'll circle around to the bus.'

In a few minutes, the bus approached the bus stop. Partha kept a distance until the bus had entered the bus stand compound and then he picked up speed. He turned off the headlights but kept the parking lights on. Near the entrance, Partha stopped the car.

'Give me one minute,' Harish said.

He jumped out of the car and started to run. There was a guard's post but the guard wasn't in it. He found a stretch where the wall ran low and scaled it. Once on the other side, he landed in an untended stretch of the compound with overgrown bushes. There were streetlights that lit the surrounding area but there were plenty of unlit patches as well. This suited Harish. He ran clear of the bushes and through the unlit areas, all the time keeping the bus within sight. He came up to a shed close to where the bus had stopped. He leaned into the shadows and watched the bus. The bus door was straight ahead at a distance and had come to a complete halt though its lights were still on. The engine stayed on for a few seconds, then the lights went out and then the engine. The driver got out, stretched, and walked off into the bus stand building. The conductor walked alongside him without speaking. It was a typical bus stand, with a canteen and washrooms. There were other buses parked in bays but this late in the night there was little activity about the place.

Partha parked the car outside the bus stand area, and he and Saheb got out and walked into the bus stand. They walked slowly so they wouldn't approach the bus too quickly. They watched for movement around them but there was very little. They saw the lone guard sitting near the office chatting with a man wearing a canteen worker's uniform. They looked in the direction of the approaching driver and conductor. The canteen worker talking to the guard got up and walked up to the canteen booth. He shook awake a teenager who was sleeping inside. The teenager got up and wordlessly stood at the canteen booth. Groggy passengers began to emerge from the bus. They took a few moments to stretch and look around. Some of them headed in the direction of the washrooms, the others in the direction of the canteen.

From his position of better vantage, Harish kept his eyes on the bus door. No one who'd stepped out so far looked remotely like Varaprasad. Harish thought Varaprasad was doing the smart thing. It is better to wait, not seem overeager. It was better to walk out like he was in no hurry. Harish admired this kid: he showed courage and good sense even under tremendous pressure.

Then it occurred to Harish that perhaps Varaprasad was not on this bus at all. It was just the sort of niggling doubt that popped up under pressure. It was true that they'd just gone along on the assumption that he was on it. Partha's apprehension that he could convince the driver to drop him off along the way somewhere was also a possibility. Or perhaps he had a friend who lived close to the highway and had gotten off there. He could stay with the friend indefinitely until things cleared up. It was also possible that the man who'd gotten on the bus was not Varaprasad at all—maybe Mr Kumar's source had simply gotten it wrong. Or what if Varaprasad didn't plan to get off in Kadapa? What would they do then? Follow the bus around until he got off? Harish shook off the doubts and told himself to focus. He remembered that the informant had said that Varaprasad had bought a ticket to Kadapa, so the bus conductor would most likely not let him travel beyond this point. Also, as he had reasoned earlier, Varaprasad was most likely to have stayed on the bus. But Harish decided he wouldn't leave anything to chance. If he saw the driver and conductor walking back towards the bus, he would just run ahead and get on the bus to take a look around. It was a risky move with uncertain outcomes, but he knew he couldn't let the bus leave without being sure.

Just then, there was some movement inside the bus again. A small movement in the windows and then a man appeared at the door. He hesitated at the door for just a second before getting off. He had a haunted look about him, his face was gaunt, his glasses oddly accentuating the sunken depths of his eyes, his cheekbones protruding through the days-old stubble. His khadi kurta was crumpled and his jeans dirty. And on his shoulders was a bulky backpack. He looked like a junkie.

He got off the bus onto the platform and started to walk very quickly. He didn't look around, as though he didn't want to see what was out there. He walked straight, eager to get out of the light of the bus platform, into the darkness. Harish held back for a few moments and started to move. Almost immediately, he stopped and pulled back into the shadows.

Another man emerged from the bus. His appearance was skinny and slight. He also walked briskly. He quickly caught up with Varaprasad, who turned around in alarm. But the man walked right past him and on towards the gate. Varaprasad stood rooted in his place for a moment and then started to walk again.

From their position in the bus stand, Partha and Singh Saheb also saw Varaprasad get off the bus and then the other man overtaking him. They then saw Varaprasad starting to walk again after a moment's hesitation. Varaprasad walked past where they were standing and made for the gate; he hardly noticed them standing in the shadows. Something about the other man bothered Partha. He had no luggage with him. Though that was not altogether strange—many people made day-trips to Bangalore and from point to point on such bus routes. But why had he taken so long to get out? The answer could be easy enough—he'd fallen asleep. But in these particular circumstances, that explanation didn't satisfy Partha. He gestured to Singh Saheb and indicated the man walking way in the distance. Singh Saheb nodded.

Partha and Singh Saheb stayed where they were, watching Varaprasad walk towards the gate. The other man had a big lead on Varaprasad now. He then disappeared from view as he turned at the gate and the compound wall blocked their view. Singh Saheb stayed put, keeping an eye on Varaprasad, moving about within the bus stand so as not to lose sight of him. They didn't want to approach him with people around especially when they knew he would react with terror. They planned to let him walk out of the bus stand and then they would drive up to him on the road. Harish too would be close by on foot.

At this time, Harish began to circle back through the bushes towards the road. Partha and Saheb walked back to the car. Partha pulled out, keeping the headlights off.

Varaprasad turned left at the gate and walked in the direction the other man had taken. As Harish pulled up near the compound wall of the bus stand, he remained close to the wall but didn't jump over. If he did, he would be directly in Varaprasad's path but a substantial distance away. He moved along slowly for a little bit and came to a stop. He found a position from where he could peep over the wall and see the road clearly. When Partha and Saheb pulled up in the car, he would jump over the wall and intercept Varaprasad. It was necessary to keep Varaprasad from running, which he was bound to try to do. Harish figured that even after they had him under control, it would take a lot to convince him that they were not going to harm him.

Varaprasad walked quickly and seemed to know clearly where he was going. Perhaps he was going to a friend's or relative's place in town. Or he was trying to reach a point from where he could set out for home. Whatever his plan was, he walked on without hesitation. He looked around once in a while, but other than that he looked straight ahead as he had in the bus stand, as though unwilling to see anything that was not in his direct path. He was walking very fast and Harish wished Partha would bring the car around quickly. At the current pace Varaprasad would come up to the point where Harish was hiding very soon. Just then, in the far corner Harish saw Partha's car turn onto the road and heard its engine. Varaprasad didn't seem to notice it.

At that moment, Harish picked up movement that made him freeze. It was at the corner of his eye, from a lane branching off from the main street. There was a flickering of light and a figure emerged from the shadows and dashed directly in the direction of Varaprasad. The sound of slippers slapping against the road ricocheted in the air. Harish reached up and pulled himself onto the wall. Varaprasad looked up and to his side.

But before he could move the figure had slammed him into Varaprasad.

Harish was over the wall in a second. He ran the fifty or more feet to Varaprasad as fast as he could. Partha and Singh Saheb had also driven up by then. Singh Saheb had jumped out of the car. He was the first to get to Varaprasad. Varaprasad had dropped to the ground and the skinny figure was standing over him. Singh Saheb took a grip on the skinny man. When he squirmed and pulled away, Singh Saheb hit him—a sharp, quick slap to the head. The man fell to the ground as Singh Saheb still held onto his shirt—he was dazed but not hurt. It was the same skinny man who'd gotten out of the bus after Varaprasad.

Varaprasad himself looked disoriented. Partha and Harish were beside him.

'Don't be afraid,' Partha said. 'You're alright now.'

Varaprasad looked up and around. He looked at all of them with terror in his eyes. He could see the three men had taken positions around him and so he didn't run. Partha indicated to Harish to step out of his way.

'You're free to go if you like,' Partha said. 'But just hear me out first.'

Varaprasad didn't know what to do. He looked around and swallowed loudly a few times. Before he could catch his breath, there was another sound. He looked up. As did Partha and Harish.

'They're coming,' Harish said, almost under his breath.

Partha and Singh Saheb turned in the direction of the sound. A Tata Sumo was gunning down the road towards them. The skinny man, still in Singh Saheb's grip, pulled himself up and waved out at the car. The Sumo manoeuvered into place, blocking Partha's car. The driver stayed behind the wheel, the others rushed towards them. Saheb slapped the skinny man again—harder this time but with the man's slight frame, Singh Saheb was afraid of doing too much damage with a serious hit. The man went sprawling.

Partha could make out Shiva in the haze of the streetlight. He was flying directly in the direction of Varaprasad. Partha got himself right in the way. Harish positioned himself to guard Varaprasad from the other direction.

Partha intercepted Shiva and twisted him just slightly away, using his momentum against him. Shiva nearly fell but recovered almost miraculously—he had the agility of an acrobat. He turned towards Partha. It was then that Partha realised that Shiva had his knife out. He felt a slash at his hand. He didn't make the mistake of trying to grab the knife, instead he threw a short, powerful punch at Shiva's throat. It found its mark. His head fell forward and he gagged. Partha hit him in the face then. He went for the body but Shiva had recovered. His fist shot out at Partha's face. Partha swerved out of its way but it caught a side of his head. Partha recovered and flung his right arm at Shiva wildly. It landed on Shiva's shoulder but didn't do much damage.

At the same time, Harish was fighting off two men. They were not very skilled but they were strong. Harish managed to knock the first one to the ground with a hit to the chest. The other man was stronger and dashed at Harish, knocking him back into the wall. Harish was out of breath. Recovering quickly, Harish slashed downward with an elbow into the man's back. The man let out a cry. This gave Harish the chance to reach down and get his arms around the man's neck. Harish didn't let go. He strengthened his grip around the neck and held him in that position, choking him. The man began to lash around with his hands. Harish kept him close, tightening the grip. When the man began to weaken, Harish let go and hit him on the head. The man slumped.

In the meantime, Singh Saheb had rushed to the SUV door and grabbed the driver through the window. The driver managed to push open the door. Singh Saheb yanked the door fully open and grabbed the man again. There was a struggle with the driver. Just as he was getting the upper hand, another man rushed towards Singh Saheb. Saheb punched the driver and turned to the other man. The skinny man saw his opportunity and slipped away.

As this played out, Partha sensed a change in Shiva's posture. Shiva was getting frustrated with Partha holding him up. He had the knife firmly in hand and he was ready to plunge with all his force at Partha. This was an opportunity. Partha leaned in the direction of Shiva, giving him a better target. Shiva thrust forward. Partha grabbed hold of Shiva's collar. Shiva lashed at him with the knife. Partha stayed out of the way and used Shiva's temporary loss of balance to his advantage—he crashed into him putting his entire weight into it. Shiva crashed into the wall and fell.

Partha turned around just in time to see the driver crash into Singh Saheb. He thought he saw a knife flash in the light. Partha darted forward to help him. Partha went directly for the driver and knocked him down. By the time he'd subdued him, he turned and saw he'd made a mistake. Varaprasad was running. He'd gone over a hundred metres and made for a lane. And Shiva had started after him. Shiva was definitely sluggish from his crash into the wall, but Partha knew he'd recover. A trained, tough man like Shiva would be able to recover quickly even after the hit he'd taken. The next thing he saw made Partha's blood go cold. Ahead of Shiva, a man darted right at Varaprasad and crashed into him. Varaprasad cried out. He pushed the man away and staggered into the lane. Partha saw the man in the street light. It was the skinny man who'd run off from the scuffle. He'd been watching from a distance all along, just waiting for an opportunity. The skinny man got to his feet and staggered after Varaprasad.

Harish and Saheb had more or less subdued the other men. They were now trying to secure them.

'Harish, that lane!' Partha said, running hard in its direction.

'Go!' Harish said.

As Partha turned the corner, his heart skipped a beat. There was no sight of anyone as far as he could see. In the street light, Partha could see streaks of blood on the ground. Partha cursed to himself. He ran into the first street in the maze of streets in front of him. He looked around for more signs of blood but it was unevenly lit and he couldn't see much of the ground. The streets were deserted. He ran straight ahead looking to his right, trying desperately to catch a glimpse of any of the three men. Partha guessed they were close to the highway because he could hear sounds of trucks passing by. He caught a glimpse of movement in a parallel street. He dashed in that direction. He rounded the corner and saw exactly what he feared: Shiva leaning over Varaprasad. The skinny man had Varaprasad's backpack opened up.

Partha crashed into the skinny man. That had the effect of drawing Shiva's attention away from Varaprasad. Partha tried to dash the skinny man's head against the wall—he didn't particularly care what the outcome would be. He felt the head make contact but he couldn't be sure if it was strong enough. He didn't have time to try again; Shiva came at him. In the grapple, Partha got Shiva by the neck with one hand and punched him in the abdomen with the other. Shiva fell to his knees and held himself up there. He was out of breath. Partha saw him clutching onto a cellphone. Partha grabbed him around the neck and pulled back. He was determined not to let go. Shiva began to choke. He dropped the cellphone. Partha kept up the pressure. He held on for as long as he could.

Looking to his side, Partha caught a glimpse of Varaprasad. He saw immediately that he'd been stabbed. He had to help him out but he had to deal with Shiva first. Partha could feel Shiva weaken. But he had one last trick in him. He gashed an elbow into Partha's knee. Partha let go. Shiva had extraordinary resilience—a last gear that nobody could see coming. He managed to pull himself up and he pulled away.

Partha understood what was happening. Shiva was injured and weakened and wanted to get away. Shiva turned and ran—he could not afford to be captured. Partha's leg hurt but he was otherwise okay. He limped a little but he ran after him. Shiva saw Partha come after him and picked up speed. He was in a zone now, one beyond the limitations of his injuries, he ran out of the colony and onto the road.

He didn't see the truck right in his track. It slammed into him. Even at the moment of impact, Partha knew that Shiva was dead.

*

Partha didn't waste time there, he returned to where Varaprasad lay. From a distance he saw the prone Varaprasad struggling with the skinny man. They were struggling with the backpack in one hand and the knife in the other. The skinny man looked up and saw Partha in the distance as he passed under a streetlight. He let go of the backpack, and wrenched himself free. He ran in the other direction. Varaprasad tried to get up and follow him but he slumped. He was losing a lot of blood. Partha didn't run after the man. He bent down to take a closer look at Varaprasad. Varaprasad pulled away from him.

'I won't hurt you, okay?' Partha said. 'We're not the ones trying to hurt you. We just fought off the people trying to kill you.'

Varaprasad eased up a little. He was breathing heavily.

Partha called Harish on the cellphone. He picked up immediately. He was somewhere in the maze of streets around. Partha gave him a few directions.

'The guy from the bus is on the run,' Partha said. 'Try to intercept him.'

'I'm on the way.'

'The others are secure?'

'They'll stay. You've got the psychopath?'

'He ran onto the highway and got hit by a truck.'

'He's gone?'

'He's gone.'

'Good.'

Partha hung up. He turned to Varaprasad again. He saw where the cut was. It was bleeding badly.

'My name is Partha Rao,' Partha said. 'We've been hired by someone from Mohan Krishna's family.'

Varaprasad's face showed dismay.

'We know that Prakash is the one who drove the girl to her death,' Partha said. 'We're trying to find proof against him. We think the laptop has it.'

Varaprasad looked too weak to react.

'Can you walk?' Partha asked.

He knew the answer himself. There was no way. Partha called Harish again.

'Can't find him, Partha!' Harish said, his breathing a little heavy. 'There's street after street here.'

'Forget about the guy,' Partha said. 'We need to get Varaprasad to the hospital immediately. I need help carrying him out of here.'

Varaprasad began to shake his head frantically.

'The phone!' he whispered. 'The phone!'

'What?' Partha said.

'He's got her phone—her message to Kalla Prakash…'

Partha picked up the phone that Shiva had dropped on the floor and showed it to him. Varaprasad shook his head.

'This is yours?' Partha asked.

Varaprasad nodded.

'We'll have to let it go,' Partha said.

He reached over and picked up backpack. He pulled out the laptops. One of them was badly busted up, perhaps from the time the skinny man had crashed Varaprasad into the wall. From Varaprasad's reaction Partha guessed this was Priya's laptop. Partha put them back in. He took out his own phone and called the police. He told them their location and told them to give him directions to the nearest hospital—a man was dying. The policeman asked where they were presently.

'You may have gotten a call about a truck running over a man,' he said. 'We're very close to that place.'

By the time Partha heard Harish approach, Varaprasad was in and out of consciousness.

22

They didn't wait for the police to arrive on the scene. They put Varaprasad in the backseat of the car and drove to the government hospital by themselves. They left the other men tied up on the road, took away the car keys and their cellphones, and deflated the Sumo's tires. By the time they got to the hospital, Varaprasad was unconscious. The doctors were reluctant to act—as was to be expected in an obviously criminal case—so they waited. Within minutes, a journalist armed with a camera reached the hospital. Partha told the journalist to go ahead and get footage of Varaprasad lying on the gurney. Invasion of privacy or the inappropriateness of the content for a news broadcast didn't really figure on his list of concerns. His top concern was protecting Varaprasad's life and putting the story out would help do that. The only precaution he took was to ensure that he, Singh Saheb, or Harish were not caught in the frame. The police arrived a few minutes later. The doctors got to work after that, while the police spoke to Partha and Harish. Singh Saheb remained silent throughout.

On the way to the hospital, Partha had made two quick phone calls. The first was to Seema. He gave her a quick update, saying they had Varaprasad but he'd been stabbed. She didn't ask for any details; she only asked what they needed. Partha asked her to call Vishwanath immediately. She'd have to convince him to send his local news crew out to the hospital. He told her he'd forward her the exclusive cellphone he could be reached on at all times of the day and night. Seema already had it. That impressed Partha: on the networking front, there was little that Seema didn't have covered.

Second, he called a contact of Harish's in the Andhra Pradesh police and handed Harish the phone. The contact could be trusted enough to be told who the stabbing victim was and request protection.

'It'd be good if he could be moved to a Hyderabad hospital,' Harish said. 'And the news that he's been found and stabbed will be breaking in a few minutes,' he added casually.

'I'm not surprised,' the officer said drily and hung up.

On the way to the hospital, Partha and Harish agonised over what to do with the laptop. Should they hand it over to the police or should they say that the skinny man from the bus had grabbed it along with the cellphone? They could have the hard disk removed and the data salvaged in a very short time. Harish was confident of getting past any encryption. But Partha was reluctant.

'We'll have to hand it over to the police,' Partha said. 'It means the NPP gets access but still.' Partha looked over at Varaprasad. 'They're going to put him on the critical list. Seems wrong to mess up evidence in light of his ... stabbing.'

'You mean possible—' Harish said and mouthed 'murder'.

Partha nodded.

'I suppose you're right,' Harish said. 'Even if we turn it in later they'll say we tampered with it.'

'Turning it in later is not a real option.'

'You've lost your killer instinct, Partha,' Harish said with a sigh. 'A couple of years ago, we'd have been driving this kid to some quack and have the computer cracked by daybreak.'

'Yeah well, we're getting old.'

Harish shook his head dejectedly.

'So we let the kid get stabbed,' he said, 'we didn't take Shiva alive—though I'm not sad about that—we let the laptop get busted, and we lose the cellphone. Man, am I glad we made this trip!'

Partha nodded. 'It's a disaster,' he said.

Harish shook his head in frustration.

'If only the kid hadn't run!' he said. 'We were just getting on top of things there.'

'He was scared of us too.'

'Yeah.'

'We should have anticipated it,' Partha said. 'I thought the guy attacking Singh Saheb had a knife. I wouldn't have left his side otherwise.'

'It all happened too quickly. As it always does.'

Partha nodded once again. 'We need to get our story straight,' he said.

Harish turned to Singh Saheb. Singh Saheb nodded and said nothing.

The police were less than impressed with the story they told them. The local inspector demanded to know what the three of them were doing there and just who the men bound to the street light outside the bus stand were. The story Partha told was largely true. He said they'd been hired by a private party to look into Priya's suicide—they were not willing to reveal the identity of the party. They were on the lookout for Varaprasad because they believed his life was in danger. They'd received a tip-off that he was on this bus—once again, they refused to say from whom the tip came—and they rushed to Kadapa fearing that he was in danger. By the time they got here, the men had already attacked Varaprasad. They got into the fight to save him but Varaprasad ran and Shiva ran after him. Shiva ran right onto the highway, trying to get away from them, and got hit by the truck.

'Why didn't you just tip-off the police?' the inspector asked.

'The boy's running from the police as well,' Partha said. 'He's terrified. We would have brought him along once we'd convinced him it was safe.'

'I'm sure you would have,' the inspector said sarcastically. 'You'll wait at the police station until we decide what to do.'

'That's fine.'

'You'll wait even if it isn't.'

'What we've done is be helpful to the police department, inspector. I hope that's factored into your final decision.'

'What are you talking about?' The inspector was not pleased with Partha's confident tone.

'Look, if it weren't for us this boy would have quietly been murdered and his body dumped. The whole police department would have gotten flak for not finding the boy in time. The Kadapa police in particular would have been blamed for not preventing it. Unreasonable as that is, you know you'd be blamed. Right now, the boy may be in a critical condition but he has a chance. We also got hold of the laptop, which is vital to the Priya suicide case. And though he died in an accident, you'll find that the dead man, Shiva, has a huge criminal record. He's also the one responsible for two murders committed in Hyderabad earlier today.'

'How do you know?'

'I told you already. We've been making enquiries in this case and we're pretty sure about this. You can check the evidence yourself and come to a conclusion.'

The inspector chewed the tip of a fingernail for a few seconds.

'Finish your point,' he said.

'My point is that the story can play out in two ways. One, we got here and got into a fight and you guys were called in after everything ended. Two, we called and gave you a late-night tip-off, and you guys turned up, broke up the fight, and Shiva was killed on the run.'

The inspector seemed interested, though he made an effort not to show it. He wiped his finger on a handkerchief and looked at Partha.

'You'll wait at the police station, as I said,' he said. 'Until we do a preliminary check, I can't say anything. Don't talk to the media in the meantime.'

'We won't,' Partha said.

Partha got his arm patched up for the knife slash from Shiva. Then they were taken to the police station. Their cellphones were taken away and they were cut off from the outside world. After the excitement of the night and given their forced idleness, the tiredness began to tell on them. All three men dozed off in their chairs. When they woke up, the constables in the station were taciturn but gruffly friendly. They had some breakfast brought in from a roadside stall nearby and asked them to pay. Singh Saheb seemed to have slept most soundly of them all. When he woke up, he seemed to enjoy the breakfast as well.

'Should we read something into the fact that we're not in the lockup?' Harish said, grinning. 'And that they sent out for our breakfast?'

'I guess it's a sign we're not being treated like criminals.'

'Not yet anyway.'

'Yeah.'

'The inspector seemed to like the idea of being the saviour in this story. Maybe that's why he's told them to be nice to us.'

Partha shook his head.

'I think it's Seema working behind the scenes,' he said.

Harish laughed. 'She probably knows the inspector's birthday and wedding anniversary by now,' he said.

'I wouldn't be surprised.'

The men who were with Shiva had been brought to the police station and locked up. Partha and the others were not allowed anywhere near them. By around 12 noon, the inspector returned to the police station. He'd just returned from the bus stand. The story was building up in the media and he looked tired.

'You kept important information from me,' he said.

'What's that?' Partha asked.

'Day before yesterday, you made a complaint to the Hyderabad City University police that you were attacked by this man, Shiva.'

'That's right.'

'So you were in a fight with the man a couple of days earlier and he turns up dead today.'

'Are you suggesting we pushed him in the truck's way?' Harish said.

'How do I know you didn't? There might be more to the story than you're telling me.'

'Yes, this man attacked me the day before yesterday,' Partha said. 'And we filed a police complaint. Those are the facts.'

The inspector drummed silently on his desk.

'I'm just saying there are several ways this can be looked at,' he said. 'Not just the way you suggested.'

Partha saw where this was going. 'That's true,' he said. 'You could say you got an anonymous tip-off saying that there was a fight near the bus stand, you landed there and found us all in the fight and that we all took off running.'

'Yes, that's right. But I wouldn't do that. Because you would contradict it, saying that you brought Varaprasad to the hospital before the police arrived. Your journalist friends would corroborate it.'

'Yes, they would. So what if we say that you were tipped off by one of your sources and you arrived on the scene and scared them off. Shiva was killed in the chase and one man got away, but you're going to find that man soon. Your action saved Varaprasad—at least got him to the hospital. We were not even on the scene. At best we got here after everything was over. I'll work it out with our journalist friends. They're not interested in these minor things; they're also keen on the overall story playing out right.'

'It's already been worked out.'

'With the news channel?'

The inspector shook his head. Partha nodded knowingly.

'Seema?' he said.

The inspector nodded tiredly. 'She is very persuasive,' he said.

'I agree.'

'Persistent too,' the inspector said, with a half sigh.

'She can be.'

The inspector didn't react.

'There is the matter of the men who were with them,' Partha said. 'Their version will be different.'

'They're local goondas,' the inspector said. 'They won't be giving any statements to the press.'

The inspector leaned back in his chair. 'I want statements from you just in case it comes out that you were here,' he said. 'The statements can say you got here looking for Varaprasad on a tip-off but everything was over by then ... Is that clear?'

'It is,' Partha said. 'Only one channel knows we were here. We can keep it from coming out.'

Harish nodded. Singh Saheb maintained his silence. Harish had to nudge him to get him to nod along. The inspector seemed satisfied.

'We'll record your statements then,' he said.

Over the next hour they narrated a highly-edited sequence of events, but still refused to divulge their sources. As they were about to leave, they passed by the inspector's room.

'Can you tell us anything at all about the men who were with Shiva?' Harish asked.

The inspector shrugged indifferently.

'They're local rowdy-sheeters, most of them,' he said. 'They said Shiva had hired them earlier for local jobs. He called from Hyderabad two days ago and told them to be on the lookout for Varaprasad. Today, he told them he was going to join them.'

'They don't belong to his revolutionary group?'

'No such affiliation. They work with political parties around here most of the time. The man who got away seems to have been in touch with Shiva as well. The others say they seemed to know each other well.'

'Must be a member of Shiva's group,' Partha said.

'Maybe. We're circulating a sketch based on all your descriptions. We'll get him, but the cellphone is almost definitely gone for good.'

It was a depressing thought. It was another reminder of the extent to which their trip had been a failure.

'It shouldn't be too much of a setback for the police,' Partha said hopefully. 'You can directly access Priya's emails and phone calls from the service provider. Even backed up photographs and stuff like that.'

'It is still a loss,' the inspector said.

'It was a smartphone. Most of those things are backed up to cloud apps.'

'We'll see.'

'The contents of the phone will come out though,' Partha said. 'I'd watch CNEWS in the next twenty-four hours to find out.'

'CNEWS?'

'They seem to have a jumpstart on this news story.'

'Hopefully, we'll salvage something from the laptop. But the damn thing is broken very badly. The media will hound us about what's on it.'

Partha turned to go.

'This thing isn't closed yet,' the inspector said. 'If we want to talk to you we'll call you back.'

'We're available,' Partha said.

*

They returned to the hospital. Singh Saheb stayed in the car and Harish and Partha went in. The media was out in force by then. It would be a struggle even to get close to the entrance of the ward where Varaprasad was admitted. Partha and Harish took care to stay out of sight and looked around for a bit. In an adjoining corridor they had a bit of luck. The constables who'd arrived at the hospital first the previous night were still on duty there. They allowed Partha and Harish to talk to the doctors. Varaprasad, they were told, had improved but was barely conscious. The doctors were considering allowing Varaprasad to be moved to Hyderabad in an ambulance the following day. The doctors weren't categorical about it but they gave the impression that Varaprasad was more or less out of danger. Varaprasad's family and some students were already on their way to Kadapa. They'd start for Hyderabad together as soon as the logistics worked out. The police would provide security for the journey.

Partha and Harish decided to start for home. It was difficult to say when Varaprasad would be in a condition to speak. Even if he was, they wouldn't have access to him that day. It was better to cut their losses and figure out what to do next in Hyderabad. They expected a story about Prakash to break soon if the cellphone had reached anyone significant in the opposing camp. What Prakash would do in retaliation would be important.

They drove into Kadapa town and had lunch at a restaurant. They then started off for Hyderabad. Partha called Seema on the way back.

'The inspector went for the deal,' Partha said.

'It was the smart way to go,' Seema said. 'Worked out for everyone.'

'How did you get his contact anyway?'

'Harish isn't the only one networked with AP officials.'

'Very cool. We didn't salvage much from this trip though.'

'Let's see where the chips fall.'

'Any progress on the media ownership front? Any patterns?'

'Am pulling at a thread—the one I meant to mention to you about last night. Still working on it.'

'Okay.'

'I'm going to call Malvika and give her an update. Also an update on what's likely to hit the news soon.'

'Tell her Prakash could get aggressive.'

'She'll know that already.'

'I suppose.'

'The initial polling on Anil's statement is overwhelmingly positive,' Seema said. 'That should give her some comfort.'

'That's a positive sign.'

Partha was about to hang up and then something occurred to him.

'Seema, you still there?' he asked.

'Yeah.'

'Wanted to pick your brain about something.'

'About what?'

'Occurred to me this morning. If there was a journalist you'd want to speak to on Leftist violence in the early 1980s, who would it be?'

'Journalist? I don't know that many journalists here. I'd talk to the seniors, I guess: Kasu Rama Rao, Balakrishna Prasad … and …'

'Vishwanath?'

'Yeah. That's right. Vishwanath.'

'It hit me that he covered the districts bordering Orissa more than anyone else back then. It's what made his reputation as a journalist.'

'You think he'll be able to tell us something about Prof. Hussain?' Seema asked.

'Perhaps. But not just that. Back then, he must have been covering Mohan Krishna intensively as well. He'd know behind-the-scenes stuff that nobody else knows. There's a lot more to this background picture than we're able to see right now.'

'That's true.'

'I'll need you to go with me on this one too.'

'Why?'

'Vishwanath is always suspicious of me. You're persuasive: he'll be a little more forthcoming with you.'

'Ah, flattery.'

'Did it work?'

'No.'

'See, I don't have your knack for winning over people! I'll see you later today.'

Harish had taken the first turn at driving. Partha took an hour-long nap and then, finding himself well-rested and his arm wound not too severe, took the wheel. Singh Saheb said he'd never driven an automatic transmission vehicle and didn't want to start now. He slept through the entire drive. They reached the outskirts of the city early in the evening. They avoided much of the city traffic taking the Ring Round. They dropped Singh Saheb off where they'd picked him up—Harish would take care of the payment for his services later. The last stretch, which was close enough to their Banjara Hills office, took over forty-five minutes. They got to office late in the evening. Seema was waiting for them.

'You boys seem to have made it out of the fight alright,' she said. 'Sounded dangerous with a dreaded criminal being killed and all.'

'I need a drink,' Partha said.

He went to his cabin and returned with a bottle of single malt. They took glasses from the cafeteria area and sat in Partha's cabin.

'Malvika seemed to freak out at the news,' Seema said. 'She doesn't know how Mohan Krishna will react.'

Neither Partha nor Harish responded.

'What do you think we should tell her?' Seema said.

Partha and Harish looked at each other.

'Tell her we'll get back to her tomorrow,' Harish said. 'Everything will have to wait until tomorrow.'

23

The news of Shiva's death broke that evening. The police deliberately kept Shiva's identity hidden for much of the day, maintaining that they were investigating and trying to establish the victim's identity. Initially, it was seen as another highway accident and the focus remained on the news that Varaprasad may have been found. Seema had to persuade Vishwanath to withhold footage from the hospital in exchange for a head-start in breaking the news. In the afternoon the police gave the go ahead. TNN broke the news. Half an hour later the police put out a statement that Varaprasad had indeed been found but he was in a critical condition. It was several hours later that they released Shiva's identity. Even CNEWS had stayed silent on Shiva's identity all day. But when it became clear that these two news stories were directly related—the news exploded on TV.

The police held a press conference in the evening. In it, they went with the version the inspector and Partha had agreed upon. There weren't any credible witnesses on the scene to dispute it. The police version was that they'd received an anonymous tip-off that Varaprasad was on the bus and may be harmed. They were unable to verify the source and thought it to be a prank call. But not wanting to take any chances they kept a watch on the bus stand. When Varaprasad arrived and was attacked, they were able reach the spot to save him and recover the laptop; unfortunately, he was wounded in the attack. Shiva died trying to evade the police. And somewhere in the melee an accomplice had gotten away unnoticed with Priya's cellphone. The report also said some minor accomplices were taken into custody and were being questioned.

This news fed a frenzy but there was little information to go on. Police and hospital sources were tightly controlled and nothing new emerged. News also came in the morning that Varaprasad was out of danger but too weak to respond to any questions.

Partha came into the office early and watched much of the coverage on the TV in the common area. CNEWS talked in agitated terms about the carelessness of the police in handling the matter. They lamented the loss of life and asked if Shiva could not have been saved. They wondered why it could not be described as an extra-judicial killing. The anchors also raised questions about Varaprasad, asking how he was tied into the whole story. How did he know Priya, and why was his role in her suicide not being seen to be suspicious?

For Partha, the line CNEWS had taken was not surprising. In fact, it was along expected lines. But he was waiting for a bigger story to break. If the contents of Priya's phone were to surface in the press, he was convinced it would happen on CNEWS. And it would happen very soon. Their opponents had suffered a setback—Shiva had been killed and the laptop had fallen into the police's hands. They would have to mount a counterattack soon. If the phone contained anything about Prakash as Varaprasad had indicated, he expected that content to be aired that morning. He was surprised it hadn't happened already.

He watched for over an hour but there was no mention of the phone. This was surprising. It might just be that they were having trouble cracking the phone's security mechanism. But Partha doubted that. That was a problem they would have anticipated and been prepared for. Even the pattern of news coverage that morning just didn't fit. Partha had expected a build-up to a big reveal. What was playing out on air, however, was a defensive tactic: the painting of Varaprasad as an unreliable character. The aggression was missing.

Partha thought through some possibilities but nothing was convincing. He looked at his phone, which he'd put on silent since the previous evening. He had four missed calls from Malvika. Partha had sent her a message simply saying he would call back soon. As he looked at the screen another text message from her flashed on the screen: 'URGENT: MOHAN K WANTS TO MEET YOU IMMEDIATELY—CALL ME AT ONCE!' Partha sent her another text instead: 'We'll meet if he's willing to reveal what Prakash has on him.' Partha's phone rang. Malvika again. This time, Partha picked up.

'You know what Prakash has over Mohan Krishna!' Malvika said. 'He controls a ton of his businesses!'

'With that kind of leverage, Prakash can expect Mohan Krishna's support,' Partha said, 'but not that Mohan Krishna would let his own son take the fall.'

'You don't understand what it's like in families with wealth and power.'

'You said your main concern was getting Anil out of this mess,' Partha said. 'There isn't any document, photograph, or anything else that suggests Anil was at fault. I don't see anybody worried about some material about him surfacing. The only things against him right now are public perception and the fact that he and his family won't point fingers at Prakash.'

'Mohan Krishna is worried—'

'He's worried that with the phone out there Prakash's name will come out. And if that happens, Prakash will retaliate.'

'But he's already retaliated. Prakash knows you guys were on the scene at Kadapa, and he says he feels betrayed.'

'He knows we were there?'

'Yes.'

'That's interesting.'

'He has some contacts in the NPP and he got it from a senior police official.'

'Okay,' Partha said. 'So what does he want now?'

'He's not bargaining, he's all set to retaliate. Mohan's trying to placate him. He's even offered to make Prakash the CEO of Swayambhu Films Ltd.'

'The holding company that controls most of your family's companies?'

'Yes. Mohan Krishna always kept the CEO position from him because he it would give him too much control and power. It would make Mohan Krishna a mere figurehead in his own empire. Now he says he's got no option but to give Prakash the job.'

Partha considered this for a moment.

'So Mohan Krishna wants me to hand over the material we have?' he said. 'And to reassure Prakash we're dropping everything?'

'It has to be done, Partha,' Malvika said. 'Everyone out here has too much to lose. If Prakash panics and starts lashing out at the family, that'll be the end of it all.'

'Tell him we were following the guy who attacked me at the university. That we didn't know we'd find Varaprasad there.'

'Mohan wants you to convince Prakash in person.'

Partha didn't reply.

'Partha?' Malvika said.

'I'll meet Mohan Krishna and Prakash in a day or two,' Partha said.

'That won't do; that's too late!'

'Malvika, listen to me. This thing runs very deep and we're closer now than ever to figuring it out. Tell Prakash whatever he wants to hear—stall him for the time being.'

'Mohan wants you to stop your efforts right now—everything. If Prakash thinks you're still active, that's trigger enough to act against the family.'

'Is that what you want as well? For us to stop?'

'I have no choice.'

'You called us in even when nobody wanted you to. Didn't you?'

'I know, but this is far more complicated than I thought. Too much is at stake.'

'If you want us to stop, we'll stop,' he said, his tone low.

'What do you think I should do?' she said.

'I think,' Partha said slowly, 'that you should do what's best for your family.'

'Then I want you to stop all work,' Malvika said. 'You can raise a bill and Mr Ramakrishna will pay.'

'Alright.'

'And I'd like copies of all the material you've collected to be handed over to us.'

'It'll take us a day but we'll get it to you.'

'And you'll stop pursuing this whole matter.'

'Fine.'

'I hope this is the right call, Partha.'

'I think it is.'

'Thanks for your help. I wish this could have ended better.'

'Don't worry about it.'

''Bye, Partha.'

''Bye, Malvika. In case Mohan Krishna wants to see me in a day or two, please tell him I'm available.'

Malvika didn't say anything. She was perhaps unsure about how to respond to that. Partha hung up.

*

Partha walked over to Seema's cabin.

'We've just been fired,' Partha told Seema.

'Never liked the idea of working for Mohan Krishna anyway,' Seema said.

'Me neither.'

'We're not going to stop, are we?'

'No.'

'What prompted the firing?'

'Prakash knew we were at the scene.'

Seema frowned.

'How did Prakash know that?' she said.

'NPP contact of his who talked to a police source. I'm guessing Prakash already knew about our involvement but now he's using it against Mohan Krishna to clinch things in his favour. But this is what I found really interesting: where's Prakash's desperation to retrieve the phone? Why is he more concerned about shutting us down?'

'You think he's already safe? He's already cut a deal to save himself?'

'Sounds like it. Mohan Krishna's offering him the CEO job at Swayambhu Films to keep him quiet.'

'Wow! What's he got on Mohan Krishna?'

'Obviously something that cuts deep. And here's something else that's interesting: CNEWS hasn't uttered a word about Prakash.'

Seema's eyebrows shot up.

'That is interesting!' she said.

'I think we can agree that the story will break there?'

'That's definitely been the way it's played out so far.'

'The phone's out there, its contents don't appear on CNEWS, and Prakash is not frantic. There's definitely something going on there.'

'A deal's been cut for sure.'

Partha nodded.

'The other big question is where do the university and Prof. Hussain fit into all this?' he said. 'I just hope we'll get some insight into that from Vishwanath.'

Seema squinted her eyes a little.

'I hope we're not off on a wild-goose chase while things blow up around us,' she said.

'I don't believe what happened in the 1980s is a distraction,' Partha said. 'I think what started back then is coming to a head now.'

Seema nodded.

'I have something on the CNEWS front,' Seema said. 'Something that explains the hostility to Mohan Krishna but not a lot else.'

Partha's eyes widened. He couldn't speak for a moment.

'Are you serious?' he said. 'Wow, that's huge! And you've been walking around keeping it to yourself, acting like it's not a big deal!'

'It wasn't easy,' Seema said with a tired smile. 'I just got done with it. We'll need Harish to follow Vikram, the actor. Find out who he meets, what his business interests are, and what he's been up to of late.'

*

As they drove out to Vishwanath's office, Seema filled Partha in about what her team had dug up.

Quietly, behind the scenes, they'd sifted through an enormous amount of data. Splitting the work between in-house staff and freelancers they regularly used, Seema systematically broke down media ownership patterns in the industry as a whole. In the first category she put people who owned media houses openly. Owners were explicitly mentioned in filed documents and they had known offices with clear addresses. These companies were transparent in terms of ownership, but even with them, one often ran into walls when enquiring about the sources of funds. This information was protected with confidentiality clauses and with the use of obscure holding companies, companies that had a mix of directors from the parent company and outsiders. Sometimes these jointly-held companies used the main media company's addresses for their offices even though they were distinct entities.

Even where a fair amount of information was available in the public domain, to untangle the web of ownership was not easy. Often, obscure companies held small stakes in the media company and sent one off on a wild-goose chase. Also, many of these media houses had investments from private equity funds or institutional investors. Much of this was bona fide investment. But occasionally you would find that the private equity fund had overvalued the media company and no convincing basis for the valuation was given, which suggested money laundering of some sort. And all too often these news organisations had money coming in from tax havens.

In the second category were media companies where the ownership was not as openly declared. These companies employed obscuring techniques similar to more openly-owned companies, with the difference that principal owners stayed largely unknown while proxies were shown as owners.

Splitting the task amongst different groups and breaking them into categories, Seema had teams scrutinise all active media channels. She worked on the assumption that contacts, companies, and relationships existed in clusters rather than in isolation. So, a private investor who held a stake in a media company was likely to have invested in it because of a prior business association with the media company owner. So, it made sense to check if the two parties had invested together in another sector, say real estate. This was true even if there was money from political corruption involved. The money had to be routed through registered companies, so these kinds of linkages could be found. Not easily, but if one had access to the right kind of people, documents, and the grapevine. Seema allowed herself to be guided even by rumours of who was invested in what company and which politician had invested in which channel. These threw up patterns almost immediately.

She saw that if companies linked to Prakash were clumped

together, there was a pattern of aggressive buying. But even with that, he remained a relatively small media player. A potentially powerful player but one who'd come late to the game. The old, dominant news channels, which also had a newspaper presence, controlled the market share. Rumour was that Prakash had tried to buy into a big player but had been rebuffed, leading to a bitter running feud between the two. This confrontation had left Prakash weakened. Also, filings showed that Prakash's acquisitions had come at great expense. And media organisations, being notoriously unprofitable, weakened him further financially. Despite the high cost, he had an enviable acquisition in one company—News Stream—and he would at least have a voice at the table.

Seema was struck by the fact that if Prakash had joined forces with Mohan Krishna to counter the current media onslaught, they would have been a formidable force. But Prakash had done little more than put a few obfuscatory stories out there. It seemed that he had made everything conditional to Mohan Krishna keeping his name out of the scandal. It also seemed that Mohan Krishna was entirely helpless against this man. He was a minor player as far as direct media ownership went—the one channel favourable to him—the unfortunately named HydNews—had little viewership. Mohan Krishna's entire political party would be without a voice if Prakash went against him.

Another ownership pattern that Seema was able to see was the one led by Ayesha. This was far more conventional. It had the stamp of the ruling National People's Party all over it. They already had TV stations owned by their party members, now there was some new effort to acquire a less-openly identified news channel. It was to be headed by a popular journalist and would appear more independent. The ownership had an odd mix of very prominent financial institutions and obscure directors. There was tax-haven money involved here as well.

The actor, Vikram, a rival of Mohan Krishna's, also had a major stake in a TV channel but he was considered a marginal player in the news media business. He had political ambitions but his run in politics had been indifferent. His real intention in launching a party was the hope that the bigger parties would offer him a deal. While he couldn't win legislative seats, he had nuisance value: he could play the spoiler and split the vote share of bigger parties. Political parties however had chosen to ignore him, leaving him in a limbo.

The smaller news channels like CNEWS were even harder to figure out. Members of these boards tended to be small-time players, people with no other connections to media or politics. It took serious effort to track their antecedents. Seema started off down that path but it proved too vague and so she changed tactics. She focused instead on the office addresses given in the documents filed with government agencies. Many of these addresses were obscure and had no connection with anything else. But having gotten her teams to collate all the addresses, she began to check if any address appeared repeatedly or were even close by, like in the same building. Patterns began to emerge. Several addresses that turned up in the filings of big companies turned up in the filings of small, unknown channels as well. If not the exact address, it was the address next door, or nearby, or on a different floor of the same building. Seema had different teams collate the addresses, but she analysed them herself. She started connecting the smaller channels to the bigger ones. Often, it was a political party that linked them together. And then it was easy to figure out the political party's media influence as a whole.

Seema's breakthrough began with the discovery that Vikram's Daily News had a major investor who seemed to have invested in CNEWS as well. This was an industrialist from Andhra Pradesh. His name was not officially on any of the documents but his office address turned up several times in CNEWS filings. That he had allowed his office address to be used showed that he probably had an interest in the channel. When Seema checked further, the so-called board members were actually the industrialist's personal staff. This was not uncommon. In a deal where the industrialist was funneling his own and Vikram's money into the media, these kinds of obscuring tactic would be standard practice.

Seema then opened up other details of Daily News and CNEWS and compared them. It turned out they had one common director—that director was the NRI investor, Chary, whose name had come up earlier. The next piece of information that turned up was even more useful: the industrialist from Andhra Pradesh was a cousin of Chary's and a business partner in many ventures. Seema's informal enquiries with a journalist friend further confirmed that three of the main journalists at Daily News were also consultants at CNEWS. This was not openly acknowledged and the journalists didn't even visit the CNEWS premises but they drove content from behind the scenes. This was enough to link Vikram with CNEWS. But Seema wanted to make doubly sure.

She accessed Film Chamber data—where film producers were registered and filed their business information—she found that a property from which CNEWS operated was leased by a dummy company owned by Vikram. It was the clinching evidence she needed.

'Vikram and Mohan Krishna have always been rivals,' Seema said. 'Mohan Krishna pulled much farther ahead as an actor and in wealth and influence, but Vikram is always trying to show himself to be an equal. But the question remains: is this rivalry enough to create a major controversy like this? Does Vikram even have the capability?'

They were coasting through traffic at the time. Partha drove.

'Vikram's got his own following,' Partha said, 'but he is no match for Mohan Krishna. But he's just the sort of weasel who'd get involved in a conspiracy. He might even want to be a part of a conspiracy just so he can pull Mohan Krishna down. But my guess is that he's in it for a political quid pro quo. He does this and he gets a political alliance, maybe a party ticket, or even a Rajya Sabha membership.'

'The question is—who's he conspiring with?'

'That's anybody's guess. But if Prakash feels confident that Vikram's CNEWS won't reveal his secret, they must be in it together. Or they've struck a deal. That still doesn't explain CNEWS's proximity to the source at university.'

'Prof. Hussain and Ayesha may have wanted to act through a proxy. But there's nothing in ownership or funding information to indicate they are working together.'

'Why would they trust a wild-card like Vikram if they had an option? They have enough media resources of their own.'

They pulled up close to the TNN office.

'What're we here to talk to Vishwanath about again?' Seema said, getting out.

'We're here to gossip,' Partha said.

'What?'

'You'll see.'

24

They sat in the small, cramped conference room on the first floor. The usual tea with milk and sugar was served in small white cups. A plate of biscuits was left out on the table but only Vishwanath ate from it.

'We wanted to thank you in person for your help in Kadapa,' Seema said.

'And that's why you're here?' Vishwanath said, with a sly smile.

'Yes.'

'You're not here to ask for another favour?'

'No.'

'In that case, you're welcome. It was just business, of course. We've got the lead on Varaprasad's story—we're up in the ratings after that breaking news.'

'I'm glad,' Partha said.

There was a brief silence.

'Why're you really here?' Vishwanath asked.

'We wanted to talk to you about something,' Seema said.

'You want information?'

'It isn't that kind of information—' Seema said.

'Oh, so that's the agenda, is it? You need some information.'

'It's not current information,' Partha said. 'More like background information—something that happened a very long time ago. I doubt we'll find it in any archival material because it was most likely suppressed. But someone like you who's been in the field for as long as you have would know.'

'What kind of background information?'

'You covered Mohan Krishna's hometown just when he became a huge star.'

Vishwanath laughed.

'Why not ask the man himself?' he said. 'You're close to him; you're going to be his media consultant as well!'

Seema laughed.

'Not really,' she said. 'Partha told you what he had to back then.'

'And now you're going to tell me what you need to in order to get information,' Vishwanath said. 'It's always fun talking with you people.'

'Only thing we can offer you is that if anything comes of it we'll share the information with you on a priority basis,' Seema said.

'Like the other day—you scratch my back and I scratch yours?'

'Yes.'

'And this has to do with Mohan Krishna?'

'Him and his family,' Partha said. 'We think there's something hidden there.'

Vishwanath looked sceptical.

'You're going to know what we suspect just by the questions we ask,' Partha said. 'And it's up to you to answer or not. It might just give you a jump on where the story will go next.'

'Why choose us for all this information sharing?'

'You guys at this channel don't have a vested interest in this story,' Seema said. 'This is true both at the level of journalists and owners. I know this because I've checked it out in some detail.'

'Alright. But why waste time with the past at this time? In the midst of all the drama going on in the present, you want to go back to those times?'

'It might be where all this started off. Something forgotten that becomes relevant again.'

Vishwanath sighed.

'Isn't that always the case?' he said. 'You go about your life assuming something's over until it resurfaces years later.'

*

'It's my guess—and that's all it is,' Partha said, 'that there was a rumour about Mohan Krishna back then, something that people whispered about but it never became a news story.'

'There are lots of such rumours,' Vishwanath said. 'There tend to be about all public figures.'

'But something more than just an affair with another star or a land grab—something more troubling.'

'Like the casting couch, you mean?'

'I suppose it could be. I don't know. But in this industry, I don't think Mohan Krishna ever felt threatened by a casting couch story. He could have dismissed them out of hand or suppressed them.'

Vishwanath nodded. He stroked his stubble and seemed to be concentrating genuinely.

'At his peak nobody would have even dared accuse him,' he said. 'He could destroy careers. Even outside the industry he was very powerful.'

'Yes, I've heard there were stories about his family committing atrocities, grabbing lands, and even torturing people.'

'Was Prof. Ahmad Hussain one such victim?' Seema said.

It took a moment for the question to register. Vishwanath looked surprised.

'I'm impressed,' he said, 'I didn't think you'd be able to dig that up.'

'We stumbled upon it. So was Prof. Hussain a victim?'

'Yes.'

'It's a shocking incident,' Partha said. 'But it's not something that will trouble Mohan Krishna today. And it's nothing

Prof. Hussain can back up with evidence for sure. I figure the story we're looking for is something that can damage him today. Something perhaps more easily suppressed in those days but damaging to him and the entire family today.'

Vishwanath grimaced and shook his head.

'Nothing comes to mind as such,' he said. 'The usual rumours you associate with actors. His appetite for sex was talked about a lot. People said he'd badgered every woman he had any influence over into sleeping with him. It was said he'd go to his native place and insist on very young women and adolescents being sent to him. Rumours like that were all over but I doubt there's anything that'll come out about those stories now.'

Partha had been listening intently to this.

'They might be of interest,' he said.

'Really?' Vishwanath said. 'They're virtually gossip.'

'Even then ...'

Vishwanath was growing restless. But Partha was focused and unhurried.

'How about the 1980s?' Partha said. 'Something that was rumoured about him then?'

'I don't know if it was the early-or-mid 1980s but there was a rumour that he had an affair with a woman from his hometown, a student. It wouldn't have been unusual as such but it happened to be someone from his own community. She was the daughter of a well-respected doctor. She was a student in Madras at the time, and came into contact with Mohan Krishna somehow.'

Vishwanath paused to take a sip of his tea.

'When she died suddenly,' he said, 'there was all kinds of speculation going around.'

'She died?' Seema said.

'Road accident apparently.'

'Why don't you tell us the whole story?' Partha said.

'Well, there isn't much that's known for sure,' Vishwanath said. 'What you have to understand is that Mohan Krishna was a rich, successful star by then but a big part of his wealth and clout at the time came from marrying up, so to speak. You know he'd married the daughter of a local MLA, who belonged to the same community. His father-in-law had a lot of money and he was one of the reasons Mohan Krishna was politically influential in the region. The community support was a major source of strength for him. Mohan Krishna couldn't afford to alienate them. He did what he wanted to behind the scenes, but had to take great care to appear humble and one with his community in public.'

'I get that.'

'I think everyone accepted that he would fool around but Mohan Krishna couldn't indulge in adventurism like a second marriage. His father-in-law and the community wouldn't allow it.'

'And he felt pressured to marry this girl?'

'The rumour was that he did. Apparently the girl's father, though only a local doctor, was influential in the region because he was also a social worker. He treated poor people for free, lived simply. He was considered a saint of sorts by the local people. As he belonged to the same community as Mohan Krishna, this scandal could have turned his community supporters against him.'

'So it was serious trouble for him.'

'It was. I think the girl was star-struck and much younger. In any case, when he realised the girl was in love and it wasn't just a one night stand, he became worried. He was apparently trying to get her married off to someone else but she wasn't willing to be shrugged off like that. She must have realised by then that she'd been deceived.'

'So his personal life would have been a mess, his goodwill within his community would have collapsed, and he would have had political problems?'

'The stakes were huge for him.'

'So how did she die?' Seema asked.

'As I said, in a road accident.'

'Seriously?'

'Yes.'

'That was convenient for Mohan Krishna.'

'It was odd. If I remember correctly she was in an auto rickshaw and it was hit by an Ambassador car. It was on a highway on the outskirts of the city. The car and the driver didn't have anything to do with Mohan Krishna. So that was that. Even the girl's father didn't follow up on the rumours—in those days nobody wanted a scandal.'

'But still … doesn't sound like anything Mohan Krishna should be too concerned about now,' Seema said.

'Actually, come to think of it, there might be,' Vishwanath said, more alert now 'And the real story might be here. Again, these are rumours entirely, of course. But this was the time Prakash started becoming indispensable to Mohan Krishna.'

'This is getting interesting,' Partha said.

'It was said,' Vishwanath continued, 'that the story never really got out because of Prakash. He persuaded her to keep things under wraps. He's supposed to have promised her that Mohan Krishna would marry her but she'd have to wait for a more conducive time. That Mohan Krishna couldn't afford the scandal or the political backlash just then but would go through with it at the right time. Prakash won her trust so completely that she would seek him out whenever she felt insecure. She trusted him entirely.'

'That's why he became Mohan Krishna's right-hand man?' Seema said.

'So the rumour goes. From this time on Prakash's rise was meteoric. Those who know how ruthless he is say that he got the girl killed. There are three kinds of speculation about this thing. One, that Prakash proved so loyal that Mohan Krishna trusted him with everything important after that. Two, that Prakash had something to hold over Mohan Krishna and that's why he held absolute power over him. Three, it's a mixture of both—loyalty and the unspoken secret hanging over Mohan Krishna's head.'

'I'd say the last sounds most likely,' Partha said.

'I think so too,' Vishwanath said. 'But there's no way to be sure about it.'

'It makes sense though,' Partha said. 'Mohan Krishna is not the sort to keep Prakash around for long if he was defenceless against him. Why should he keep a potential blackmailer around and even make him party to all his business plans? Prakash must have kept Mohan Krishna from turning on him by holding onto some kind of proof that would come out if he was harmed. But he could have also convinced Mohan Krishna that it was in their mutual benefit to cooperate. After all, Prakash couldn't have risen as much as he did without hitching his wagon to Mohan Krishna's. And Mohan Krishna benefited hugely from Prakash—financially and in dominating the industry. Over time, Mohan Krishna must have come to believe that whatever Prakash held against him has become less and less important. That would have allowed him to go about his life without any serious concerns.'

Vishwanath became even more animated now.

'The story was that Prakash had the girl's accusations in writing,' Vishwanath said. 'The more fanciful story goes that she had recorded statements on tape and Prakash preserved them, first on cassettes and then on CDs.'

'You think such material really exists?' Partha asked.

'Vikram, the actor, once claimed once that in a drunken moment Prakash admitted there was,' Vishwanath said.

Partha's eyes widened.

'Yes, it's true,' Vishwanath continued. 'He actually said that in an interview to a colleague of mine but Mohan Krishna made a call to the editor at the time and the story wasn't published.'

'And the story went away?' Partha asked.

'It disappeared,' Vishwanath said. 'This rumour itself was years old at the time, and I don't know how Vikram knew about it. It was the right editorial decision because Prakash would have just denied it back then. For Prakash it would have been killing the golden goose.' Vishwanath's tone had taken on a hurried quality. 'But maybe his equation with Mohan Krishna has changed now!'

'Maybe it has!' Seema said. 'Think about it: any material from that time would be most damaging now. Priya's suicide puts them in a context that could be toxic for Mohan Krishna. The headlines will read: "Like father, like son". Even if it is decades old, the story would become relevant again.'

'Even today it would be a serious blow to his clout within his community,' Partha said. 'His political career would be over before it started.'

Vishwanath was downright excited now. 'I need to get some of my people on this background story,' he said.

Partha nodded.

'You're not going to try and dissuade me?' Vishwanath asked.

'Would it help?' Partha asked.

'No. This information is fair game.'

'Go for it.'

*

The moment they were in the car, Seema stopped him.

'You handed him that story,' she said.

'Couldn't be helped,' Partha said.

'It could have,' Seema said. 'You could have cornered Mr Ramakrishna and gotten this information from him.'

'He wouldn't have told us. He's too much of a loyalist.'

'In these extreme circumstances he would have.'

'Well, bad luck then.'

'Bad luck?'

Partha looked at her and shrugged.

'There's something else I want to learn from Ramakrishna,' he said. 'I didn't want to ask that of Vishwanath. I think it might well be the most important angle of all this. Something we've all been missing.'

Seema shook her head impatiently.

'But you don't mind this information being out there?' Seema asked.

'No,' Partha said. 'Do you?'

'No. I hope Mohan Krishna burns in hell. But was it the smart move to do it right now?'

'I don't mind Vishwanath playing that angle up. If you're indifferent to Mohan Krishna's secret being protected it has one positive fallout.'

'What positive fallout?'

'With the information out there, Prakash's hold over Mohan Krishna is broken, and with that Anil's troubles could be at an end.'

'I guess.... Well, tell me this then: what's the information you want from Ramakrishna?'

'I'm just taking a shot in the dark.'

*

Seema drove while Partha called Mr Ramakrishna. He answered on the first ring itself.

'When are you coming here to meet Sir?' he said.

'Soon,' Partha said. 'I'm trying to tie up some important loose ends first.'

'You've not been keeping me informed and it seems you're not forthcoming with Malvika either!'

Ramakrishna's tone was accusatory.

'You know how I work,' Partha said. 'I don't report like an employee; I get results.'

'What results? You've found nothing that clears Anil's name! And now other things are going out of control. You don't seem to understand how bad things are.'

'From where I stand, things are moving in the right direction.'

'How can it be the right direction when the cellphone and laptop have fallen into others' hands? We should have had them in ours. Why didn't you keep them?'

'A man died in the process—that was one good reason not to keep them. The other reason was that if we kept the laptop we would not have been able to use any of it as evidence, even in support of our cause. We believe that the contents of the laptop would help Anil so we didn't want to compromise it in any way.'

'But Sir is in trouble now. He's going to have to give control of his empire to that fellow, Prakash.'

'That's got nothing to do with me. It's for the family to deal with. If I can help out Anil, I will.'

'They're not two separate things! You protect the whole family!'

Partha was silent. Mr Ramakrishna let out a snort of exasperation.

'Come and meet Sir immediately!' he repeated.

'I will. Soon.'

It was Mr Ramakrishna's turn to be silent.

'Fine. So why did you call me?' he said after a moment.

'I'm trying to figure out how this media game is playing out. I think you might be able to help.'

'Our rivals are ganging up, the government is not helping us—that's what's happening. What's to tell—it's all evident!'

'You know that a consortium led by Ayesha, Prof. Hussain's daughter, has consolidated control over a significant section of the media?'

'She's Prof. Hussain's daughter?'

'You didn't know that?'

'No. We'd heard about here; that she had close connections with the ruling party at the State and Centre. We knew she was buying control on their behalf before the elections.'

'How is it that you didn't know she was Prof. Hussain's daughter? As a political party you should have done a background check of your rivals.'

'We thought she was a player in the media, no more than that,' Mr Ramakrishna said defensively.

'If you'd checked at all you'd have seen there was an important link,' Partha said in an impatient tone. 'Especially when Prof. Hussain has a history with Mohan Krishna going back decades? Mohan Krishna's family tried to kill him at one point.'

Ramakrishna let out a small gasp.

'You think that's what's going on here?' he said. 'Are they behind everything that's happening?'

'They may be.'

'So it's them and the ruling party!'

'I thought you'd be aware of Ayesha's parentage.'

'She was just a proxy for the NPP! We didn't need to dig up much more about her.'

Partha spoke in a grave tone of voice.

'Have you been following up on Prof. Hussain through the years?' he asked. 'He is a known victim of Mohan Krishna's, and so a likely enemy.'

'We kept track of him a little bit but he could never do anything more than write an article or two!' Mr Ramakrishna said. 'In recent times he's been writing a little more so we did watch out for him but he didn't do anything particularly threatening, especially since we started planning the party launch.'

'Anybody else from that time who could be a threat?'

'Back in the 1970s and 80s? I don't immediately know. Why do you ask about that time?'

'There is definitely a connection to Left groups. We've seen that with the student groups. Even the man killed in Kadapa the other day belonged to a radical Left group. But this was a man who took orders. He did not act on his own.'

'It was all so long ago.'

'I'd like you to recollect.'

'There were so many of these young activist sorts—it's hard to remember.'

'Anybody in significant positions right now—journalist, academic, politician? Someone still active and around?'

Ramakrishna was silent.

'There was another student activist. Fellow came all the way from Delhi. Apparently sent by the Communist Party high command there. I can't recollect his name—yes, Ramdas, I think.'

'Prof. Ramdas?'

'Yes, I think he's at the university now.'

'You're sure about this?'

'Yes, yes. He was picked up by the police in the first week after he arrived. He was a hardcore communist—brainwashed and a hardliner. He was sent to direct the activities of some violent, radical group out here. But he got caught almost immediately after his arrival. Funnily, he cracked in front of the police the easiest. They say he started talking after being slapped once or twice and revealed the names of several activists. But he was a cunning chap. The police later complained to us that he didn't reveal the names of the members of the radical group. He just gave up genuine student activists like Hussain. His party in Delhi worked through political circles to get him out of police hands. But it was through his information that we were able to catch Hussain and others. The damned superintendent of police was hostile to us and wouldn't act on Hussain. Some local policemen were good though: they gave us the information.'

Partha took a deep breath. Everything fell into place. They had allowed themselves to be played. He'd allowed a prejudice, a blindspot, to mislead him terribly.

25

'They're going to try to kill Varaprasad!' Partha said to Seema. 'We've got to get to the hospital!'

Partha then dialled Harish's number and waited impatiently for him to pick-up even as he gave directions to Seema. Harish's phone kept ringing but there was no answer. In times like these, when they were under pressure, Harish generally made sure he was reachable unless there was something pressing. Partha hung up. They drew up to a traffic light and when the light turned green, took the right turn.

'The police are guarding him,' Seema said.

'Student union members and faculty will have access,' Partha said.

'Friends or faculty could kill him? Are you serious?'

'Yes, I'm serious.'

Partha pulled up the University Campus Police Station inspector's number they'd been given on the night of the incidents on campus. The inspector had asked Partha to call if he recollected anything of use or if anything else occurred. He dialled and waited.

'There'll be a hue and cry if people aren't allowed to meet him,' Seema said. 'The media would go ballistic accusing the police of a cover-up.'

'The doctors can say he's still critical,' Partha said.

'And they'll do that on your say-so?'

'They'll do it if the police ask them.'

The inspector picked up. Partha rattled off his concerns for Varaprasad's safety as quickly as possible. The inspector, who was at a crime scene in the vicinity of the hospital, said he'd check about the security arrangements but responded coldly to the idea of blocking access to Varaprasad.

'You'll deal with the controversy it causes?' he asked.

'Let them just enforce visiting hours rules strictly,' Partha said. 'When we get there I can explain in more detail.'

'Family and friends are not allowed into the room except during visiting hours but they do hang around in these hospitals,' the inspector said. 'It's hard to move them out without creating a problem. And visiting hours start off informally from after 4 p.m. even though they officially start only at 6 p.m.'

'I understand, sir,' Partha said. 'But his life's in danger and I've warned you.'

The inspector just clucked his tongue irritably.

'Fine,' he said. 'But only for a few hours.'

Partha was hoping for some such response: it was a high-profile case and the inspector wouldn't want to be accused of complacency if anything happened to Varaprasad.

'Thank you,' Partha said.

'But you better reach the hospital quickly and give me an explanation,' the inspector said.

'We're on our way right now.'

Seema drove as fast as she could through the traffic. Partha tried Harish again but to no avail.

'You want to tell me why you're acting crazy?' Seema said. 'Just what did Ramakrishna tell you?'

'He confirmed a hunch,' Partha said.

'What hunch?'

'That the man behind everything that's happening at the university is Prof. Ramdas!'

'What?' Seema said, her head snapping in Partha's direction. 'What are you talking about?'

'I can't get into the details now,' Partha said, trying to call Harish again, 'but Ramakrishna confirms that Prof. Ramdas was in Srikakulam in the 1980s.'

'He didn't mention that when he told us about Prof. Hussain!' Seema said.

'He belonged to a ruthless and ultra-radical group. He was caught and gave up information about a lot of student activists. He was responsible for Hussain's capture by Mohan Krishna's people.'

'Oh my God!'

Partha looked restlessly at the traffic in front. Seema accelerated, darting onto the wrong side for a moment to overtake the car in front.

'He sent Shiva to deal with Varaprasad in Kadapa,' Partha said. 'He's got thugs on campus and credibility amongst students—if he uses them to get to Varaprasad, that's the end of it.'

Traffic slowed down around a Metro construction bottleneck. Partha rubbed his chin nervously and glared through the windscreen. Seema showed no emotion. She waited with grim determination for the traffic to move and looked out for opportunities to forge ahead.

Partha's phone rang sharply. Harish's name gleamed on the phone screen. Partha didn't allow him to speak.

'We're on the way to the hospital,' he said. 'Varaprasad is in danger. I need you to get clarity on Satya's guys ASAP.'

'That was what I was on when you called,' Harish said. 'We tracked down a guy. Had to chase him around first. He used to work for Satya.'

'Listen, Harish, I think they were working for Vikram or some proxy of his. See if you can get confirmation of this.'

'You're sure about this?'

'It's a damned good chance.'

'And see if they've seen or heard of Prof. Ramdas.'

'Prof. Ramdas? What the hell are you talking about?'

'Can't explain now but it's very important. Press them on this.'

'Okay.'

*

They neared the hospital. As soon as they entered the compound, Partha jumped out and headed for the hospital building while Seema went in search of the first parking spot she could find. From a distance, Partha made out a familiar face. It was Raghav—whom he recognised immediately—and with him were two other students. The student's union office-bearers were here; did that imply the radical group was also there? Partha made directly for the hospital entrance. The portico was crowded with people. The lone guard on duty tried to move people along to keep the way clear but he seemed to have accepted that the students were there to stay.

The students moved to block Partha's path. A constable was sitting nearby but he was on his phone. Partha didn't have the patience for this. He pushed Raghav out of the way. Raghav reeled but the other students closed up the gap. The constable came rushing up.

'What's going on?' he demanded.

'I'm trying to get into a government hospital,' Partha said, 'and these people are in my way.'

Partha's look stayed on Raghav. He barely acknowledged the presence of the constable.

'You know what happened the other day,' Partha said to Raghav. 'Don't make me do it again.'

Raghav kept his gaze steady but a flicker of hesitation showed in his eyes.

'What's the problem here?' the constable asked.

Partha's gaze didn't shift from Raghav.

'You won't be able to withstand the kind of beating the others got,' Partha said. 'And don't think I won't give it to you if you get in the way.'

Seema came up to the portico just then.

'Is CI Sir here yet?' she said to the constable. 'We're here to see him.'

The constable's expression eased a bit.

'He'll be reaching in a few minutes,' he said. 'He mentioned someone was expected.'

'I know your instructions were to keep everyone including students under control and away from Varaprasad,' Seema said.

'Yes…'

'Are these the only students here?' Seema asked gesturing in the direction of Raghav and the others.

'These boys said they were friends of his and they've been here since the morning,' the constable said. 'Even the family said they were friends so we let them stay. They say they want to help protect Varaprasad.'

'Which floor is he on?'

'Second floor, madam. End of the corridor on the right.'

The constable looked past them to the building entrance. Another constable had come to the hospital entrance. He looked tired and bored.

'Why're you out here?' the constable in the portico said. 'Why aren't you at the room?'

'They've taken him for tests,' the second constable said. 'He's not in the room.'

'What tests?' Raghav said. 'The doctors didn't mention anything when they came on rounds.'

The second constable shrugged.

'Some nurse came and said they'd ordered an ultrasound,' he said. He turned to the constable in the portico. 'You go inside now. I'll take this post.'

'Who's with Varaprasad now?' Partha asked.

The second constable gave Partha a curious look.

'They're here to see inspector sir,' the constable in the portico said. 'He told us they would be coming.'

The second constable nodded. 'One of them is with Varaprasad,' he said indicating to Raghav and the other students. 'He said he'd go along to help because the ward boys were not available.'

Raghav looked surprised.

'One of us?' he said. 'Your people wouldn't let us wait near the room so we're waiting out here. We're the only ones here.'

'He said he was one of you,' the second constable said, looking perplexed. 'Said he would go along so it wasn't a strain on Uncle and Aunty. Varaprasad's parents didn't say anything.'

'They know only me and Vikranth!' Raghav said angrily.

'I told you not to allow anyone near him!' the constable in the portico shouted.

'You said no visitors,' the second constable said defensively. 'It was a nurse who came and said there was a test.'

Partha and Seema rushed inside.

'Take us to the test area!' Partha said as he brushed past the second constable.

The second constable looked unsure for a moment.

'Go with them!' the constable in the portico said. 'I'll call the inspector!'

'Second floor!' the second constable called out.

Raghav, skinny and fast, bolted past the constable in the portico and through the entrance. He was gone before the constable could react. But his friends weren't as fast. The constable in the portico merely raised his hands sideways and grabbed them. He gave them a gentle push back and pointed a finger at them. They were done: they weren't getting in. Raghav ran after Partha and the others. They rushed up two flights and down the corridor to the right of the stairwell.

'Radiology!' the second constable shouted.

They ran down the corridor to the end. The radiology department had a deserted look about it. Two nurses sat chatting at a desk in the corridor. They looked a little startled when a bunch of people ran up.

'Has the boy's ultrasound started?' the second constable asked a nurse sitting at a desk.

'What ultrasound?' the nurse behind the desk said irritably. 'There's nobody in there right now.'

'Nobody's come here?' Partha asked.

The nurse shook her head.

'Maybe they took him back to the room?' the second constable said hopefully. The worry was beginning to tell on his tone: he'd abandoned his position and now Varaprasad's location was unknown.

Partha turned around and scanned the hospital corridors. It wasn't encouraging. This was a massive quadrangular design with interconnected corridors going all around. Each corridor had too many rooms to allow for a quick check.

'Where's his room?' Partha asked.

Raghav pointed to a corridor at a distance—past the lifts.

'End of that corridor,' he said. 'Room 466.'

'I'll go check the room and call you,' Seema said, starting off.

Partha turned to the constable.

'Was Varaprasad shifted onto a wheelchair?' he asked.

'No, they had to take him on a stretcher,' the constable said. 'He's not able to sit up.'

'Stretcher with wheels?'

The constable nodded.

'If you have to take a patient to another floor is the lift the only way or is there a ramp?' Partha asked the nurse.

'Lift,' the nurse said. She pointed to one at the far end of the corridor. 'That one and there's another on the other side of the building.'

'When they left the room, which direction did they go?' Partha asked the constable.

'I'm not sure,' the constable said, trying to concentrate. 'I can't remember.'

At the lifts, there was a security guard tasked with keeping people from going towards the wards before visiting hours. The constable asked the security guard if a man on a gurney had been wheeled into either of the lifts in the past few minutes. The guard shook his head.

'I think I saw a stretcher go that way,' the guard said, pointing to a corridor across the quadrangle, on the other side of the building. 'But I'm not sure.'

Partha looked across at the long corridor with several doors. Part of the corridor was open and the end part was walled-off. At the end of each corridor was a small lobby that joined it with a perpendicular corridor. There were four large corridors on the floor, each forming one side of the quadrangle, each with a large number of rooms for them to search. They weren't going to find Varaprasad quickly if he was wheeled into a room. And if the aim was to harm Varaprasad, they could be doing it right now.

Partha's phone rang.

'He's not in his room,' Seema said. 'But his father says his mother went along with him.'

*

He hadn't counted on the mother being so insistent. An illiterate woman from a small town should have taken the nurse at face value. The nurse had spoken with the matter-of-fact authority of a hospital worker. The father, though nervous, deferred to her. The mother was unfazed. Even when the man told her he'd go along to help and that only one attendant was allowed in the radiology department, she insisted on going along. She said she would leave her son's side just before the test commenced, and even then, only if the doctor ordered her out. Through this argument, Varaprasad lay exhausted after the exertion of shifting him from the bed onto the gurney. He was silent and his eyes were shut.

The man was not happy. The corridors were never empty and they would soon be thronging with people. As they wheeled the gurney slowly through the corridor, he was all too aware that time was running out. He could not ask Varaprasad any questions without running the danger of his mother raising an alarm. He would have to wheel Varaprasad into one of the rooms. There he could silence the mother as well if needed. He felt the syringe stick out of his pocket. He lowered his hand and pushed it inside. The nurse could give Varaprasad the injection saying she was prepping him for the test. The mother was unlikely to make a fuss about that.

The man pushed the gurney with one hand. He raised his other hand to his eyebrow as was his habit, almost a nervous twitch. He touched the scar that ran up from the eyebrow through the forehead. He lowered the hand to the stretcher frame and pushed. As they approached the end of the corridor, they were running out of options.

'Should we check this room, sister?' he called out to the 'nurse' who was guiding the gurney up front. His tone was as deferential as he could muster.

They stopped. The mother looked at the man questioningly.

'We may have to wait a few minutes if someone else is inside,' the nurse said to the mother.

'They have to prepare him for the test also,' the man added.

The 'nurse' opened the door. Several faces turned in her direction: two patients on beds and their attendants. She shut the door matter-of-factly. She moved on to the next. She tried to turn the knob but it was locked. She turned back and shook her head. The man nodded in the direction of the end of the corridor.

The area at the end of the corridor looked like a disused nurse's station. The space was walled off and access to the adjoining corridor was also boarded up. It was a cramped space, just about enough to fit two hospital beds. A few boxes were stacked there. Past the nurse's station was an exit leading to a staircase. As they drew closer and caught a better look at the space the man's face eased up. He almost smiled: it was ideal. Now he'd have to get rid of the mother.

'Why're we waiting here?' the mother asked, looking around at the bleak nurse's station. 'Where will they do the test?'

'It's the third room in this corridor, Aunty,' the nurse said, pointing back into the corridor. 'But it's occupied right now and there's no other waiting space. We have to prepare him here only now.'

The nurse turned to the man.

'He's very weak,' she told him. 'You have to help him get his shirt off and to put the lotion on. Then he can start drinking water.'

'Drinking water?' the mother asked.

'Yes, you have to drink a lot of water for this test,' the nurse said. And then she slapped her palm against her forehead dramatically. 'I forgot the water bottle! I'm telling you about drinking water like you should know and I myself forgot! Aunty, it's better we give him safe water. Can you bring a water bottle from your room?'

The man looked at the 'nurse' with awe. She was really into the role now. He was genuinely impressed.

The mother looked uncertain. Then she looked at the man.

'Aunty, I can't change his dress by myself,' the nurse said. 'I need his friend's help. And you can't help me as well as he can. The room is not so far away, please bring a bottle of water.

Otherwise, we'll have to wait for a long time. They might even allow someone else go in first because he's not ready.'

The man had to strain every nerve in his body not to laugh. Or even to outright applaud. He really liked this girl. The mother hesitated for a moment and nodded. She looked at the man.

'Take care of him,' she said to him. 'I'll be back very quickly.'

The man watched as Varaprasad stirred a little. He was awake but groggy and disoriented. Everything was working out. The man felt the syringe in his pocket.

'Don't worry, Aunty,' the man said. 'I'll take care of him.'

*

It was at that precise moment, when Varaprasad's mother stepped back into the corridor, walking fast, looking down at the floor that Raghav spotted her.

'Aunty!' he shouted out loud, unable to control himself, giving in to a combination of excitement and relief.

The lady looked up, surprised. She continued to walk towards Raghav; Raghav rushed down the corridor. Raghav's voice had carried clearly enough to cut through the noise of the hospital corridor. Partha and the constable, who were questioning a ward boy on the other side of the hall heard the shout and rushed down the direction of the corridor as well.

The 'nurse' peeked out from the nurse's station. The man too took a step outside the nurses' station and looked down the corridor. The sight of men rushing down the corridor took him by surprise. And then he recognised Partha at a distance in the background. Instinct took over. The man grabbed the syringe out of his pocket and pulled off the protective cover.

Behind him, the 'nurse' let out a little shriek. She turned and ran, through the exit leading to the stairs. Varaprasad's mother turned around, completely stunned.

'Syringe!' Partha shouted to no one in particular. But it rang out loud and clear.

The man turned to the prone and helpless Varaprasad. He didn't have time to look for a vein to inject it into. He grabbed Varaprasad's leg. He palmed the syringe with his thumb on the plunger and raised it like a knife.

The man's arm had begun to swing downward when Raghav slammed into him. The man staggered back a few steps. Raghav tried to grab his arm but the man managed to shake him away. Raghav reached for the arm with the syringe and tried to hold onto it. Raghav was skinny and slight; the other man was much stronger. But the adrenaline coursing through Raghav's veins now gave him the strength and focus to hold on. The man pushed Raghav away, making him stumble but Raghav held on to the arm. The man looked up and saw Partha and the constable running up. He made an instant decision. He dropped the syringe and thrust his knee into Raghav's side. Raghav shouted out and let go—he went sprawling. The man's hand was free now; he ran for the exit. He shot through it and down the stairs. The constable ran after him.

Partha stopped near Varaprasad and began to examine if he was harmed. Raghav struggled to his feet and made to run towards the stairs.

'Stay here,' Partha said, in a loud but calm voice.

Raghav looked at Partha for a moment undecidedly.

'Making sure Varaprasad's safe is more important right now than catching that man,' Partha said. 'He seems alright. Help me get him back to his room.'

Raghav nodded. Varaprasad's mother ran up to Varaprasad and asked if he was okay. Varaprasad seemed to respond more from impulse as he nodded. The lady began to sob. Around the corner Partha saw a sub-inspector and a few constables running up.

Partha stepped away from the gurney and stood clear as the sub-inspector ran up. He was an athletic looking man of moderate height with an air of command about him. A constable stayed with him while another ran into the stairwell. The sub-inspector looked at Partha with a businesslike distrust.

'He's alright,' Partha said, nodding in Varaprasad's direction. 'The man who just ran tried to inject something into him but he was thwarted by this student.' Partha pointed in Raghav's direction. 'The syringe is still there.'

The sub-inspector looked at Raghav and then down at the syringe. He gestured in the direction of the syringe to the constable with him to collect it and moved over to check on Varaprasad. Varaprasad was more alert now but still a little dazed. His mother still sobbed by his side.

'You alright?' the sub-inspector asked, stepping up to Varaprasad.

'Yes,' Varaprasad said, his voice weak.

'We'll get him back to the room immediately,' the sub-inspector said turning to Partha. 'You're to come with us. Inspector sir wants you to wait near the room.'

Partha nodded. He went over to one end of the gurney and began to push. The constable and the Raghav helped it along. The place was more crowded now, as visiting hours had begun. The sub-inspector walked ahead, telling people to clear the way. They wheeled him past the lifts and into the corridor where his room was.

Seema stood outside room 466. But there were other people waiting as well. The sight of them jolted Partha's senses. He almost stopped in his tracks but thought better of it and kept moving forward. Standing behind Seema, a little to the side was Prof. Ramdas along with three students. A visibly anxious and out-of-breath Vikranth also came into view.

*

Prof. Ramdas's look was cool and hard. He momentarily turned to look at Vikranth and then his gaze settled on Partha again. The sub-inspector waved everyone away.

'Varaprasad, I must speak to you immediately,' Prof. Ramdas said.

Varaprasad stared at him but did not respond. He was wheeled into the room by a constable and Varaprasad's father. Only his parents were allowed into the room with him.

'Nobody is going to speak to him,' the sub-inspector said, posturing more aggressively. 'Who're you?'

'I'm Prof. Ramdas from the university. This boy is my student and I must be allowed to speak with him.'

'Somebody tried to harm him just now. My men are after them. Until we have clarity on it, nobody other than his paremts will be allowed to see him.'

Prof. Ramdas raised his hands angrily and let them drop to his side.

'I suppose these are the people who're deciding Varaprasad's security now!' Prof. Ramdas said gesturing towards Partha and Seema.

Prof. Ramdas seemed to have no patience for a pretence of cordiality now. Partha thought it likely that he knew from his sources—perhaps the skinny man who'd gotten away with Priya's phone—that Partha and Harish were on the scene at Kadapa. And that it was his plan that had just been thwarted at the hospital. Prof. Ramdas had no patience left for interference from the likes of them now—he had to get to Varaprasad.

'We have instructions from the CI,' the sub-inspector said.

'Who has received instructions from these people?' Prof. Ramdas said.

The students around Prof. Ramdas made vague noises in assent and dutifully scowled to show their disapproval of Partha and Seema. Despite the circumstances, Partha had to exert himself to hold back a grin. The students moved forward and blocked Partha from the room door. The sub-inspector watched them cautiously but did not react.

'The CI received a tip-off about a threat to Varaprasad's life from them,' the SI said, holding his ground. 'We can't ignore it.'

Prof. Ramdas glanced in the direction of Partha.

'Maybe they organised the threat to his life,' Prof. Ramdas said.

Seema shook her head in disbelief.

'They seem to have helped save him just now,' the sub-inspector said.

'They're good at creating such dramas.'

The sub-inspector gave Prof. Ramdas a weary look.

'Even if that was true,' the sub-inspector said, 'it doesn't worry me right now because they're not going to be given access to the boy. The same goes for you. We can't ignore a tip-off about a possible threat to his life.'

'I'm not asking you to ignore anything,' Prof. Ramdas said forcefully. 'You must protect him, of course. It's your duty. But I'm asking you to appreciate how frightening it is for ordinary people to see the police hold a person incommunicado from his friends and well-wishers at the say-so of a private party.'

'Sir, even if you gave me the tip-off we'd secure him in the same way.'

'Do you know these are people with vested interests? They represent Mohan Krishna's family.'

This was another cue for the students. They tried to look angrier still and nodded solemnly. The SI stepped in the way and made the students step away from Partha. The room door opened and Varaprasad's father stood at the entrance. He looked anxiously around to see what the altercation was about.

'The only people who can make a decision about who is allowed in are the patient himself and his parents,' the sub-inspector said. 'We'll go by their wishes.'

The SI addressed Varaprasad's father.

'I'm telling them I'll only let anyone in if you say so,' he said to them in Telugu.

Varaprasad's mother rushed to the door. She shook her head vigorously. The sub-inspector turned to Prof. Ramdas.

'That's the decision then,' he said.

'The parents are being misled,' Prof. Ramdas said.

'My son will not meet anyone,' the father said in Telugu.

Partha decided to get into the fray.

'So if people disagree with you they're being misled?' he said to Prof. Ramdas.

The sub-inspector looked at Partha suspiciously for a moment but did nothing. Prof. Ramdas gave him a hard look.

'You're smug because you're able to manipulate the system,' he said.

'You're smug because you can manipulate impressionable students,' Partha said.

One of the students began to swear at Partha. Partha ignored him.

'There is no matter of principle here, Professor,' Partha said. 'You want to be able to reach Varaprasad either to intimidate him or to harm him. I doubt you can harm him with all of us around now—your little plan for harming him was just thwarted. But you would still want to intimidate him.'

'How dare you accuse me of such a thing!'

'I dare. Take me to court if you like. Or do you not believe in the Indian judiciary?'

Prof. Ramdas's face was flushed with anger but he recovered control impressively quickly.

'A man trying to suppress his client's role in a young girl's suicide is going to lecture me on motives?' he said.

'I'm not lecturing you; I'm stopping you,' Partha said. 'I'm not going to stand around listening to self-righteous nonsense from the likes of you. A man who gave up the names of dozens of his comrades to the Srikakulam police—and this was in his idealistic youth.' Partha said the last part with deliberate emphasis.

Prof. Ramdas didn't reply and he betrayed no reaction. The students continued to glare at Partha but their fervour seemed a little dampened. They were thrown by this comment and by the confidence with which it was spoken.

'Lies,' Prof. Ramdas said.

'I'm sure your friend Shiva would have also agreed that I'm lying.' Partha looked at the students. 'I'm talking about the radical Leftist who was killed in Kadapa trying to kidnap or kill Varaprasad.' Partha returned his look to Prof. Ramdas. 'You didn't give up radicals' names in Srikakulam but you gave up Prof. Hussain. Perhaps the students should ask him?'

The sub-inspector and the students both looked on with surprise.

'What is this nonsense?' one of the students said, but his tone betrayed an uncertainty.

The glances of the students began to shift in the direction of Prof. Ramdas; he sensed a subtle change in mood. Suddenly, he laughed.

'I was told you were a liar,' he said, 'but I didn't realise you were this proficient.'

'So call my bluff,' Partha said. 'But you can't. Prof. Hussain won't back you. And your confession to the police is still available, I'm told.'

Prof. Ramdas smiled and turned to the students.

'You should take notes,' he said. 'He's giving us a class on how propaganda works. He's stating lies and building on them. It all starts to sound true after a while.'

Partha laughed. 'With a difference,' he said. 'I'm willing to put it to test—we can verify with Prof. Hussain or the police. What test can you offer?'

Prof. Ramdas didn't reply.

'By the way, I don't think your little alliance with Vikram and his CNEWS is going to get much leverage either,' Partha said.

Prof. Ramdas's smile didn't leave his face but it froze. Seema couldn't help but wonder if he was going too far. She resisted the temptation to turn and look at him. Was he trying to get a reaction from Prof. Ramdas? He had succeeded in doing that already, in some measure. She just hoped he wasn't doing it to win an argument.

'Another channel has got the story Prakash is bargaining with,' Partha said. 'So the story's going to run before you can make your deal with Prakash—'

'I don't have to stand here and listen to your rubbish!' Prof. Ramdas said.

'If the family pulls together and covers up its secrets, your one chance to crush Mohan Krishna is gone.'

Prof. Ramdas took a moment to recover and then he smiled.

'You're talking nonsense,' he said. 'The truth is that a young girl was killed because of that family's exploitation and we're working to bring that truth to light. You're trying to prevent that by keeping us from seeing Varaprasad. You've convinced him and his family that his friends and teachers pose some threat to him. And having created that fear you're going to suppress the evidence.'

Partha smiled back at him. This was a good comeback because the motive he was attributing to Partha was entirely believable. Even so, it was a defensive move. Prof. Ramdas was fighting on two fronts now: one, to convince his students that his motives were sound and so, be able to retain his influence over them; two, to try get to Varaprasad and convince him not to speak against him.

'It is our moral obligation,' Prof. Ramdas said, 'to see that this boy doesn't unknowingly become an accomplice in your conspiracy.' He turned to the sub-inspector. 'I demand to be allowed in now!'

Only one of the students with him seemed equally emphatic. The others were far more subdued. The sub-inspector was entirely unmoved and unimpressed. He shook his head.

'We refuse to leave this place without meeting him!' Prof. Ramdas said. 'We object to this conspiracy by the police and these fixers!' Prof. Ramdas turned to Varaprasad's father. 'They're all going to manipulate you people and fix the responsibility for that girl's death on your son! Tell him to come to his senses and meet with me immediately.'

Varaprasad's father's eyes widened. His expression was one of hurt before it acquired a tinge of anger.

'My son has done nothing wrong!' he said.

'Your son got involved in things he doesn't understand!' Prof. Ramdas said. 'And he's done things that are illegal. He isn't some angel—his hands are not clean. You tell him that! And tell him to see sense and let me help him.'

Partha was surprised by Prof. Ramdas's behaviour. He'd expected someone with his presence of mind to deal with this setback with poise, to leave the scene in a dignified manner. It was clear now he wouldn't be allowed one-on-one access to Varaprasad; it was also known that Priya's computer was now with the police and out of Varaprasad's hands. But here Prof. Ramdas was making a scene and drawing attention to himself, acting like he had a lot to lose. Partha had to wonder just what other information Varaprasad had. Why was Prof. Ramdas this desperate to reach him? What was left for him to conceal? Perhaps he hoped all of Varaprasad's material was encrypted—so convincing him to cooperate would mean keeping Ramdas's secrets.

'What's all this?' the sub-inspector asked.

Varaprasad's mother covered her face and began to sob. The strain of the situation was getting to her. Varaprasad's father looked plain frightened and he didn't even try to conceal it. There was a moment of confused silence all around.

'Varaprasad doesn't want to see you.'

The voice was calm and firm—able to command attention even though it was not raised. It was Vikranth. He'd stood by all this while almost unnoticed. Now everyone turned to look at him.

'He understands the implications of everything you just said and more,' Vikranth went on. 'But he won't see you. I've spoken to him. And the answer is no—he will not meet you or ever be influenced by you again.'

Prof. Ramdas's face flushed.

'He's ... a member of the party!' he said.

'Not anymore,' Vikranth said. 'And neither am I. Varaprasad understands that anything he's done while he was a member of the party may come out now. He's willing to face the consequences.'

'You're turning your backs on your friends and on your cause!'

'We're turning our backs on you. And on being used for your agenda.'

'The cause is the only agenda!'

'I'm not going to get into an argument with you,' Vikranth said. 'Varaprasad went on the run because he was caught between people like Mohan Krishna, Prakash, and you. He went on the run because the truth about Priya's death would never come out if he trusted you. The truth will come out now—however ugly it is.'

Prof. Ramdas stared at Vikranth.

'Varaprasad wanted to meet them when I spoke to him this morning,' Vikranth said, nodding in the direction of Partha and Seema. 'He says Partha saved his life. They're the only ones he'll meet.'

Prof. Ramdas's face darkened with disbelief and stifled rage, first at Vikranth and then at Partha. He suddenly shoved away the students standing in front of him and walked away towards the staircase.

26

A look of confusion fell upon the students who had accompanied Prof. Ramdas. They seemed hostile to Vikranth as long as Prof. Ramdas was present but now they were at a loss about what to do. The attending doctor came up just then and went into Varaprasad's room. On the way in, he told them not to crowd around the room. Varaprasad's parents and the sub-inspector followed the doctor inside. A few minutes later, Varaprasad's father came out and asked Vikranth to come in. It appeared they trusted him intimately. The others gathered outside moved away. The three other students hung around undecidedly for a few moments and then dispersed. Partha and Seema found a couple of chairs in a corner nearby and sat down.

'How long have you suspected Prof. Ramdas?' Seema asked when they'd settled down.

Partha shrugged. 'I guess I never closed off the possibility that he was involved in some way,' he said. 'But after my initial anger with Prof. Hussain wore off, I felt he would not have done things in this messy way—as I said, it was a hunch.'

Seema nodded.

'Did it strike you as odd that Prof. Ramdas took a call on how to deal with me and the students all by himself?' Partha asked.

Seema frowned. 'It didn't at the time,' she said.

'Because you thought he had that kind of goodwill with the students?' Partha asked.

'Yeah.'

'That's what I thought too.'

'So he kept the fact that he was in Srikakulam from us to deflect blame unto Prof. Hussain.'

Partha nooded. 'It's a minor echo of what happened back then,' Partha said. 'Ramdas gave up information about Prof. Hussain so that he and his violent fringe group could be protected.'

'Why did you think Ramakrishna might know something?'

'I called Ramakrishna because this connection between Mohan Krishna and the Leftists bothered me all through,' Partha said. 'I thought it probably had origins in the 1980s. Why were these radicals in the university at all, going so far as putting one of their most ruthless killers in the field?'

'From the outside it just looked like university students reacting emotionally to Priya's death,' Seema said.

'Some of them must have been,' Partha said. 'I fully expected some student protests, but on the whole, whether it was Vikranth or anyone else, they only talked about their ideology or some general sense of injustice.'

'And not about Priya herself?' Seema said.

'I didn't meet a single person who spoke about her. Then there was the involvement of radical groups, which made the possibility of a purely emotional outburst unlikely. And after my run-in with Shiva it was clear that the students weren't acting independently. That convinced me that the driving force of this university unrest wasn't Priya's death in itself.'

'Right.'

'If anyone, I thought Varaprasad might be acting from a personal angle and not an ideological one,' Partha went on. 'The others who have every reason to be personally vengeful—her parents—had gone into quiet grieving. That made me think the key to the whole thing was in the connection between the campus and the radical groups. When Shiva died that lead just got cut off.'

'So Varaprasad was the one person left who probably knew the connection between the university and rest of this mess.

That's why you thought he was in immediate danger when the Ramdas connection fell in place?'

'Exactly,' Partha said. 'Temporarily, my focus shifted to what Prakash might do but I knew that what Varaprasad might reveal if he pulled through was key. And he's in delicate health—having access to him briefly is enough to harm him.' Partha paused. 'See, the media wars, the intra-family wars, and the political wars were all very real but to me the picture just didn't feel complete. Nothing warranted this level of activity in the university—it was always the key. '

Seema looked in the direction of Varaprasad's room. Varaprasad's father emerged from it briefly, speaking on the phone, and then went back inside. Seema turned to look at Partha again. A look of curiosity came over her face.

'Why were you angry with Prof. Hussain?' she asked.

'What?' Partha asked with surprise.

'In the car you said you were able to see more clearly when your anger with him wore off.'

'I did think he sent me into a trap,' Partha said defensively. But there was a hint of sheepishness as well. He let out a small laugh. 'He knows how to push my buttons—he always questions my integrity and motives.'

'And he thought you were no good for his daughter,' Seema said with a smile.

'And that,' Partha said with a weary grin. 'The daughter who can do no wrong though she pretty much does what I do.'

'So you realised these are not relevant factors in this case?'

Partha nodded. 'When I looked back with some perspective, I just couldn't see Prof. Hussain at the heart of something like this,' he said. 'I couldn't see him be this cynical. Initially, I thought I was unable to be objective about Prof. Hussain and suppressed the possibility that he was vengeful and calculating. But then, if you look at how it all panned out, how Prof. Hussain put me in touch with someone and those very people turned on me, and how Prof. Hussain dropped out of sight—it was all very crude and unsubtle. Very unlike Prof. Hussain.'

'It didn't help that we were spoon-fed the connection between the Leftist movements, Prof. Hussain, and Mohan Krishna,' Seema said. 'We should have been wary.'

'It was dropped right into our laps. And we just went along with it. Later, I wondered why Prof. Ramdas would give up his comrade and colleague so easily. He could have just kept quiet and let us find out in time. He gave us information we'd have dug up anyway; but he fed us information in the form he wanted, editing out his own involvement, and threw us off-scent.'

'He played it just right.'

'He did. Later, even when I recollected Vikranth's conversation with Shiva. I saw just how firm a grip Shiva had on him. Vikranth was terrified. That was in strong contrast to Prof. Ramdas's seemingly affectionate and hands-off relationship with the students. So I had no reason to tie the two together.'

'Even I got caught up in the story he gave us. I spent the bulk of my time tracking Ayesha's moves because I was sure it involved Prof. Hussain's.'

'We all took the bait,' Partha said with a slight shake of his head. 'Now I think Prof. Hussain left town upon realising that Prof. Ramdas was taking this whole Mohan Krishna matter into his own hands. My involvement in it must have pressurised him further. He wanted to stay out of it and perhaps he didn't want to expose Ayesha to it all. She was making quiet media moves for the NPP and wouldn't have wanted to get dragged in.'

Seema squinted her eyes thinking something through. 'So those two men hired to follow you were killed because it would somehow lead back Prof. Ramdas's direct involvement?' she said.

'Perhaps,' Partha said thoughtfully. 'But I think it more likely it'll lead back to Vikram.'

Seema raised her eyebrows. 'How do you figure that?' she asked.

'I can't know for sure…' Partha said. 'But from the very beginning the murders baffled me. If these men following me were radicals they could have just left town and gone underground. These were just hired hands, blunderers at that—good for light surveillance but no more. I don't believe someone as careful as Prof. Ramdas would have been directly in contact with them. Shiva was in touch with them—he even knew I'd thrashed one of them. So could Shiva have killed them because they were in touch with him? Possible, but unlikely. A man who operates in the field directly and is a known criminal and fugitive need not kill to conceal his identity. It's more likely that these men were hired by their ally, Vikram, and they couldn't allow that link to come out.'

'It was that important to keep that link secret?' Seema asked.

'Think about it,' Partha said. 'If Harish got to those men we'd have worked our way back to Shiva very quickly and it would have also brought Vikram into the spotlight. Plus, establishing the connection with CNEWS would have handed us a big win in the perception game if we made it all about the conspiracy driving the news story. Most of Mohan Krishna's problems would have ended with that. It would have also allowed us to turn the heat on those students, Sirisha and Biren, and shine a light on them and their credibility as well. In that sense, you had to cut off that link if you didn't want it to lead back to the university and eventually to Prof. Ramdas.'

'Vikram and CNEWS were their main weapons in this war,' Seema agreed.

'Yeah,' Partha said. 'So, the way I figure it: Vikram hired the men who were following me. The guy following me probably reported to Satya that I knew their identities; Satya tipped off his employer or Shiva directly. Prof. Ramdas and Shiva in turn told the students to pick a fight with me and film it. The students took matters into their own hands, which forced Shiva's intervention. Prof. Ramdas diffused the situation because you were talking about prosecuting attackers and counter-spinning the story. Sensing that we were a more serious outfit than they'd assumed up front, and not having any direct control over Satya and his men, they decided to get rid of them because they could lead us to Vikram's involvement.'

Seema shook her head but didn't respond immediately.

'Priya's dead, two small-time crooks are dead, and now they wanted to kill this boy,' she said after a while. 'And it's not even just that: Prof. Hussain had to tolerate working with the man who betrayed him for thirty years.' She ran a hand through her hair. 'He was lucky to get back into the mainstream,' she said almost to herself. 'He wouldn't have had the luxury of choosing his colleagues.'

Partha nodded. Seema shook her head again but this time to clear it.

'Now that Varaprasad is safe, Prakash will be their focus, right?' she said.

'I think so too,' Partha said. 'Varaprasad said there was a message on Priya's phone to Prakash. The fact that Prakash's name isn't coming out in CNEWS even though they have the phone confirms what we knew all along—they were never going to reveal it. Their real targets are Anil and Mohan Krishna. But they're probably using the message to put pressure on Prakash to hand over the material he has on Mohan Krishna—which they know of from Vikram. That's why Mohan Krishna is placating him with the CEO offer and we were fired. But I think Prakash will want assurances from Ramdas that nothing Varaprasad has will ever come out. So they were to get to Varaprasad one way or the other.'

27

A few minutes later, the inspector of the university police station arrived. He gave Seema a quick smile and nodded at Partha in a more business-like manner. He said the constables were unable to catch the man with the scar and the nurse. They seemed to have an escape route worked out beforehand. They had jumped a compound wall and disappeared. But the police had a good description of the man and were confident of nabbing him soon.

'I suppose you were right about the risk,' the inspector said to Partha.

'Yes,' Partha said. 'And what happened here after the attempt on Varaprasad further confirms my suspicion.'

The sub-inspector stepped out of the room.

'Our people weren't able to catch the suspects, sir,' he said.

'They reported to me already,' the inspector said. 'What happened here just now?'

'Things got very heated, sir,' the sub-inspector. 'That Prof. Ramdas from the university was here. He was accusing us of collaborating with these people to keep him from seeing Varaprasad.'

'Ramdas is always accusing us of something or the other,' the inspector said. 'But what the hell is all this about?'

'Sir, Prof. Ramdas wants to meet Varaprasad to persuade or intimidate him,' Seema said. 'Varaprasad knows things about the circumstances of Priya's death. The computers are already with you but they want to keep him from revealing whatever else he knows. It must have been their fallback option if they couldn't harm him first. Luckily, we got here in time and started looking for him.'

'It was this boy Raghav who saved Varaprasad,' Partha said. 'That guy who ran away was trying to inject

Varaprasad with something. Raghav grabbed his arm and wouldn't let go.'

Raghav first squirmed uncomfortably in his place when everyone looked in his direction. He then looked away with seeming indifference.

'And your people stopped Prof. Ramdas from going in to talk to Varaprasad,' Seema said. 'So he was upset. But when that student leader, Vikranth, told him Varaprasad wouldn't see him, he finally left.'

'What kind of information does Varaprasad have?' the inspector asked.

'We don't really know for sure,' Partha said. 'I thought the laptop and phone were the extent of it. But Varaprasad was on the scene right after Priya's death. Also, Vikranth told me he had access to her laptop for months before her death and he knew her personally. We all got so caught up with the evidence part of it we ignored the fact that he was a witness as well. He probably knows what exactly drove her to suicide.'

The room door opened and the doctor stepped out. The inspector took him aside and spoke to him for a while. He then went into the room to speak with Varaprasad and his parents. It was ten or fifteen minutes later that he came out. He beckoned to Partha.

'He wants to see you people,' he said. 'I'm not sure I should be doing this but I will. But only on the condition that any information that he shares with you will be shared with us.'

'We have no problem sharing information with the police,' Partha said. 'But if he tells us to keep something confidential, we will.'

The inspector gave Partha a harsh look. Then he let out a half sigh.

'Fine,' he said. 'But enough damage has been done because of all this secrecy. Someone got killed in Kadapa and there's this whole media drama. Let's keep in mind that we all want the truth to come out and share information. All right?'

Partha nodded. The inspector gestured to his subordinates. 'Allow them in,' he said.

*

The room was small and cramped. Varaprasad lay in bed, the backrest a little elevated, a blanket covering him till his chest. He was hooked up to a heart-rate monitor and had an oximeter on his index finger. He wasn't allowed to sit up straight for fear of exerting pressure on the wound on his abdomen. He looked weak and extremely fragile. The days of being on the run, the days and nights of extreme stress, and the wounds from the attack had all taken their toll. It would now be a slow, tortuous path to recovery.

Varaprasad's parents squeezed into the space between the wall and the bed. They looked at the visitors with some anxiety. There were two chairs on the other side of the bed. In a corner of the room, a constable was seated on a chair. There was a moment of awkward silence. Varaprasad's father gestured to Partha and Seema to sit down. They declined and moved the chairs out of the way to the front of the bed so the parents could sit. After a few moments of hesitation, the couple moved over and sat down. They were exhausted as well.

Varaprasad didn't have the strength for small talk or pleasantries.

'I think I can trust you,' he said, 'because you took a risk to save my life. And because you handed over the material to the authorities. Vikranth too feels we can trust you. I've made some copies of the material and sent them out. But you're the only ones seriously capable of bringing it into public light.'

'We'll do whatever we can,' Partha said. 'But you don't really need us now—the police have the material. They can leak it if they like.'

Varaprasad gave a slight shake of the head. 'One of the reasons I ran,' he said, stopping to catch his breath, 'was that I thought the police could be manipulated by Mohan Krishna. So there's nothing they'll find on the laptop.'

'You've erased everything?' Partha said.

'Everything,' Varaprasad said. 'The software I ran on it leaves nothing behind. Even forensics people will get little out of it.'

'So the entire evidence is out there in the copies you made?'

An almost playful smile came onto his lips; he glanced upwards at the ceiling.

'A lot of it is in the cloud,' he said softly. 'Everyone ran after the laptop, as I thought they would, but a lot of it is where it's always been. What's not in the cloud is in the pen-drives I sent out—the communications of the last day. I couldn't allow those to be lost. The single most important piece of evidence is the last Skype call between Prof. Ramdas and Priya.'

He winced with pain and couldn't speak for a little while. They waited for him to be able to speak again.

'I want the truth about Priya's death to come out,' Varaprasad said.

'It's what we want too,' Seema said. 'We're not here to protect Mohan Krishna's interests. We got involved because we believed that Anil was not guilty of driving her to suicide. We have no obligation to protect Mohan Krishna himself.'

'Anil's only fault is that he's an idiot,' Varaprasad said. 'It was Prakash that Priya was in a relationship with. Anil's just a rich kid. Caught up in his own world—his cars and video games.'

'Did Prakash drive her to suicide?' Partha asked.

Varaprasad shook his head with effort.

'I wish I could say he had,' he finally said. 'He's a scum who deceived her. But it wasn't him.'

Seema leaned forward.

'So was it just her state of mind?' Seema asked. 'Depression or something like that?'

Varaprasad shook his head.

'She was driven to killing herself,' he said. 'By Prof. Ramdas.'

*

As they left the hospital room, Vikranth unobtrusively slipped a pen-drive into Partha's hand. Partha slipped it into his pocket. The policeman in the room didn't notice it. When they emerged into the corridor they found that the number of people hanging around in the corridor had dwindled. The inspector had left and the sub-inspector was preparing to leave himself.

'We need to find a place to talk,' Partha said to Vikranth.

Varaprasad had asked them to talk to Vikranth at length. He himself didn't have the strength to speak for long but he'd told Vikranth everything he knew.

'I know a coffee shop close by,' Vikranth said.

'You're okay talking to us in the open like that?' Seema said.

'It seems I've picked a side. It's out in the open now.'

Another student, along with Raghav, volunteered to take Vikranth's place at the hospital and remain with Varaprasad's parents. Now as visiting hours ended and the crowds thinned out, Partha noticed that a group of students waited in the hospital compound. They were all known to Vikranth. Most of them remained in the hospital compound to ensure Varaprasad's safety while two accompanied Vikranth to the coffee shop. They found a Café Coffee Day a short distance away. The two students who'd accompanied them, who seemed to see themselves as a security detail for Vikranth, sat at a table nearby and didn't interact with Partha or Seema.

'I thought you were very close to Prof. Ramdas,' Partha said. 'He gave the impression he was looking out for you.'

Vikranth smiled bitterly.

'I thought so too,' he said. 'Until that day when Shiva attacked you. I realised we were caught up in a bigger game. And we were expected to carry out Prof. Ramdas's and Shiva's orders. I didn't sign up for that.'

'You were running your own movement?' Seema said.

'That's the impression we initially got,' Vikranth said. 'That it was our movement and he was mentoring it. That day, I realised we were being used.'

Vikranth shook his head.

'You know, after that experience, I thought of Prof. Ramdas's connection with violent elements like Shiva,' he said. 'Funny thing is, when I thought it through, it didn't surprise me.'

Partha looked at him inquiringly.

'So much of Prof. Ramdas's ideology is about justifying violence,' Vikranth said. 'It's merely a question of whose violence he chooses to justify or whose cynical actions he finds acceptable.'

Partha and Seema were careful not to prod or rush Vikranth. He was unburdening himself and it looked like he needed to.

'That's the ideology they spread around here,' Vikranth said. 'In fact, they always stop just short of saying violence is alright. Or they smuggle it in through the backdoor, just talking about victimisation or some other such thing. The victimisation may be a fact, but so is the fact that they're suggesting violence as a valid response. Then they imply the primacy of ideology. They pander suspicion about everyone and everything. The more emotional students slowly turn radical.'

Vikranth let out a short, nervous laugh. 'You don't know what I'm talking about, do you?' he said.

'We do,' Partha said. 'It's a way of creating an enemy to fight.'

'It's not just outsiders,' Vikranth said. 'You're an enemy if you're not extreme in your ideology. If I look back now and see how Prof. Ramdas undercut a moderate like Prof. Hussain—it's frightening.'

'How did he do it?' Partha said.

'He'd quietly badmouth him to start with,' Vikranth said, 'mock him and sideline him when he could; keep students away from him. Which is sad because everyone knows that while Prof. Hussain is not active in campus politics he is one of the best professors in the university. He mentors students, especially from small towns and weaker sections, and ensures they get jobs or higher degrees.'

Vikranth took a sip of his tea.

'The bottom line for me was this,' he said, 'I wasn't going to get involved in murder. I certainly wasn't going to let the union get involved in it. So I distanced myself from Prof. Ramdas. He retaliated, turning some sections of the union against me. Luckily, the majority were with me.'

Vikranth looked around the café in an unfocussed manner and then back at his tea again.

'The rival group even tried to attack me at the hostel,' he said quietly. 'That's when the union turned on itself—it's split now. But it left no doubt that the union was being used by Prof. Ramdas for his own agenda.'

He paused and looked at Partha and Seema.

'You know, even before Varaprasad told me, I suspected he drove Priya to suicide,' he said.

He smiled when he saw the expressions of surprise on their faces. He seemed to be expecting the reaction.

'It was just a hunch,' he said. 'But I suspected. Once you change your opinion about someone you start wondering about everything to do with them.'

'I don't follow,' Partha said.

'See, Priya's family was very close to Prof. Ramdas at one time,' he said, 'and then abruptly they cut themselves off from him. They were also members of the party once but now don't even exchange greetings. I know it's not much to go on, but it bothered me. Only Priya continued to be in touch with him, considering him to be her mentor. She reached out for guidance while she was here at the university and even after she'd left. She grew up with the ideology; she could never break free entirely.'

'How do you know about Priya's family?' Seema asked.

'Through Varaprasad,' Vikranth said. 'He's a close friend of mine and he got to know Priya quite well.'

'He didn't tell you any of this stuff until now?' Partha asked.

Vikranth shook his head.

'He kept everything to himself then,' he said. 'He was afraid someone would rat him out. In fact, I was initially upset that he hadn't come to me for help and ran. But, in retrospect, it was the smart choice: back then I would have tried to convince him to hand over everything to Prof. Ramdas and allow him to deal with it.'

Vikranth laughed bitterly.

'Anyway,' he said. 'The news about the attack on Varaprasad was the final straw. That Shiva had tried to attack him and died trying to escape removed all doubt about what was going on. After that, most students—except the really brainwashed ones—lost their faith in Prof. Ramdas.'

'How come you guys are all over the hospital?' Partha asked.

'We were waiting at the hospital before the ambulance from Kadapa arrived,' Vikranth said. 'Some of us know Varaprasad's parents so we were at hand to help them. We had to reach them before Prof. Ramdas did. I was able to speak to his father on the phone. We were prepared to protect him ourselves if the police didn't help. But the police were already on alert because the case was so high profile. This afternoon, some of the more radical sorts turned up demanding to see Varaprasad. But a policeman was put inside the room so we were reassured. I stepped out for just a little while and I got a call that Varaprasad had been moved by some outsider. I rushed back here.'

'You got to speak to Varaprasad right after he was brought here?' Seema asked.

'Yes,' Vikranth said. He looked at Partha. 'He said you'd told him your name in Kadapa. He later asked the inspector in Kadapa who confirmed your name. He wanted to see you after he got here. He told me to contact you; I was going to do that later today.'

'We'll need you to tell us what he told you,' Seema said. 'In as much detail as you can remember.'

*

'How did Prof. Ramdas come to trust Varaprasad so intimately?' Seema asked.

'Varaprasad's brilliant with technology,' Vikranth said. 'He's a second-year Master of Computer Applications student. He tops his class without much effort. Prof. Ramdas, on the other hand knows nothing about technology. He can manage to send and receive email—that's the extent of it.'

Seema was jotting down a few notes. Vikranth looked at her.

'You mind?' she asked.

'No,' Vikranth said.

'To entrust him with handling communications with Priya—that's a whole other level of trust,' Seema said.

'Varaprasad's idealistic—he was willing to act on his beliefs and he hero-worshipped Prof. Ramdas. He thought he'd found his ideological mentor. Prof. Ramdas saw that.'

'Okay.'

'The party was thrilled to have Varaprasad on their side. He's extremely capable and they had use for him. So they gave him a lot of importance—that drew him in further. And he felt he was part of a larger cause, an ideal. For the past year or more he's been doing everything from setting up their websites to securing internet connections.'

'When do you think his break with Prof. Ramdas began?' Partha asked.

'He got to see a lot of the inner dealings of Prof. Ramdas and the party. Some of the scales dropped, he says. Then he saw Priya becoming a pawn in a game—that was the breaking point.'

'He tried to stop it?' Seema asked.

Vikranth shrugged animatedly. 'How could he?' he said. 'He was totally at sea himself! By the time he saw what was really happening, it was too late.'

'There's no question of blaming him, Vikranth,' Seema said. 'I was just asking if the break with Prof. Ramdas came because he tried to intervene.'

Vikranth nodded.

'Eventually it did,' he said. 'But the fact that he was involved in dragging her into a trap haunts him. He can't forgive himself.'

'Whatever happened, it couldn't have been his fault,' Partha said. 'And he took huge risks to bring out the truth.'

'That's what I told him,' Vikranth said. 'See, he became quite close to Priya in her last months. He would go to her house almost every week to check her laptop and phone.'

'Why would he do that?' Partha asked.

'So she could communicate with Prof. Ramdas without leaving any unwanted traces online. His job was to back certain things up and wipe clean unwanted and seen communications from both her phone and laptop.'

'What kind of stuff would he save?'

'Primarily stuff about Prakash—anything she said or any material on her devices that related to him. But from a sense of caution Varaprasad backed up all her conversations with Prof. Ramdas as well.'

'Prof. Ramdas didn't know?' Seema asked.

'No. He really is clueless about technology. Varaprasad would save things to other email addresses and clean up signs of the transfer. He also had ways to retrieve emails Prof. Ramdas thought he had deleted. In the initial stages he says he saved the emails because he liked the discussions on ideology. When they turned darker, he saved them just to be safe.'

Partha leaned back in his chair.

'So what does Varaprasad want conveyed to us?' he said.

'He wants me to tell you exactly what happened in Priya's last days,' Vikranth said. 'And then help you figure out the contents of the pen-drive.'

Seema looked up from her notebook and nodded.

'Okay to interrupt if I need details?' she asked.

Vikranth laughed.

'Sure,' he said. He took a breath and started to speak. 'See, Varaprasad could see Priya was in a fragile state. She'd lost the film and was disillusioned about Prakash. In some conversations with Varaprasad she would be angry with herself for letting her guard down and getting into that relationship. Her psychological issues aggravated everything.'

'What kind of psychological issues?' Seema asked.

'At times she was so anxious and depressed, she could barely function. She wouldn't leave the house for days on end. At other times she would seem remarkably well-adjusted, positive.'

'So these were like depressive episodes?'

'I suppose so. I don't know. Varaprasad says bipolar disorder but he is not sure. Perhaps her parents would know what the problem was. But in a way it doesn't matter one bit. It wasn't any illness that killed her. It was someone using it to drive her to suicide.'

Vikranth looked at them as though daring them to question the statement. Seema simply nodded.

'Varaprasad says the positive days didn't just happen by themselves,' Vikranth said. 'They were tremendous acts of will, a result of a struggle with herself.'

'What she managed to accomplish all by herself was remarkable,' Seema said. 'Even if it came to a tragic end, she followed her ambition with remarkable grit.'

'That's what makes it absolutely diabolical,' Vikranth said. 'Prof. Ramdas was fishing in these troubled waters. He worked with cold calculation through it all. Varaprasad initially thought the computer stuff was about Prof. Ramdas helping Priya gather material against Prakash. It was some weeks ago that he began to suspect that Priya was being lured into a trap. When Prof. Ramdas's purpose became clear to him, he was shocked. But by then, it was too late.'

Vikranth finished his tea in a long gulp, looked around for a moment, and then drank from the bottle of water on the table. He seemed troubled by the thought of it all.

'Because he'd grown quite close to Priya,' he went on, 'Varaprasad tried to dissuade her from doing anything drastic. But she was in a state of frenzy because of her psychological problems and the manipulation had gone too far. She was also cut off from her parents.'

'Why?' Partha asked.

'Mainly over the influence Prof. Ramdas had over her,' Vikranth said. 'Then it was other things. Her parents never stopped her from entering the film industry but they were not thrilled about it. Then with the reversals she was facing, she just went into a shell. Some mistaken notions of failure and shame, I think. Her parents tried hard to reach out to her, but she was too far gone by then.'

'And the more isolated she got, the more influence Prof. Ramdas had?' Partha said.

'Yes,' Vikranth said. 'Varaprasad wanted to dismantle the elaborate communications network he'd set up between Priya and Prof. Ramdas but he didn't for a couple of reasons. One, Priya herself was in an uneven state of mind and had grown dependent on Prof. Ramdas. She suffered from paranoia and being suddenly disconnected from him might have driven her into a panic. Second, he was plain scared of Prof. Ramdas and the party. All Varaprasad could do was ask her to talk to some friends. But the friends—this Sirisha and that guy, Biren—too were involved with the party and they did nothing to help her. In fact, they always led her back to Prof. Ramdas.'

Vikranth collected his thoughts for a second, as though making sure he didn't forget anything important.

'Around this time, Varaprasad chanced upon an email that Prof. Ramdas had sent out to Priya. He was stunned. There was only one purpose to that email: Prof. Ramdas wanting to drive her insane.'

'How was he doing that?' Seema asked.

'It was subtle,' Vikranth said. 'But what the email left to be assumed was as important as what it said. You don't directly say to a person "you're a failure, you're a disgrace, a sellout, a disappointment—your situation is pitiable but hopeless".'

Seema stopped taking notes and looked up at Vikranth.

'But you talk to them like each one of those things were absolute truths,' Vikranth continued. 'Things everyone else holds against them. Things they find repugnant. You keep saying it to them. That's enough burden to crush anyone. Even in better circumstances.'

Vikranth became aware of Seema's unblinking gaze.

'Anyway,' he said, looking away from Seema, 'Varaprasad installed spyware on Priya's laptop the first chance he got. He worried that if he placed it on Prof. Ramdas's computer, some other party member who had access to it may find it.'

'Were there others who had access to his computer?' Partha asked.

'No,' Vikranth said. 'But Prof. Ramdas has a suspicious streak. He tried to bring another student into the loop a while ago but when Varaprasad pointed out a careless mistake he'd made, Prof. Ramdas got rid of him.'

'Okay.'

'So the spyware was set up to record all Skype communications as well,' Vikranth said. 'The day of her death, Priya got on a Skype call in the evening. Varaprasad came to know about the Skype call from a reference Priya made to it in a message she left for Prof. Ramdas. Prof. Ramdas responded as well.'

Vikranth took a breath.

'The way it was done was this,' he said. 'Priya accessed an email account and left a message in the Drafts folder. This could be done safely. Varaprasad had set up a system on both Prof. Ramdas and Priya's computers to access the account anonymously. The IP addresses were concealed and all their internet activity was without a trace. He had used a TOR router to mask their activity—no one could see details of it. It would have been tough even for investigators to find.'

'Harish's sources in the police said they hardly found out anything of relevance about Priya's internet use from the service provider,' Partha said.

Vikranth laughed. 'That's Varaprasad!' he said. He then turned a little serious. 'He regrets being so good at what he did now. Still he's done his bit to save the evidence.'

Vikranth broke off as another round of beverages was brought to the table. The moment the waiter left, he continued.

'On the night before Priya's death Varaprasad logged in and saw an email from Priya in the Drafts folder,' he said. 'It terrified him. Her email was a farewell message, it declared her intention to go through with the suicide. In it was also a mention of a scheduled Skype call the next night. Varaprasad knew that Prof. Ramdas had broken down Priya's defences and pushed her to the brink of commiting suicide. He had convinced her she'd be a martyr for a cause.'

Seema made notes rapidly. Partha listened taking care not to show any expression.

'The next day, Varaprasad went to her house to convince her to get help,' Vikranth said. 'But students close to Prof. Ramdas were there and he couldn't speak to her. He was now scared they were suspicious of him and didn't know what to do. He went back to the hostel. He was convinced he would go to jail for his part in it if Prof. Ramdas and the others turned on him.

'But that night, Varaprasad was in a frenzy and started for her house disregarding the consequences,' Vikranth said. 'He was on the way when he got a call. It was from Prof. Ramdas himself. He asked him to cover up Priya's email activity and the account they had created. He also told him to meet Shiva and another man near Priya's house in a couple of hours. They were to use the key he had to retrieve the laptop from her apartment and sanitise it entirely. He also asked them to copy the contents of Priya's phone as there would be a video message to Prakash on it. That would be Prof. Ramdas's leverage with Prakash so he wanted sole control over it. So Varaprasad was told to check for it and copy it in Shiva's presence. Shiva would then dispose of the laptop as it was too risky to try to return it to the apartment.'

'Pretty thorough,' Seema said.

'Yeah, very,' Vikranth said. 'But Varaprasad figured they wanted a couple of hours of buffer to make sure she was dead. He rushed to the apartment hoping against hope that she was alive.' Vikranth paused. 'She was gone by the time he got there. But Varaprasad managed to collect himself. He logged online from Priya's computer, using her Wi-Fi. He changed the passwords for the email and Skype accounts so Prof. Ramdas and others couldn't access it—Varaprasad's email and phone number were already in the settings for account recovery. He checked the data to see that incriminating evidence against

Prof. Ramdas was still on the laptop. Most importantly, he got the recording of the Skype message Prof. Ramdas had with her that evening from the spyware folder. He also copied the contents of her phone, including a message to Prakash. After that, he grabbed the devices and ran.'

Vikranth paused for a breath.

'He showed remarkable presence of mind and courage,' Partha said. 'What he did wasn't easy.'

Vikranth looked at Partha and Seema by turns.

'It was unbelievably brave and resourceful,' he said. 'He knew that the evidence would be destroyed if left there. This evidence was also the only proof of what had really happened to Priya and he would not allow that to die with her.'

'How did he make it out of the city?' Partha asked. 'It must have been late at night.'

'There are a lot of BPO and software people in the area Priya lived,' Vikranth said. 'There are shared autos and even cabs available at all times of the night. So he collected cash from an ATM and took an auto towards the airport. He took another auto to the highway and flagged down a truck headed to Chennai to throw them off the scent. Next, he headed to Bangalore.'

'Wow,' Partha said softly. 'It's good he's not a criminal.'

'He'd never get caught!' Vikranth said. 'In Bangalore, he hid out in some cheap lodge. He got hold of three pen-drives from the local market and copied all the evidence onto them. He managed to mail two of them out as well. Both packages have been received—I called and checked with both of them earlier today. Varaprasad doesn't want to share whom he sent it to with you right now—he wants to protect them.'

'That's fine,' Partha said. 'We don't need to know.'

'The third pen-drive and his own pen-drive were with him,' Vikranth said. 'His own pen-drive he wasn't too concerned about after he'd made copies. But the third pen-drive he concealed on his person and held onto it even when he was semi-conscious. That's the one I've handed over to you now.'

'He headed homeward because he was running out of cash?' Partha asked.

'He was also traumatised,' Vikranth said. 'And yeah, he was running out of money in Bangalore as well and didn't have any way of getting more. He knew he couldn't go home, but he trusted friends and relatives would conceal him.'

Vikranth paused and took a deep breath.

'Varaprasad trusts that you'll be able to bring this to light,' he said. 'He doesn't think the other two people who have the pen-drives can do it as effectively. They may be well-meaning and they'd try for sure but they're not likely to have the reach you do.'

Vikranth stopped, unsure if he should go on.

'I'm too cynical about the world to expect that justice will automatically follow,' he then said 'Whether justice is done by Priya or not, the world should know what happened to her. That's the responsibility he's entrusting you with now.'

*

As they drove back to their office, they received a phone call from Harish. Partha put it on speaker.

'I have a confirmation,' Harish said right away. 'The guy from Satya's gang confirms they were hired by Vikram to follow you and keep an eye on our office. After the murders they were paid off and told to disappear for a while.'

'Did anything promising turn up on Prof. Ramdas?' Seema said.

'Sort of, but it's not concrete,' Harish said. 'Vikram owns a guest house in Jubilee Hills. On a hunch I downloaded a photograph of Prof. Ramdas from the internet and showed it to a guard at Vikram's guest house. He says he recalls seeing him come to meet Vikram at the guest house. Now that's vague as hell and he had an incentive to lie because we were paying him. So I'm trying to confirm it.'

'So you're going beyond the pale …' Partha said.

'Of the strictly legal?' Harish said. 'Yeah. I'm trying to get a confirmation through a guy in the telecom company.'

'I wouldn't exert myself too much on it,' Seema said. 'We seem to have enough incriminating stuff on Prof. Ramdas now. And we've got Varaprasad's data.'

'You do? That's terrific!' Harish said. 'But there's other movement too. News is breaking about something from Mohan Krishna's past. They're not saying what exactly yet.'

'Which channel?' Seema asked.

'TNN. Vishwanath's channel.'

'Yeah, we expected that,' Partha said. 'And if CNEWS or any of Prakash's channels start leading with it we'll know Prakash has broken with Mohan Krishna.'

'I'll keep you posted,' Harish said and hung up.

'I have missed calls from Malvika,' Seema said, holding up her phone.

'We'll call her a little later,' Partha said.

'Why? She's no longer our client.'

'But this thing isn't over yet.'

'So if she wants you to go meet Mohan Krishna, you'll go?'

'I will. But not right away.'

28

Priya's emails to Prof. Ramdas started off innocuously enough. There were a few hundred of them, the first of which was exchanged about a year earlier. Partha, Seema, and Harish divided up and read through them painstakingly, shutting out the rush and pressure of the outside world. Vikranth joined them later that evening. He filled in the gaps and helped reconstruct what had happened. With what Varaprasad had told him about Priya Vikranth was able to put it all in context. As they put things together, a picture began to emerge.

The first few emails from Priya stopped just short of being chirpy but radiated a general sense of optimism. Priya said she was lucky to get a great start in the film industry and to meet the kind of people she had. Prof. Ramdas's replies were terse, often dismissive.

'If you're as happy to be in the film industry as you say,' Prof. Ramdas wrote, 'then I don't see the need to declare it so insistently. Perhaps you seek my approval. That's entirely unnecessary. If you really sought my approval, you'd have sought it before taking the decision and not as an afterthought. As for approval, I would have given it if I didn't believe the industry to be disgustingly shallow and exploitative. I cannot change my opinion that anyone who is part of it or even comes into contact with it is debased. It is an opinion based on years of observation and struggle against its abuses.'

But Priya persisted in writing to him. She tried to convince him that the industry was not inherently bad and that it was possible to be a part of it without being compromised as a person—it was possible to build a meaningful life there. After several of the following emails went unanswered, Ramdas sent a single line in reply.

'A meaningful life?' it simply read.

Priya wouldn't relent. She argued her case; she defended her pursuit of her ambition.

'Ultimately, you have to pursue your talents and be true to your aspirations,' she wrote in an email. 'One can't lie to oneself and live in a half-hearted way. Perhaps being successful gives you the standing to do things for your beliefs, things you can't do while struggling through life yourself.'

The response was prompt and curt.

'I see you've picked up the industry's penchant for inanity.'

Prof. Ramdas's tone remained sarcastic and hostile but he didn't terminate the correspondence. It was as though he enjoyed the power he held over her, power he'd held for a long time. Thread after thread of emails revealed a protégé-mentor relationship going terribly wrong.

From things mentioned in the emails, facets of Priya's early life began to emerge. Her parents being part of the party, she had joined its theatre group as a child. Her parents were non-teaching staff at the university and they were in the ideological thrall of faculty members who were party office-bearers. Prof. Ramdas was an active leader of the theatre group. He guided its members as they put on street or stage plays with Leftist themes. In her teen years, Priya grew even more involved with the group.

In one outburst, Priya alluded to what had happened at the time.

'I stayed with the group because I believed in you, because you were my mentor,' she wrote. 'Even after my parents left the party, I stayed on.'

This seemed to cut Prof. Ramdas to the quick.

'Your parents' commitment to ideology was skin deep,' he wrote. 'Their judgement was shallow. In a struggle, to make common cause with enemies of an enemy—strategically and ideologically—is entirely correct. It is necessary. If people adopt the language and interpretation of the state, then the party is better off without such people. To talk of nationhood, terrorism, and separatism at a time of war! Perhaps I was wrong to expect more from you. Have you inherited the same weak-heartedness? Perhaps you have. Your weakness for the industry betrays the same bourgeois thinking your parents never overcame.'

This rupture between her parents and Prof. Ramdas was a consequential one in Priya's life. It found mention in several messages. It seemed to have disrupted her life at many levels. In one message, Priya alluded to the treatment meted out to her by other group members after her parents had fallen out with the party. She referred also to how she was virtually cut off by the group because she was associating with another theatre group in the city. This was not an easy thing for her to endure—being cut off from the people she'd grown up with. She was isolated. It was never the same after that, even when she'd disassociated herself from the other city theatre group, and was allowed back into the fold.

'Please don't play the victim,' Prof. Ramdas wrote. 'You maintained your contact with that group secretly. You merely stopped performing with them. It was through this group that you developed this silly fascination with the film industry. Did you really think I didn't know this?'

Priya's response to the email revealed a darker and more tragic side to this mentor-protégé relationship. Here lay the fault in that dynamic that was to tighten like a noose in later years.

'I knew even then that it was you who'd instructed the group members to cut me off,' she wrote. 'But I maintained perspective all through. It was the ideology you were protecting. You were being true to your beliefs and I respected that.'

From other mentions in emails and from details Vikranth was able to add, a picture of what happened next began to become clearer. Priya returned to the fold, chastened and further diminished. She even joined the university theatre arts programme on the advice of Prof. Ramdas. This was against the will of her parents. They had suggested she get away from there, move to a different city and make a fresh start. But it was the shadow of her mental illness that held her back.

It was evident from some of the emails sent to Prof. Ramdas and Prakash that Priya was all too aware of the phases of darkness she tended to slip into. But it was the Drafts folder that provided a true understanding of what she was going through. These were emails written out and never sent, for want of a person she could share them with.

These emails revealed her at her most vulnerable. She was insecure, suspicious of those around her, and highly susceptible to self-hate. A constant emotion through these phases was fear, and from that fear came virtual paranoia. She could see no good in anything she did or was involved in. She saw no worth in her life and tended to turn on herself. She attributed the worst possible motives to her actions and was harder on herself than anyone could have been on her. Each time, she was at great risk of self-harm. When the despair grew too strong, she turned to familiar places and people. She could not be by herself. It was at the onset of one such phase that made her decide to stay on at the university after her Masters' and to pursue a PhD programme in theatre arts. Her parents' resistance to this exasperated her, causing a temporary rift between them.

A little later, when the film offer came her way, things with Prof. Ramdas grew strained once more. Prof. Ramdas invoked what he saw as Priya's duplicitousness in an email.

'Your participation in our theatre group was just a part you were playing,' he wrote. 'You played the penitent follower but it was never sincere. At the offer of a tawdry film role, you dropped everything and ran after it. Do you deserve to be trusted after that?'

The context for this was not entirely evident from the emails. The conversations Varaprasad had had with Priya were needed to fill in the gaps. This was in response to the opportunity that had come Priya's way; the opportunity that would take a turn for the tragic. Priya was spotted by a young assistant director who worked for Keshav when he visited the university. Keshav had just returned from the USA after completing a filmmaking course and was in the process of pitching his film to stars in the Telugu industry. The assistant director was convinced she was right for the movie. At his repeated requests, Priya sent Keshav her portfolio. Keshav auditioned her and was genuinely impressed. He was about to pitch the movie to Anil and he wanted a newcomer for the heroine's part.

A few months later Keshav managed to get Anil onboard. There was uncertainty about whether the star family would accept Priya as star. The uncertainty dragged on for several months even after rehearsals commenced. Priya did her best to be acceptable to everyone in the star's family. And then one day, she got a call from Keshav: she was accepted. Priya was euphoric.

She took stock of her situation objectively. She realised that she would have to embrace this opportunity fully. Even if that that meant being disconnected from her old circles. It was a time when her mental state was one of optimism and drive. It was a time when it was easy to imagine that her problems emanated from circumstances rather than an illness. Any way you looked at it, this was too big an opportunity to miss. She made her decision: she would strike out on her own and make it in the industry.

She announced the offer to the theatre group. She was immediately cut off, just as she'd anticipated. She tried hard to placate Prof. Ramdas, persistently reaching out to him, but he was angry and standoffish. Priya then threw herself into her work and her new world. She tried to make new connections with the people around her, those she met professionally and those she met through Anil and Keshav. But enthusiasm proved a poor shield in a place as harsh as the film industry. For one, the work paid virtually nothing and she had to make do on money her parents sent her. Then the delays began. Soon after, rumours began to circulate that she was to be dropped from the film. She tried hard to get other offers and to build a network but nothing materialised. She could sense the underlying hostility when she tried to be a part of the film world or even tried to associate with Anil's family. She could see judgement in the eyes of people around her who questioned her ability to be a mainstream star. She heard their sniggering and saw mockery in their smiles. As the spiral began to take hold, she felt Prakash's attention turn in her direction. Initially, she was suspicious and kept her distance, but with all her insecurities and isolation, she became unsure. It was somewhere in that flux that the relationship began. She'd been taken in by a seasoned conman.

The spiral that eventually resulted in her death started when she was dropped from the film. The announcement was casual and irreversible. Prakash said there would be other films and other filmmakers, but none of them materialised. Priya didn't expect him to create opportunities for her, but it was becoming clear to her that she was being handled. She realised that despite being alert to it, she had fallen prey to the kind of deception that was common in the industry.

She made two fateful decisions at this time. The first was that she decided to shield her parents from this reversal. She sensed that they would understand but theirs was a relationship where some distance had already set in. She also knew her parents lived with severe constraints already and she wasn't willing to place a greater burden on them. The second decision, which was more difficult, was to try to return to the only world she knew—the world of the university and her old friends. The first indication of this came in an email she wrote to Prof. Ramdas.

She talked of reapplying for the PhD programme the following year as the deadline had passed that year. She sought his advice on working with the theatre group of an NGO in the meantime. Both her mentor and her friends refused to respond. They ignored her emails and phone calls. Desperate, she landed up at Prof. Ramdas's office one day. He saw her briefly and told her not to return.

Priya poured out her state of mind into an honest, searing email written to Prof. Ramdas that evening. The signs of depression and paranoia showed through clearly. She spoke of hopelessness and the overwhelming sense that it was all pointless. She spoke of how she sometimes did think of ending it all. She reminded him that she'd suffered from such thoughts all through her life and he was aware of it. She also mentioned her disillusionment with the industry. She mentioned the affair with Prakash; the thought that she'd allowed herself to be in a sleazy affair filled her with disgust, she wrote. At times she feared who else knew of the affair and if any compromising material of her existed.

The next day, two friends from her old circles—Sirisha and Biren—got in touch with her. She welcomed them wholeheartedly. In an email sent out that night, she thanked Prof. Ramdas profusely: she knew he'd sent them to see her, concerned as he was for her safety. 'You've sent me a lifeline,' she wrote.

Her friends commiserated with her and brought with them the guarded possibility of Prof. Ramdas being open to letting her back into the group. They didn't mince their words. Priya had proved unreliable and uncommitted to the cause—Prof. Ramdas was deeply disappointed in her. He also believed her to be irretrievably compromised ideologically, and he didn't think he could ever trust her again. It was only the thought that he'd known her from her childhood that convinced him to give her a chance.

In response, Priya made a series of confessions, all of them by email. She agreed that she'd been unfaithful to the cause, she'd been untrue to their ideals, and she didn't deserve trust. She now knew how shallow and vicious this world she'd stepped into was, and she would do anything to get away from it.

Her friends laid out the conditions under which Prof. Ramdas was willing to be in touch with her. But he would not be in touch directly, they said. From then on, he would reply to emails sent to a particular email account. The one condition overriding all others: he decided what to respond to and what not to. Priya agreed.

Sirisha and Biren also gave Priya several instructions about how to backup and store communications and phone records that she got from Prakash. Prakash was taking a lot of precautions to keep their relationship a secret, they pointed out. She would be left open to scandal or blackmail from him and have nothing to hit back with if she didn't take precautions of her own. This is what prompted her to start saving up her phone logs, even recording some of her phone calls. She did it compulsively, in the haze of rising fear. The audio files of those recordings were all on the pen-drives Varaprasad had created.

It was at this time that Varaprasad was sent to her house for the first time. He was to back up her data. He even convinced her to allow him to set up one of his several email accounts as a recovery address for her account.

While Prof. Ramdas was at a disadvantage when it came to technology, he knew what he wanted as far as safety measures went. And what he wanted was control of Priya's account in case of an emergency. He also wanted safety of his own communications. He took both very seriously. Varaprasad suggested he get a cellphone with 4G connectivity and use it in personal hotspot mode to log into his account. This satisfied him. A SIM card was easily disposed of and cellphones are frequently lost. Varaprasad wasn't even sure how his SIM had been procured but Prof. Ramdas was confident of using it. It was a prepaid connection that was topped up regularly. The only thing he could make out was that caller ID identified it to be a number registered in Madhya Pradesh. This was the first thing that made Varaprasad pause and think about what exactly was going on. Prof. Ramdas's precautions were excessive by all measures. When he tentatively broached the topic with Prof. Ramdas, he was told he was being careful because the party was always under attack. In this case, Mohan Krishna was a known enemy of the party and Priya was entangled with his family. Extreme caution was entirely warranted. Prof. Ramdas even lowered his voice and told Varaprasad that he wasn't sure if Priya wasn't being used by Mohan Krishna's family to get back at the party in some way. That was the reason, he said, he was being so cautious about admitting Priya back into their circles. He then spoke darkly about Mohan Krishna's imminent entry into politics and said they had to be most careful now. Varaprasad was convinced.

In the initial days, Varaprasad saw some of the emails exchanged. He didn't think much of it. Prof. Ramdas, he figured, was being tough on Priya but there was some sense in it. With mild curiosity he observed a pattern where Priya was never entirely accepted back into the fold but she was not allowed to leave either. Occasionally, Prof. Ramdas would write positively to her, saying he wanted her back in their circles and would allow it in time.

In the coming weeks and months, Varaprasad saw Prof. Ramdas's growing concern about the email accounts. On one occasion he even got Varaprasad to promise that he would not access the email accounts without his permission. By this time, Varaprasad had begun to grow disillusioned with Prof. Ramdas and the party. And he had begun to suspect that what was underway was an ensnarement of Priya. So he took a risk: he began using the computer's email management system to save emails offline. He also started to save things to the Google Drive account associated with the email, which he knew Prof. Ramdas knew little about. He shared some of the contents on this Google Drive account with other email accounts he'd set up or saved them offline. He also used his access to Ramdas's devices to discreetly insert his own email accounts and phone number in the account recovery settings. And as he was the one sanitising Priya's computer and phone, he began to make copies of its contents.

He had set up several such ways of keeping track of what was happening but he himself didn't access them much. He was busy with university and other things. He was also afraid of what he would find out.

It was one such visit to Priya's house that changed things for him. The sight of her in a distracted, miserable, and terrified state shook Varaprasad to the core. He tried to calm her down the best he could. They had become friends over the past few months. She told him why she was overwrought. She told him she'd turned to Prof. Ramdas for guidance after what seemed to think were grave personal mistakes—she had led a self-centered and shallow life. She had debased herself following these weak impulses. She had created the conditions where a rigged and exclusionary system could exploit those impulses to toy with her. They never had any intention of letting her succeed in their industry—she was a wide-eyed fool for them to lead on, laugh at, and use. Priya said she saw meaning in Prof. Ramdas's view that she should become an instrument for something bigger than herself but she couldn't think of what. She once again spoke of believing that to die was better than to live like this. Varaprasad also noticed that she had gone into a state of paranoia where she believed her laptop was hacked, her phone tapped, and that her house was being watched. Varaprasad told her she needed medical treatment and that she should get in touch with her parents. But she was vehemently opposed to that. She said that nobody could understand the difficult and unique position she was in. The last thing she wanted was to involve her parents in dealing with the mess she'd created. She dismissed out of hand any notion of seeing a counsellor.

Varaprasad was troubled by all this. He spent a lot of time with her that day. When she'd calmed down a little, he copied the contents of her computer onto his hard disk. He took the material back to his hostel room. That night, he locked himself in his room and went through the contents of the laptop and her emails. What he found there shocked him.

Through the emails and the Skype calls, Varaprasad saw a clear cut, coolly calculated, dark design. Prof. Ramdas would invoke ideology when talking about the film industry and society as a whole. He spoke of the ways in which they exploited poor people and women. He spoke about how she had debased herself wanting to be one of them. He spoke of how she'd been compromised and he even suggested that she'd stooped to sleeping with Prakash because she wanted a toehold in the industry. When Priya protested, he bullied her. He asked her to look within and ask if she was really naive enough to believe that a married man with a reputation for being a womaniser was about to turn a new leaf for her. If not, how did she allow herself to be seduced? Priya put up a fierce defense but he wore her down meticulously, persisting until her resistance wavered.

Prof. Ramdas often denounced publicly the illiberal values that society imposed on people, but he used those very values to try and target Priya. The insinuation of petty scandal and regressive thinking, which Priya intellectually rejected but feared all the same, was a lethal vulnerability. The thought of what her parents would think of her, of her ambitions, and how they'd cope with social reactions tormented her. Prof. Ramdas was keenly aware of this niggling and pernicious doubt, and he used it to the full.

Over the next several weeks Prof. Ramdas wrote or spoke to her almost everyday. He talked about the unfairness of a system that reinforces itself, making the unfair seem fair. And then he spoke in even more abstract terms. He spoke of living and dying for a cause. Priya was emotionally exhausted by now. And then, in one Skype video Varaprasad found on Priya's computer, Prof. Ramdas began to push his agenda more openly. When she mentioned thoughts of killing herself, Prof. Ramdas responded slowly and deliberately:

'Sometimes,' he said, 'a compromised life can be redeemed by having something to die for. Unless you think it better to live as an object of pity and ridicule? Or build some pathetic life as a small-time employee in some small-time place—strive to live the life of a petty bourgeois, living from shopping discount to shopping discount. After the vaulting ambitions you've pursued—to live like that! There is a way to overcome it ... to become a symbol—a symbol of exploitation, of someone who wouldn't accept living on others' terms, but chooses to sacrifice for a larger cause. Live a wretched life or choose a useful death.'

He never told her what her death would accomplish, but it was implicit that it would be used to target Prakash and Mohan

Krishna. All of it repeatedly brought her to the prospect of suicide. It was very much on her mind, something she was always in danger of drifting towards, and now the notion was tied up with implications beyond her personal story and her bitter circumstances.

The tone of her emails became disquietingly composed.

'I've thought about everything you've said,' she wrote in one of them. 'You say the only way to redeem myself is to sacrifice myself. That the choice is between a wretched life or a useful death. My reply is "I choose the latter".'

Varaprasad was terrified. He was frightened for her safety. And he was frightened for his own. He had not signed up for something like this. He did not want any part of it. And he didn't want his life ruined by being associated with driving this girl to her death. He had no idea what he could do to stop it. He was out of his depth and paralysed by the fear that what he had done was illegal. He also knew his credibility was low: he could always be accused of having tampered with evidence as he controlled Prof. Ramdas's and Priya's computers. Only damning video evidence would corroborate his story.

He avoided speaking to Prof. Ramdas the next day and tried to reach Priya. She wouldn't answer her phone. He even tried to get hold of Priya's parents' telephone number, but this is when he realised he didn't know anyone who knew her personally. Varaprasad decided go to Priya's apartment. When he got there, the door didn't open immediately. When it finally opened, it wasn't Priya who answered. It was Sirisha. She demanded an explanation as to why Varaprasad was there.

Varaprasad showed presence of mind. He said he had discovered some problem with the computer's files and that he had to destroy files on it more thoroughly. The girl was suspicious, saying she had not been informed of any such thing. Varaprasad told her he knew more about technology than Prof.

Ramdas did and that she was free to call him to see if he should be let in. She did. Prof. Ramdas asked to speak to Varaprasad. When Varaprasad made up something that sounded important he agreed to let him do it this time, but told him not to go to Priya's place without his prior permission. Varaprasad agreed and went inside.

Priya saw him and said hello but Sirisha took her inside. Biren, who was with Sirisha watched over Varaprasad as he tinkered with the computer. Varaprasad didn't dare talk to Priya in the presence of these people. He left without speaking to her at all.

That night, he began to panic. He did not know what to do. Going to the police was out of the question with all the stuff he'd done with the computers. He couldn't see any way out of this that didn't have serious consequences for him. Late that night, he decided to act—he could not let her die. He set off for Priya's house once again. He hoped to convince Priya to give him her parents' number and he would call them over to the house.

He was halfway there when he got the call from Prof. Ramdas asking him to go to Priya's house to clear out the laptop and cellphone.

It was when he was on the run in Bengaluru that he saw the video clip of Prof. Ramdas's final message to Priya.

'Your death will be for a great cause,' he said. 'I guarantee it. It is not an act of vengeance, it is an expression of human anguish. You must show the courage to act. The time for thinking is over. If you did not find meaning in life, I will ensure it has meaning in death.'

*

It was late at night by the time they got through all the material. Vikranth left for the university accompanied by his two friends and two people Harish deputed. A silence fell over the office; the mood was heavy and there was little talk. They picked at leftover pizza and drank coffee before getting back to work.

Harish and Seema worked at putting the emails and videoclips in order. Partha went into his cabin, typing out a brief note giving details of the entire story. He then wrote out elaborate notes about the people involved in the story and made references to specific video clips. The three of them then put it all together, connecting emails and clips to the writeup. It took a few hours to complete.

When done, they copied the emails and video clips from the pen-drive onto a Google Drive account using IP-masking software. They then sent out alerts to a few contacts—some of them abroad—sharing specific files on the Google Drive account with them. Within minutes there were queries. To those who showed interest and followed up, they began to give access to the full stash of emails and videoclips. They then sent requests and recommendations to those who'd responded. Some of the people they approached would put this material out on social media anonymously.

It was almost dawn by the time they were done. They prepared to go home.

'Let's catch a little sleep while our invisible friends spread the word,' Harish said.

'We should have a couple of hours,' Partha said. 'You'll have to handle the queries when I'm out tomorrow morning,' he said to Seema.

'That's fine.'

'I'm guessing you'll meet Mohan Krishna tomorrow?' Harish asked Partha.

'Yeah,' Partha said. 'But I'll have to talk to Malvika first thing in the morning.'

'So for now we just wait?' Seema asked.

'Yeah,' Partha said. 'Let it cook online for a while.'

29

The next morning Partha pulled up Malvika's number on his phone. She'd called him several times that morning but he had put his phone in silent mode. He hesitated before calling. There was a buzzing sense of guilt at the back of his mind when he dealt with her or Mr Ramakrishna. It wasn't a position he'd been in before: one where he might be working against the interests of a client. At the same time, he had never felt as sure of what he had to do. He dialled the number. Malvika picked up after the first ring itself.

'Where did this story about Mohan Krishna's past come from?' Malvika said, getting directly to the point.

'Telugu News Network's editor, Vishwanath, used to cover the Srikakulam area in the 1980s,' Partha said. 'He believes these old rumours are connected to what's going on now.'

'They've got nothing to do with what's happening now!'

'You should have told me about these rumours. Or Mr Ramakrishna should have. Do you know how good the headlines on this story sound?'

'They're not relevant.'

'The "like father, like son" stories are enough to make them relevant. And this scandal's going to shake Mohan Krishna's support within the community—how can they not?'

'The rumours are not true!'

'Good. Then advise Mohan Krishna to take TNN to court.'

'What?'

'They can't possibly have any proof—they're just running rumours. They've got nothing—and nothing's going to turn up—to corroborate them.'

Malvika didn't reply.

'Trust me, Mohan Krishna is sure to win in court,' Partha said.

'It might be better to ignore it,' Malvika said. 'Why dignify such rumours with a comment?'

'If the rumours aren't contested, people will take them to be true. There hasn't even been a statement from you people so far.'

Malvika went silent once again.

'Malvika, the only possible reason not to issue a legal notice is if you're afraid that proof will turn up,' Partha said.

Malvika still did not speak.

'Are you really telling me Prakash doesn't have some such proof?' Partha said, changing his tone a bit. 'It would be devastating if Prakash said the allegation was true. He wouldn't even have to produce proof.'

'We have to stop the story,' Malvika said. 'You have to do something.'

'We can't stop it,' Partha said. 'It's out there and only going to get bigger.'

'You have to get hold of Priya's phone—we have to put Prakash on the defensive.'

'We can't. And getting leverage on Prakash wouldn't help stop the story. It's an independent TV station running it, not him.'

'Stop telling me what can't be done—come up with something to counter TNN!'

'We no longer work for you. You fired us.'

'You're rehired.'

'We don't want to be. Malvika, I know you mean well and you think you're doing what's right. But I told you right at the start, I didn't want to get involved with the business of bailing out stars from a scandal. My stand hasn't changed. I signed on to help Anil get off the hook. If any part of the material Varaprasad had comes out, he will be. He's in no danger now.'

Malvika started to say something but smothered it. She seemed uncertain of what to say next. Partha could imagine there was relief at his assurance about Anil but also concern about what the family still faced.

'I can understand the strain you're under,' Partha said. 'But you have to understand that it's perfectly right for me to take this stand. I have no interest in Mohan Krishna's image, his political career, or his past.'

'You've been forthright on this from the start,' Malvika said. 'But Mohan Krishna's asked me to convince you to come see him. He's hoping to get some information or help from you.'

'Isn't that the real reason you were calling me early this morning?'

Malvika exhaled. 'Yes, it was,' she said. 'This time it's serious, Partha. He's not requesting anymore. He's making threats about what he'll do if you don't turn up. It has implications for me too—I brought you in.'

'Alright then,' Partha said. 'I can be there in an hour.'

'Really?'

'Yes.'

'That's great! I'll tell him.' There was relief in Malvika's voice.

'Malvika, there was just one more thing,' Partha said.

'What's that?'

'I'm afraid to even ask you this.'

'What's that?'

'I used to know a lot about the industry some years ago. I had a lot of contact with insiders. This was around the time you were still acting.'

Partha paused. There was complete silence at the other end.

'You must have heard of some of the rumours out there,' Partha said. 'Rumours concerning you.'

'Yes,' Malvika said.

'They were vicious.'

'About whom?'

'Mohan Krishna.'

'You're being kind. They were vicious to me really. Everyone assumed they were true. It's more titillating that way.'

'I know the rumours about you weren't true,' Partha said.

'Are you sure?'

'I couldn't be more sure. Many insiders admired your spirit. They thought nobody could resist Mohan Krishna and survive in the industry.'

Malvika laughed.

'No one dared not report to Mohan Krishna's guest house when called?' she said.

'But you did. He even had to swallow his pride and act with you because you were so popular.'

'It's nice to hear this version for a change. Most people like to believe the one where I report to the guest house. That's what actresses do, right? It's just business?'

'So it was true that he tried to pressurise you?'

Malvika didn't say anything.

'And you still married into this family?' Partha said.

'You seem to disapprove,' Malvika said.

'It's not for me to approve or disapprove. I just don't understand.'

'I loved Vishnu. He loved me. What's not to understand?'

'Did Vishnu know about this?'

'This happened early in my career and I didn't even know Vishnu back then. And nothing happened. So I guess it doesn't count.' Malvika laughed, as though at what she'd just said.

'That's why the family resisted the marriage at first? Like it was your fault?'

'Vishnu is a good man, Partha,' Malvika said, a sort of weariness in her voice. 'And I'd seen men in the industry, I'd seen how things worked here. He wasn't like the rest of them. I knew I could trust him. And I wasn't going to let go just because the family was regressive. Even they've opened up to me a lot since then.'

'And now you want to help Mohan Krishna?'

'Once you're in the industry, once you're famous, you don't go back to being an ordinary person again. It's like riding a tiger. Everybody knows you, everybody wants something from you—they want to exploit you, or exploit your name, or your wealth. Once you're in the industry, you're afraid to ever have to leave it. Some aren't bothered by it, but I know I need a foothold to stay on here. So I accept it as a fact of life and deal with it.'

'I suppose Priya must have felt that despair too—to come so close to stardom and risk losing it all.'

Malvika sighed. 'She must have,' she said. 'I honestly hadn't thought about it that much. It must have been terrible.'

'Mohan Krishna is collapsing under his own weight now, Malvika. How can you want to defend him?'

'Come on, Partha.'

'I just don't get it.'

'You're not that naive, Partha. I'm sure you know what it's like when there's a superstar in the family. Mohan Krishna is more than just someone who earns a lot of money—he's an industry. Everyone in this family lives off him. All our businesses, all our political influence, every bit of relevance we have today revolves around him. My husband doesn't have a career of his own, he makes a living doing what Mohan tells him to do. It's like that for everyone in this family. And that's only family—what about all those who run businesses with us, who work with us, producers? You think any of our lives would be the same again if Mohan falls?'

Partha didn't say anything immediately. He got up and stepped over to the kitchen counter where he'd put down his laptop. Its screen was blank, having gone into power-saving mode. Partha ran his finger over the touchpad.

'So you made up the story about Mohan Krishna not

wanting any outside interference,' he said. 'You knew I wouldn't work with him directly?'

The laptop screen came alive. The story was spreading slowly but steadily on the internet and on social media. Even some lower-end film news websites and blogs had started picking it up.

'Yes,' Malvika said.

'Mr Ramakrishna knew I'd refuse so you were prepared to convince me. We were working for Mohan Krishna all the time.'

'I was prepared to make you see that it was about helping out Anil.'

'You did convince me of that.'

'And not much else, it seems. What else did you figure out?'

'I figured that your in-house fixers couldn't handle a story of this size, especially with Anil's name being thrown around. And with the family at war with itself, you couldn't trust anyone completely. Mohan Krishna needed to be seen to be doing nothing. So you brought us in.'

'When did you figure out that Mohan Krishna had signed off on your involvement?'

'From the very beginning, really. Mr Ramakrishna acting independently, going against Mohan Krishna—it just didn't add up. You telling us that we had to work under the radar so Mohan Krishna wouldn't be upset also didn't make sense. He was always going to find out. And any advice we gave got acted upon—whether it was asking you to do interviews or have Anil address a press conference, Mohan Krishna gave his consent to. All this was confirmation.'

'Why did you stay on? You dislike Mohan Krishna—you could have walked away.'

'There was a young girl dead—caught up in the schemes of others. If there was anything I could do about it, I wanted to. And I believed Anil was innocent.'

'Will you help us now?'

'Mohan Krishna doesn't need my help right now. He needs to be making deals to limit the fallout. I'm sure that's what he's doing as we speak.'

Partha was about to hang up.

'Partha?' Malvika said.

'Yes.'

'Vishnu and I genuinely care for Anil, like he is our own son. That part stands on its own; it's got nothing to do with anything else.'

'I know that.'

*

Partha checked in at the office on the way to Mohan Krishna's. He ran into Harish on the way in. They then gathered in Seema's office.

'We found two phone calls from a number Prof. Ramdas uses to a number associated with Vikram,' Harish said. 'Both calls were made yesterday afternoon, both from the hospital area. It may have been a panic reaction after the students turned against him.'

'Are you sure about the number being Vikram's?' Partha said.

'We got confirmation from Satya's people. Satya used to speak to Vikram directly on it.'

'It still isn't a lot to go on.'

'No, it isn't. But we were able to look up logs of this number going back several months. The SIM was taken in the name of a part-time worker of Vikram's. So we looked up phone calls to this number and we found several calls from this number to Prof. Ramdas's number. His phone is not in his own name either. But it's the phone number that Vikranth gave us—the one Varaprasad used to contact him on.'

'That's fantastic,' Partha said.

'How does that help us now?' Seema said.

'It's absolute confirmation of our theory,' Partha said. 'I now know what exactly to expect when I get to Mohan Krishna's.'

'What does he want to see you for?' Harish said, with a questioning look.

'It's an ambush of sorts,' Partha said.

'Want me to go with you?' Harish said.

'No.'

'Call me if you need help.'

'I will. But I don't expect it'll be that kind of ambush.'

Harish nodded.

'The story's catching on well,' Partha said to Seema. 'But keep pushing the pace. Stick to the plan.'

'Don't worry about it,' Seema said.

Partha hesitated for a moment. Seema and Harish looked at him expectantly.

'It's the right thing to do,' Partha said, with a shake of the head. 'But it will end up hurting some good people as a result.'

30

It was déjà vu. Partha was in the waiting room at Mohan Krishna's house again. He expected to be called in sooner this time: Mohan Krishna himself was waiting for him. The guard had ushered him through the gate immediately. This time, the compound wore a deserted look; there were no fans, no hangers-on. Even the TV set in the waiting room was switched off. Just a few minutes after he was seated, an attendant asked Partha to follow him into the house. Even the house was quiet. Their footsteps echoed through the corridor as they walked through.

The corridor opened out into a grand hall, which resembled something out of a European castle. Doors opened out on all sides of it. Outside a grand door sat Malvika and Mr Ramakrishna. They nodded at Partha, making bare minimum eye contact. The attendant led Partha directly in. Malvika and Mr Ramakrishna did not follow.

The room was as grand as the hall. Its ceiling rose high and on two sides, large, arched windows had views of the landscaped gardens outside. The wall paper was a patterned red; the curtains maroon and gold. It looked like a room out of the palace at Versailles, only gaudier. At the centre of the room was an arrangement of sofas. Long sofas stretched parallel to each other. At the head of arrangement was a large single-seater chair. It had the appearance of a royal court about it, perhaps not by accident.

Mohan Krishna was seated at the head of this sofa arrangement. His legs crossed regally, his head held aloft at an angle. He was speaking as Partha was led in. There were two others in the room, both of whom listened keenly, almost reverentially. One of the two—Vishnu—Partha had met personally. The other was a man Partha had never met but recognised—Prakash. Mohan Krishna continued to speak as the attendant led Partha in. He showed no sign of noticing that someone had come into their presence. The attendant came to a stop near the long end of the sofas and waited to be noticed.

Mohan Krishna continued speaking. He was talking about admirers. Partha stood a step behind the attendant and listened intently. Mohan Krishna said his fans, who were spread around the world, were flooding him with offers of help and donations. They all wanted to contribute to the development of the state, he said. He only had to announce his developmental programmes and the fans would flood the state with billions of dollars. Indian-born entrepreneurs and IT workers in Silicon Valley were the same way, he said: every one of them expected the state to enter a golden era when he entered politics.

He paused at this stage. Vishnu half-turned to look at Partha but stopped himself when he observed Mohan Krishna still had a far-off look in his eyes. Mohan Krishna started to speak again.

It would be the end of corruption as well, he said. As for the state itself, caste equations were important to manage, so he was paying them some heed, but his film career was proof that he was adored across region and community. They would win regardless of how these other political equations worked out. The others eagerly agreed.

Unable to put it off any further, Vishnu glanced in Partha's direction. He turned back to Mohan Krishna and whispered something. Mohan Krishna nodded slightly but didn't look in Partha's direction; he gazed out of the window instead. He then took a deep breath, as though coming out of contemplation. He finally turned in Partha's direction. He gazed at him expressionlessly for a long time. Partha gazed back, only taking care to keep his gaze unfocussed so it was non-confrontational. Vishnu beckoned for Partha to sit down.

Partha sat down on the side opposite Vishnu and Prakash. He was aware all through that Mohan Krishna would be watching him closely for a sign of submission. Some stars needed that to feel comfortable. In this situation, where he was already wary of Partha, he would be looking for it even more acutely. Partha avoided giving a hint of either docility or aggression. He stayed quiet, waiting for Mohan Krishna to set the tone of the conversation.

'You finally found the time to see us,' Mohan Krishna said.

Partha smiled.

'I didn't want to come see you with half-baked information,' he said.

'Your need to get information is not more important than my need to get information, is it? I may be wrong, please correct me if I am.'

'Not at all. We were tracking a story that I thought might interest you—I wanted to come to you only when we had complete information about it.'

Mohan Krishna looked up at the ceiling for a few moments before he looked back down at Partha.

'See, Partha,' he said, his tone kind, 'there is no bit of information out there that I am not aware of. You understand that?'

'You're very well-informed, I'm sure.'

'I might require some small clarification from time to time, but I hope you don't think you know anything I don't know.'

'No, I don't think that at all.'

Mohan Krishna observed Partha for a few moments; suddenly, he smiled.

'I am happy with the work you've done to try clear my son's name,' he said.

Vishnu and Prakash also smiled.

'Thank you,' Partha said.

'But I'm sure you realise that I make the decisions in this matter.'

'Yes, sir, I do realise that.'

'So now you must submit your findings to us and then leave it to us to decide what to do with them.'

Partha didn't respond.

'You will hand over all the material you have collected—big and small—and then forget about this matter,' Mohan Krishna said. 'You will do nothing—I repeat—nothing more in this matter.'

Mohan Krishna's voice had an edge. This was not an instruction, it was a warning.

'My sister-in-law—great lady that she is—was impatient to get information that would help Anil,' he said, 'so I allowed you—and her—to play for a while. But ultimately these kinds of problems are not solved by petty detective work but by serious players sitting down and coming to an understanding. I'm sure you know this already.'

Partha saw a small smile come to Prakash's lips. Partha nodded.

'I do realise that,' he said.

Mohan Krishna smiled beneficently once again. 'And?' he said.

'All the material we have with us will be delivered to you by this evening.'

Mohan Krishna did not speak.

'Actually, it's better that my people go with you back to your office and collect it.'

Partha hesitated and then nodded.

'You will hand over all your copies,' Mohan Krishna said.

'There's no such thing as all copies with this kind of material, sir,' Partha said. 'Things are backed up in different places. There are associates and private investigators we collaborate with who have bits and pieces of information as well.'

'You will not get smart with me, Mr Partha,' Mohan Krishna said. 'You don't realise what kind of reach I have. If you imagine you have proven yourself by getting this far in your investigation, you are fooling yourself. You won't last five minutes against me.'

Partha nodded and looked down. Then he raised his head and looked Mohan Krishna in the eye.

'I don't doubt that at all, sir,' he said. 'That's exactly why we take precautions of our own. We back up data in a manner that it can't be reached. Associates at the firm—three of us—take precautions so we protect each other. We also have provisions so our associates all over the country and our lawyers can get access to material in a crisis. This is so they can use it to bail us out of trouble, you understand. Of course, this is only if they need to.'

Vishnu frowned. He shifted uneasily in his chair.

'Are you saying you've shared this information with outsiders?' he said.

Mohan Krishna gave Vishnu a dark look.

'Not at all,' Partha said. 'We just have protocols in case something happens to us. We have to trigger an alarm or give them a scenario in which to act. Otherwise, nobody has access to anything except us. Please be reassured.'

Despite that last sentence, the three men looked less comfortable now.

'We're happy to give you copies of whatever we have,' Partha said. 'But what we're happiest to give you is our word that we won't share this information with anybody.'

He looked at Mohan Krishna as he said this. Mohan Krishna stared back coldly. After a few seconds he allowed himself a small smile.

'It seems Partha speaks the same language as we do,' he said.

'Yes, sir, I do,' Partha said. 'Please don't worry about it.'

'You'll receive whatever Ramakrishna promised you,' Mohan Krishna said.

'Please don't worry about that. We were glad to be of help.'

Mohan Krishna's smile had a touch of condescension to it now, as though he had the situation entirely figured out. Partha smiled back at him.

'It must be hard to be at the head of such a large empire of influence,' Partha said. 'I cannot imagine the complexity of it.'

Mohan Krishna stroked his chin.

'It's like being a father to a family of thousands,' he said. 'It's like being a ruler. You can't understand the strains it comes with.'

'I'm sure your impulse would have been to defend your son, but you had to exercise a lot of restraint.'

Mohan Krishna smiled.

'No father should have to go through it,' he said.

Partha nodded. 'But as head of the family,' he said, 'and head of all the business and political interests of the family, keeping damaging material about you from coming out was priority. I can understand that.'

Mohan Krishna's smile froze.

'Don't talk rubbish!' Vishnu said.

'Vishnu,' Mohan Krishna said, his voice soft. 'I'm speaking, aren't I? Don't interfere.'

Vishnu shifted about in his chair angrily. Prakash looked uncomfortable but did not say anything. His smile was gone now.

'See, Partha,' Mohan Krishna said. 'There are people who depend on me. It could be family members, it could be producers, politicians, businessmen—anyone. If I am damaged, they are all damaged. If I remain strong, I can protect them all. Including my son.'

'I understand.'

'And we've been able to work things out. We've been able to sort out all misunderstandings. The damage can be controlled now.'

'Except, a young woman is dead.'

Mohan Krishna's gaze rested on Partha. It was not hostile but watchful.

'It's a terrible tragedy,' he said. 'But we're practical men and must deal with this problem practically. We will do something for the family a little later. Definitely. That is not just a promise to you but a promise to myself. It should not have happened.'

Partha said nothing.

'But you understand that we must come to an understanding now to diffuse the situation?' Mohan Krishna said.

Once again, Partha did not react.

'We must be ready to deal with all parties—we must come to agreements,' Mohan Krishna said, 'There must be give and take.'

'How do you propose to do that?'

Mohan Krishna's look was guarded. He didn't want to reveal any information to Partha that he didn't already have. He preferred Partha reveal what he knew instead.

'Why don't you guess?' he said. 'It'll also help me see if you really appreciate the full situation and what is expected of you.'

'Well, sir, what's in the public domain now is broadly speculative,' Partha said. 'The actual evidence is not with anybody including the police—I understand the laptop's hard-drive has been badly damaged. Even Priya's emails and other materials are not with the police. If Varaprasad can be handled, that's the end of it.'

'Good. What else?'

'Now I'm just guessing, but I figure that Prof. Ramdas has material against Mr Prakash here because they have Priya's cellphone. Mr Prakash has some information about you.'

Prakash's look was hostile. It seemed he didn't like his deeds spoken about out loud.

'They could have released the material against you by now,' Partha said to Prakash. 'They had Vikram's political and media support in all this as well. In retaliation, whatever you've got on Mr Mohan Krishna would have also come out.'

Mohan Krishna didn't say anything.

'But that's where things took a dramatic turn,' Partha said.

Mohan Krishna looked at Partha and nodded.

'Go on,' he said.

'Two students—Varaprasad and Vikranth—turned against a certain Prof. Ramdas,' Partha said. 'Varaprasad especially has become high profile and has taken precautions to protect himself by spreading the material around. Now both these students trust me—they trust me with the material they have and they trust me to act on their behalf. That material, apart from being damaging to Mr Prakash here is damaging to your enemies as well. That's what's brought them running to you, back to the negotiating table.'

Mohan Krishna smiled. 'Mutually Assured Destruction,' he said. 'MAD. That's what kept the world from facing a nuclear holocaust during the Cold War. You hold a threat over me and I over you. But we all go on living. Thriving even.'

'If all parties step away from the brink. If nobody fires their missiles…' Partha said.

'Then it's as though the nuclear weapons never existed. You can even continue to fight each other, but you don't mention certain things. That's all.'

'I'm sure you have other material on Mr Prakash?'

'In business, everyone has something on everyone else.'

'But you needed Varaprasad's material secured for this deal to go through? That's what will get Prof. Ramdas to hold back the material Mr Prakash has shared with him.'

Mohan Krishna was silent.

'Prof. Ramdas has had Mr Prakash at his mercy since Priya's phone came into their possession,' Partha said. 'It's incriminating. It was not Anil but Prakash who was in a relationship with Priya. My guess is they approached him the morning Priya committed suicide. Vikram knew Prakash had material on you. But Prakash must have turned them down at the time—he knew he could use his leverage with you to shield himself. He used this time to consolidate his position in the family's businesses. Your combined clout could have kept the contents of the phone and laptop from coming out when the police eventually got hold of them. But when the phone fell into Vikram and Prof. Ramdas's hands, he couldn't fight the pressure anymore. So he had to make a deal with them. But with material about Prof. Ramdas and Prakash falling into my hands, you needed to see me urgently.'

'Let's say you are right.'

'For the sake of argument only, of course.'

'Only for the sake of argument.'

'But it's not going to be an easy victory for anybody. They have material against you. You must have material against Mr Prakash. The students have material against Prof. Ramdas. I have material against him. And everything would come out if this fight went on.'

'In a war, the extent of damage is hard to estimate or control.'

'But things can be controlled in peacetime.'

'That's why peace is a wonderful thing.'

Partha smiled. 'In some situations,' he said. 'But just to tie things up, Mr Prakash and Prof. Ramdas came to you with an offer—everyone backs off.'

'Let's say you're right, once again.'

'But for the deal to go through you have to deliver me. More specifically, you have to deliver Varaprasad and his evidence through me.'

Mohan Krishna was impassive. The other two watched Partha keenly.

'He must be here—Prof. Ramdas?' Partha said.

Mohan Krishna nodded.

'We might as well have him join us.'

*

When Prof. Ramdas walked in, Mohan Krishna and the others rose and made way for him to sit close to Mohan Krishna. Mohan Krishna ushered him to a seat and sat down only after he had. Prof. Ramdas sat next to Prakash. He evaded Partha's look initially. When he eventually looked at him, he smiled. Partha smiled back.

'The material against Prof. Ramdas is incredibly damaging,' Partha said, smiling still. 'I don't think he can imagine the extent of it.'

Prof. Ramdas matched Partha's smile steadily.

'It doesn't matter,' Mohan Krishna said. 'Whatever the extent of it is, it will never come out.'

'It contains emails, video clips, and even Skype calls between him and Priya,' Partha said.

Prof. Ramdas's smile hardened. He couldn't have known about the Skype calls being recorded.

'It shows clear abetment of suicide—actively driving someone to suicide really,' Partha said. 'It would completely exonerate Anil. Even Mr Prakash here would be able to come out of it alright. He'll face some heat because of the inappropriateness of the affair but even he should be fine. There is one message from the night when Priya killed herself that is damaging. But if that's kept out, he should be fine.'

There was a long pause. Prakash's look eased up a bit. A degree of surprise registered on Mohan Krishna's face.

'As I said,' he said slowly, 'it doesn't matter.'

'No, of course not,' Partha said. 'Because in releasing any such material we expose Mr Prakash to scandal and unless

Prof. Ramdas is protected, the material Mr Prakash has given him—about you—will come out.'

Prof. Ramdas smiled. 'Checkmate,' he said simply.

Partha nodded with a laugh. 'Checkmate,' he said.

A thought suddenly seemed to occur to Partha.

'Prof. Ramdas hasn't handed over any material to Vikram?' he asked.

'He hasn't,' Mohan Krishna said.

'What does he get from all this?' Partha asked. 'A ticket or some other political sop?'

'He's a minor political player,' Mohan Krishna said dismissively. 'He's onboard with whatever Prof. Ramdas decides. He'll be taken care of.'

'So it works out well for everyone,' Partha said.

Prof. Ramdas's smiled faded. Mohan Krishna was quick to notice this.

'You will hand over the material you have,' Mohan Krishna said sharply. 'And you will convince the students to keep quiet. Tell them their access to media is completely shut off. Even this TNN will back down now—they have no evidence against me and if they try to push any story against me, Prof. Ramdas, or Prakash, they will face our combined power. They can't afford that. Tell the students we've worked out a deal with the state governments here and in AP and will suppress any evidence out there. Nothing will ever come out—make it clear to them. But if they cooperate, they will be looked after. If they don't, there will be a price to pay.'

'Done,' Partha said.

Mohan Krishna eyed Partha for a moment and then smiled fully. He got up and extended a hand. Partha shook it. Prof. Ramdas also rose and shook Partha's hand. As did Prakash and Vishnu.

'I'll have the material dropped off by this evening,' Partha said. 'I don't need your people to accompany me.'

Mohan Krishna nodded. Partha started to walk away. He stopped and turned around after taking a few steps.

'Oh, I almost forgot something, sir,' he said.

Mohan Krishna looked at him.

'I've been tracking a story since last night,' Partha said.

'Yes?'

'There are a set of videos that are about to go viral,' Partha said. 'They turned up posted on Russian and Eurasian sites—hard to trace their real source. But links to those have been sent to all the major state and national news sites—I gather this happened when I was on the way here. Even international news channels have received the links, I believe. Again, from unidentified emails.'

'What videos?'

'If I could just finish. These links have been sent to advocacy groups, political parties, activists, government and police officials—everyone. They're trending amongst student groups on all social media. It's early yet, but news channels will be covering reactions of students from all over the country soon. They've no choice because they're all over the internet now—they have no real say in the matter. I also understand they're being shared on P2P sites.'

'What material?' Mohan Krishna said, a hint of stress telling in his voice.

'You really don't know what I'm talking about?' Partha said.

'You wouldn't dare!'

'They're about Prof. Ramdas. Most of them, at least. One addresses Mr Prakash. I don't know who's responsible for all this. I just wanted to check with you about what to do. How should we react to all this? How do we manage it?'

Mohan Krishna's eyes reddened, taking on a bloodshot appearance.

'You're finished!' he said.

Prof. Ramdas looked stunned.

'I'm sure you'll try,' Partha said. 'See, Prof. Ramdas and his friends now have a choice. They can keep your secret and work with you, or Prof. Ramdas can take one for the team. I wonder which one he'll take considering how much he despises you and how much time and effort he's spent trying to fix you. I wonder if he hasn't come here having stashed a copy of the material with Vikram. One can't control everything, after all.'

Mohan Krishna began to breathe heavily.

'Some of the missiles are already away, it seems,' Partha said. 'Mutually Assured Destruction, you said. You're at the mercy of the other side now. If they decide to die themselves and not take you with them, you'll luck out.'

Mohan Krishna staggered forward, the rage making him uncoordinated. Vishnu had to step in his way and restrain him.

'If you have a go at the students,' Partha said, 'know that we're bringing their security threat to the attention of every agency in the country and every other source we can. The finger will point right back at you. We're already uploading all kinds of material that we can potentially use against you. You hit us, we hit you.'

Partha looked at Prof. Ramdas and Mohan Krishna with now unconcealed contempt.

'You're at two ends of an ideological divide,' he said, 'but both of you have deaths to answer for.'

He walked out. Malvika and Ramakrishna tried to speak to him but Partha kept walking.

31

The détente didn't hold. CNEWS ran the story accusing Mohan Krishna of deceiving a young woman in his early years of stardom. Her death in suspicious circumstances only added to the speculation connected to it. It played out in bulletin after bulletin. Scratchy tape-recordings of the woman's accusations and a stack of yellowed letters accompanied the story. Legal action on an occurrence decades-old was out of the question but the story took a political toll on Mohan Krishna. His support within the community was split; in particular, he lost his support amongst women and young people. He was forced to put off launching his political party. He hoped to wait it out a few years—counting on public memory being short—to try to win back his community's support. It was wishful thinking. He'd become an object of contempt and mockery—it was not easy to come back from this.

Prof. Ramdas also released all other material he had against Mohan Krishna, including stories about his family's excesses during the days of unrest in the 1970s and 80s. These evoked less interest but inevitably brought out stories of Prof. Ramdas's own actions at the time. Partha was pleased to see that many of these stories appeared in channels Ayesha was associated with. It may not have been outright retribution but it was close, and well-deserved.

Prof. Ramdas's attempts to keep the focus on Mohan Krishna did not work. There was too much damning evidence against Prof. Ramdas. He was arrested. The party and a few intellectuals and academics tried to argue that Prof. Ramdas was being targeted for being against Mohan Krishna, and the establishment as a whole. This too found a few takers but they remained a minority. The student community—in large part—

turned against Prof. Ramdas. More stories against him started coming out from within the student unions. Legal proceedings against Prof. Ramdas began and he faced the prospect of long-term imprisonment. The police, under pressure from the government, decided to be lenient with students who might have been drafted into Prof. Ramdas's activities. No action was pursued against Varaprasad, Vikranth, and others like them. Sirisha and Biren were allowed to go without charges in exchange for cooperation.

Prakash was arrested soon after. He was charged with withholding information pertaining to Priya's suicide. Priya had sent him messages in her last few days. The last one—the message sent on the day of her death—accused him of being exploitative. Prakash had tried to conceal all these messages. This, along with the material found on Priya's laptop and phone, were enough to arrest him. His resources—political and financial—were all diverted to keep him from going to jail for a long time. It was not a good position for a man with enemies to be in. Business rivals capitalised on the opportunity to reveal his malpractices and to undercut him in the film industry.

Anil came out of it all looking like a victim. But he was damaged as well, tainted as he was by association. His film launch was put off indefinitely and the family went into low-profile mode, hoping to ride out the storm.

Ironically, Malvika and Vishnu became the mainstays of Mohan Krishna's family holdings. Within the family, there was acknowledgement of the fact that they couldn't be held responsible for bringing in Partha. Mohan Krishna himself had signed off on it after all. In any event, they were now the relatively non-controversial face of the family. They were entrusted with protecting the family's still-considerable wealth and interests.

The students came out of it well. The disgrace of Prof. Ramdas ensured that Varaprasad and Vikranth became student icons. Varaprasad's role in setting up communications for Prof. Ramdas was seen as an act of misguided loyalty and no more. He was discharged from all responsibility on that count. His courage in saving the devices and ensuring that the evidence against both Prakash and Prof. Ramdas was preserved made him a hero. Even Vikranth's steering of the union away from the influence of Prof. Ramdas won him praise.

Vikram's involvement was harder to prove. He denied being in a conspiracy; instead, he claimed the moral high ground, saying he had used his influence to ensure that students got a sympathetic hearing and platform. Several revelations from the investigation into Prof. Ramdas's actions, made Vikram's claims hard to believe. He was able to escape formal legal action but his indirect control of CNEWS attracted the Enforcement Directorate's attention and eventually the channel, which was already unprofitable, shut down. The perception that Vikram used a young woman's suicide to score points against a rival and his son further weakened Vikram's political prospects. He had gotten involved in the matter hoping to shape perceptions. At the end of it, he was left with significantly weakened image and influence.

Mr Ramakrishna was deeply upset with Partha. In an angry phone call, he threatened retaliation of some kind whenever the time was right. Partha spoke to him patiently. He wasn't free of guilt when it came to Mr Ramakrishna, but after some consideration, he felt that he had no choice but to do what he had done. So Partha apologised, but explained that he knew Mr Ramakrishna's vulnerabilities as well—things that could damage him deeply. He also reminded him that he'd been honest about his disinclination to get involved in the first place. Mr Ramakrishna himself and Malvika had insisted on it. Partha said he understood that Mr Ramakrishna was hurt and that he hadn't acted against Mohan Krishna lightly. But it was Mohan Krishna who had tried to use Partha's skills without appearing to have done so; he'd merely turned the tables on him. Ultimately, he wasn't going to become party to this cover-up so he had to act as he had. The conversation seemed to calm Mr Ramakrishna down somewhat and they called a truce of sorts. Mohan Krishna himself kept Mr Ramakrishna at a distance for a while, choosing to blame someone for the fallout. But he enjoyed the trust of Malvika and Vishnu, and they sought out his advice and assistance in business matters.

*

Partha, Harish, and Seema went back to life in their little grey zone. Over a month later, the three of them met at Partha's apartment. Partha had invited them over saying he had a message he wanted to convey. It was a lazy day, with no real work or meetings of any sort. They'd dealt with the fallout of the story and worked behind the scenes to insulate themselves, but they'd never had the occasion to just talk about everything that had happened. This afternoon, over beer, margaritas, and takeaway Italian food, the conversation drifted in that direction.

'So why'd we get involved in all this in the first place?' Harish asked with a grin. 'I'm not complaining; just asking.'

Seema didn't say anything but she looked in Partha's direction.

'Seemed like the right thing to do,' Partha said slowly.

'At what point did you know it was?' Harish asked.

Partha shrugged.

'Almost immediately, I think,' he said. 'When I realised that we could get involved without having to defend Mohan Krishna. More importantly, I knew that in a battle between Mohan Krishna and Prakash, neither would walk away intact.'

'Still doesn't answer why.'

'No.' Partha interlaced his fingers and fidgeted a little. He didn't reply.

'It struck you that she was depressed?' Seema said.

Partha looked up at her and didn't speak for a long moment.

'She must have been depressed—she killed herself,' Partha said almost dismissively.

Seema and Harish didn't say anything.

'It occurred to me that it must have been hell,' Partha said. He said it with an air of casualness and had a sip of beer. 'And then they were all going to play politics over it.'

'Turned out to be worse than that,' Seema said. 'To be psychologically manipulated, driven to commit suicide—and then used to wage an ideological war.'

Harish looked uncomfortable. He sat up and coughed softly.

'Feels to me like she was tough,' he said. 'Not easy navigating an industry like this but she showed grit. Fought for her place, even developed a persona to cope with it.'

'My God, yes,' Seema said. 'Coming from a modest, conservative background as she did, it must have been really hard. She even had the resilience to handle the movie being taken away from her.'

'I think she did,' Harish said. But that was exactly when she got manipulated into a downward spiral.'

'If she'd been left alone, she'd have been fine,' Partha said. 'But Ramdas saw an opportunity.'

'And when he mixed it up with ideology …' Seema shook her head. 'Diabolical.'

'All those years of indoctrination paid off for him,' Partha said.

Partha finished up the beer he was drinking. He got up to fetch another. When he returned he stretched a little.

'One thing I'm still a little unsure of,' he said. 'Did that scum, Prakash, keep Priya's getting the role tentative for months just to keep her insecure?'

'I spoke to Varaprasad about it a bit,' Seema said. 'He thinks Prakash did that on purpose. I do too. She was told the family would have to approve, so she reached out to everyone. That's how she came in touch with him.'

'Wonder why she got involved with Prakash at all,' Harish said.

'We'll never know for sure,' Seema said. 'But Varaprasad feels Prakash was playing a sport he'd mastered. He charmed her—wouldn't approach her directly, presumed nothing, came off as earnest. He would discuss cinema and the film industry with her—even impressed her with his insight into it. So she actually thought him to be thoughtful, intelligent, and even sympathetic. He'd played the long game and Priya was not prepared for it. Her defences were up for the direct advance but not this elaborate set-up.'

'When exactly do you think Ramdas got in the middle of all this?' Harish said.

'I think her affair with Prakash was the key for him,' Partha said. 'Ramdas knew of the material against Mohan Krishna through Vikram—this was a way of getting to Prakash. He must have thought that he could use Priya to destroy Mohan Krishna's son and his political ambitions with one blow.'

Seema smiled sardonically.

'They came together to kill that girl,' she said.

'And came close to getting away with it,' Harish said. 'Both of them at least!'

'God bless the internet,' Partha said dryly.

There was laughter but it was thin. A heavy silence followed. Harish finished off his can of beer; he crushed the can and got up to go get another. Suddenly, Partha let out a laugh.

'Man, this party's a downer,' he said.

'We didn't get paid—that's the real downer,' Harish said. 'Is this how we're going to do business now?'

Partha grinned.

'We'll try to get paid the next time,' he said. 'My hands were full getting Ramakrishna to stop making threats. Asking for payment would have been a bit much.'

Harish stopped. 'So there's going to be a next time?' he asked. 'And soon?'

Partha nodded slowly. 'I think so,' he said.

Harish slapped his hands together. 'It'll be good for you, you'll see!' he said. 'You've looked more alive these past few days than you had since we moved here!'

'Harish!' Seema said.

'Should I not have said that?' Harish asked, looking puzzled. 'Doesn't matter—he knows what I meant, don't you Partha?'

Partha laughed. 'Yeah, don't worry about it,' he said.

Harish grinned. 'I'm off now,' he said, chugging the new can of beer. 'Leave on this high note.'

He left. Partha and Seema remained seated, sipping their drinks.

'He's happy!' Seema said with a laugh. 'I was getting a little worried about the tension between you two.'

Partha shrugged. 'Don't worry about those tensions,' he said. 'No matter how much Harish disagrees with me or even gets upset, I know I can rely on him. I hope he knows the same about me too.'

'But is this a good decision for you?'

Partha didn't reply immediately. 'I think it is,' he said. 'This feels quite good—the way it all turned out.'

Seema smiled. 'I'll admit it feels okay,' she said.

'Are you okay with us becoming more active?' Partha asked.

Seema pondered it for a moment. 'I think so,' she said. 'It'll disrupt my quiet life right now, which I happen to like. But some part of us likes this kind of excitement—it's who we are.'

Partha nodded. 'It is who we are,' he said.

A curious look came into Seema's eyes.

'Speaking of who we are, Partha,' she said. 'I figured something out finally.'

'What's that?' Partha asked.

'I thought back to some of the important crises you handled. And then I thought about how Prof. Hussain questioning your ethics bothers you.'

Partha sat up a little in his chair.

'And I could see quite clearly,' Seema went on, 'that you never get involved unless you think you're on the right side.'

Partha looked uncomfortable. 'Once you're in the middle of the fight, the lines between right and wrong are more blurred,' he said.

'You do things you normally wouldn't. And that makes you question who you really are.'

Partha didn't answer. He looked away for a while.

'Oh by the way,' he said as casually as he could. 'I got a call from Prof. Hussain.'

'Seriously?' Seema said.

'Yeah.'

'What'd he say?' Seema demanded. 'Did he tell you why exactly he took off and stuff? Did he tell you what happened all the way back in Srikakulam?'

Partha shook his head.

'He didn't talk about any of that,' he said.

'What then?'

'He said I should have dinner with him and Ayesha next time she's in town,' he said.

Seema made a face.

'That's it?' she said. 'I just can't wait until the next time Ayesha's in town and to hear about where you went and if the meal was any good!'

Partha nodded and half-raised his hands defensively.

'But he wasn't calling on his behalf,' he said.

Seema gave him a questioning look.

'He was calling on behalf of Priya's parents,' Partha said. 'He said they were pleased with our efforts to bring the truth to light.'

There was a brief silence. Both Seema and Partha sat back in their chairs, looking out past the sit-out at the view of the city.

'That's approval,' Seema said.

'It is,' Partha said.

The city below looked grey and murky for the most part. There were a few patches of colour and light. The noise of people and vehicles continued.

Acknowledgements

I would like to thank my father, who had the heart to delight in this book's acceptance for publication even as he struggled to breathe. He passed away last June after a long and difficult struggle with a lung ailment.

I would also like to thank my mother, a genuine mystery novel fan who returns manuscripts unread if they fail to hold her interest--even if those manuscripts happen to be written by her son! She approved of this one.

My brother and sister-in-law were supportive as always through the writing of this book. My brother also read through the novel in manuscript form. My two very dear nieces, Meghna and Medha, also had something to do with the writing of this book: their persistent and pointed question 'how come you're a writer but have only one book out' spurred me to get to work on this one!

I am grateful to Dr Vamsee Juluri, friend, author, and media studies professor at the University of San Francisco. He was the first to read the manuscript and respond with great enthusiasm and warmth.

I am also grateful to my editor at Westland, Karthik Venkatesh, whose advocacy for this book helped see it through. His editorial inputs and suggestions were always on point and the many ways he has contributed to this novel are greatly appreciated. My thanks to Shradha, whose edits, comments, and queries enriched this book tremendously. Thanks also to Gautam Padmanabhan (CEO, Westland) and V. K. Karthika (Publisher, Westland) for showing faith in this book.

Several friends and family members have been of great help through the writing and editing of this book. I am especially indebted to Lt. Col. Kiran Golla (Retd.), a valued friend who not only helped me with technology-related inputs but also read through the book to see if anything was amiss.

Other intrepid readers of the typo-ridden manuscript include my uncle, Mr. B. M. Sharma, and two close friends, Amit Gopal and C. Satish Kumar, who also read through the manuscript patiently and provided valuable feedback and encouragement. I am grateful to them all.

I would also like to thank Joshua Mohr, a terrific author, creative-writing instructor, and editor. I can recommend him very highly in all three roles as I've read his books, attended a workshop he taught, and received his valuable feedback on the structure of this story.

I would also like to express my thanks to Mr. P. K. Manvi, Dean, Ramoji Academy of Film & Television (RAFT), who encouraged me to keep writing whenever I wasn't in the classroom or in a discussion with students.

The editing of this book was completed through a very dark phase in my life, much of it spent dealing with a parent's terminal illness and its aftermath. As always, it is close family and friends who get you through such testing times. My heartfelt thanks to them all.